ON THE RUN

RUN

Kirk House Publishers

ON THE RUN

RUN

DENNIS F SMITH

ON THE RUN © Copyright 2021 Dennis E Smith

ISBN: 978-1-952976-26-1
LCCN: 2021914962

Illustration of man in trench coat 151774747 © Hwitte | Dreamstime.com
Cover and interior design by Ann Aubitz

First Printing: August 2021

First Edition

Published by Kirk House Publishers
1250 E 115th Street
Burnsville, MN 55337
Kirkhousepublishers.com
612-781-2815

To Billie Rogers,
the love of my life,
who always keeps me on my toes

Note: The words *might could* is grammatically correct; a respectable and often spoken Southern colloquialism.

Part I

ONE

• • •

"**B**uck, you've got to come over, quick. There's a body in the bathtub."

"Ha! Very funny, Avery."

"It's not funny, you idiot, it's true. Now get your butt over here and help me figure this out," Avery said into his cell phone.

"For real, *a body*?"

"Well, no, it's actually a skeleton. But what's the difference? It's dead."

"Somebody put a skeleton in the bathtub we hauled out to the dumpster this mornin'? What sick bastard would do somethin' like that?"

"No, no. It's in the house. When I started taking out the bathroom floor, *another* bathtub was under the floor itself, with a skeleton in it. And it's black."

"It's black?" Buck paused. "Like a mummy? I thought you said it was a skeleton."

"No. The bathtub's black. Porcelain, I think, and it's shaped like a big heart."

"Okay, Ave, that's enough. You're pullin' my leg, right?"

"Believe me, Buck, I know it sounds like the Twilight Zone, but it's *a real* skeleton. There's even clothes on it."

"Uh, okay. Did you call the cops?"

"Are you kidding? They'll start asking questions, and after them it'll be the reporters. One way or another, somebody's going to figure out Avery Gillis doesn't exist. Then what do I do?"

"What about the—"

"Buck, you're not listening. Get your scrawny ass over here, *now!* But you've got to keep this quiet, do you hear me? Not a word, especially to that ditzy girlfriend of yours. So hurry up." Avery ended the call and stuffed the phone in his pants pocket. He knew Buck wouldn't let him down.

Within seconds the phone vibrated against his thigh. It had to be Buck. He ignored the call and remained seated on an outdoor stone bench, hesitant to go back inside to the black, porcelain, heart-shaped tub he found under his bathroom floor, complete with a fully clothed skeleton with a bullet hole in its skull—an even better reason not to call the cops.

The bench Avery sat on was part of a large garden patio overlooking a small lake. A towering oak stood nearby, shading the house and garden from the afternoon sun. His Arch Street home in Little Rock, Arkansas was built of natural stone and glass. Some attributed its unusual curved design to Frank Lloyd Wright.

Avery stared across the sloping foreground, past the oak and the lake. His mind was focused elsewhere, on his two friends and co-workers who got him into this mess, and on him having to disappear off the face of the earth or end up like them—dead.

Thirty minutes later, Buck found Avery in the master bathroom, now a remodeling nightmare. Avery stood in the gaping hole in the floor, holding a pair of scissors.

"What are you doin', Ave?" Buck said.

Avery dropped the scissors. "Damn it, Buck, scare the crap out of me, why don't you?" He picked up the scissors and boosted himself onto the cluttered bathroom floor, his legs dangling into the hole. "How'd you get in?"

"I used my key," Buck said, holding it up. "The one you gave me so I could work on the house when you're not home."

"Oh, yeah, sorry. I'm just rattled, that's all."

Buck moved closer to the hole and tilted his head. "Damn, Avery, you weren't kiddin', were you?"

"You think I'd make a joke about somebody being dead?"

"Well, no, but this *is* freaky. So what's with the scissors?"

"I was going to cut off his clothes and—"

"Avery, I hate to interrupt, but is that, uh," Buck pointed to his forehead, "a bullet hole in his skull?"

"That's what I figured. Unless he had a tiny third eye."

"Right. You and your humor." Again, Buck stared into the opening. "Man, this is gettin' crazier by the second. If you were gonna murder somebody, why like this?"

"You're asking me? All I know is, after you left, the flooring popped right out, and the joists were all makeshift. Somebody must have been in a big hurry to cover it up."

Buck kicked debris out of the way and sat down on the toilet. "So who is he?"

Avery shrugged. "How the hell should I know? I looked for a wallet, but came up empty, so I'm calling him Mr. Bones."

Buck made a face. "Mister *Bones*? That's twisted."

"I suppose. But it's apropos, don't you think?"

"From your way of thinkin', sure. But now are you callin' the cops?"

"Honestly? I thought about it, but no way. How many stories have you heard about people finding a body buried under their house?"

Buck scratched his goatee. "A few, I guess."

"Exactly. And every time they become headline news all over the country. In no time the cops *and* the FBI have a court order to rip up the floors, plus the whole yard, looking for more bodies."

"Well, maybe."

"Maybe, my ass. That's what they do."

"Geez, Ave, now you're talkin' about stuff I hadn't even thought of. How about we grab a beer and talk about this someplace else? Just bein' in here with this guy creeps me out."

They sat quietly in comfy leather recliners in Avery's spacious living room, each tugging on their bottle of beer. Finally, Buck set his drink on the coffee table. "Maybe you *should* call the cops, because what if more bodies *are* buried around here? There could be a serial killer runnin' loose out there."

"I thought of that," Avery said, "but then it hit me. This guy wasn't buried, he was hidden. Serial killers are into pain and torture, not putting dead men dressed in expensive suits in bathtubs. It had to be something that wasn't planned, you know, a spur of the moment thing. And because he's a skeleton, it had to be some time ago."

Buck stretched his long arms. "Right. Then maybe the cops won't make such a big deal about it."

"Are you living in la-la land, or smoking weed? Finding dead bodies *is* a big deal, no matter when *or* where it happens. And telling the cops will expose who I really am. It's already hard enough pretending to be some guy named *Avery Norbert Gillis,* from somewhere I've never been. You think I want to start all over again with another new name? No way."

"*Norbert?*" Buck laughed. "You're already a nerd and now your middle name's *Norbert?* You never told me that."

"I knew you'd laugh."

"Right. So maybe I should start callin' you Norbee for short." Buck laughed again and held out his beer bottle in a mock toast. "Hey, *Norbee,* cheers!"

"You do and I'll start calling you Roebuck. That's still your middle name, isn't it? *Roebuck?*"

"Okay, okay."

"Or better yet, I should call you *Luther.*" Now Avery laughed. "That's what you get for having James for a last name, *Luther Roebuck.*"

"All right, already. Uncle, uncle." Buck held up his hands in mock surrender. "I'll stop if you will, okay? Middle names *and* Luther, they're out. Deal?"

Avery smiled and raised his beer. "Deal."

"You know, I can't believe I didn't think of this before," Buck said. "Why not leave Mr. Bones where he is? I'll rebuild the floor and put the new shower right over him. Who's to know?"

"Duh." Avery pointed to his temple. "Remember your friend Joe, the plumber? He's coming Monday, two days from now to install the new plumbing like he did in the guest bathroom. Unless you can do it?"

Buck shook his head. "Oh, crap, you're right."

For a few moments, they watched through the glass patio door, as the trees turned to silhouettes in the waning evening light.

Buck broke the silence. "So, uh, where do you plan to put Mr. Bones without someone findin' out?"

Avery's fingers tugged at his brown scraggly beard. "First, we buy some heavy-duty trash bags, and latex gloves so we don't leave fingerprints on anything. Then stuff Mr. Bones and his clothes in a bag, triple line it, and bury it somewhere in the woods."

"Jesus, Ave, sounds like you already have a place in mind."

"I do. I was thinking about somewhere up in the Ozarks with lots of trees and undergrowth. But then I thought, with us not being locals, we'd be easier to remember if somebody saw us. It's weird how people who live in the sticks have a funny way of noticing strangers and asking too many questions. It's like they don't trust people they don't know."

Buck laughed. "And you think people livin' in Miami or the Caymans do?"

Avery shot Buck a nasty look.

"Yeah, yeah, I know, you never lived in any of those places." He leaned closer to Avery and whispered, "Just like your real name's not *John*."

Avery stiffened. *John, Miami, the Grand Caymans.* A name and places he wanted to erase from his memory. His first attempt to hide in Ohio lasted a mere three weeks. He was lucky to escape with his life. Two months later, still shaken, but with a better plan, a lean, six-foot-tall, thirty-two-year-old man clad in Levis and a T-shirt, with the new name of Avery Norbert Gillis, arrived in the capital city of Arkansas. Sporting a fresh beard and a growing head of hair, his clean-cut appearance and million-dollar lifestyle, along with his real name, were now something of the past.

Buck sighed. "Sorry, I was just tryin' to make a point, that's all."

Avery looked away.

Buck cleared his throat. "So go ahead with your Mr. Bones idea."

Avery shifted his weight. "Between then and now I changed my mind. I think we should bury him somewhere around here, where we're both familiar faces. That way we're less likely to raise suspicions."

"That's probably true," Buck said.

"Tomorrow we can scout out all the wooded areas close by. Some look pretty dense like they haven't been touched in years. I was hoping you might think of a place."

Buck shrugged. "Not really. I've only lived in Little Rock four years, and not out here south of town. But you keep sayin' *we*. What do *I* have to do with this mess?"

"Well, for one thing, we need a truck, and since I don't have one, it's best we use your F-150," Avery said.

"*My* truck?"

"For sure. Putting a shovel and trash bag in the bed of a pickup is a lot easier than trying to cram them into the trunk of my car. Then we can pick a wooded spot along one of the side roads hereabouts. I'll drive, and when nobody's coming, you hop out, grab the shovel and the bag with Mr. Bones, and disappear into the woods. After you're done, I'll cruise by and get you."

Buck held up his hand. "Wait a minute. You want *me* to bury him? It's *your* house, *your* idea, and *your* Mr. Bones."

"Right. But from what I hear, poison oak and ivy are all over these woods, and I swell up like a blimp if I even get close to it. If I remember right, you're immune; it doesn't bother you at all."

"Yeah, but—"

"Think about it, Buck. With all that poison stuff, who in their right mind tramps through those woods anyway? I figure no one. Hikers go places where there's a trail, hunters, too. That's why it's perfect. And if someday somebody does find Mr. Bones, no way the law could tie him to me."

"Okay, but what about the SOB who killed him? He'd know," Buck said.

"Yeah, assuming it *was* a he. And if he is still around, I'm sure he couldn't wait to call the cops and tell them it was him who did it and *my* house is where he hid the body." Avery laughed. "If you ask me, the guy's more likely to send me flowers and a thank you note."

"Maybe, but he murdered the poor guy and got away with it. We'd only be helpin' him. If you tell the cops, there's a chance they could find out who did it and put him in the slammer, and—"

"And give the dead guy's relatives some closure?" Avery interrupted. "It's a good thought, but by the time they get closure, there's a chance I will too, right between the eyes, just like Mr. Bones. Look, I hate to sound cruel, but he's dead already and I'm not. With all due respect for the departed, can you blame me for trying to keep it that way?"

"No, no. You're right. I was just thinkin' out loud." Buck finished his drink.

Avery could hear it in Buck's voice; it wasn't the right thing to do. But as uncomfortable as he was being Avery Gillis, involving the police was even more fearful. What other choice did he have?

"Here, let me get you another beer." Avery took Buck's empty to the kitchen and returned with a cold bottle.

"Look, if you want, I'll do it on my own, okay?" Avery said. "If I get caught, I won't say a thing about you knowing, I promise."

"What about the poison oak and ivy?"

"I guess I'll have to chance it. I'll wear gloves and extra clothes. I'll start looking for a place tomorrow morning. But if I pull this off, can you keep this on the down-low, you know, not say a word to anyone? Could you do that much for me?"

"Yeah, I suppose." Buck took another drink. "What the hell, why don't I just help you?"

"Really? You would do that?"

"Why not? You think I want you swellin' up like a blowfish? I'd feel guilty. Then I'd have to knock off work to be your nurse-maid and put up with your constant bitchin' and moanin'." Buck held up his bottle. "Here's to success, *Norbee*." He smiled.

"Thanks, *Luther*." Avery smiled back.

"Besides," Buck said, "what good are brothers if they don't have each other's back?"

TWO

• • •

The pair carried their empty beer bottles to the kitchen.

"If we're going to do this early tomorrow, you should stay over," Avery said. "Or do you have a hot date with Polly tonight?"

"No, she canceled on me. Couldn't get a babysitter for Mary Jo; her mom backed out at the last minute."

"That sucks," Avery said.

"Yeah, but it's okay. We're on again tomorrow. I'm pickin' her up around noon."

"Lucky you after all." Avery gave him a thumbs up. "Then let's get this thing planned out so you can make your date."

Buck nodded. "But let's eat first. I'm starved."

"Okay by me. How about we go into the city and eat at someplace decent?"

"Sure," Buck said. "There's a new Italian restaurant on West Markham. I hear it's good. Then we can swing by my place on the way back. I need some different clothes if I'm gonna be trampin' through the woods."

"And while we're out, I can buy some latex gloves and big heavy-duty bags," Avery said.

"Right. But don't sweat the gloves, I've got some in my shop—

better than latex."

Avery shrugged. "Sounds perfect. Now let's go."

To keep their conversation private, eating someplace decent turned out to be inside the cab of Buck's pickup in the parking lot of Home Depot. They sucked on their soda cup straws and dined on extra spicy Popeye's Chicken from the drive-through a few blocks down.

"Do you want to help me put the bones in the bag? It sure would go a lot faster," Avery said, licking his fingers after his last bite of chicken.

"I'm still eatin', can't you see?" Buck said.

"Not the chicken bones, dummy, *Mr. Bones*, back at the house. Do you want to help take him apart?"

"Damn, you sure know how to kill a person's appetite. No wonder you don't have a girlfriend." Buck nudged Avery.

"Not funny, Buck. Are you going to help me or not?"

"Like hell. It's creepy enough I volunteered to bury him."

"Okay, Wimpy, then I'll do it myself," Avery said.

"Bein' a wimp has nothin' to do with it."

"Then what is it?"

"Jesus, Ave, all your life you pretend like nothin' gets to you. So now, if hackin' Mr. Bones into pieces and dumpin' him in the woods is better for you, then no big deal—just do it. But I'm freaked, okay? This guy was a person, a live human being for God's sake. You talk about him like he's an old washrag you get rid of. I know I can't be cool like you, pissin' things away with your whacko humor, but sometimes your stoic attitude is more than I can handle."

Avery had never thought of himself as stoic, but it wasn't the first time he'd heard it. As far as being cool, he wished he was but knew he never would be. And his sense of humor, what was wrong with it?

"When we get back to your place I'm hangin' out in front of your flat screen," Buck said. "Mr. Bones is all yours."

"Sure, okay. Which spare bedroom do you want?"

"I'll take the couch, thanks," Buck said, then smiled. "Why? You spendin' the night in the master suite with Mr. Bones?"

"Yeah, we're spooning together."

Buck laughed. "I'd like to see that."

"Are you kidding? I'm closing the bedroom door and sleeping wherever you aren't."

"Why don't you throw him in the bed of the truck?"

"Yeah, right. And take a chance an animal gets into the bag? That's all I need, some dude driving down Arch Street, and there in his headlights is a raccoon dragging a human skull across the road. Talk about freaked out." Avery made a funny face. "Or, if I'm really lucky, the guy will have just left Hawg's Tavern after knocking down a few too many and think he's hallucinating—until the next day, that is—when it comes out Mrs. What's-Her-Face from down the road went ape-shit because her faithful dog, Rex, showed up at her back door, tail wagging, with a slobber laden skull clamped in his jaws. Then what would I do?"

Buck laughed again. "You crack me up."

"So how about I stick Mr. Bones *inside* the cab of your truck? I could prop him up behind the wheel, ready to drive."

"Like hell. How about *your* car?"

"I think I'll stick with the bathroom. Besides, how many years has Mr. Bones been in there already? One more night won't hurt."

"Whatever. You deal with it," Buck said. "I'm watchin' Saturday Night Live. Just keep Mr. Bones *out* of my truck."

Buck wanted to call Polly, so Avery went into Home Depot alone. Fifteen minutes later he returned.

"What's the word, lover boy?" Avery asked, climbing back into the cab.

"Don't know, Polly didn't answer. Probably readin' Mary Jo a bedtime story or somethin'."

"I know you hate it, but how about texting her? She might even answer."

"Maybe that's your style, but I think it's impersonal, when all you have to do is answer the damn phone."

"No need to get defensive, Buck. It was only a suggestion."

"I hear you. I guess I'm just old school. So did you find the right bags?"

"Extra heavy-duty," Avery said, holding up a green box with yellow lettering.

Leaving the parking lot, Buck had just turned onto Markham when Avery tapped him on the arm. "Look, there's a craft store. Turn in. I need to buy some scissors."

"What happened to the pair you had?"

"They don't cut worth crap. So turn in already."

Buck pulled into an empty space, killed the motor, then looked at Avery. "What are you *really* doin'?"

"I told you, I'm buying a pair of sharp scissors."

"Yeah, but that's bullshit," Buck said. "You wanna stuff this guy in a trash bag and then bury him in the woods. And now you're all worried about *how* you cut off his clothes? Why should it matter? It's crazy enough you wantin' to take precautions wearin' gloves. But now you have to be Mr. Neat with special scissors when it won't make a fart's worth of difference how you do it." Buck shook his head.

"I know this guy deserves justice, but right now I can't give it to him," Avery said. "All I'm trying to do is give him a little bit of respect."

"By buyin' a pair of scissors?"

"Yeah. And cutting off his clothes and putting them *and* him in the bag in a respectful way." Avery paused. "I know it sounds weird, but you asked."

"And dumpin' him in a hole in the ground is respectful? That's dumb-ass crazy."

Avery backhanded Buck on the arm. "Look who's talking, you volunteered to do it."

"Okay. If it makes you feel better, go buy your friggin' scissors."

When Avery returned, he held up his new pair of long pointed scissors. "Look, just what I need."

"Jesus, Ave, it's a good thing Mr. Bones is already dead. Those look lethal."

"They're called sewing scissors, for cutting cloth. They're really sharp."

"No joke. So did the guy ask you what you wanted them for?"

"*He* was a lady, and when I told her, she wanted to know if she could help." Avery laughed.

●●●

Buck turned into the driveway of his remodeled bungalow in the Hillcrest area of Little Rock. He bought it as a repo fixer-upper three years earlier. The neighborhood, once *the* place to live, had fallen on leaner times, but thanks to motivated souls like Buck, Hillcrest was making a comeback.

He went inside while Avery waited in the truck, listening to Buck's *Led Zeppelin II* recording, the one with "Whole Lotta Love" on it. When they were growing up, Buck played it so often Avery hated it. Now it reminded him, except for the death of his parents, growing up hadn't been so bad after all.

When Buck returned, he dropped a shovel in the truck bed, tossed a pair of boots and a sports bag in the back seat of the cab, and climbed into the driver's seat.

"Did you bring the gloves?" Avery said, in an anxious voice.

Buck gave him a blank stare.

"What?"

"This is crazy, that's what. If we get caught, your identity cover's blown for sure."

Avery grimaced. "So you think it's better to call the cops and take my chances?"

"I don't mean the cops, and you know it. I'm talkin' about your Marshal buddy, Roger. Isn't that his name?"

"Tell that asshole? He hates me."

"Yeah, but I read somewhere that nobody ever gets found in Witness Protection."

"Except for me, last year, when somebody leaked my whereabouts. But they'll never admit to it," Avery said. "The only good thing about it was, I wound up here."

"But aren't the Marshals like the FBI, able to put the hush-hush on the local cops and make stuff go away?"

"That's what I've been told. But if it's true what they say about the police and the Fed's disdain for each other, why would the cops play along, especially if it's Roger they're dealing with? The cops would probably call a press conference just to piss him off, even if it meant hanging me out to dry. And why would Rog care? It's no sweat off his balls. All he'll do is relocate me, give me another new name and say, 'Deal with it,' just like he did the last time."

Avery stared into the night. "Somebody out there wants me dead. And if somehow they found me once, by rocking the boat I'm afraid they'll find me again. Here things are good just the way they are, so the cops are out, the Marshals, too." He put his hand on Buck's shoulder. "You're another reason not to call them. If the Feds ever find out we're related, it could be bye-bye Little Rock for me, and I don't see you relocating."

Buck sighed. "I think you're right. But with us havin' different real last names, and after all this time the Feds haven't found us out, it's like you said, we're good. So screw Roger." He started the engine and backed out of the driveway.

Avery nodded his agreement. "Did you bring the gloves?"

Buck grinned. "I brought the whole damn box. Enough for both of us, *and* Mr. Bones."

THREE

• • •

Buck grabbed the TV clicker and flopped onto Avery's living room couch.

Avery went to the master bedroom, and wanting to hide his discretion, closed the door and pulled tight the curtains covering the full-length wall-to-wall, ceiling-to-floor window, as well as those over the sliding glass door on the opposite wall.

Armed with his new scissors and wearing a pair of Buck's thin nitrile gloves, he entered the master bathroom, placed a green trash bag within reach, and awkwardly lowered himself into the heart-shaped tub. *How symbolic,* he thought, as if sinking deeper into an abyss.

Two dark stains covered Mr. Bones's gray pinstriped suit jacket. A light blue dress shirt was underneath. Avery's plan was simple: cut away the clothing to expose the skeleton, separate the bones at the joints, put them into the bag, gather up the clothes and stuff them in afterward.

Keep it clinical, he told himself. Thinking about the person who had once worn the pricy suit would only weaken his resolve. Avery squatted down and gently lifted the edge of the sleeve of the left arm and began to cut.

Methodically he snipped away in patterns that reminded him of his grandmother preparing material for a patchwork quilt. As he went, he lifted away the panels of cloth and placed them in an orderly pile on what remained of the bathroom floor.

Quite by accident, he discovered a small folded piece of yellowish paper, partially bloodstained, in an inside coat pocket. Avery opened the notepaper and observed three sets of letters positioned around a hand-drawn circle containing three additional letters.

He shrugged and placed the stiffened paper on a loosened floor tile, apart from the growing pile of carefully cut cloth.

Upon reaching the collar of the jacket, each cut of the scissors made contact with Mr. Bones's skull, and with every 'click' Avery flinched. A knot formed in his stomach.

The heavily stained shirt came next. His eye caught a small bullet hole, then another. A third hole appeared in the middle of Mr. Bones's violet silk tie.

As Avery cut away the last of the shirtfront, he shuttered. Layer by layer he had stripped away any dignity Mr. Bones might have left, and perhaps his own as well. The knot in his gut tightened.

He looked like a contortionist as he turned around in the tub, trying not to step on Mr. Bones. "Damn," he mumbled. Here he was, treating

Mr. Bones with the care he would give a dozen raw eggs, yet knowing in minutes he would dismantle him bone by bone and stuff him into a garbage bag.

He unbuckled the skeleton's black belt, gave it a gentle tug, and pulled it off. With a single cut down each pant leg, and again with Mr. Bones's boxer shorts, the material fell away, revealing the stark white hipbones, femurs, and lower leg bones.

"Hmm." Avery's lips parted into a wry smile. The naked Mr. Bones was still wearing dress shoes and argyle socks. How to remove shoes and socks from a skeleton? Avery's answer was to not even try. He gingerly lifted the left shoe and slid the edge of the trash bag under it. He did the same with the other foot, then pulled the bag under the skeleton toward its knees.

Avery could feel his hands sweating inside the thin blue gloves. If he stopped now to dry his hands and put on new gloves, he feared his resolve would weaken. No, he could not allow himself to feel compassion *or* guilt.

Avery placed bone by dismembered bone into the green bag. At last came the skull. As he lifted the orb, there came a rattling sound—the sound a small stone might make inside a wooden box. He tilted the naked head. A short rattle was followed by a soft thud on the clothing that remained on the bottom of the black tub.

Puzzled, Avery placed the skull in the bag with the other bones and returned his attention to the small object he heard fall. He picked it up. It was metal. Not once had he thought it would be a spent bullet.

It took little time for him to find the other three slugs. Two that pierced the suit coat of Mr. Bones and one that forever ruined his designer tie. As Avery gathered up the remaining parts of clothing from the bottom of the tub, he heard a metallic scraping sound against the porcelain finish. Avery lifted the soiled cloth, exposing a shiny object. His nitrile fingers retrieved the object—a brass shell casing, which no doubt belonged to one of the bullets that killed Mr. Bones. Avery searched the tub for others like it. He found none. "Hmm, looks like you missed one," he said, as if speaking to the unknown assailant. He placed the casing on top of the bloodstained note.

Something moved inside the green bag. Avery snapped his head around. The motion stopped as an eye socket appeared to peek out of the opening. Avery gasped and looked away. He couldn't help but think Mr. Bones was giving him the evil eye for what Avery was doing to him. As Mr. Bones continued to watch, Avery slid the pieces of cloth into the bag, which pushed the skull further in. He snatched up the four spent slugs, tossed them in, and pulled the zip tie to seal the bag. Out of the tub, he hurried to encase Mr. Bones and his belongings into two additional bags, each one tied shut with a separate zip tie.

At last, Avery breathed a sigh of relief. He removed his gloves and dried his sweaty hands, turned off the lights, and closed the bathroom door behind him.

He found Buck asleep on the couch while the TV played an infomercial for Wonder Bras. Avery crashed in the first of the two spare bedrooms, the one farthest from Mr. Bones. He tossed and turned throughout the night, while Buck slept soundly in the living room, and Mr. Bones rested quietly amongst the debris on the bathroom's cold tile floor.

FOUR

• • •

A very drove. Buck rode shotgun. For an hour the pair scoured various side roads feeding off Arch Street, the meandering two-lane road that made its way south out of Little Rock.

"You didn't say, but did you find the bullet?" Buck asked. "You know?" He pointed to his forehead.

"Huh, you must be blind," Avery said. "Didn't you notice the stains on his suit coat? He was shot three other times."

"Are you kiddin' me?"

"No. And before you ask, I found the slugs and threw them in the bag along with Mr. Bones. If the cops ever find him, maybe they can match them to another shooting and nail the SOB who did it."

Buck nodded. "Makes sense. So I take it you didn't find out who he was."

"Not a clue." Avery fudged his answer. In his haste, he had forgotten to add his other findings to the bag—the blood stained piece of paper from Mr. Bones's jacket, and the .380 caliber shell casing. At that point he wasn't about to cut all the zip ties and start again. For now, the paper and the shell casing lay in the bottom of Avery's sock drawer. Maybe he'd tell Buck about them—maybe not. But were they clues? Without a doubt.

Just past 7:00 a.m., Avery turned Buck's dual-cab Ford pickup onto a seldom-traveled side road. Both agreed it was the best of the forested areas they had considered that morning. Another factor was cell phone reception. There was none, and in today's age of rampant cell phone addiction, an area more likely to be avoided.

"You sure this is the road with the big dip in it?" Buck said.

"Yeah, I remember that giant oak where we turned. You better get ready."

Dressed in boots, overalls, and a dark blue zip-up jacket, Buck pulled on a black knit cap. "You drive off, I check out the woods, then you come back by in twenty minutes."

Avery stopped at the bottom of the swale. "Just make sure you find a good spot."

"I know, Ave, I know. We went over it ten times." Buck checked the time on his wristwatch. "I have seven after. See you in twenty." He stepped out of the truck, closed the door, and made his way into the woods.

Avery gunned the motor and the Ford shot up the slope, onto the level road. He saw no cars ahead. His eyes scanned the rear-view mirror. The road was clear. About a mile from the swale he turned the pickup around, pulled onto the shoulder of the road, and checked the time.

Avery gave a shrill whistle as he came to a stop in the dip. Buck popped out from behind a tree and hurried toward the truck. "I found a great spot," he said.

"Good. Do you have the gloves?"

"Right here." Buck held them up in his hand. "Damn, Avery, you're more nervous than I am."

"Yeah, maybe, but we can't afford to make any mistakes."

"You're tellin' me? If I get caught while you're out toolin' around, I'm the one holdin' the bag, if you know what I mean."

"Ha, ha. Now go, before some fool comes flying down the road and kills us both. Wouldn't that be poetic justice?"

Again Buck checked his watch. "Ninety minutes, Ave, and make sure you're on time." He pulled on the gloves and turned toward the bed of the truck.

"Buck!" Avery yelled. "Make sure you dig the hole deep enough."

Buck flipped him the bird, grabbed Mr. Bones and the shovel, and retreated into the woods.

Avery didn't wait for Buck to disappear before he hit the gas pedal, leaving a patch of burned rubber on the roadway. Out of the swale, he checked the rearview mirror. No one was behind, but a car approached from 100 yards ahead. He watched the car pass, then followed it in the side mirror as it descended into the dip, then just as quickly reappeared up the other side.

Relieved, Avery headed back toward Arch Street. He thought about surprising Buck with a dozen Shipley's donuts but reconsidered. What if he had a flat tire, or a wreck, or God forbid, was stopped by a cop? He'd panic.

Instead, Avery drove to his house where he maneuvered the pickup between the tall pines near the entrance to his driveway. He turned off the ignition, reclined the seat, and gazed across the small lake that bordered the property. He couldn't stop thinking about Mr. Bones. Who was he? Did he have a family? Maybe he did deserve a bullet in the head.

At the appointed time, Buck bounded for the pickup, threw the shovel in the bed, and jumped into the cab. "Hit it," he said, out of breath.

Avery accelerated out of the swale. "Well?" he said.

"Well, what? I buried the guy, okay. I know you want to hear all the gory details, but first, let me get these gloves off. My hands are sweating like mad."

"Enough to leave DNA on the bag?"

"No, I was extra careful. This is the *third* pair I used, and not wantin' to litter, I stuffed the other ones *in* the bag with Mr. Bones, along with the hairbrush I snuck off your dresser." Buck smacked Avery on the arm and laughed.

Avery didn't smile.

"Jesus, Ave, give me a friggin' break. And watch where you're drivin', you're goin' off the road!"

Avery corrected his steering. "So tell me, really. How'd it go?"

Buck turned his head to the open window and was silent. Finally, he said, "If you must know, it was a gruesome thing to do. And I'm not proud of it."

Avery bit his lip. "I hear you. While you were out scouting the woods, there I was, with Mr. Bones in the back of the truck like a sack of garbage I needed to get rid of. The sad part is, that's how part of me thinks. And you're right about me being stoic. I think it started when Mom and Dad died."

"But you were only four," Buck said.

"And you were six and somehow you handled it just fine, but not me. I swore I wasn't going to feel pain like that ever again. That's why I say I don't care and push people away. And then, on the rare occasion, when I do get close to someone, things go haywire."

"And you believe it's your fault?" Buck said.

"That's the way it keeps playing in my head," Avery replied. "It's like I'm stuck being this way, no matter who I'm with."

"But you don't have to be."

"So you keep telling me. But right now I don't want to talk about it, okay?"

For the remaining minutes it took to drive home, both men were quiet.

Avery turned the truck into his driveway.

"Say, Ave, why don't you go with me and Polly to Hot Springs today? It'll be fun."

"Thanks, but—"

"Come on. Do you wanna stay here and be miserable, feelin' sorry for yourself *and* Mr. Bones, or have some fun with us? I'm gonna rent a boat. We can find a spot, swim and relax, and put Mr. Bones behind us. So how about it?"

Avery shrugged. "What about your, uh, alone time with Polly, *without* the kid?"

"Don't worry, you'll be home in plenty of time for us to, uh, do other things."

"And Polly would be okay with it?"

"Sure, why not? She knows you; we've been out together before. I'll tell her you're in the dumps and need company."

"Yeah, because we spent the morning sneaking off to bury some murdered guy named Mr. Bones."

Buck laughed. "How about sayin' you just broke up with your girlfriend?"

"Right. And when she starts asking me questions, then what do I say?"

"Tell her it was a long-distance relationship with a gal in New Orleans, you know, where you tell people you used to live. Just think about what you said the last time you broke up with somebody. It'll be easy."

Avery scoffed. "Easy for you maybe. Every relationship I've been in, she dumped me first."

"Damn. You really are a nerd."

"Don't remind me, okay?"

Except for Polly's incessant talking, Avery did enjoy his day on the lake.

Back at home, he closed his bedroom door and spent the night on the living room couch, trying to distance himself from his encounter with Mr. Bones and the black, heart-shaped tub. And worse, what he had talked Buck into helping him do about it.

FIVE

• • •

J oe, the plumber, arrived the next morning as scheduled. Minutes later, Avery made an emergency call. "Buck, Joe's gone bananas over the tub. He wants to take it home so he can show it off and then sell it on the Internet."

"So?"

"Think about it, Buck. He's going to tell everybody he knows from here to Dallas. With my luck, it'll go viral, and some eager TV reporter will show up to do a human-interest story. Then I'm screwed. Talk to the guy, will you?"

As it turned out, other than knocking out an entire bathroom wall, the tub would have to remain where it was. Buck would build a floor over it like before, except this time done properly.

In a few weeks work on the master bath would be finished, with a large granite-tiled shower securely built over the porcelain tub. It also would complete the six-month makeover of Avery's entire house.

What remained uncertain, however, was how long Avery would continue to bolt awake in the middle of the night with visions of Mr. Bones's eye socket staring him in the face, and his long, ossified finger pointing to the extra hole in the middle of his forehead.

SIX
● ● ●

By the first Monday in October, Buck and his two co-workers were applying the finishing touches to the master bathroom. In the kitchen, Avery was about to microwave a Shipley's donut when his *other* cell phone rang—the one issued him by the U.S. Marshals Service. The call was from Roger Haslock.

In Miami, because of an anonymous tip, Avery's employer, the investment firm Monetary United International (MUI), was under investigation for offshore money laundering. Threats were made against the suspected whistleblowers, Avery's two colleagues, Malcolm Westbury and Nelson Decker. Because they were friends and shared similar jobs, Avery was also threatened, even though he said he wanted no part of it.

Nelson Decker was the first to die. He fell down a flight of stairs and broke his neck. An accident, the Miami newspapers reported. Days later, Malcolm Westbury wound up like Mr. Bones, with a bullet hole in his head. *That* was no accident, it was a message. Certain he would be next, Avery quickly agreed to cooperate.

Given a new identity, he was placed in the U.S. Marshals Witness Protection Program and sent to live in Ohio. Within weeks an attempt was made on his life. Who leaked his whereabouts, no one knew. Assigned a second new name, he was relocated to Arkansas.

Deputy Haslock said the Government phone was for Avery's protection, so the Marshals could better protect him from those who wished him harm. They could also monitor his every call, and with its built-in GPS, track his every move. Although he promised to use the phone for all his calls, he lied.

Avery usually carried the phone with him, except when he would rather the deputies not know his whereabouts—like when he needed to bury a dead body in the woods. When caught not having his assigned phone with him, he would say he forgot and left it at home, and because it happened infrequently, the Marshals let it slide.

For his other calls, Avery used a burner, or throwaway phone, so he and Buck could talk freely without detection. Also important, he could call people and places he didn't want the Marshals *or* his brother to know about. The ringtone was always set on vibrate.

Avery touched the screen. "Hold on, Rog," he said, and walked out the front door, onto the garden patio. "Okay, what do you want?"

"Avery, you don't sound happy to hear from me," Roger said.

"I already got an earful from your watchdog, Jerry Joyce, an hour ago. So what is it now?"

"Didn't he tell you? The Supreme Court's back in session and re-fused to hear MUI's appeal. The lower Court's ruling stands; everything Malcolm Westbury gave you concerning MUI is now admissible."

"Like I said, Jerry already clued me in: He gave me the subpoena, and next week I go to Miami to testify. So either tell me why you really called or I'm throwing your frigging phone in the lake."

"Okay, okay. IRS and Justice are on my ass to make sure you show up with *everything.*"

"What about the info Malcolm gave you when this all started?"

"Don't jerk me around, Avery. The Court made its ruling, and now you have to comply with the subpoena. That means either you show up with those CDs or kiss your get-out-of-jail-free-card goodbye. It's all part of your immunity deal, so don't tell me you don't remember."

"But how do I know I'm safe *after* I turn them over? That's what I'm worried about."

"Because you've got it in writing."

"So did Native Americans, Rog, and look what happened to them."

"You mean the Indians? Okay, but that was way back then. Things are different now."

"Yeah, right. Instead of just screwing them, the Government's adopted a new equal opportunity policy: now you screw everybody."

"Avery, I know you're anxious. Who wouldn't be in your situation? And despite your cynicism, I promise you'll be safe. Then afterward, you can keep your Avery identity or we'll get you a new one. We'll protect you like we've been doing all along."

"You mean like you protected Nelson and Malcolm?"

"That wasn't on us and you know it," Roger said.

"Then what about Ohio, when my first alias was Robert Gable, where you said I should dye my hair, grow a mustache, and wear fake glasses? A lot of good that did. Which reminds me: did you ever catch the SOB who tried to kill me?"

"No, but—"

"Then whoever it was is still out there, right?" Avery said.

"It's what we're assuming. That's why, wherever you are, you'll have someone like Jerry to keep tabs on you."

"Yeah, and every time I see Jerry, he's driving his shiny black car and wearing the same loud blue suit, pretending to be my insurance agent. He might as well put a flashing neon sign in his rear window that says, *DEPUTY JOYCE, BORN TO SERVE.* Honest, Rog, Jerry has cop written all over him. Someday the wrong person's going to take notice and I'll be dead."

"Okay, I'll talk to him."

"You told me that before."

"All right, all right. I'll make sure he listens this time, okay?"

"Yeah, sure, when pigs fly. And you should know all about that, right?" Avery said.

"Listen here, you ungrateful piece of shit, I've had it with your smart-ass attitude. We want those disks."

"I'm tired, too, Rog, of you making me play this hide-and-seek game, and it's me doing all the hiding. It's like *I'm* the criminal."

"*It's like I'm the criminal,*" Roger mocked. "With your know-it-all Ivy League degree, you want us to believe it never entered your mind that writing a computer program to help people hide taxable income from

Uncle Sam might be illegal? In case you've forgotten, you're not getting one dime of the whistleblower reward money. As far as I'm concerned, you're just as guilty as the assholes who bought into your scheme. The only difference is, you got lucky by getting immunity, *and* you get to keep your million-dollar condos and six-figure bank account. So stop with the victim act already, I'm tired of hearing it."

"Right, but what good are the condos and the money when I'm in Witness Protection?"

"You should have thought about that beforehand. So I'm not asking, I'm telling you, turn over the goddamned disks or I'll cut you loose."

"If I'm such a low life criminal, maybe I should forget where I keep Malcolm's evidence. Better yet, I could delete it all. Then poof, your big-time case would be history."

"And so would you, dickhead. Do you really think that's going to stop certain unsavory characters from hunting you down? With no Witness Protection, a slip of the tongue that you're hiding out in Hick City, Arkansas—along with your new look photo—you'll be dead meat inside a week."

"I bet you'd do it, too," Avery said.

"Damn right I would, and sleep like a baby just after I read your obit. So stop your bitching and listen to me. Your past life is over; John doesn't exist anymore; only Avery Gillis has a chance to survive. Besides, what other choice do you have?"

Abruptly, Avery ended the call, cursed, and returned to the kitchen. This time he placed two glazed donuts into the microwave, then went to the hallway and yelled, "Hey, Buck, I need to see you. It's kind of important."

The Marshals' phone rang again. Avery opened the refrigerator and tossed it in the vegetable drawer.

Buck appeared in the doorway. Avery handed him a warm donut on a napkin and a mug of coffee. "Let's go outside."

Buck followed Avery through the living room, out the sliding glass door, to the pool. They sat down at a round table, shaded from the sun by a large umbrella rising from the table's center.

"What's up?" Buck said.

"You know, last night I told you the Marshals want me in Miami to testify?"

"Yeah, and you might not be back for two or three months. So?"

Avery looked around. "I've got myself in a bind."

Buck laughed. "Who'd you piss off this time?"

"It's Rog. He wants me to turn over more evidence, so I need a couple of those thumb drives I sent you for safekeeping."

"What are you talkin' about?"

"You know, the small box I sent to you when this all went down, with the USB flash drives in it?"

Buck took a bite of donut and gave Avery a blank stare.

"You're good, Buck, I'll give you that, but this isn't funny."

"And I'm not laughin', okay?" Buck leaned closer. "Or, uh, do you need to ask me *a question?*"

Avery rolled his eyes. "Oh, yeah, I forgot. Okay, Buck, *when's the last time you got laid?*"

"Jesus, Ave, you and your damned *secret code.*"

"Kind of stupid, huh?" Avery gave a sheepish grin. "But what's on those flash drives got two people killed and me into this mess. I'm just sorry I had to involve you in it."

Buck smiled. "You had me fooled. After not hearin' from you in months, out of the blue I get this box along with a cryptic handwritten note: Hide these. If someone knows you have them, you could end up dead. Which reminds me, I never did thank you for makin' me paranoid." Buck raised his coffee mug toward Avery. "Thanks, *Norbee.*"

"Sorry, *Luther,* but I had to leave them somewhere safe, and you were the only option I had."

"Then stop apologizin' already." Buck finished off his donut.

"The thing is, they haven't stopped looking for them. They've searched the house, my car, the storm cellar, everywhere."

"Don't they have to have a warrant to do that?"

"Probably, but they either deny it or say, 'So call the cops.' Anyway, Rog said I have to show up in Miami with the data on those drives, which means they're going to follow me like a hawk to find out where they're stashed."

"But if you're givin' him what he wants, what's the big deal?"

"Because I'm not, and after the phone conversation we just had, I think he knows it, too. He'll have me watched 24/7, trying to find where I keep the data and if anyone's helping me. Between now and when I leave, they'll check my every move, my phone calls, and every person I come in contact with, and you can't be one of them."

"And here I was thinkin' our biggest worry was Mr. Bones."

"I wish it was that simple." Avery finished his coffee. "How close are you to being done? I need you gone, ASAP. Your helpers I'm not worried about."

"Except for cleanin' up, we're pretty much finished. I could be gone in ten, easy."

"Good. Then I need you to make a delivery—the number one and two thumb drives from the box. I need to turn them into four CDs before I leave town."

"Do you have a plan?"

"Tonight I'll go out for dinner. I was thinking about that new Italian place you talked about on West Markham."

Following a brief but hushed conversation, they rose and turned to re-enter the house.

Buck put his hand on his brother's shoulder. "So when *was* the last time you got laid?"

"Jesus, Buck, you really know how to hurt a guy, don't you?"

SEVEN
● ● ●

L ater that morning in Little Rock, Avery placed a new sports bag he had just purchased into the trunk of his car.

"What are you up to, Avery?" a man's voice said.

In response to the unexpected voice, Avery's body jerked, and his head banged against the trunk lid. "Damn!" he cried out.

"Oh, sorry, Avery, I didn't mean to startle you."

Holding his hand to his head, Avery turned. "Jesus, Jerry, did you have to sneak up on me like that, or is that part of your job description?"

"Like I said, I'm sorry," Marshal Joyce replied.

"Look at that!" Avery held out his bloodied hand, then retrieved a paper napkin from inside his car and held it to his wound. "So why are you here anyway?"

"There's been a change of plans. You're flying to Miami tomorrow night, not next week. I'll pick you up at nine o'clock sharp, so be ready. And don't bring any change of clothing."

"You're joking, right?"

Jerry Joyce shook his head. "Because we're not interested in blowing your cover, we bought you all new clothes—suits, shirts, ties, shoes and socks, everything. By the time you appear in public, you'll be the same clean-shaven, classy looking guy you used to be. You're sure Roger didn't go over this with you?"

"I'd remember if he did. But the last time we talked our

conversation got cut short. So is that all? Can I go now?"

"There is one other thing—who's looking after your house?"

"What are you talking about?"

"With you being so anal, you haven't said anything to Roger or me about somebody taking care of your house. And because you know you could be gone for months, it means you've got somebody lined up already. So who is he? Or is he a she? We need to run a check on them. Your life could be at risk and you wouldn't know it."

Run a check on Buck? Avery thought. He coughed, pretending to have something caught in his throat. "Look, just because I'm a neat freak doesn't mean I'm always thinking straight, especially right now, okay?"

"So you don't have anyone in mind?"

"How could I? All my friends are dead or on your Do Not Call list."

"No need to be defensive. I'm just doing my job," Jerry said. "Besides, after you spent all this time fixing up your place, why let it run down. Roger and I talked, and we've decided, if you don't have someone, I should live at your house, pay your bills, drive your car—that kind of thing."

"I suppose I don't have a choice, do I?" Avery said.

"Not if you want to keep things looking normal. And if anyone asks, I'm a good friend, house-sitting while you're away on a consulting job. I'll stop by this afternoon to iron out the details," the deputy said. "Think of it this way, for as long as you'll be gone, now you won't have to winterize your house."

"Uh-huh. So what about *your* family? What do you tell them? 'See you in a few months,' and they have no say?"

"With all the time I have to spend protecting clowns like you, I don't have time for a real family."

"Geez, Jerry, you really bleed Marshal red-white-and-blue don't you?"

"Even though you don't appreciate my efforts, Avery, I'll take that as a compliment. Besides, living at your place without you around, I can sleep in every day."

Avery smirked. "Now can I go?"

"Sure, after you show me what's in the bag you put in the trunk."

"It's new, Jerry, and it's empty. I bought it to take to Miami." Avery popped open the trunk and grabbed the bag. "But first, let's see your search warrant."

"You're in Witness Protection. I don't need one."

"And I'm supposed to believe that? I wonder what my new attorney would say?"

"You mean the one you just hired?" the deputy said. "He's in Miami, so screw him and hand it over."

Avery shoved the bag into Jerry's chest. "Here, knock yourself out, bozo, but the CDs aren't in there."

After a quick look, Jerry handed it back. "I don't get it, Avery. Why do you keep pushing our buttons? We hide you from the bad guys, take extra precautions to get you to Miami and back, and all you do is bust our balls about it. Why?"

"Because I want my life back the way it was and it won't ever happen, that's why. Look at me, what the hell kind of life is this? You want me to lay low, but never contact my old friends, and don't make too many new friends, and if I do, make up stories about a life I never lived. Plus, I can't work—you say it's not safe—and all the while Rog tells me, 'Stay upbeat, think about the future.' Are you kidding me? What frigging future? And when I told him as much, he said to stop complaining, stay home, watch TV, read books, and if I'm still bored, play with myself. He actually said that."

Jerry tried to cover his laughter. "But Avery, you've got to have thought about the alternatives. A year ago you were on the fast track to Federal prison when your two pals bought the farm, and somehow you lucked out and wound up with all the evidence, which got you off the hook and in Witness Protection."

"*Lucked out?* What kind of lame thinking is that?" Avery said. "Sure, I took the money, wrote the program, did what they asked and looked the other way—we all did. It was stupid, okay? I admit it. And look what happened: my two friends get murdered, and now I have to hunker down like a hunted animal. How's that lucky?"

"Because the Justice Department struck a deal with you, that's how. Instead of serving time or winding up dead you're living here in Little

Rock. Under the circumstances, you *are* lucky."

Avery breathed a sigh. "On some twisted level I suppose you're right, but as far as being upbeat about my future, who are you jokers kidding? No matter how this thing strings out, my future's in the crapper. I hate to unwind your spin, Jerry, but the way my life is going, I feel anything but lucky."

EIGHT
• • •

The new Pasquale's Italian Restaurant sat near the end of a large L-shaped strip mall on West Markham. Parking for the myriad of shops was more than ample. Avery arrived as promised, close to 6:30 p.m. He scanned the lot for just the right place.

Buck was early. His gray F-150 was parked near the exit lane, several rows deep from the mall storefronts. Avery recognized the small ding in the left rear bumper, and pulled in between two cars a short way from Buck's empty pickup. He cracked open the passenger window a few inches, locked the car with his keypad, and casually angled his way between cars to the front door of the restaurant.

Although early in the week, Pasquale's was busy. Avery waited while the hostess checked for single seating. Before she could return, the bell on the door jingled and in walked Jerry Joyce.

"Avery, what a coincidence. We picked the same place to dine," Jerry said. "I didn't know you liked Italian. Imagine that."

"Imagine, my ass," Avery said. "If you have to follow me around, can't you at least wait outside so I can enjoy my dinner?"

"Not a chance," Jerry answered. "We're on you like glue, so get used to it."

"So I've noticed, all day."

"Sir," the hostess said to Avery when she returned, "it'll be a few minutes before we have a single table setting available."

"Excuse me, Miss," Jerry said. "Do you have an open table for three? Avery's my friend and we just happened to show up at the same time. That way he won't have to eat alone. Our other friend should be here any minute now."

"Yes, sir, I believe we do," she said. "Follow me, gentlemen."

"See, Avery, I told you I was looking out for your best interests," Jerry offered.

As Avery followed the hostess to the table, he slipped his hand behind his back and gave Jerry the finger.

"What other person?" Avery said, after they were seated.

"Hold on." Jerry speed dialed his cell phone. "He's having dinner, so come on in," he said, and hung up.

Avery whispered, "Is this really necessary?"

Jerry leaned in closer. "We went over this this morning. I'm just following orders, okay? And, yes, I don't want to have dinner with you either. But right now it's what I get paid to do, so the less attention we draw to ourselves the better. If the conversation stays civil, maybe we can enjoy our meal and all go home somewhat happy. So, how about it, Avery? Deal?"

Avery drummed his fingers on the tabletop.

"How about I pick up the tab," Jerry said. "Will that make your dinner more palatable?"

Avery exhaled. "Okay, but with one stipulation."

"I don't think you're in a position to demand anything."

Avery leaned forward. "It's not a demand, Jerry, but a simple request. Tail me if you want, but back off. People hovering over my shoulder make me nervous, sometimes to the point it gets ugly, and you don't want me to go there. So I'm asking you to give me some space. Like when I go home tonight, promise me your Marshal pal will park his butt at the end of the driveway, not outside my front door, okay? *Deal?*"

Jerry hesitated, then nodded in the affirmative.

A man approached the table and sat down next to Jerry.

"Avery, this is Deputy Lance Briscoe."

"I remember you," Avery said. "You're the guy who followed me around in Sports World, where I bought my bag. Or were you shopping for matching jockstraps for you and Jerry?"

"Avery," Jerry snapped, "our deal?"

"*Sorry*, Deputy." He faked a smile.

Their dinner conversation was minimal. Finished, Avery said, "Excuse me, gentlemen, I have to hit the head."

"I'll check it out," Deputy Briscoe said.

Avery gestured. "I'm just going to pee, that's all. I promise."

"I know, but you don't have a choice," Jerry said.

Avery sighed. "Go ahead, Lance, you've got your marching orders."

Once outside the restaurant, the deputies walked Avery to his car.

"Jerry, I have to ask you a question," Avery said. "Did you follow me today because you thought I had those disks secretly stashed in the sporting goods store, or they were somehow hidden here in the men's room? Is that it?"

"Not even close," Jerry said. "We want to know who's helping you."

Fortunately, Avery was leaning against his car or he might have fallen over. "Helping me?" he said weakly.

"Contrary to TV movies and public perception, we're not dumb," Deputy Briscoe offered.

"Lance is right," Jerry added. "Malcolm gave you those disks in Miami, and we know you didn't have them when you were relocated here. And now, suddenly you're Houdini, and you can magically pull them out of your ass? I don't think so."

"Believe what you want if it makes you feel better," Avery countered.

Jerry rolled his eyes. "Look, Avery, whoever it is, I'm sure they think they're doing you a favor. Our experience says it often results in the exact opposite. If they slip up it could blow your cover. And after your close call in Ohio, it could cost you your life. So tell us and we won't charge them with obstructing justice, a felony offense I might add. We'll let them walk away, scot-free."

"You're kidding, right?"

"Marshals don't joke when it comes to people breaking the law," Lance said.

"No, I mean I can't believe you seriously think someone's helping me." Avery forced an innocent grin, similar to the one he gave his grandmother whenever she caught him with his hand in the cookie jar. She never fell for it once.

NINE
•••

"Avery?" Buck's sleepy voice said.

"Sorry, but I had to call."

"Damn, Ave, it's two a.m."

"I know, but I couldn't wait any longer."

"Don't tell me I screwed up?"

"No, I got the flash drives, just like we planned. But I *was* surprised to see your truck already there."

"Yeah. Originally I was gonna take Polly to the Whole Hog Café—you know, the one just down from the Italian place—slip the thumb drives through your car window and have dinner at the same time. But then she couldn't go, so I ate early and waited for you to show, made the drop, then met up with Joe for a few beers."

"Polly does that a lot, doesn't she—cancel on you?"

"Yeah. But it's her mom who's the hang-up. Says she'll babysit, then ka-boom, somethin' comes up and she can't."

"Do you think she's trying to torpedo your relationship?"

"I don't think so. She's an uppity-up with the city. Polly says she's always schmoozin' with somebody. But I can't blame her, wantin' to hang out with adults rather than spend her nights with a five-year-old. Besides, she usually makes up for it, like she did the week when you went with us to the lake. You know, after my trek in the woods?"

"How could I forget?"

"So if you got what you need, why the hell call me at this hour?"

"A couple of things that can't wait. First off, the Marshals are certain somebody's helping me, and they want me to give you up."

"Are you shittin' me?"

"No, but if you want to walk away I can't blame you. Maybe you should."

"Yeah, well, the last time I checked we're still brothers, so screw 'em, I'll hang tight."

"Okay," Avery said. "But let me tell you what else. That asshole, Jerry, is coming to live here, *in my house*, the whole time I'm gone. So forget about looking after the place."

Buck swore. "How can he do that? It's your house."

"My guess is he wants to search the place from top to bottom for the MUI data. So let him look, he won't find squat."

Buck laughed. "Just think, maybe he'll dig up the yard and find another skeleton. Wouldn't that be somethin'? With your luck, it'll be *Mrs. Bones*."

"Very funny, Buck, but these guys are serious."

"I got that already. When exactly is it you leave?"

"Tomorrow. That's why I'm calling tonight. After I hang up I'm taking out the SIM card and throwing it and my phone in the lake, along with the thumb drives. It's a good thing you have copies."

"Okay, but then how do we talk?"

"Until I get back, we don't. It's too risky."

"All right. Then what happens?" Buck said.

"First, pick someplace to eat where we can meet—I'm guessing sometime in January. Then when I show up, we'll pretend to be surprised to see each other. And bring a new burner phone with you. I'll casually pick it up."

"How about the Whole Hog on Cantrell? I'm hooked on their pulled pork sandwiches."

"Okay, make it a Friday," Avery said.

"Sure, but you really think you'll be gone that long?"

"That's what I'm told."

"Isn't it risky bein' in Miami all that time?"

"No. After I testify they'll hide me somewhere else until my hair and beard grow out again. But it's not Miami that worries me. It's this damned disk thing that keeps me up at night. I think it all goes back to Malcolm."

"Your friend who got murdered?"

"Yeah, him. And after running it through my head a thousand times, I think I figured it out."

"Figured what?"

"Who killed my friends, and why they're looking for CDs, not flash drives."

TEN
• • •

Deputy Jerry Joyce arrived after dark to transport Avery to the airport to meet Roger Haslock and the private jet destined for Miami. "No offense, Avery, but I have to ask. Do you have the CDs?"

Avery thrust his hand into his new sports bag. *"Abracadabra."* He pulled out four CDs and held them up to the deputy's face. "I've had them all along, Jerry, right here under your nose," he lied. "The Boss, Elton John, Bon Jovi, and the frigging Beatles—or so it would appear." He grinned like a Cheshire cat.

• • •

After entering through a special gate at the Little Rock airport, Jerry drove the car onto the tarmac and stopped alongside a waiting plane near a darkened hangar. Avery exited the car and mounted the short flight of steps leading into the sleek twin-engine Learjet 60XR where Roger and another deputy were waiting.

Following a short conversation, Avery flashed Roger the set of CDs. Expressing relief, Roger offered Avery his choice of seats for the three-hour flight to Miami.

"What about my beard and long hair?" Avery asked, picking a seat.

"We'll get you all cleaned up when we land in Miami," Roger said.

"You mean others are going to see me looking like this?"

"A few deputies. But don't worry about the pilots," Roger motioned toward the cockpit. "They don't know why we're here."

"What about my new lawyer?" Avery said.

"You'll meet with him *after* you get to the courthouse, just as you asked, which doesn't make a whole lot of sense. He's your attorney for God's sake. He can't disclose anything to anyone without your permission. You know that."

"Right. But thanks to my last attorney, a bomb magically appeared under my car after you hid me in Ohio. But you always forget that part."

"Are you serious? Who do you think warned you? You're welcome, by the way, for us saving your ass," Roger said.

"Yeah, but you never caught the guy who did it. And what about my lawyer? You said it was him who leaked my address, and you didn't bust him either."

"I have to agree with you about your prick attorney, but we had no concrete proof to charge him," Roger said. "So what made you change your mind about needing a lawyer now?"

"Because I'm tired of you guys stepping all over me."

A second Marshal cleared his throat. "Deputy Haslock, if I may interrupt, we need to get this flight going. Avery, or should I say, John, try to relax. There'll be plenty of time for questions later."

Avery reclined in a single plush leather seat, took out his cell phone, hooked up his earbuds, and dialed in his favorite playlist. His new sports bag containing the four CDs rested in his lap, secure in his folded arms.

● ● ●

"John, John," Roger said, shaking Avery's shoulder.

John? "Huh, what?" Startled, Avery's body jerked awake. He pulled off his earbuds.

"Wake up, John, we're almost there."

Avery rubbed his face to clear the cobwebs, then squeezed his bag to make sure it still held the CDs.

"Listen, you'd better get used to being *John* again, even when you talk with your new attorney," Roger said.

"Yeah, I got it, I'm John again. What time is it anyway?"

"Almost one a.m.," Roger said. "As soon as we're off the plane we'll get you a shave and a haircut. Then in the morning we'll do your make-over."

"Makeover?" Avery said.

"Yes, we have to do something about your two-toned face."

"My what?"

"Part of your face is tanned, but not where your beard is," Roger said. "Somebody's bound to notice. We have someone who'll make you look a hundred percent like your old self. Then we'll parade you in front of the courthouse."

"The Dade County Courthouse, with all those high-rise buildings around it? No way, Rog. A sniper could gun me down before I got up the steps."

"No, no. It's the newer glass building on Miami Avenue."

"Oh, great, it has to be fifty yards to the front door. Are you *trying* to get me killed?"

"Don't worry, John, you'll be protected like Fort Knox, trust me. Besides, it's the best place to accommodate the press."

"I thought you were sneaking me in and out."

"Get real. Today you'll be the biggest thing on TV."

"But why?"

"Because the Government wants to scare the shit out of people— all those assholes avoiding taxes—thanks to MUI and your programming skills. When they see you walk into that building to testify, the more likely they are to turn themselves in, to try to get a better deal and stay out of jail."

● ● ●

Later that morning, in the street adjacent to the courthouse, Avery exited the Marshals' black SUV. One hand held fast to the shoulder strap of his sports bag, while the other pressed a copy of *USA Today* close to his face. His head remained down, his eyes fixed on Roger's shoes, not daring to look aside in fear his rubbery legs would collapse completely.

The police had difficulty holding their ground against the pressing crowd. Avery, flanked by Roger and numerous law enforcement personnel, forged their way through the gauntlet of clicking cameras and crazed reporters screaming their inane questions. In what seemed an eternity, Avery followed Roger's polished black Florsheims into the building.

Once inside, the doors were quickly closed and secured, which muffled the din of frenzied reporters.

"Now that wasn't so bad, was it?" Roger said. "Just like that, we got two for one."

Avery looked at him, puzzled.

Roger slapped Avery on the shoulder. "We walked slow enough to appease the press, *and* nobody put a bullet in your head. Like I said, piece of cake, John, piece of cake."

Roger and his posse marched Avery to a private security elevator and up several floors, down a corridor, and into a room. A wooden table with matching chairs stood in the middle of the room. Framed pictures of the Everglades hung on the beige walls. As Avery prepared to set his bag on the table, a second door opened and a man entered.

Roger pointed to Avery. "That's him."

"Okay, John, let's have 'em," the man barked.

"Who are you?" Avery said.

"I'm Richard Glenn, and I need to verify the disks you brought."

"Here, let me help," Roger said, and grabbed hold of Avery's bag. "They're in here."

"Hey, that's mine!" Avery yelled as he struggled for control of the bag.

"Not anymore, John. You're on our turf now," Roger countered.

Two court police officers pinned Avery against the wall as Roger took the bag and pulled out the CDs. "Here you go." The detective handed them to Richard, who immediately left the room.

"I guess this means I'm getting screwed, huh, Rog."

"Easy, John, easy," Roger said. "You'll get your deal all right; your immunity *and* your Witness Protection, exactly as promised. Except now, *we* have all the evidence and don't have to fart around anymore trying to figure out where you hid it. I'm surprised though, after all your efforts to keep us guessing, I expected to see more fight in you."

"Geez, Rog, what can I say? It's the way you sweet-talked me into it. I never could resist the persuasive arguments of a real asshole."

Roger stepped toward Avery. "You want to mess with me, Avery— I, uh—" His face turned red. "I mean, *John*?"

Avery didn't respond.

"I, uh, I need to pee," Roger said. "Just don't let this son-of-a-bitch leave the room 'til I get back. Clear?"

"Yes, sir," was the unison response.

The two officers loosened their grip on Avery's arms and directed him to a chair at the table. Another handed him his sports bag.

Before Roger returned, Richard Glenn barged into the room. "Is this some kind of joke?" he said, pointing a finger at Avery.

"What? I brought what you wanted," Avery replied.

"Like hell you did. Where's the rest of it?" Richard said. "You know, the foreign stuff."

"It was my understanding that I'm testifying before a *Federal* Grand Jury. I may not be a legal scholar, but it seems to me they're only involved with the wrongdoings of *American* citizens, not foreigners dealing with MUI through the Grand Cayman Islands. And that's what I gave you, the files regarding citizens of the United States doing business in Florida. But go ahead, correct me if I'm wrong, *Dick*."

"I'll do just that, wise guy," Richard countered, "because that's not what the subpoena stipulated."

"It said I had to show up, and that's what I did."

Just then, Roger re-entered the room. "What's going on?"

Richard Glenn explained his side of the story.

Roger rubbed his chin, not happy. "John, I warned you about not having an attorney, because he could have set you straight about the sub-poena *before* you left home. It's more than a simple subpoena, it's a *sub-poena duces tecum*, which means you show up along with *all* the CDs. But you didn't deliver, did you?"

"Okay, I didn't. So?"

"*So?* That's the best you've got?" Roger laughed. "John, you failed to comply with a court order, and for that bonehead move you win the grand prize: which means your Witness Protection deal is off, and you're going to jail."

Avery clenched his jaw and pressed his hands together to keep them from visibly shaking.

"Is there something brilliant you'd like to say?" Roger chided.

"I think I need to speak with my attorney," Avery said, in a half-hearted voice.

"Ha! Little good he'll do you now. But sure, John, it's your screw-up."

ELEVEN
• • •

A well-dressed woman entered the room and cleared her throat. "Excuse me for interrupting," she said. "John, my name is Margret Nylander. I'm chief counsel for the government and will be presenting our case to the Grand Jury. I'm certain the Marshals are looking out for your best interest, but it's times like these that people become, let's say, overly anxious, and say things they normally wouldn't, or *shouldn't* say." She looked directly at Roger.

"Gentlemen, I need the room," she said. "Deputy Haslock, would you please locate John's attorney? I believe Mr. Greene's waiting in the lobby. I'm sure we wouldn't want to violate John's civil or legal rights any more than we already have, now would we?"

"No ma'am," Haslock said, embarrassed, then turned to Avery. "I still can't believe you hired Martin Greene as your lawyer."

"Deputy Haslock," Ms. Nylander scolded.

"Yes, ma'am."

Ms. Nylander watched Roger and the others exit the room before she sat down opposite Avery.

"If this is another ploy—"

"John, let me talk first, then you can protest," she said. "First, I need to clear up certain comments made earlier. Yes, you are correct in that today we only need the information you gave us. You did, however, violate the conditions of the subpoena. It requires *all* the remaining MUI data."

Avery's back stiffened.

"But no," she motioned with her hand, "you will not go to jail or be removed from the Witness Protection Program. But we will have to work out the details."

Avery exhaled. "Thank you, but how do you know what was said?"

"Since you arrived, your conversation was being monitored from the adjoining room, where I heard every word. But I assure you, John, for now, that listening device has been turned off."

"Why are you telling me this?"

"Besides your lawyer, I may be the only person in this building who wants what's best for you. I also need your trust, which is asking a lot, especially with what happened with your last attorney. And from what I just witnessed, you seem to have difficulty with the Marshals as well."

"Can you blame me?" Avery said.

"I think it's Deputy Haslock's habit to be contentious."

"I think it's how they're all trained. Jerry acts the same way."

"Jerry?" she said.

"You know, the deputy where I live."

"Except for Roger's slip of the tongue, calling you Avery, I don't know your new identity *or* where you live. In fact, if I were to inquire about your new name or your location, I'd face a firewall of resistance, and you should be glad. Any contact I have with you, I'm required to go through the U.S. Marshals Service, as I did with Roger to get you here."

For the first time today, Avery breathed more easily.

"But as I said, I need you to trust me. That's why I confided in you," she said. "For us to go after MUI and those hidden accounts, your Grand Jury appearance is vital. Then once this whole thing is over, you can disappear and start a new life."

"Now you sound like the Marshals."

"That's because I'm a pragmatist, John. The way I see it, it's your one way out, so why not make the best of it?"

"I know it sounds logical, but my gut says I'm going to wind up like

Malcolm."

"Under the circumstances, I understand."

"No, Ms. Nylander, I don't think you do, because there are things you don't know. So please, let me explain."

She checked her designer wristwatch. "All right, but make it quick."

"Okay. To begin, it was Nelson and Malcolm who were going to turn over evidence to the FBI, not me. But when Nelson died, Malcolm came to see me the night before he was killed. He wanted me to have a copy of all the account data from MUI, here in Miami *and* the Caymans, because he thought Nelson's broken neck was no accident. He said I had to help, just in case.

"Anyway, it was Malcolm's idea to transfer all the data from flash drives onto CDs, and put them in plastic cases with different album covers, you know, artists like Elton John, The Stones. He said if somebody broke into his place or searched him, they'd be looking for the thumb drives, not CDs—because these days, only an idiot would store data on CDs. Anyway, he said he was giving them to the FBI the next morning."

"Then how did *you* get the disks?" she asked.

"I didn't. He gave me flash drives."

Ms. Nylander looked puzzled. "Then why did you give us CDs?"

"Because the next day, a man from the FBI called me and said the Government was screwed because Malcolm was dead and *the CDs* were missing. He asked me if I had them or a copy, and I said something like, 'Yeah, he gave me the data.'"

"That sounds reasonable. What's your point?"

"Ms. Nylander, from the beginning, the FBI said disks or CDs, *never* flash drives; the Marshals, too. At first I thought they were using the wrong terminology, coming from a bunch of older guys stuck in last century's technology. But now I don't think so, because the only other person who knew the data was on CDs was the FBI guy Malcolm was meeting."

The prosecutor buried her face in her hands.

"Ms. Nylander?"

She pressed her hands to the table and spoke in a hushed voice. "You're saying an agent of the Federal Bureau of Investigation was somehow involved with Malcolm's murder?"

Avery nodded. "That's why I'm afraid, and why I haven't told anyone except you, right now—not even Roger."

She paused for a moment. "Did the agent give you his name?"

"He did, but I don't remember. But if he was the one who murdered Malcolm, it makes no sense for him to tell me his real name. If anything, he would have used an alias."

Nylander agreed.

"Is there some way you can find out who Malcolm *was* supposed to meet?" Avery asked.

"Hmm." She tapped her pen on the table. "Without tipping off the agent, it would be tricky." Again she paused. "But I do know a person with connections, so it might be possible."

Avery nodded his approval. He was beginning to like this lady.

"Let me go back a minute," she said. "If the person who killed Malcolm took the CDs, why would he need to ask if you had a copy?"

"Because a decryption code was required to open them. It's mnemonic, with a series of fourteen jumbled numbers, letters, and symbols no one would ever guess—and it wasn't written down. I figure the killer didn't think about a code before he shot him."

"But you know it?"

"Of course, I have it memorized," Avery said in a matter of fact way.

"I see. But why didn't you just turn over the data after Malcolm died?"

"Because if I did, they said Witness Protection wasn't necessary. But my gut said something different. Whoever killed Nelson didn't have to. It was Malcolm who had the data. I think they were both killed just because they agreed to cooperate. That's why I hid everything Malcolm gave me, to make sure they put me in Witness Protection. It's why I didn't bring you everything today—afraid they'll kick me out."

"The Marshals think you gave it to someone else to keep, but they don't know who," she said. "Is that true?"

Avery hesitated. "Because I'd like to keep them guessing, I'd rather not say."

Ms. Nylander nervously tapped her pen on the table. "You're not making this easy for me, are you?"

A sharp tap on the door interrupted their dialog.

TWELVE

● ● ●

Roger Haslock stepped into the room followed by a noticeably shorter man. Roger wore a grin on his face. "It took a while to find him, but here he is, John, your new attorney. It appears the esteemed Mr. Greene is conflicted because the evidence you hold may well include the names of crooks, I mean clients he presently represents. He expressed his apologies and sent—"

"Thank you, Deputy Haslock," the short man interrupted. "I'll take it from here." He patiently waited until the Marshal left and closed the door behind him. "Ma'am," he said, turning to Ms. Nylander, "my apologies for taking so long in coming." He then extended his right hand to Avery. "John, my name's Raymond Bryce, I'm here as your counsel. Call me Ray if you like. Mr. Greene filled me in on your case as best he could."

Avery hoped Raymond Bryce's legal skills were reflective of his firm handshake rather than his considerably small stature, wrinkled suit, or his unruly hair, with touches of gray. After exchanging pleasantries, Mr. Bryce sat down, his feet barely touched the floor.

Ms. Nylander took little time to explain Avery's Grand Jury testimony and the information he was expected to provide. "Do you have any questions?" she said when finished.

"Yes, I do," Mr. Bryce began. The toes of his shoes pressed the vinyl flooring while he adjusted his chair. "On my way up from the lobby, Deputy Haslock expressed his, let's say concern, because my client failed to provide information regarding the names of foreign investors doing business with MUI in the Grand Caymans. Is that correct?"

"May I explain?" she said.

"Of course."

"Just because MUI operated in the Caymans, does not preclude that all transactions began or ended there, especially given your client's creative programming skills." She eyeballed Avery.

"What we're looking for," she continued, "is a trail of American investments filtered from Miami through the Grand Caymans and then beyond. It's important to keep in mind this perspective: in the Caymans, *all* Americans are foreigners, hence the term, foreign investors. That's why we need the evidence your client still holds, not only to prove our allegations, but for the IRS to track both the money and the investors themselves."

"What about non-Americans. Are you after them, too?" Mr. Bryce asked.

"Is that question aimed at helping John, or other clients you may represent?" Ms. Nylander replied.

Mr. Bryce's body stiffened. "I take offense to that comment, Madam Prosecutor. I'm surprised a person of your position and reputation would ask such a thing."

"Oh, please, counselor, save your grandstanding for the press and the courtroom. Considering you came here at the behest of the infamous Martin Greene, I assume you are similarly connected."

The lawyer cleared his throat. "Ma'am, other than being roommates at law school, and sharing a common desire to be damn good lawyers, our paths are not further connected, unless you count exchanging birthday and holiday phone calls. In case you hadn't noticed, this ten-year-old suit and my worn-out pair of shoes should belie any suspicion that I circulate in the client world of Martin Greene. I've only recently moved to Florida to get back on my feet. I'm recovering from"—Mr. Bryce cleared his throat—"being ill. I think Marty threw me a bone to help me out. My question was simply an attempt to quantify exactly what John is required to relinquish and what he is not."

"He gives us everything. I'll make sure you're provided with a copy of the Court's ruling and the subpoena—it's very specific—plus a copy of everything we have pertaining to John." She wrote on a notepad.

"Thank you, ma'am," the attorney said.

"And, my apologies, Mr. Bryce. Perhaps I was a bit harsh."

"It's ancient history, ma'am. It's all forgotten. And please, Ms. Nylander, call me Ray."

"I appreciate that, Ray." She turned to Avery. "John, do you have any questions?"

"About the Grand Jury? No, but I'm still worried about turning over the other CDs, especially after, uh, you know." He nodded at Ms. Nylander.

"What's he talking about?" Mr. Bryce asked.

"Don't tell him, Ms. Nylander. I don't want anybody else to know."

"But, John, I'm your attorney. I'm sworn to secrecy."

"No offense, Ray, but so was my last lawyer. Besides, I think it'd be safer for you not to know."

The attorney gave Ms. Nylander a questioning look.

"Mr. Bryce—Ray, one of John's concerns is what harm might befall him by turning over the data."

"Then let me ask you again, Ms. Nylander, about foreign investments made through MUI, and I don't mean by Americans. Are you being pressured by other countries to turn over names and figures?"

"Not yet," she said. "But it's something we do anticipate."

Mr. Bryce turned to Avery. "Even when caught, individuals who cheat the IRS seldom, if ever, resort to violence." Mr. Bryce rubbed his stubbled chin. "But professional criminals, especially those in foreign cartels, are malevolent creatures of habit when it comes to people who mess with their money or threaten their lifestyle. The mere fact they think you now have, or *ever* had this information, puts you in danger. The murder of your friends Nelson and Malcolm bears witness to that fact."

"Does that mean I'm not crazy being afraid every time I start my car?" Avery said.

"The way these people operate, no, you have every right to be," Mr.

Bryce answered. "And speaking as your counsel, and being a life-long criminal defense attorney who has at times represented these nasty people, I'd advise you to stay in Witness Protection forever, or else find a dark cave somewhere and never come out."

"But I'm already tired of hiding, and it's only been fourteen months," Avery said. "I've got to do this the rest of my life? Can't you announce to the world that I'm done with this and I refuse to cooperate with the government, ever?"

"Yes, I could. But as I said, whether you do or don't, if they ever find you, you're a dead man."

"Don't you think that's a rather harsh opinion?" Ms. Nylander said.

"I don't," Mr. Bryce said. "Why else would John be in Witness Protection? Or would you like to check with the Marshals Service?"

"You don't have to," Avery interjected. "Every deputy I met told me the same thing."

"All right, Ray, I get your point," she said.

"Good," he said. "But what's bothersome is you wasting your time if you think any of these foreigners will wind up behind bars or give up any of their money. The only person at risk is John."

"How do you figure?" she said.

"It's the way you're going about it, ma'am. Your first mistake was to parade John in front of the press as the great whistleblower. Yes, you're going after Americans citizens for fraud and tax evasion, while behind the scenes other countries negotiate with our Government over John's precious data from MUI. The problem is, before long, everybody will know what's going on. And because it takes governments so long to act, all the crooks will have disappeared, along with their money. Meanwhile, John's only way out is to reinvent himself as a new person or live the rest of his life in fear in Witness Protection."

"You make it sound so bleak," she said.

Their banter continued for several minutes before Ms. Nylander checked the time and changed the subject. "John, I need to speak to you privately about, well, you know."

"You'll do no such thing," the attorney said.

"Mr. Bryce, I assure you, after we talk, John is free to tell you anything he wishes regarding our conversation."

"It's all right, Ray, I'll be fine," Avery said.

The attorney slid off his chair and exited the room, still unconvinced.

"Unfortunately, John, I believe Mr. Bryce is right about the prosecution of non-Americans, and he's not the first person to voice that same opinion. Or do you disagree?"

"No, I'm sold," Avery said.

She nodded. "And with a rogue FBI agent out there, you're in even greater danger. That's why I suggest you settle things with Mr. Bryce, then ditch the U.S. Marshals and disappear."

"Huh?"

THIRTEEN

• • •

Following Avery's Grand Jury testimony, he met privately with his attorney. "Ray, thanks for coming. As much as I'd like to say I don't need you, I do."

"Of course, how may I help?"

"I want you to sell my two condominiums. One here in Miami, and another one I own in the Grand Caymans. You keep five percent of the sales price. Is that agreeable?"

"In addition to your original ten thousand dollar retainer, what kind of money are we talking about?"

"It's prime property, so unless you're holding a fire sale the condos should net me close to six million, even if you go through a real estate agency. Under the circumstances, I have no qualms about giving you a big slice. Just don't take too long."

Mr. Bryce grinned. "Of course, I'll agree to that."

"Good. Set up a separate bank account, and when it's all done, transfer my share to my Swiss Bank account—I'll give you the number," Avery said. "Everything is still held under my real name, so keep it that way. And pay the government whatever I might owe in taxes. The last thing I need is more trouble with the Feds."

"Yes, of course, but you know you have to give me power of

attorney?"

"I do, but only for the bank account and the sale of the condos."

"That's understandable. Considering the rumors I hear about your last lawyer, I'll try to rectify your faith in our profession. I'll bring along my secretary to notarize the documents."

"Can she be trusted?" Avery asked.

"Implicitly. *He* is someone I've known for years."

"Okay, as long as he doesn't know what I'm up to."

"I'll make sure," Mr. Bryce added.

"I also need a simple will. You know, in case I don't make it."

"All right. Who's the lucky beneficiary? Or are there more than one?"

"Just one. But is there any way I can fill in the name later? I don't want anyone to know."

Raymond Bryce laughed. "I believe you, and if I thought you were married I'd say it's your mistress, because you wouldn't want your wife to find out until *after* you were dead."

"Very funny," Avery said. "But if the wrong person learns who he is, then they can find him, which means they can find me, too."

"I understand your life's in danger, but come on, this is not a public document," Bryce said. "But if it will make you feel better, I won't keep a copy for my files."

"Yeah, okay," Avery said. "His name is Luther Roebuck James."

The attorney wrote it down. "Does he know you're doing this?"

"No, he'd be a nervous wreck. So when I croak, I want it to be a surprise."

"And if he dies first, he won't ever have to be disappointed. Is that what you're saying?"

"Right." Avery smiled. "Can you have everything ready by tomorrow morning?"

"Of course."

"Good, because I have one other thing for you to do. After I sign the papers, I need you to withdraw thirty thousand in non-sequenced twenty-dollar bills from my bank's savings account, and another twenty Gs in hundreds. Which means you'd better add that account to your power of attorney."

"You do know, any transactions over ten grand and the bank has to report it to the Feds? I'll have to fill out paperwork saying where the money's from and where it's going. I'll need your social, date of birth, street address, the whole nine yards."

"Oh, yeah, that's right. Tell them I'm making a down payment on a yacht, or I'm going gambling; say whatever will get the cash. And use my Miami condo address. Will that work?"

"Sure, but let's stay with the yacht. That way I can keep a straight face."

"Of course," Avery said. "Stick the cash in a nondescript sports bag. I need it three days from now."

Mr. Bryce cleared his throat. "What the hell's going on, John—power of attorney, selling your condos, fifty Gs in cash?"

Avery sighed. "Here it is, Ray. I'm going to disappear. So when you bring me the money, I need a ride out of town. I'll give you directions when you pick me up. Then hopefully, you'll never hear from me again."

"You're leaving Witness Protection? Are you insane?"

"In fear for my life is more like it. I've thought about what you said when we met with Nylander, and after speaking with her, I've made up my mind. So, yeah, Ray, sane or insane, I quit. I'm out of here."

Mr. Bryce shook his head. "I don't agree with your decision, but I do understand it."

"Good, because I need you to sell it," Avery said.

"Sell it?"

"After I ditch the Marshals, I want you to hold a press conference and announce to the world I'm on the run, that I'm not cooperating—even though I did—and say I didn't turn over anything from MUI, especially the Caymans."

"I understand." Mr. Bryce nodded. "But how will I know if you've succeeded in getting away?"

"I'll text or call your cell phone, so I need the number. I'll simply say, 'I'm free.' That's when you call the media."

"Have you figured the odds of succeeding at this?"

"Better than I've got going now, that's for sure," Avery said.

"You seem so certain."

Avery lowered his voice. "Ray, trust me, I think the person who murdered Nelson and Malcolm is an FBI agent—or a friend of his—and that's no joke. He already tried to kill me with a car bomb. That's why I have to vanish. Otherwise, with his connections, he'll eventually ferret me out, and then, *bang*, I'm dead."

Mr. Bryce's eyes grew big. "Does anybody else know about this?"

"Only Nylander, and now you," Avery said.

"You think telling her was wise?"

Avery shrugged. "I had to tell somebody, and for some reason I trust her. If I told the Marshals, they'd think I'm blowing smoke up their ass."

"You may have a point. But what can Nylander do?"

"She knows someone who might be able to track down the agent. But because there's no guarantee, she said I should run away."

Bryce looked shocked. "It was her idea? That's crazy! If someone finds out, her career's in the tank. She could serve time."

"Only if somebody rats her out." Avery stared at his attorney.

Mr. Bryce nodded his understanding.

"Then if we're still good, that's all I'm saying."

"We are, but beyond that, I know nothing." Mr. Bryce brushed his hands together. "Do you know where you're going to hide out?"

Avery paused. "Not exactly. I'm still working on it."

"Then let me make a suggestion. I know a man with a boat on the Gulf. For a price, he'll take you to South America. I can give you the details when we meet."

Avery shrugged. "Sure, I'll take it. It might come in handy."

"All right, but you didn't hear about it from me."

Avery agreed. "Listen, Ray, I have to warn you. If someone from the FBI contacts you, watch your back."

"All right, but hopefully they'll catch the guy."

"Great, but who's going to catch him, the Bureau?"

"I get it," Mr. Bryce said. "But what about me selling your condos and moving money around? Won't the Marshals step in?"

"They're more likely to wait for me to make a withdrawal. Then they can follow the money. That's why I need the fifty thousand now. By the time I run through that, you'll have transferred my condo money to my numbered Swiss account. As soon as that happens, I'll change the account again, then they'll never find it *or* me."

Avery gave the lawyer his financial details, then pulled up one of his pants legs and wrote Bryce's cell number on the flesh of his calf.

MUI Whistleblower Flees

MIAMI – Mr. Raymond Bryce, attorney for the Monterey United International whistleblower, John Hammer, released a statement today confirming a rumor that his client has fled the Government's Witness Protection Program. Persons from the U.S. Marshals Service, as well as those from the Department of Justice declined comment.

Last week, in a scheduled appearance before a Federal Grand Jury, Hammer refused to cooperate, a source reported. He also failed to turn over sensitive client investment information from MUI offices in Miami and the Grand Cayman Islands. An anonymous official from the Justice Department said, "John told me he feared for his life."

Bryce confirmed this report by saying, "I'm sure the threats against his life, plus the constant haranguing by Justice officials, is what drove John to do what he believed was in his best interest."

The attorney stated he had no knowledge of John's whereabouts, where he was going, or how to contact him. "Clearly, he's flown the coop," Bryce said.

FOURTEEN

•••

Federal Prosecutor Margret Nylander had convinced Roger Haslock and the U.S. Marshals Service to go along with the story that Avery had fled their custody. Unwillingness on the part of the Marshals turned cooperative when Avery revealed his theory regarding the deaths of Nelson and Malcolm. After discreetly checking with unnamed sources, Deputy Haslock concurred, and believing there was no other logical explanation, he pledged to cooperate with the ruse. But even among the Marshals Service, only a select few would know of the deception.

Part of the deal was for Avery to surrender the remaining MUI documents involving the Grand Cayman Islands to Ms. Nylander upon his return to Little Rock. For now, she and her team would begin work using the data Avery had given them. The other part was the assurance Avery would remain in Witness Protection. Meanwhile, the general public would be told that Avery, in possession of the coded data from both Miami and the Caymans, had run away and therefore the Grand Jury inquiry regarding MUI would be suspended—again, all lies.

"By tracking these people and their money from behind the scenes, it will make our efforts more productive if people think you've disappeared," Nylander told Avery. "And with you supposedly missing, it should also make it more difficult for the rogue FBI agent to find you, don't you think?"

"What other choice do I have?" Avery said.

Before arriving in Miami to testify, Avery had wanted little to do with Roger and the U.S. Marshals. But now their attentiveness to his well-being was almost reassuring. Almost.

Avery stressed to Roger and Ms. Nylander that his attorney, Raymond Bryce, be kept in the dark regarding his supposed flight from Witness Protection. Avery trusted Mr. Bryce from their first meeting, but only so far. He was, after all, a lawyer.

And although Avery promised to surrender *all* MUI documents to Ms. Nylander, it seemed so final. Any leverage he had would be gone. It meant trusting her *and* the Federal Government to keep their word. It wasn't Margret Nylander he worried about.

• • •

Two weeks into the New Year, and the return of Avery's brown beard and full head of hair, the Marshals believed it was finally safe for Avery to return to Little Rock. Where the Marshals had kept him in hiding, he wasn't sure. It did convince him, however, he was never going to be comfortable living forever under the thumb of the Marshals and Witness Protection, even in Little Rock. But what was his alternative? To his consternation, even with 5.8 million dollars from the sale of his condos now hidden in a numbered Swiss bank account, he had no clear answer.

FIFTEEN

• • •

The first Friday after arriving back in Little Rock, Avery went to lunch at the Whole Hog Café on Cantrell Road in hopes of finding Buck. Grabbing a soft drink from the self-serve machine, he headed for an empty table.

"Hey, Avery," a voice said.

Avery turned to see Buck's plumber friend, Joe, sitting in a booth.

"Long time no see," Joe said. "Buck said you've been out of town."

"Uh, yeah. I was doing some consulting. How about you?"

"Workin' with Buck on some condos near downtown. He went to the head. Oh, look, here comes the SOB now. My turn." Joe exited the booth. "Hey, Buck, look who's back?"

Avery and Buck shook hands and exchanged a casual greeting.

"Did you eat?" Buck said.

"No, just ordered. Waiting for them to call my number."

"Then take a load off."

Avery squeezed into the booth across from his brother.

"You doin' okay?" Buck asked.

"Besides trying not to be bored, *and* freezing my nuts off, am I still a hunted man? What does this beard tell you?"

Buck laughed. "It's good to see you, too."

Avery smiled back.

Buck leaned closer. "You know, it scared the crap out of me when the news said you'd ditched the Marshals and was on the run. You could have told me before you left."

"I didn't know myself until it happened. But you got my postcard, right?"

"Yeah, a week later, and all it said was, '*Don't believe everything you read*,' signed with a smiley face. What the hell kind of message was that? I half expected you to never come back."

"Well, here I am. What you heard in the news was all BS," Avery said. "I'm still in Witness Protection, but right now that's a good thing."

Buck hunched his shoulders. "Because?"

"It has to do with convincing the FBI I've gone walkabout. I'll fill you in later."

"Sure, which reminds me." Buck checked to see if anyone was watching, then slid a cell phone across the wooden tabletop. "It's a burner, like before. I programmed in my number and set it on vibrate only."

Avery slipped the phone into his coat pocket. "Thanks. I'll call you tonight."

"Better wait 'til tomorrow. Polly might be stayin' over."

"Might be? You two still playing that game?"

"Me and her? I keep tellin' you, it's her mother. Polly and me, we're solid."

"For your sake, I wish I could believe that."

"What's not to believe?" Buck said. "The only thing *I'm* playin' is my guitar. And thanks to her, I practice every day."

"I know Polly keeps saying it's her mom who can't babysit, but something's not right about her. And I'm not talking about her mother."

"If you really thought that, how come you never said, or are you just jealous because you can't get your own woman?"

"Look, I'm not saying she's a bad person or anything, I just don't think she's the one for you. Call it a hunch. Besides, I thought by now you'd have gotten tired of being put off half the time and moved on."

"Moved on? Geez, Avery, I'm thinkin' about buyin' her a ring."

"A friggin' ring? Seriously?"

"I'm just thinkin' about it, okay. And if I remember right, most of your hunches don't amount to jack."

"Yeah, well, you got me on that one."

"Number one-seventeen," a voice called out.

"That's me," Avery said. "But I should eat at another table, in case Deputy Jerry walks in."

"That's all right," Buck said, "I've got to get Joe's lazy ass back to work. Call me tomorrow, but make it after ten."

"Sure," Avery said. "By the way, when was the last time you got laid?"

Buck rolled his eyes. "Talk about playin' games."

"I need those other flash drives," Avery whispered.

"But I thought—"

"I changed my mind. I'll explain tomorrow." Avery stood and gave Buck a friendly slap on the arm. "Sorry I got on your case about Polly."

"No worries," Buck replied.

"Then good luck tonight." Avery gave Buck two thumbs up, grabbed his soft drink glass, and turned to lay claim to his barbeque ribs, potato salad, and side of beans.

SIXTEEN

• • •

As promised, Avery was ready to turn over MUI's Grand Cayman documents to Federal Prosecutor Margret Nylander. After a clandestine meeting with Buck to collect the two remaining thumb drives, Avery transferred their contents onto four CDs with easily readable lists of names, dates, amounts of money, corresponding account numbers, and any redistribution of funds from MUI in the Caymans to other foreign entities. When finished, he returned *three* thumb drives to Buck for safekeeping.

On the designated morning, Avery met Jerry Joyce in the parking lot of the Clinton Library. Jerry drove to the airport where they waited near an isolated hangar for the arrival of Deputy Roger Haslock. Within minutes the sleek Learjet approached.

"Don't leave the car," Jerry told Avery. "Let him come to us. We don't want to risk you being seen. The tinted glass will keep you hidden."

Roger disembarked, walked to the car, and crawled into the back seat with Avery. Following a short conversation, Avery handed Roger the CDs. Everyone agreed to continue with the disk motif to avoid arousing undue curiosity.

"So this is it?" Roger said.

"Everything you need is on those CDs. One for people who live in the U.S. and Canada; one for Central and South America; one for Europe and Asia; and one for the Pacific Rim and other countries. The disks are marked accordingly."

"Thanks, John. Or should I say Avery from now on?"

They shook hands, and Roger left to board the private plane to return to Miami. Jerry drove back to the Clinton Library where Avery had parked his car.

Avery pulled up the collar of his jacket against the chilly air and walked to the levee overlooking the Arkansas River. Rather than take in the view, his mind was on his exchange with Roger. Avery hadn't lied to him, but then again, he hadn't been completely forthcoming either. Roger did have the data Ms. Nylander requested, just not all of it. Although it wasn't Avery's original intention, it was something he had stumbled upon.

During the process of transferring the MUI data onto disks, Avery recognized the names of 18 prominent American politicians, all with squeaky-clean reputations: two Governors, five Congressmen, one Congresswoman, and six U.S. Senators, one of whom was campaigning to be his party's next Presidential candidate, plus three former Senators and one former Vice President.

He moved the 18 names and their account information to a separate flash drive, then deleted them from the CDs he handed over to Roger. He gave that flash drive to Buck.

Avery smiled to himself. If ever he needed a bargaining chip, this might be worth a great deal; an ace in the hole should he ever need one.

He also came across an important 19th name, but after a short pause, he pressed the delete button and kept no record of it. He would never mention it, not even to Buck. Was it ethical? Of course not. But considering his situation, it would only complicate his already tenuous position. The account balance had read $15,672,353.03. The name on the account was his.

Now Avery Gillis had a second numbered Swiss bank account only *he* knew about—or so he thought.

SEVENTEEN
• • •

It happened on the 13th green.

To Avery's delight, in early March a warm spell hit the city. Spring was on its way. Now he could escape the confines of his house and play golf without wearing thermals.

Growing up, he played golf with Buck and their grandfather, and was a member of the varsity team in high school and his Ivy League college. After arriving in Florida, he took lessons and became a three handicapper. Since coming to Little Rock, golf had become the one thing he looked forward to. It took him outside where he could breathe. It gave him the illusion of freedom from the Marshals and the rules they insisted he follow.

The Marshals cautioned him against playing golf because it was the one common thread he had with his previous life. Avery persisted, however, saying if he only played on public courses, the likelihood of someone tracking him down was next to impossible. The Marshals relented, as long as he only played on weekdays and late mornings, when fewer people played and he was more likely to play alone.

This particular day, Avery ventured to the public course situated along the Arkansas River, off Rebsamen Park Road—one of his favorites. He played the front nine by himself, and had just hit off the 10th tee when a lone man pulled up in a golf cart.

"Howdy," the man said, exiting his cart. "The starter suggested I join you on the back nine since I don't have time for a full eighteen. Is that okay?"

Avery couldn't help notice the man's attire—overdressed, especially for a public course. Even the logo on the ball cap covering his bald head matched that of his high-end brand of clubs.

Avery tried to smile. "Why don't you play through, I'm in no hurry."

"Thanks, but I don't have to be back in my office that soon," the man said. "Besides, I hate playing by myself, don't you?"

Avery hesitated. "I suppose," was the best he could muster.

The man pulled the driver from his bag and walked toward Avery. "I'm Karl, Karl with a K. Last name's Casey with a C." With a broad grin he extend his hand. "How about you?"

"Avery," he said in return, not giving his last name, and secretly wondered whose god he pissed off to deserve playing with *this* guy.

From the beginning, Karl peppered Avery with questions. The very reason Avery preferred to golf alone was to avoid having to recite his rehearsed lies and answer innocuous questions about who he was and what he did for a living. His responses would prompt further curiosity because Avery lacked any hint of a Southern drawl, which required him to produce even more fairytale stories as to why he lived in Little Rock.

The pair had only played two holes and Karl Casey's verbal barrage had driven Avery to distraction. It also didn't help that the guy was taller and outweighed Avery by 40 pounds. Not only did he hit the ball a mile, he hit it dead straight. On the 12th green, Avery missed a four-foot putt for birdie and settled for a five.

"Tough break, but nice par," Karl said, as the pair walked off the green.

"Thanks," Avery tried to say in a pleasant voice.

"That's three straight pars. Damn, you're good."

"You play a good game yourself."

"Thanks. But, no, I mean it. Where'd you learn to play so well?"

Rather than blurt out, "Taking private lessons in Miami," Avery said, "I don't mean to be abrupt, Karl, but the reason I play by myself is to clear my mind and enjoy the green surroundings, and that's difficult to do when people talk to me, because then I feel obliged to answer." He forced a smile. "Sorry, it's nothing personal."

Karl cleared his throat. "Well then, my apologies, sir. From now on my small-talk lips are sealed." He ran his fingers across his mouth and walked ahead to his cart.

The golf course's picturesque par four, 330-yard 13th hole ran alongside the curved banks of the Arkansas River. Both golfers managed to safely negotiate the narrow fairway and land on the elevated green in regulation. Neither player spoke.

The secluded two-tiered green lay on a small point near a bend in the river. With water on one side, a tall stand of eucalyptus trees guarded the green on the other and ran back toward the tee box. One hundred yards across the river's expanse, on the opposite bank, lush vegetation and native trees covered the rugged terrain with no sign of civilization.

As Avery was away, Karl pulled the flagstick. Avery's long putt came to rest three inches left of the hole.

"I'll give you that one," Karl said.

Avery walked toward the hole.

Karl glanced back toward the open fairway, then said, "Nice up, *John.*"

Avery's knees buckled. Blood drained from his face. The putter fell from his hand. The unexpectedness of Karl's words rendered him speechless.

Karl gave Avery a crooked smile. "Jesus, John, don't faint on me. If I was here to kill you, you'd be dead already." He reached down, picked up Avery's ball and putter, and handed them to him.

"Thanks," Avery said weakly. His hand pressed against his chest. "Who the hell are you?"

"I think we'd better stick with Karl," he said. "Your prosecutor friend from Miami, Margret Nylander, sends her regards."

"Nylander?" Avery sucked in a few breaths to regain his composure. "Yeah, okay, but did you have to scare the bejesus out of me? Couldn't you just knock on my front door?"

Karl smiled again. "From the get-go you pegged me as an obnoxious, loud-mouthed fool. For a man marked for death, you need to pay more attention to how easy it is for someone to get close to you. The next time you might not be so lucky."

Avery rolled his eyes. "*She* told you how to find me?"

"Hell, she doesn't even know your bogus name, let alone where you live. Which says if I can find you, so can that scumbag FBI agent. And I didn't stop by your house because I don't know where you live, just where you play golf. Besides, I wouldn't want to inadvertently tip my hand to your Marshal friends."

"They don't know you're here?"

"Are you serious? Roger Haslock would have a shit-fit if he knew I'd found you." Karl glanced back down the fairway. A twosome was about to tee off. "We need to talk someplace private. I'll explain more then." He replaced the flagstick, picked up his ball, and with Avery, walked to their carts.

They returned to the clubhouse and then to the front seat of Avery's car.

"How'd you find me?" was Avery's first question.

Karl nodded. "I figured out you were in Little Rock because the Marshals Service has the bad habit of using the same private air service to move high-risk people around. Couple that with the fact that major airports keep meticulous records of planes that land and take off, and it didn't take long to find out Transcontinental Air had four flights into Miami within three days of when you testified. Only one of them was in the dead of night—it had to be your plane. And when I tracked down the two pilots, they said the flight was from Little Rock, but didn't know any of the details."

"They just told you? They didn't ask questions?" Avery said.

"Of course, but once I flashed them my credentials, they gave it up, *just like that*." Karl snapped his fingers.

"Okay, but I could be living in the boonies somewhere."

"Huh, not really. Small towns with nosey locals aren't good places to hide high profile people. Little Rock, on the other hand, is perfect— easy to monitor, but enough population for strangers to blend in. Except for your weakness, I might never have found you."

Avery raised his eyebrows.

"Golf. You're good at it, and good golfers just can't give it up. That's what I counted on. So I photoshopped your face and made up several composites, including one with a beard and long hair. When the weather changed, I flew in and started visiting public courses, and there aren't that many in these parts. I said I was a Federal agent and it was important I find you. I flashed your pictures around, and *bingo,* it only took five days. The guy in the pro shop called me as soon as you headed for the first tee."

Avery shook his head in disbelief. "If Nylander sent you, what does she want?"

"There's a small problem she hopes you can resolve," Karl said.

"Sure, what is it?"

"By last month, news of the Grand Jury's impending indictment of MUI officials began to leak out—as if that's any big surprise—and guess what? Two Congressmen paid her a personal visit to fess up. In private, of course, no doubt trying to cover their respective asses. But for some reason their names failed to show up on any of the files you turned over. Would you care to explain that?"

Avery's stomach churned.

"Don't tell me, you decided to hold out a few names, important names I'm guessing, to ferret away another trump card—is that it?"

Avery shrugged. "Can you blame me?"

"Nice try, but let's get something straight. You *used* to hold the cards, apparently the entire deck. But those days are over. Nylander's goodwill has reached the end of its rope, and unless you want to find yourself hanging at the end of it, get over yourself."

Avery's body slumped.

"How many names are we talking about?" Karl asked. "And I'm not in the mood for some bullshit answer."

Avery's fingers nervously tapped the steering wheel. "Eighteen."

"That's it, eighteen?"

"Yeah, no bullshit. And they're all politicians. If there were more, then I missed them," Avery said. "And one's making a run for President. Will Nylander go after him, too, or chicken out?"

"Actually a little of both."

"Talk about a bullshit answer; what's that supposed to mean?"

"You do know how many names are on the list, right?" Karl asked. "The *big* list."

"Yeah, but—"

"Hear me out before you go ape-shit, okay? There's enough names and accounts to keep Nylander and the IRS busy for who knows how long. So instead, a public announcement will be made next month, saying any U.S. citizen who invested money with MUI, who filtered it through the Grand Caymans to avoid paying Federal taxes, is going to be prosecuted by the IRS for tax evasion, resulting in fines and possible imprisonment, *and* their names will be made public. *Unless*, that is, they voluntarily turn themselves in and pay a thirty-three percent across-the-board tax on their deposits. And to further guarantee everyone's cooperation, their names will never see the light of day."

"You can't be frigging serious?"

"I told you not to get all pissy. It's a win-win for both the government and the people involved. The government rakes in billions with little expense, and those involved are saved from public scorn and humiliation. A person would have to be crazy not to do it."

"Right, and all these politicians avoid being exposed so they can be reelected as upstanding citizens, when they're really douche-bags," Avery said. "Figures."

"You're one to talk."

"*Me?*"

Karl laughed. "Let's see, you want these *douche-bag politicians*—as you call them—punished somehow instead of letting them off. It's ironic you would even think that, let alone say it. If there's anyone who's a criminal, it's you, for writing that computer program to begin with." Karl pointed his finger. "Then, when cornered, you demanded a deal—no jail time *and* to be put in Witness Protection—as if you were somehow entitled. And now you have the balls to complain about politicians? Instead of going to prison where you belong, you get a free pass to start life over again, compliments of two dead friends and the United States Government. It's like your very own lifetime entitlement."

Avery wanted to crawl into a hole.

"Which reminds me. Nylander thinks she's missing one more name on that list."

"No. I told you already, eighteen, that's all."

"So the millions paid to you under the table in the Caymans just vanished into thin air?"

Avery's mouth opened but nothing came out.

"I know, you bought two luxury condos, drove an expensive car, and had a six-figure bank account. But that was all from your Miami salary. Add to that your Caymans money and the numbers don't add up."

Avery exhaled in frustration. "How do you know all this?"

"Easy. You're not the only one trying to save his own skin. It seems your old boss at MUI couldn't talk fast enough."

Avery's head flopped back against the headrest.

"He said you raked in over fifteen million, but Nylander can't find it." Karl stared at Avery.

"I deleted it."

"You—" Karl stopped in mid-sentence. "Holy shit. And Nylander said you were smart."

Avery's head was spinning. He turned to Karl. "Look, I screwed up, okay. I already told her that. But honest, I deleted my account because I was afraid, that's all."

"Of what? Fifteen million dollars?"

"No. Nylander said she was going to prosecute everyone, no exceptions, and I would have been one of them. Look, I get it: the Marshals, the IRS, nobody likes me. I was afraid it'd be an easy excuse to kick me out of Witness Protection or throw me in jail. Either way, I'd be dead for sure. That's why I did it."

Karl hesitated, then smiled. "Wait, don't tell me. You put it in an untraceable foreign bank account, didn't you?"

"Uh, yeah, but I was never going to tap into it."

"Ha." Karl threw up his hands. "I take it all back, you *are* cunning. But at this point it doesn't matter. Nylander wants a list of those names, and *yours* better be on it, otherwise she *will* prosecute you."

Avery nodded. "In that case, do I get to keep what's left?"

Karl laughed. "First you don't want anything to do with the money, then five seconds later, as long as you can skate, you want it back. Damn, you've really got a set of brass ones."

"I'm just asking, that's all."

Karl laughed again. "There's always a chance. But to hold out on her like that, she may take it all just for pissing her off, especially with that *delete* story of yours."

"But I told you—"

"Save your breath," Karl interrupted. "With fifteen mil at stake, no one will believe you."

What could Avery say?

Karl's expression turned serious. "Look, just bring the names and accounts, *all* of them, to the airport tomorrow morning. On paper, disk, thumb drive, I don't give a shit. Just get them to me, six-thirty sharp. I'll be in front of the Skycap kiosk. It's a dinky-assed terminal, so you can't miss it. And don't be late, I want to try to catch a flight."

"Yeah, okay," Avery said, scratching his beard. "But what about the FBI guy? If it was so easy for you to find me, why am I still alive?"

Karl shrugged. "I can only guess, but for him it has to be slower going, especially not wanting to give himself away. But he did try my method about two weeks ago, which means he's guessing you may still be in Witness Protection. Anyway, the two TA pilots said a man identifying himself as a Bureau agent contacted them. But both were hesitant to cooperate, seeing it was by phone. The agent said he'd contact them again."

"Did he tell them his name?"

"He did, but it was the name of an agent who left the service fifteen years ago and has since died. The phone number he gave was untraceable."

"And he didn't call back?" Avery said.

"No, but if he does, the pilots will hem and haw, then reluctantly tell him your city of departure was Houston. And if he checks the airport logs for that time period, it will show a TA plane landed and then departed twenty minutes later, destination, Miami. If he bites, you just might be home free here in Little Rock."

"You had them alter the flight records? You can do that?"

"Of course." Karl puffed out his chest. "My security clearance is above anything those Bureau bastards only have wet dreams about."

Avery made a face. "So you're like, CIA, or—?"

"I'm not saying," Karl interrupted. "And it's better we leave it at that. But I have another question for you: where's your attorney, Raymond Bryce?"

Avery felt a sudden chill. "He disappeared didn't he?"

Karl nodded. "Nylander was hoping Bryce was in touch with you somehow, to ask about the missing accounts, but she couldn't find him."

Rather than blurt out, "Yeah, he hopped a boat to South America," Avery said, "I don't know. When did it happen?"

"Fifteen days ago Bryce told his secretary he was taking the day off. 'Going to the Keys,' he said. Then poof, he was gone. The next day his secretary called the police, who alerted the Marshals and the FBI. Instead of the Keys, the Bureau learned he went to the bank and moved the bulk of his account offshore, less $30,000 in cash he took with him."

"Any other clues?" Avery asked.

"He bought a bus ticket to Mobile, Alabama, where he got off and walked away, *alone*, carrying a single bag. That's where they lost him. But he hasn't used his passport to leave the country—at least legally—so maybe, like you, he's holed up in the U.S. somewhere."

For a moment, Avery was silent. "He's hiding from the FBI agent, isn't he?"

"It's a damn good guess."

"But why would he need to run away?"

Karl shrugged. "My guess is, he learned something he shouldn't have, and thought it was life threatening."

"Then what am I supposed to do?"

"For now, stop playing golf and do what the Marshals tell you."

Avery groaned. "And be completely bored to death?"

"Yeah, well, your choice."

"Choice? You said that before. What's to choose?"

Karl looked Avery in the eye. "With that FBI asshole out there, the Marshals can protect you for only so long. But if you want to survive, spend less time feeling sorry for yourself and pay more attention. And start planning before it's too late."

"Planning for what?"

"To disappear," Karl said, "except this time for real."

"Are you trying to scare me?"

"Hell yes, you need to be afraid, because unless you change your ways, one of these days he *will* find you." Karl got out of the car, but before closing the door, he leaned back in. "Look, not that it'll do any good, but if you want my advice, learn how to become a fucking chameleon. Right now you stick out like a pine tree in a fruit orchard."

"What?"

Karl shook his head. "Look at you, with your wild long hair and a bird's nest for a beard. A blind man could spot you two blocks away. If you don't want to be found, start looking like everyone else. Then make plans for a life that doesn't include the Marshals *or* golf. Which means, if ever the opportunity strikes, be ready to do the most unlikely of things. In your case, disappear and leave it all behind—something your attorney apparently pulled off. Then, not even I can find you. Unfortunately, you pissed off an untold number of crazy rich bastards with guns. Turning over those files will cost them millions, and when it comes to money, rich people *never* forget. So, like I said, it's your choice, transform or fucking die." Karl closed the door and walked away.

That night, Avery related to Buck his troublesome visit from Karl with a K and having to meet him at the airport the next morning.

"Isn't that kind of dramatic, *transform or die?*" Buck said.

"It's probably all BS, just trying to scare me." Avery forced a smile.

"So you wanna hang at my place a few days for what reason?"

EIGHTEEN
• • •

Thump, thump . . . thump, thump, thump!
Pounding on the ceiling-to-floor glass window of his master bedroom startled Avery awake. After staying up late to watch a movie, he had drawn the curtains to give himself a better chance to sleep in. Someone was yelling.

"Avery, Avery, wake up, it's Buck. Wake up!"

Alarmed by Buck's frantic yelling, Avery threw back the covers, and dressed only in briefs, quickened his pace to the front door. As he unbolted the lock, Buck pushed his way in.

"They found him, Ave. They found Mr. Bones."

Chills ran through Avery's body. "Please tell me this is your idea of a joke."

"Believe me, I'd like to, but it's true. Here, read it yourself." Buck jabbed the folded *Arkansas Tribune* in Avery's chest and pointed to the column.

Human Skeleton Found in Woods
LITTLE ROCK – Yesterday, south of Little Rock, state utility workers stumbled upon a shallow grave containing the remains of a human skeleton sealed inside a garbage bag. The workers were said to be on a surveying project.

Hanna Jackson, an official with Pulaski County Coroner's office, confirmed the skeleton was in their custody, and efforts were being made to determine the identity of the remains. She stated, "Because of the evidence found, this is being treated as a homicide. We are cooperating with local law enforcement officials, and any further evidence our office uncovers will be shared with those authorities in a timely manner."

Jackson declined to disclose the nature of the evidence they uncovered, or the exact location of the skeleton's discovery.

Avery handed back the paper. "Here, let me get dressed. I'm cold all of a sudden." He returned to his bedroom.

Minutes later he joined Buck in the living room and flopped onto the couch. "Damn. I knew this would happen."

"Why do you always say that?" Buck said.

"Because every time things start going the right direction, I get blindsided. Last week it was that creep Karl Casey, and now this."

"Oh, come on. They only *found* Mr. Bones. You said it yourself, why would anyone come knockin' on your door?"

"Right, but you just did. And you were in such a panic about it you scared the crap out of me. Why didn't you call?"

"I tried, but your phone's always on vibrate. And for sure I wasn't gonna call you on your government phone. Besides, I figured you'd wanna know right away."

"Yeah, well, you could have at least waited until a decent hour," Avery said.

"Easy for you to say, but I buried the sucker, remember?"

"And according to this story you must not have done a very good job." Avery stood and began pacing the floor.

"You're just sayin' that because they said it was a shallow grave. But you try diggin' a friggin' hole out there. Weeds, roots, rocks, all that shit in the way and I'm supposed to dig a really deep hole and then cover it up, all in ninety minutes? I'd like to see you try it." Buck threw up his hands. "I swear, Ave, the hole was totally covered."

Again, Avery collapsed onto the couch. "You're right, you're right. I'm sorry. Besides, the only way they could tie him to being here is if the person who killed him came forward, and that's illogical."

"So was findin' Mr. Bones in the woods," Buck said.

"Right. And while you're at it, is there anything else you want to shoot full of holes?"

Buck laughed. "How much time do you have? I'll get my list."

Avery flipped Buck the bird. "Instead, how about we go get breakfast and talk about something else, anything but Mr. Bones. And you're buying for scaring the shit out of me."

"It's a deal. But if I'm buyin', we're goin' for donuts. I need a sugar fix."

NINETEEN

• • •

For Avery, Friday afternoons were the worst. Rather than go out, he hunkered down with a regimen of self-consuming activities to get himself through another dull weekend without falling into abject boredom. It didn't help that the Marshals were on him to keep an even lower profile due to his supposed flight from Witness Protection.

A cold beer in hand, he settled into his recliner, ready to watch the movie adaptation of Steven King's *Shawshank Redemption* on cable TV. It must have been the 43rd time he'd seen it. Considering his circumstances, he loved it more than ever. Andy, the hero, an innocent man unjustly convicted, quickly adapts to the abuses of a corruptly run prison, plans his escape, and scams the crooked warden as a bonus. He flees to Mexico, rich, to begin again and live free. Avery could only wish.

Ding-dong.

Startled, Avery jumped out of his chair with the unexpected sound of the doorbell. He peeked through the glass panel at the side of the door and saw two clean-shaven men dressed in suits. One appeared to be in his early 40s, the other man older. Avery hesitated.

Thump! Thump! One of the men pounded on the door. "Mr. Gillis, or whoever's in there, we saw you through the glass, so open up."

Avery didn't budge. "What do you want?"

"We're with the police department. We just want to talk."

Avery tried to control his breathing. "You don't look like cops to me."

After a moment, one of the pair held his badge against the glass panel. "We're detectives with the Little Rock Police Department. We're legit, so come on, open up, it's starting to rain."

Avery turned the bolt lock and opened the door, but only wide enough to peer out.

"I'm Detective Frank Pearl," the younger man said. "This here's Detective Tony Trainer. Sorry to startle you."

"What's the problem?" Avery said.

"You are Avery Gillis, right? The homeowner?" Frank Pearl said.

"Uh, yeah, but like I said, what's this all about?"

"Look, pal," Detective Trainer said, "we're not here to bust your balls if that's what you're worried about. We just have a few questions, that's all. So how about it? We're getting wet out here."

Avery's gut said he'd already be dead if they weren't real policemen. But they *were* cops, and that could only lead to trouble, regardless of what the detective said. Yet, not to let them in was illogical. "Yeah, sorry. Come on in."

"Thanks," the pair said.

Avery led the men to the living room where they formally introduced themselves, then sat on the couch. Avery turned off the TV and sat in his recliner. "So what's this about?"

Frank Pearl removed a notepad and pen from his pocket. "Mr. Gillis, we're looking for information regarding two men. One of them is Samuel Uronski. His friends call him Sammy."

Avery scratched his beard. "I never heard of him."

"Okay." Frank wrote on his notepad. "How about Arthur Bateman? Do you know him?"

"No, don't know him either."

"You're sure—Arthur Bateman—his name doesn't ring a bell?"

"Yeah, I'm sure. I said I don't know him."

"That's strange, Mr. Gillis," Frank said, "because county records show you bought this house from him eighteen months ago. Does that jog your memory?"

Avery paused. "Look, if he was the one who owned this place before me, I never met him. The only person I saw was the real estate lady and a notary when I signed the papers. If he owned the house, I didn't pay any attention, okay?"

"It's all right, Mr. Gillis, I was just asking," Frank said.

"I hate to interrupt," Frank's partner said, standing up, "but is it possible for me to use your bathroom? Sorry, but I really need to take a leak."

"It's down the hall from where you came in, first door on the right, you can't miss it."

"Thanks," Detective Trainer said, then disappeared.

Frank Pearl looked around the room. "Nice digs. Did you redo the house yourself?"

Avery hesitated. "Most of it I contracted out. Why?"

"Just asking. Whoever it was did a good job. So are you from around here?"

"Uh, no I'm not."

"Then how'd you find this place? It's kind of out of the way, don't you think?"

"If you must know, I found it on the Internet."

"Oh, so you came from somewhere else then?" Frank said.

"No, I was living in a condo and wanted out of the city."

"In Little Rock?"

"Of course. Isn't that what I said?"

"Actually, you said you weren't from around here, or is that not right?"

Avery glared at Frank. "I didn't say *where* I was from, Detective. So why don't you stop beating around the bush and tell me what you're really after? Otherwise, I think you and your pal should leave."

Frank tapped his pen on the coffee table. "I just wondered if there was any connection between you and Uronski, or Bateman, that's all."

"If you say I bought the house from Bateman, fine, but I don't know him, *or* the other guy." Aver threw up his hands in disgust. "Okay?"

"No need to get defensive, Mr. Gillis, I believe you." Again the detective tapped his pen. "I do have one other question. Do you know a man named Parker MacAfee?"

Avery shook his head. "No! I don't know him either."

"Thank you, Mr. Gillis, I'm sorry to have bothered you," he said coldly. He tucked away his pen and pad, stood and yelled, "Hey, T, aren't you finished yet?"

Detective Trainer appeared from the hallway. "Thanks for the use of the head." He waved.

Avery escorted the detectives to the front door.

Frank Pearl handed Avery a business card. "If anything comes to mind, Mr. Gillis, please give me a call."

In your dreams, Avery thought. He locked the door, then pressed his back against it. After a few deep breaths he retreated to his bedroom, where he noticed the master bathroom light was on. He was certain it was off before the cops came. *Damn. The detective used this bathroom, not the one off the hallway.* He pulled out his cell phone.

"Hey, what's up?" Buck said.

As best he could, Avery described the detective's visit and Frank Pearl's questioning. "I tell you, Buck, it was surreal. They did it just like on TV. You know, two detectives show up all innocent-like, make an excuse to come inside, then right away one of them says he has to pee. But it's all a ruse to snoop around your house while the first cop distracts you with a bunch of smart-ass questions."

"Did you call him on it?" Buck said.

"Are you kidding? They scared the crap out of me just knocking on my door. I didn't think about the other cop poking around until it was too late. I tell you, Buck, those cops know about Mr. Bones."

"Oh, come on. How could they?"

"Get real, Buck. Why would he use my bathroom instead of the one near the front door, especially when I told him where it was?"

"You're sure?"

"Buck, he left the light on."

"Jesus, Avery, if he was bein' sneaky, he would've turned the light *off.* And if the door was closed on the hall toilet, he could've walked right by it."

"But maybe he did it on purpose, to scare me."

"He was a cop, Ave, not Jack the Ripper. Besides, what could he know?"

Avery didn't answer.

"Nothing. Exactly. He was takin' a piss. Now stop actin' paranoid."

"Yeah, okay. I guess you're right."

"Good. So how about I come over? I'll bring a six-pack. There's gotta be a game on the tube we can watch."

"I thought you were hooking up with Polly tonight."

"Nah, her mother's got plans again. We're on for tomorrow instead."

"Okay. But with the cops being here, and all this Mr. Bones talk, I've got the creeps. How about I meet you at Hawg's Tavern instead?"

"With the Marshals pressin' you to lay low, are you sure you wanna be out in public?"

"I hear you, but right now I need a breather. Hawg's came to mind and it's just down the road. Besides, I hang out there in the afternoon sometimes and the Marshals haven't said jack."

"Hawg's it is then," Buck said. "How about I meet you around six, after I shower and grab a bite to eat? I'll fast food it."

"Okay, I'll raid the fridge, then go early and snag a booth."

TWENTY

• • •

After calling Buck, Avery opened his laptop computer. His initial Internet search for Sammy or Samuel Uronski turned up zilch. He tried several spellings—nothing. His search for the other names, Arthur Bateman and Parker MacAfee came up equally empty. He was left with knowing he bought his house from Bateman.

He googled the name *Arkansas Tribune*. They had an online archive. Access was only available with a credit card payment of $65.00. "Credit cards leave paper trails," he once told Buck. "It's not in my best interest to have one."

He sat for a moment, his fingers drumming haplessly on the computer keyboard. "Crap," he blurted out. He suddenly remembered the paper he found in Mr. Bones's pocket. The circle with the initials ABC in the middle was clear in his mind. *ABC . . . AB . . . Arthur Bateman . . . Corporation or Company.* It sounded reasonable, which now made Avery think there was more to the detective's visit than him answering a few questions.

He glanced out the window. A light mist was falling. He threw on a jacket and a ball cap and hurried outside, behind the house. An aluminum extension ladder lay against the foundation. He grabbed the ladder and propped it up against the wall.

The exterior walls of the custom-built home extended several feet above the flat roof itself. What Avery valued most about the recessed rooftop was secrecy. Without being seen from the ground he could easily access the hidden space he had fashioned behind one of the loose stones near the base of the chimney. He kept valuables there, things the Marshals and even Buck didn't know about, including the blood-stained note he had taken from the inside pocket of Mr. Bones's jacket, along with the shell casing he found in the tub. He moved them from his sock drawer to his rooftop-hiding place just before he was called to testify in Miami.

Avery began to climb the ladder when the heavens opened in a heavy downpour. "Damn," he said. Retrieving the note would have to wait.

By the time Avery reentered the house, he was soaked to the bone. After taking a warm shower, he dressed, grabbed a bologna sandwich, and made the short drive to meet Buck.

TWENTY-ONE

• • •

Avery entered the front door of Hawg's Tavern. Still unnerved by his two police visitors, he scanned the half-crowded room. No one paid him any attention. *Good,* he thought. Satisfied, he approached the bar.

"Howdy, Ave," the bartender said.

"Hey, Jake."

Jake looked at the clock on the wall. It said almost 6:00. "I don't think I've ever seen you in here this late in the day."

"You're right," Avery said. "I'm waiting for a friend."

"Anyone I know?"

"I don't think so. He's coming from Hillcrest. It might be a while."

"Pull up a stool, have some nuts, watch the tube. You want a drink?" Jake asked.

"Yeah, a draft on tap. But I think I'll wait in a booth. It's been a long day."

"Take your pick, but there aren't many left." Jake pushed the beer across the countertop. "Want to run a tab? I'll tell Sue Anne. She's workin' the tables."

"Maybe after my friend shows up." He paid Jake and moved toward an empty booth that provided a clear view of the front door, to spot Buck when he arrived. He put his drink on the table and slid onto the black vinyl seat.

Avery hadn't been seated long when a woman with a small handbag approached his table. "Oh, excuse me," she said, "I think I was sitting here. I went to the, uh, powder room." She gave him an apologetic smile.

"Sorry, I didn't realize—"

"That's okay. It's just that this is where I put my wrap when I came in." She pointed to the seat across from Avery.

"I'm sorry. I wasn't paying any attention." Avery prepared to exit the booth. "I'll go sit at the bar. I'm only waiting for a friend."

"Oh, really. I'm waiting for someone, too." She looked around. "We might could share the booth until another one opens up."

"Uh, sure. But I, uh, wouldn't want your boyfriend or husband to get the wrong idea." Avery blushed. Saying awkward things was standard behavior when he encountered a woman, any woman, unless she was old enough to be his grandmother, in which case he wouldn't blush but still wouldn't have a clue what the right thing was to say.

"No, no," she laughed and sat down. "I'm waiting for a girlfriend. How about you?"

"Uh, no. No girlfriend, I mean. He's my, uh, my friend." Avery gave a nervous smile.

"Oh, I see," she said.

Avery noticed her raised eyebrows. "No, no, he's not, I mean we're not, uh—"

"I'm sorry," she interrupted. "I didn't mean to imply—and, and I don't care. I was just trying to make small talk, that's all. I guess I'm not very good at it."

"Me either, as you can tell."

"Well then, maybe we can be awkward together until one of our friends shows up. My name's Billie Rae, by the way."

"Hi, Miss Ray. I'm Avery, Avery Gillis."

"Pleased to meet you, Avery Gillis." Billie Rae smiled. "Just call me Billie, okay?"

"Uh, yeah, okay, Billie."

"Now don't you go away, Avery. I'll be right back. I want to get a drink."

"Wait," Avery said, and tapped the bar girl on the arm as she passed by. "Sue Anne, this lady needs a drink." Avery's face flushed red. "I mean she wants to order one."

"Sorry," he said, and tried to smile.

"What do you need, sweetie?" Sue Anne said.

"I'd like a Vodka martini, straight up. Two olives."

"You got it. Back in a sec." Sue Anne scurried off.

"Do you come here often, Avery?" Billie Rae asked.

"Sometimes, but never on weekends. It's too crowded for my liking."

"Are you saying you're a loner?"

"In some ways, I suppose. How about you? Do you come here a lot?"

"No, it's my first time. I live in Hillcrest. My friend Gracie asked me to meet her here."

"Oh, really, that's where my friend lives, Hillcrest."

"What's his name? Maybe we're neighbors."

"It's, uh, Buck. Buck James."

Billie Rae bit her lip. "No, his name doesn't sound familiar. So, Avery, you said you live around here, but where are you from?"

"From?" Avery swallowed hard.

"Well, your lack of an accent says you're not from the South, and by calling me Miss Ray confirms it. Rae, R A E, is my middle name. Calling people by two names is common around these parts. Names like Bobby Dean, Catherine Ann, and me, Billie Rae. So like I said, where y'all from?" She said with a deliberate twang.

"Yeah. I, uh, I knew that, about the double name thing. I guess I'm, uh, uh—"

"Tongue-tied?" Billie Rae smiled.

Dumbfounded was more like it. It would be later that night before Avery realized Billie Rae was about his age, that she wore a touch of lipstick to go with her auburn hair, and was somewhat tall with nice legs. Although casually dressed, her clothes were high-end. The quality of a person's appearance was something Avery always noticed. Perhaps he learned it from his grandmother, who continually fussed about what he wore and the way he looked. On the other hand, she raised Buck the same way and he didn't seem to care one way or another.

"Then how about I ask what you do?" she said. "Where do you work?"

Avery had rehearsed the answer to this and other questions a hundred times. He practiced his lie over and over in front of a mirror and still felt uncomfortable. "I'm an accountant, but right now I'm out of work."

Sue Anne set Billie Rae's drink on the table, then hurried away.

"Did you work here in Little Rock?" Billie Rae asked.

"I worked in New Orleans. But when the market collapsed the company struggled, then eventually went under. So I moved here, hoping things go better." Avery had never stepped foot in New Orleans, but instead, read articles and stories about it: the French Quarter, aboveground cemeteries, drive-through daiquiri bars, and important local customs like Mardi Gras. He rented movies to watch. *The Big Easy* and *Streetcar Named Desire* were two he could remember.

"That's too bad. What company did you work for?"

Avery's stomach tightened. "Southern Mutual Equity, near the French Quarter."

"Now there's a coincidence. I was a student at Tulane and went to the Quarter with my friends whenever I could. I loved it there. So what's your favorite po-boy?"

"Po-boy?"

"Yes, you know, the sandwich?"

"Uh, shrimp, I think."

"What about beignets? You had to like them, especially from Café du Monde."

Avery was stymied. "Look, Billie, I liked the city all right, but the way my job turned out, I'd rather not talk about it if you don't mind. Besides, you haven't told me anything about yourself. What do you do?"

Billie Rae paused. "Oh, okay. I work for the D.A.'s office. At times I'm their sketch artist. Otherwise, I do legal work, but it's nothing to brag about."

"Is that something you do very often—make sketches of people?"

"I used to, but now there's this program called *Identikit*. It's a computer program even an idiot can figure out. Now I only do it on rare occasions. But I still love to draw. I wish I could afford to do it full time, but I can't." She sipped from her drink. "Now that's enough about me. I want to hear more about you, Avery, like where are your roots?"

"Roots?"

"You know, where'd you grow up, go to school?"

Stay calm, he told himself. "I was born and raised in Davenport, Iowa, went to Central High School, the University of Iowa, and got my master's degree at UCLA," he said in a robotic way, and gave Billie Rae a well-practiced, totally fake smile.

"Oh, I see," she said. "What about your parents?"

As he prepared to come up with another rehearsed response, the front door opened. Both he and Billie Rae turned their heads to see a couple enter the bar, their arms around each other's waist. The clean-shaven man was casually dressed and wore tennis shoes. His female companion wore tight shorts and a revealing blouse that turned more heads than one. It was a good bet no one bothered to check out *her* footwear.

Avery's eyes opened extra wide. He turned his head away and hid his face with his hand.

Billie Rae noticed. "What is it?"

"Are they coming this way?" Avery whispered.

"Who?"

"The pair who just came in."

Billie Rae looked to see. "No, they sat in a booth with another couple."

"Can she see us? The woman?"

"No, she's facing the other way. Why, what's wrong?"

Avery took a peek. "I, uh, I think I should be going."

"Is it something I said, or is it about her?" Billie Rae motioned toward the dishwater blonde.

"Uh, yeah, and I need to leave without her seeing me."

"Avery, I don't know what your relationship *is* or *was* with her, but trust me, Polly's not worth getting worked up over."

"You know her?"

"Polly Stonehill? I do. Her real name's Pauline Mae, but she hates it—always did—so everyone calls her Polly."

Avery gave Polly another glance. Her hand stroked the back of the man's neck.

TWENTY-TWO
● ● ●

"Look, Avery, it may not be any of my business," Billie Rae said, "but if you're upset because she's all over some guy, don't. It's the way she is."

"Are you serious?"

"Do I sound like I'm joking?"

"Well, no, but how do you know her?"

"We grew up friends. But that was years ago. Now please, tell me she's not your ex-girlfriend or something."

"No, of course not."

"Then why are you so jumpy?"

Avery squirmed in his seat. "She's my friend's girlfriend."

"Seriously?"

"Yeah. Buck said he was saving money to buy her a ring."

"He wants to *marry* her?" Billie Rae made a face. "Oh, please."

"But if he walks in and sees her with another man, he'll go berserk. That's why I need to wait for him outside, to keep him from coming in."

"Do you have a cell phone?" Billie Rae asked. "Maybe you could call him—"

"And tell him Polly's here pawing some other guy?"

She rolled her eyes. "I was thinking you could suggest meeting him someplace else."

Avery blushed again. "I'm, I'm sorry." When it came to women,

Avery always dug holes, deep ones. He took the phone from his pocket. "Do you mind?"

"If you make a call? I'm the one who suggested it." She picked up her drink and avoided looking at him.

You're right, I am an idiot, he wanted to say. Instead, he speed-dialed Buck's number.

"Buck, I'm at Hawg's. How close are you? . . . No, no, being late's not the problem. But it's pretty hectic in here, so I was wondering if . . . No, honest, it's not that . . . yeah, okay. How about I meet you outside? Then we can decide . . . Twenty minutes? Sounds good. See you then." Avery put the phone back in his pocket and took a drink.

Billie Rae turned her head. They made eye contact. The fact she hadn't gotten up and fled surprised him.

"Are you okay?" she asked. "Or are you fidgety by nature?"

"I'm sorry, Billie. But you, uh, you make me nervous."

"I can see that, but why? You don't even know me."

Avery wasn't sure where to begin. "Well, it's, it's not just you. It's women, all women. Once I get past hi and hello, I'm never sure what to say, like now. That's probably why I'm a nerd, *and* a computer geek. When I'm around people like you, you know, girls, I mean women—see, there I go again. Sorry. It's just that—"

Billie Rae held up her hand. "Stop, okay, stop. I get it. You *are* a nerd. But relax for a second, take a breath, sit back, have another drink. It's not the end of the world."

Avery opened his mouth to speak.

"And stop apologizing. I hate people who make excuses for being who they are." Billie Rae finished her drink, then devoured the two olives.

Wow, this woman has balls, he thought. He picked up his glass and polished off his beer.

"Look, Avery, you seem like a nice guy, so if you care about your friend, tell him to run the other way. She's bad news for any man who's looking for a long-term relationship." She pointed toward Polly and her male companion. "Need I say more?"

"But they've been together for eight or nine months now. He says it's the real thing."

"Nine months? Whoa. Maybe from his end they've *been together.*" Billie Rae made air quotes with her fingers. "But there's no way this is her first time cheating on him."

Holy crap, Avery thought.

"Not only that, I'll bet you a dinner I can tell you how she and your friend first met."

He raised his eyebrows. "Okay, I'll bite."

"Guitar lessons. She's the teacher, right?"

Avery nodded. "Uh, yeah, that's what Buck said. But I thought she worked at the University."

"She does, in records, I believe. But she meets most of her *men friends* giving guitar lessons, and after a month or two, she moves on to a new one." Billie Rae flagged down Sue Anne for another vodka martini. Avery ordered a second beer.

"But if you're not friends anymore, how do you know all this?" Avery asked.

"Little Rock may look like a big city, being the capital and all, but it doesn't live that way. We're like a big quilt, patch-worked together. If you look closely enough, we're all connected in one way or another. You just haven't lived here long enough to see it.

"People who grew up here still keep in touch with childhood friends—like me with Gracie, the person I'm waiting for. And now and then we all cross paths. I run into Polly several times a year. We hardly ever speak, but seldom have I seen her with the same man twice." Billie Rae paused. "But if your friend still thinks he wants to marry her, you'd better feed him this other bit of ammunition. It won't take long."

Avery checked the time. He still had 10 minutes. "Okay, *shoot.*"

"Oh," she said, pointing her finger, "you're trying to be funny." She smiled.

He smiled back.

Billie Rae lowered her voice. "About six years ago, Polly got married, to a guitar student no less. But several months after the nuptials, she was back, giving more lessons, if you know what I mean. And it wasn't too long before he found out."

Sue Anne returned with Billie Rae's vodka martini and Avery's beer. "There you go."

"Thanks," they said, and each took a drink.

"So who ratted her out?" Avery asked.

"As it turned out, nobody. One afternoon her hubby went to the airport to catch a plane. Three hours later, after weather had canceled his flight, he came home to candle lights, romantic music, and a gourmet dinner—except it wasn't for him. She and her latest fling were, uh, how do I put this, having dessert on the dining room table when her husband walked in."

"While they were—?" Avery couldn't help but laugh.

"Exactly." She nodded. "And cool as can be, he didn't say a word—just walked out the front door. Rumor has it he slashed the guy's tires."

"Where'd you hear all this?"

"Some of it came from the lawsuit, which was covered in the local paper. But most of it I heard from the slasher's sister, who happens to be a secretary in my office. I told you it was a small town."

"There was a lawsuit because he slashed somebody's tires?" Avery said.

"No. He got away with it because the guy Polly was doing was also married. The scallywag claimed the car was vandalized so his wife wouldn't find out. The suit was over paternity." Billie Rae continued to sip her martini.

"Did I just miss something?"

"Well, the husband filed for divorce and moved on, or so he thought. Six months after he left, Polly had a baby. She said the ex was the father. So for the next two years the fool paid her big-dollar child support, every month.

"But as chance would have it, for some reason the ex wanted to have a vasectomy. To do so, his doctor required him to have a sperm test to see if the operation was necessary. Turns out the guy was sterile; Polly's kid couldn't have been his. So he went to court to stop paying child support and to get his name off the birth certificate. It seemed straightforward enough. That's when her mother stepped in and made the case disappear."

"Now I'm really lost," Avery said.

"To save Polly's reputation, and herself from being ridiculed by all her rich friends, her mother paid off the ex—I heard six figures—for him to leave town and say he was the biological father if anyone ever inquired."

Avery shrugged. "And this all came from—"

"The same. The ex's sister."

Avery leaned back. "Wow, that's some story."

"No doubt more than enough to convince your friend." Billie Rae sipped from her drink.

"Yeah, if he doesn't think I'm trying to pull his leg."

"He'd really think that?"

"You'd have to meet him."

"Hmm." Billie Rae circled the rim of her glass with a finger. "Just tell him he'd better watch how he handles this."

"Meaning?"

"Meaning, going off on Polly may not be the right thing to do—although I couldn't blame him if he did."

"Wait a minute. Buck may lose his temper now and then, but he wouldn't hit a woman, no matter what."

"Good, but that's not what I meant. I was thinking more along the lines of him doing something else, like—"

"Becoming *a slasher*." It was Avery's turn to make air quotes.

"Precisely," Billie Rae said. "I know, it's a man's thing to want to lash out, but you'd better tell Buck to hold up, because if her mother thinks her precious daughter's been wronged—even if she hasn't—look out. She doesn't get mad, she gets even."

"You make it sound serious."

"It is. Her family comes from well-heeled Little Rock stock. Besides her own influences, her husband was a powerful judge with long-reaching ties. She's been known to tap into them and cause people trouble for less things than insulting her daughter."

Avery held up his hand. "I get it, thanks." He checked his cell phone for the time. "Look, I've got to leave. But I'd rather not have her see me."

"Why does it matter if you're going to spill the beans?"

"When it comes to women, Buck's a sap, he'll believe almost anything. That's how he wound up in Little Rock. And if she's been fooling him up to now, by seeing me, she might concoct some other story for him to swallow." Avery shifted his weight. "So I, uh, I hate to ask, but since you know her, is there some way you could distract her while I sneak by?"

"Is there a back door you can use?"

"Not from here," Avery said. "I'd have to walk right by her."

Billie Rae drummed her nails on the tabletop. "Oh, all right, if it helps wake up your friend. But you've got to promise to keep my name out of it, do you hear?"

He nodded. "You don't have to worry."

"Good. I'll invite her to the powder room for some girl talk. Then you leave, but make it quick. It's likely to be a short conversation."

"Okay. And thanks. I'm sorry to get you involved," Avery said.

"Don't fret. Besides, it's kept me from being bored 'til Gracie shows up." Billie Rae produced a pen and a piece of paper from her purse. She wrote on the paper, then slid it across the table to Avery. "Here's my number. You owe me a dinner, remember? Maybe two if Polly gets mouthy." She gave Avery a quick smile. "But don't wait too long." She stood, downed the rest of her martini, and walked to Polly's table.

Billie Rae raised her voice. No doubt for his benefit, Avery thought. "Hey, Polly, long time no see. I was waiting for someone when I saw you come in. Who's your friend here?"

Avery couldn't make out Polly's reply.

"I hope you don't mind," Billie Rae said to Polly's latest fling, "but I need to borrow Polly for a minute. It's a girl thing. She'll be back in a flash—promise."

Avery watched Billie Rae prod Polly toward the restroom. He put money on the table to pay for his unfinished beer, picked up her note, and pretended to act nonchalant as he exited the front door onto the covered porch. He paused only to pull up his collar before making his way down the set of steps into a light rain and the well-lit parking lot.

Once inside the dry confines of his car, he flipped on the dome light and checked the paper from Billie Rae.

Billie Rae Robinson
501-555-5972

"Whoa," he said under his breath. Avery couldn't believe his eyes. A woman actually gave him her number. He pushed his thoughts aside and stuffed the paper into his pocket.

A minute later he spotted Buck's truck pull into the lot from Arch Street. Avery jumped out of his car.

Buck no sooner turned off the motor when Avery tapped on the passenger window for Buck to unlock the door, and then jumped into the cab. "Let's go back to my house, you won't believe what I've been through."

"What the hell's goin' on?" Buck asked.

"Trust me, it's a madhouse in there, you can't hear yourself think. I should have told you to go to my place when I called."

"I thought you wanted to get away from the house," Buck said.

"I did, but I changed my mind. My place is a lot safer."

"Safer? Jesus, Ave, did somebody spot you?"

"No. I'm just saying we need to leave *now*, okay?" Avery said. "I'll get my car."

"Okay, okay. Take it easy," Buck said, as he turned over the engine.

"Stop!" Avery yelled, and grabbed Buck's arm. "Kill the engine, *quick.*"

"Now what?"

"Just do it, do it!"

Buck complied. "I thought you wanted to go?"

"Yeah, I do. But look, it's her."

"Who?"

"The woman I met, she's on the porch."

Billie Rae had stepped outside the bar, and using her small purse as an umbrella, hurried to a parked car. Quickly, the car backed out of its space and its headlamps flashed on.

"Duck," Avery said.

The brothers hunched down as Billie Rae's BMW passed by and turned into the street. The pair sat up and watched her car disappear down the road.

Buck laughed. "You're hidin' from a woman?"

"That's not it."

"No wonder you didn't want to stay. You should've said so in the first place."

"I said it's not about her."

"Then why were we playin' duck and cover?"

"She said she was meeting a friend, but something's not right."

"You can say that again. It's just like you to run the other way when some female shows you the slightest bit of interest," Buck said. "Or did you say somethin' to make her mad? She sure left in a hurry."

"For the third time, it's not what you think."

TWENTY-THREE

● ● ●

The pair hadn't been in Avery's house two seconds before Buck began. "Okay, enough stallin'. What's goin' on?"

"A couple of things," Avery said. "But first let's talk about the cops showing up."

Their 10 minutes of conjecture led them to a handful of questions but no answers.

"Enough with that," Avery said. "Now give me the keys to your truck."

"What?" Buck replied.

"You heard me, the keys, *and* your cell phone." Avery held out his hand.

"Is this some kind of trick?"

"No, it's about what happened at Hawg's."

"This is about that woman, and you want my keys?"

"I promise, it's not about her, so hand them over. If I'm wrong I'll apologize. In fact, I'll buy you a steak dinner wherever you choose. So how about it?"

Buck shrugged. "Sure, filet mignon at the Peabody. Count me in."

"Who said anything about the Peabody? You don't eat there."

"Neither do you, but you can afford it." Buck rubbed his hands together. "So that's where we're goin'."

"Don't get too excited, you still haven't coughed up your keys and phone." Again Avery motioned with his fingers.

"Oh, all right, brother, here." Buck complied.

"Be right back." After a brief absence, Avery returned with a beer in each hand. "Here, start sucking on this, you'll need it."

"Okay, I'm ready. Tell me about this woman you met," Buck said.

Avery drank more than a swallow of beer before he spoke. "It's not her, it's about Polly. She was there with another man."

"Not funny, *Norbee.*"

"Buck. I'm dead serious. She was fawning all over some guy. That's why I met you in the parking lot. I didn't want you to see it."

"No friggin' way."

"I hate to break it to you, but she's been playing you all this time. Her mother-can't-baby-sit alibis are bogus."

"That's bull. Give me my phone. She'll straighten it out," Buck said.

"I said, no phone. And you're not going to drive over to her place and have her sweet talk you with some bullshit story."

"But why should I believe *you?* You don't know squat about women."

"You're right, but I wasn't the only one who saw her. By accident, I shared a booth with another woman. She knows all about her."

"The one outside the bar? What's her name?"

"I'm not saying. Just listen for a minute and let me tell you what she said." He recapped his conversation with Billie Rae.

The remainder of the night, Avery endured Buck's fist pounding anger and foul language.

The following morning, Buck sat at the kitchen table, his cup of coffee untouched. Avery had taken a cereal bowl from the cupboard when the muffled sound of Buck's cell phone rang from inside one of the kitchen drawers. Avery retrieved it and checked the screen. "It's Polly."

"And you want me to answer it?" Buck said.

"Why not? She doesn't know what you know." Avery held out the phone. "Do I need to leave?"

"No, stay." Buck took the phone and touched the screen. "Hi . . . having breakfast . . . uh-huh . . . your mom can babysit tonight?" Buck began pacing. "And last night you stayed at home with Mary Jo because your mom had plans? . . . So that really wasn't you with some guy at Hawg's Tavern? . . . Hello, Polly? . . . Billie who? . . . No, I never heard of her . . . I'm not sayin' who, but they saw you there all right, dressed to kill, hangin' all over him." Buck circled the kitchen table.

"So every time you said your mom couldn't babysit, she actually did, so you could ring some other guy's bell, is that it? . . . Just sometimes? What the hell kind of answer is that? . . . You were gonna tell me? When, next year? Or were you gonna string me along like you did your ex-husband about your daughter being his?"

Buck stopped pacing and held the phone away from his ear.

Avery caught nearly every word of Polly's vile tirade before the line went dead.

"Did you hear her threaten me if I say anything about her ex and the kid?" Buck said.

"From what I was told, she means it." Avery put his bowl on the table and sat down. "So how do you feel now?"

"Half of me wants to puke. The rest of me's mad as hell."

"At her, or yourself?"

"I don't know, probably more at me for bein' such a sap," Buck said. "Damn, why didn't I see it?"

"Not to criticize, but that's what you say every time you break up with somebody. It's like you wear a sign around your neck: 'Wanted, a women to walk all over me.'"

Buck gave a small laugh. "You know, for being such a dork, you see right through me."

"A lot of good that does me. At least you can get a woman."

Buck sighed. "I thought Polly was different."

"She's different all right. So now are you hungry?"

"Sure, but I'm not eatin' that cereal shit. I need a donut—a whole friggin' dozen."

"You want donuts?"

"Right. With all that sugar in me, maybe I'll go comatose and forget I ever had a girlfriend."

Avery smiled. "Speaking of food, since you don't have a date tonight, how about I buy you that filet at the Peabody? That should cheer you up."

"Seriously? A filet at the Peabody? How about I order lobster, too?" Avery hesitated.

"Come on, *Norbee*, look at me, I'm depressed." He made a face.

Avery laughed. "Sure, *Luther*, why the hell not? Surf and turf."

TWENTY-FOUR

• • •

Following his donut breakfast, Buck breathed more easily. "Who's this woman who told you about Polly?" he asked.

"I promised I wouldn't say," Avery said.

"Oh, come on, you promised the Marshals not to say a lot of shit I know about and your cover's still good. Why would knowin' about her be any different?"

"Yeah, okay. Her name's Billie Rae Robinson. But the crazy thing is, she gave me her phone number, to take her out to dinner."

"She hit on you? Jesus, Avery, she must be desperate."

Avery slugged Buck on the arm. "I thought disparaging girlfriends was off-limits."

"She's your girlfriend already? Hell, you haven't even been on a date."

"You know what I mean."

"Yeah, I do. But come on, Ave, you don't wear thousand dollar suits anymore, or drive a Mercedes. With your wild looking hair and that crazy beard, either you're a slacker, or you're from the backwoods and wrestle bears for a living."

Avery didn't speak.

"Okay, I take it back. But how'd it happen, you gettin' her number?"

Avery explained how he unintentionally sat in her booth at Hawg's Tavern.

"Is she good lookin'?" Buck said.

"I guess, she wore nice clothes."

"Her clothes were nice but you don't know if she was attractive? No wonder you're hopeless with women."

Avery blew out a breath. "Okay, maybe she was. But should I call her?"

Buck laughed. "A woman gives you her number and says don't wait too long, and you wanna know what? Geez, Avery, you're unbelievable."

"But she'd already downed a couple of martinis. And there was something strange about the way she left."

"Then *don't* call her. Or better yet, let me do it." Buck pretended to hold a phone to his ear. "Hey, *Billie Boobs*, this is Avery's friend, Buck. He said you gave him your number at Hawg's while you were snockered. But because he's a dork he's too embarrassed to call, and since you're the one who ratted out Polly, how about me and you hook up sometime?"

"Okay, okay, I'll do it. Just go easy on me when things don't go well, okay?"

"Yeah, right. So where are you takin' her?"

Avery shrugged. "I don't know, I hadn't thought about it."

"Then take her to the Peabody and order lobster *and* filet mignon— exactly what I'm havin'. In fact, think of tonight as a dry run, except I'll be your date."

Avery laughed. "Very funny, *Luther*. But why the Peabody?"

"To impress her, *Norbee*. Which also means, you need to do somethin' about the way you look."

"Yeah, okay. I'll trim my beard."

"That's it? Honest, Avery, your disguise has gone overboard. You really do look like you wrestle bears, friggin' grizzlies, two at a time. And if *I* take notice, that's sayin' somethin'. So unless she's blind *and* desperate, you haven't got a chance in hell of ever gettin' to first base."

TWENTY-FIVE
● ● ●

Sunday afternoon Avery mustered up his courage to call Billie Rae. "That's right, you do owe me dinner." She paused. "How about this Thursday?"

"Yeah, sure. Can I come by and get you?" Avery said. "We'll go to the Peabody."

"The Peabody? Impressive, but I was thinking of a restaurant close to where I live here in Hillcrest. It's called The Icehouse, on Kavanaugh. How about I meet you there at seven? I'll make the reservation."

Avery phoned Buck to give him the good news.

"You know this doesn't count as a real date, don't you?" Buck chided.

"Why not?"

"Because *she* chose the place to eat, *and* you're not pickin' her up. So far, you're simply payin' off on a bet."

Knowing Buck was right, Avery also took his hint to 'clean up.' On such short notice, he scrambled to find not just a barber but a hairdresser to trim his beard *and* hair. Then he bought a decent shirt, a pair of nice slacks, and shoes to complement his upgraded appearance. Checking in the mirror, it occurred to him that Karl Casey's golf course advice might be right after all. Blending in *was* a better way to go, although *this* getup was a bit overboard.

• • •

Billie Rae was already seated when Avery approached her table. Her shoulder-length auburn hair stood out against her simple but stylish white blouse. Consciously, he tried to improve his posture.

"Billie Rae?"

She looked up. "Oh, Avery." Her fingers brushed at her hair. "I almost didn't recognize you."

After exchanging an awkward handshake, Avery sat down and picked up his menu.

"The fish dishes are excellent," Billie Rae said.

"That's good. Fish is one of my favorites."

"Really? Or are you being polite?"

"No, it's true. I see salmon listed here. Have you ever tried it?"

"I have. The way they prepare it is superb."

Their small talk continued over a glass of wine and salad, followed by the entrée.

"So, how's your friend Buck? Isn't that his name?" Billie Rae asked.

"He's recovering. And thanks for telling me all about Polly. I don't think he would have believed me without that. But what did it was when she called Buck the next morning."

"I hope my name didn't come up."

"It did, but Buck said he never heard of you. Anyway, she blew up, cursed a blue streak, and said she never wanted to hear from him again."

"That's good. Are there any details you left out?" She grinned.

"Sorry. I, uh, tend to ramble at times."

"Oh, come on, you're still nervous? I thought things were going well."

"Really? I'm not boring you?"

"If you must know, it's quite the opposite."

"You're joking, right?"

She smiled. "Let's just say you're different—not all full of yourself, expecting me to be impressed with your every word. Believe me, if you were boring, I'd tell you."

Avery opened his mouth to speak.

"And no more *I'm sorrys*. It sounds too much like whining, and if there's one thing I can't stand is a man who moans and groans."

During the meal their conversation was polite but casual. For dessert they agreed to split a serving of blackberry cobbler *à la mode*.

"Now this isn't so bad, is it?" she asked. "Being here, I mean."

"No, it's been good." Avery smiled.

"You know, when Polly walked into Hawg's the other night I got way off track."

"About what?"

"Finding out more about you," she said.

He forced a smile. "I don't like to talk about myself."

"I can understand a bit of modesty, but I'll bet your life isn't as mundane as you make it out to be."

"The last time you said 'I bet,' I lost, and here I am, buying you dinner."

Billie Rae's mouth fell open.

"I, I didn't mean it that way." Avery's face felt warm as he tried to regain his composure. "It was about losing a bet, not about being here with you."

She shook her head and laughed. "You're something else."

"I didn't mean to be funny."

"You don't have to try, believe me."

Avery shifted his weight. "Is there anything else we can talk about?"

Billie Rae set aside her napkin and placed her elbows on the linen-covered table. "Of course, but I don't know if you're up for it."

"Up for what?"

"The truth," she said. "You say your name is Avery Gillis, and you were born and raised in Davenport, Iowa. How about you start from there?"

He crossed his arms. "I don't like to talk about my past because there's nothing to tell."

"It's funny you should say that, because I actually agree with you. After spending several days in the D.A.'s office researching you, there's something odd," Billie Rae paused, "no, something irrational with what I discovered. Upon first glance, your background is squeaky clean. But looking beyond your transcripts and degrees, something wasn't right, because the more I searched, the less I found."

Avery's heart rate quickened.

"You say you graduated from Central High in Davenport, Iowa, but your name and picture never appeared in one of their yearbooks, you never joined a club, or played a sport. The same can be said for the University of Iowa and UCLA. I spoke with people from those schools, in the departments your degrees say you majored in, and not one person can remember you, and it wasn't that long ago.

"You also said you worked for Southern Mutual Equity in New Orleans, but the state of Louisiana has no record of a company ever licensed to do business by that name. I even had law enforcement search to see if you had a criminal record. But they also came up empty finding anything about you," she said. "And I find all this impossible to believe. Or would you care to provide a reasonable explanation?"

"I can't answer you."

"You can't, or won't?"

He removed the napkin from his lap and placed it on the table. "I think I need to leave."

Billie Rae leaned forward. "I would hate to spoil your evening, but if you walk out that door without me, you will be arrested and taken to jail. But if I'm satisfied with what you tell me, we'll leave together and nothing will happen to you."

"Arrested? On what charge?" he said.

"Who knows? I'm not the police," she replied.

"But that's illegal."

"Eventually they may let you go, but only after they find out who you are and what kind of game you're playing. Or perhaps you can tell *me* and save the police the trouble."

Avery rubbed his neatly trimmed beard. He needed time. But time for what, to make up another set of lies? He was already in over his head. "So you're telling me there's been a cop outside all this time just waiting to see if we leave together?"

She nodded. "I am. His name is Frank Pearl. I understand you two have met."

Avery rolled his eyes. "Now I get it. You're in cahoots with the cops. I should have figured it out after I watched you leave Hawg's."

Her eyebrows lifted.

"When we *accidentally* met, you said your wrap was on the seat opposite me, but when you left you didn't carry one, just your purse. You weren't there to meet a friend, you were there to interrogate *me*, just like now, but Polly got in the way, so you concocted a plan for us to meet again—me buying *you* dinner. And you talk about the truth."

Billie Rae blushed. "Well, you've got to admit, I did give you a heads up about Polly to help your friend. You make me sound heartless."

"I suppose, but telling me about Polly turned out to be a convenient way for you to gain my trust. And now *you* accuse *me* of not being honest."

She blew out a breath. "Oh, all right, I confess, I did follow you to Hawg's. So I can see why you feel that way."

"Do you think?"

"Yes, but—"

"Why don't you explain how you and your boyfriend, Frankie, figure in this together?"

She dabbed her lips with her napkin. "It's complicated," she said. "And Frank's not my boyfriend."

"So uncomplicate it."

Billie Rae sighed. "I'm not sure how much to tell."

"Do you need to consult with your cop boyfriend outside?"

"No. And I told you, he's not my boyfriend."

"Then why is it so important to find out about two people I never heard of and some guy who sold me his house?"

"So you don't know Bateman?" she said.

"No, but I'm sure your detective friend already told you that."

"Let me try to explain." She sipped from her glass of wine. "One night, ten years ago, my brother, Parker, disappeared and was never found. To this day I believe Arthur Bateman killed him, and so does Frank Pearl. Frank was Parker's best friend. But we couldn't prove Bateman did it because there was no evidence Parker was dead. But then two weeks ago, Parker's remains were found buried in the woods not two miles from your house," she said. "You may have read about it."

Holy crap, Avery thought. *Mr. Bones is Billie Rae's brother.* Avery wanted to vanish into thin air. "Yeah, I did, but I don't remember hearing who it was."

"It's because the police haven't made his name public. But what caught my attention was what the coroner told me. He said Parker's remains had been buried in the woods no more than a year—two at most—and they had come from someplace not exposed to the elements." Billie Rae leaned closer. "Bateman's house was the first thing that came to mind, because it had been empty for more than eight years when he sold it to you. And you're the only one who's lived there since. That's why I followed you, because Frank thought you might be connected to Bateman somehow. And until I met you at Hawg's, I was thinking along those same lines."

"What do you mean?"

She sipped another drink. "The way you showed concern for your friend finding out about Polly made me believe you're not a callous person, not the kind who would do dirty work for the likes of Arthur Bateman. But with him living out of the country, logic says, if Parker *was* there, somehow you could be involved in moving his remains, which means you have something terrible to hide and can't be involved with the police. But for the life of me, that scenario doesn't seem to fit your— how should I say this—your awkward demeanor."

Avery hesitated. His carefully planned efforts to remain aloof were being undermined by an emotion he swore he would never give in to: guilt. "Look, Billie, I'm sorry. I'd like to help you, but I can't."

Her eyes grew big. "You just admitted knowing something about Parker."

Avery made a face. "I think I've said way too much."

"It sounds like you're leaving Detective Pearl no choice."

Avery pulled his Government-issued cell phone from his pocket and spoke in a hushed tone. "If your detective friend tries to arrest me, I will make a call, and not tomorrow or next week, but tonight the police will be forced to release me, and I will disappear from Little Rock forever. There's nothing you or Pearl can do, short of killing me, to keep that from happening," Avery paused. "And any information I may have concerning your brother's sad death will vanish along with me."

For a moment, Billie Rae froze. "What information?" Her words were almost inaudible.

He didn't answer.

"Avery, you can't deny you said it. And if you don't tell me, I swear on my mother's grave I will scream." She sat up and opened her mouth.

Avery raised his hand. "Okay, okay. I found what might be called evidence that may or may not help you."

"What kind of evidence?"

He shifted in his chair. "Right now I'd rather not get into specifics, but I do have it."

She drummed her fingers on the table. "And you're serious about the police having to let you go?"

"One hundred percent," he replied.

Billie Rae heaved a sigh. "I can't believe I missed this. You're in Witness Protection, aren't you?"

Avery nodded. "That's why I'm asking, begging if you want, not to tell anyone, even your detective friend. My life depends on it."

"You're saying you messed with my brother's remains and you want *me* to help *you*?"

"That's exactly what I'm asking. Do you think I wanted this to happen? I'm just trying to stay alive. I don't want to hurt anyone. And as much as I want to help you, trusting the law is not something I'm eager to do."

Billie Rae pursed her lips. "But if you are in Witness Protection, how does bringing in the police jeopardize you?"

There was no way around it. "It's not the police I worry about, it's the FBI. If the wrong pair of eyes are watching, I'm finished."

"Oh, come on, the FBI? You're being paranoid," she said. "With that thinking, how do you know I'm not part of some diabolical scheme to do you in?"

"If you were, I'd be dead by now. Besides, I already know all about you."

"*You* know about *me?*"

"Of course. You were born in Memphis, grew up in Little Rock, and went to Hall High. You graduated from Tulane University in New Orleans, but your law degree is from Vanderbilt. Married for two years, single the last seven, you've worked for the D.A.'s office for nine. And if I wanted, I could know your FICO score or how much you owe on your two-year-old Beamer. That's how paranoid I am." Avery paused. "Oh, yeah, your birthday's May eighth, so happy early birthday."

TWENTY-SIX

●●●

A very's information about Billie Rae had come thanks to Deputy Jerry Joyce and the powers given to law enforcement by the USA PATRIOT Act of 2001.

"So you found a girlfriend," Jerry said when Avery called.

"Maybe," Avery lied. "It's just that Roger said you guys could check out somebody if I had any worries. Is that right?"

"Of course. What about this woman concerns you?"

"She made an excuse to talk to me and I found out it wasn't true." Avery's suspicions were raised when he realized Billie Rae had left Hawg's without a wrap, or meeting a friend—her pretenses for sharing a booth with him.

Jerry laughed. "You called me because some woman hit on you? That's a good one."

"Okay, don't believe me. I just want to make sure she's who she says she is. I googled her name but nothing helpful came up."

"You mean you want to know if she's somebody like you?"

"Not funny, Jerry. Will you help or not?"

"Sure, why not? What's her name?"

"It's Billie Rae Robinson." Avery spelled out her name. "She said she works for the D.A.'s office in Little Rock."

"Okay. We'll add her to the list of people we've vetted since you came to town."

"Wait a sec. All this time you've checked up on people I see and haven't told me?"

"Unless there was a problem, there was no need," Jerry said. "Contrary to your often expressed opinion, we're trying to normalize your life, not complicate it. Besides, most have been simple background checks, no red flags have ever popped up."

"Then who have you checked on?"

"You really want to know?"

"Sure, you've piqued my curiosity."

"Hmm, let's see," Jerry paused, "the last one was a couple of months back, that new attorney of yours in Miami. Bryce, I think his name was. Other than being a recovering alcoholic, he's pretty clean."

It flashed through Avery's head that Jerry failed to mention Raymond Bryce had gone missing, at least according to Karl Casey. But why would Karl lie, and why would Jerry not say? "Uh-huh. So who else?"

"Offhand, the only two I remember were guys who helped remodel your house. The contractor you spend time with, Luther James, who likes to be called Buck, and the plumber, Joe somebody—a simple guy who drinks too much, but harmless as a fly as far as you're concerned."

"You know I hang out with Buck?"

"Of course, it's our job. But like I said, he checked out fine. If he's becoming a good friend, I wouldn't worry about it."

"What do you have on him? Buck, I mean?" Avery tried to ask casually.

"What's to tell? He moved his home repair business here from Minnesota four or five years ago. Except for an unusual beginning, he's pretty much a regular guy."

"What do you mean, an unusual beginning?"

"Didn't he tell you? He was born in Australia."

"No," Avery lied. "But why's that unusual?"

"Hmm. I probably shouldn't say."

"Come on, Jerry. If he's a friend, why should it matter? It might even help."

"Okay, as long as you keep it under your hat."

"I promise. Tell me."

"At first, I thought he might be undocumented, but he is a U.S. citizen. It's his mother who's interesting. She was an American who must have been knocked up by some Aussie who wouldn't or couldn't do the right thing, so she came back to the States with the kid."

"What makes you think that?"

"My contact at the State Department said she returned to the U.S., single, with a four-month-old child, which means she had to be knocked up, right?"

"I guess. Anything else you know about him?"

"No, that's all. Just don't tell him you know about his mother, okay?" Jerry said. "What if she told him a BS story about his dad being a war hero or something? It might not sit well with him knowing otherwise."

Avery sighed in relief. Jerry didn't know the real story.

TWENTY-SEVEN

●●●

L uther Roebuck James *was* born in Australia.
His mother, Jennifer Anne Roebuck, had been recruited to teach school in the state of Victoria, along with 494 other Americans. Assigned to teach high school French in the river town of Mildura, she met and fell in love with an Australian-born teacher, Luther James. Four years later they married.

The subsequent January, when Jennifer was eight months pregnant, Luther's father unexpectedly died of a massive heart attack. Because of her impending delivery, she remained at home while Luther flew the 600 miles to Sydney to be with his grieving mother and older sister. His third day there, Luther was killed in Australia's worst commuter train accident in history, a derailment that killed more than 80 fellow passengers.

Twelve days later, Luther Roebuck James was born in Mildura Base Hospital.

Following Easter, and the Southern Hemisphere's approaching chill of winter, Jennifer flew with baby Luther to visit her parents in her childhood home of Redlands, in Southern California. She intended to return Down Under, but home felt too good, and she never did. Jennifer's parents gave young Luther his nickname, Buck.

In July of the next year, Jennifer married Jason Hammer, a former high school sweetheart she had known since first grade. Ten months later she bore a second son, John, now known as Avery Norbert Gillis. When John and Buck were four and six, respectively, John's father filed papers to adopt Buck. After all, he was the only father Buck had known. Shortly before the papers were to be signed, a drunk driver killed their parents in a fiery automobile accident on the nearby I-10 Freeway. Jennifer's parents adopted the two boys, but Buck's last name was never changed.

The newspaper article regarding the accident, as well as the obituary, read in part: *Jason and his wife Jennifer were survived by one child, John.* Had the harried Redlands reporter interviewed Jennifer's parents, rather than her husband's, the articles would have said *two* children survived their daughter. Suddenly saddled with caring for two grieving children, Jennifer's parents never got around to ask the newspaper to issue a correction. It no longer seemed important.

In Miami, when first questioned by the FBI, John was asked if he had any living parents, siblings, or close relatives. Embarrassed by his situation, and not wanting to entangle Buck, he said, "No," and showed agents a copy of the obituary clippings of his parents' death. An agent from an FBI office near Redlands was asked to verify the authenticity of the newspaper's printing, but never spoke with the original reporter.

The agent did discover that John's mother's parents, who raised him, had passed, and his father's parents had become Christian missionaries and relocated to South America 11 years earlier. Their last known whereabouts: a small coastal village near Valparaíso, Chile. The agent's report was brief. The subject in question—now Avery Gillis—is an only child with no close-surviving relatives of any consequence. The background inquiry was closed.

The U.S. Marshals Service, in charge of placing Avery in the Witness Protection Program, saw no need to question the veracity of the Bureau's findings. Yet, had the investigating FBI agent taken time to check school records, or knock on doors in the neighborhood where he was raised, Avery Gillis would not be living in Little Rock, Arkansas or anywhere near his half-brother, which might have proven better for both their futures.

TWENTY-EIGHT
• • •

"Who told you about me?" Billie Rae asked.

"The U.S. Marshals Service. They did it because *I am* in Witness Protection."

She paused. "Okay, for the moment let's say I believe your story. And if that's the case, and you suspected I met you under false pretenses at Hawg's, why did you call and agree to meet me for dinner?"

Avery rubbed the back of his neck. "First, I didn't put together you saying you had a wrap and then leaving Hawg's without one, or meeting your friend, Gracie, until *after* I called you. But then I was curious. Why would you do that? And yes, I did think about a possible connection between you and the detectives, but I, uh, hoped it wasn't true." Hard as he tried not to, he blushed.

"Oh," she whispered

"I wish you could understand how hard it is hiding from the world, afraid to make friends. To meet someone new was nice, and I, uh, just hoped you really wanted me to call."

Billie Rae shifted in her chair. "Avery, do you suppose there's a way we can stop being adversaries?"

Avery cocked his head.

"You want to remain hidden and I want my brother's killer brought to justice. It seems to me they are not mutually exclusive. We could help each other. But first I need more information."

"Like what?"

"How do I know for sure that you *are* in the Witness Protection Program and not some sociopath who seems polite and innocent but needs to be locked up forever? I'm supposed to take your word for it? And I'm not even talking about your FBI story."

"Without talking to someone in person, it could be tricky," he said. "If you call the Marshals Service they'll refuse to comment. And if you identified me by name, as jumpy as they are about me being found, I could disappear in a heartbeat. Then you're screwed, even if you don't want to be. I mean—"

She tried to keep from laughing. "I know what you mean."

"Look, Billie, all I want is to stay anonymous and live in Little Rock, which may not be a big deal to you, but it is to me," he said. "How about I promise not to leave town and you promise not to rat me out to your cop friend. Then, like you said, we could help each other."

"Interesting," she replied. "But if you do have credible evidence, you've got to realize I *will* tell the authorities. So why ask me to make a promise you know I won't keep?"

"I get that part. But who would you tell? I hear the cops collect information from people whose names never get reported to anyone."

Billie Rae nodded. "It does happen. They're called confidential informants—CIs."

"That's all I'm asking. And because you work for the DA's office, you could find the right person to set it up and keep my name out of it."

"Hmm, that might could work," she said.

"Does that mean you'll help?"

She didn't answer.

"What can I do to convince you I'm real?"

Billie Rae sat perfectly still, her gaze fixed on Avery. "All right then, answer me one question. Otherwise, I'll take my chances with my friend Frank and his pair of handcuffs."

Avery straightened up. "Okay."

"Did you find Parker somewhere in or under your house? Tell me now, a simple yes or no, or we're done here."

A lump formed in his throat. If she was bluffing, her green eyes weren't giving it away. After a moment of hesitation, he answered her with a simple, but definite nod of his head.

They sat in silence as the waiter cleared the table of everything but their wine glasses.

Billie Rae spoke first. "All right, it's a deal. But first I need to talk to a person I trust. And you have my word, your name won't be mentioned."

Avery couldn't believe his ears. "How much time do you need?"

"It might take a few days. So let's say next Tuesday. Give me your cell number in case I have to call you."

"Yeah, okay." Avery was careful to recite the number of his burner phone.

She wrote it down. "Meet here at the same time?"

Avery glanced around. "If you don't mind, I'd prefer to meet someplace outdoors, where people aren't too close by."

"How about in front of the Clinton Library?"

"I was thinking about the park along the river, just past the golf course on Rebsamen. It's not that far from downtown."

"Murray Park? I know it well."

Avery nodded. "If you don't feel safe, then have your cop-friend, Frank, tag along. He can keep tabs on me from his car."

"All right," she said. "How about we make it lunchtime?"

"Okay. Can I pick you up a sandwich and a drink?" Avery asked.

"Thank you, but no. Just be there at twelve. And use the second entrance, further down the road, past the dog run—there's several covered picnic tables. You can't miss it."

Avery leaned on his elbows. "Can I ask you why?"

"Why what?"

"I all but admitted I had something to do with your brother being found in the woods, and yet you said you still want to help me. Why would you say that?"

Billie Rae hesitated. "Someday I might explain, but for now, you'll have to trust me." She half-smiled. "Just don't say *thank you* again, all right?"

The waiter appeared with the check. Avery gave him cash, the way he paid all his bills.

"There is one other thing," Avery said. "I'm worried about your detective friend. From his visit, I got the feeling he doesn't like me. And with him waiting outside, what will you tell him so I don't get busted?"

Her finger circled the rim of her wine glass. "I'll tell him it's too early to jump to any conclusions, and we're going to see each other next week."

"Whoa. You make it sound like a date." Too late to take back what he said, Avery blushed again.

Her hand went to her mouth to cover her laughter. "I'll be sure I use different words with Frank."

Avery tried to smile.

"When we leave, I'll have a word with Frank," she said. "Then we exchange pleasantries and go home separately."

"I didn't imply otherwise."

"My apologies," she said. "Unfortunately, it's a habit I have, dealing with bossy men."

Avery nodded his understanding. "Did you drive here?"

"No, I walked. It's only a few blocks."

"Then how about I drive you home? I'd feel more comfortable knowing Detective Pearl will be less likely to arrest me if you accept my offer."

"Perhaps," she said, then chided, "Or, once you know where I live, you'll sneak back in the middle of the night and murder me in my sleep."

"Probably," he said, trying not to laugh. "But thanks to the Marshals, I already know where you live."

She sighed. "Oh, all right, I'll play along."

Avery finished his wine and deliberately set the glass at the edge of the table.

"What are you doing?" she asked.

"I wouldn't put it past your cop-friend to come in and take my wine glass for fingerprints."

"But why? I'll talk to him."

"Because that's what I'd do if I were him. And when he runs my prints through the national database, there won't a match for Avery Gillis. But there will be with the person I used to be. When that happens, both the Marshals *and* the FBI will be alerted, and somewhere inside the Bureau, that rogue agent might see it as well. Then, if the Marshals don't act fast to move me, I won't be alive next Tuesday."

With his index finger he pushed the glass off the table. It shattered to pieces on the tile floor.

Billie Rae gasped.

"Maybe you trust Detective Pearl," Avery said, "but he's still a cop."

Once in the car, Avery thought he detected someone following not far behind.

The couple exchanged a simple "Goodnight," and Billie Rae walked to her front door.

Avery waited until she opened the door. He recalled his grandmother telling him if he wanted to impress a girl, it was the polite thing to do. As he drove away, he doubted she had even noticed.

TWENTY-NINE
•••

"**M**r. Bones is her *brother*? Damn, Avery, you sure know how to pick 'em," Buck said on his phone. "And here I thought you called to say you at least made out."

"After what happened, not a chance. But you haven't heard the worst of it."

"What could be worse than you havin' the hots for some chick whose brother turns out to be Mr. Bones?"

"I only said I liked her. What I wanted to say was, she knows I'm in Witness Protection."

"Whoa. On your first date you dumped that shit on her?"

"But I didn't tell her. She figured it out. She works for the D.A.'s office, and those two cops are her friends."

"She found out who you are? I mean who you *really* are?"

"No, at least she didn't say. But that's not what I'm worried about. She thinks I'm the one who buried her brother in the woods."

"Hold it. Did you just say she knows you're in Witness Protection, but you're only worried about what she thinks you did to her brother?"

"Well, I, uh—"

"Shit, Avery, this woman's already got you hooked." Buck laughed. "And if that's the case, tell her the truth and say *I* did it. Then maybe she'll only dislike you, not hate you."

"Very funny. But I promised I wouldn't get you involved."

"Yeah, but how did she figure out you did it?"

"I, uh, suppose because I told her."

"Damn. I knew you were hopeless with women."

"Right. But there's something else you need to know." He told Buck about forgetting to put Parker's note and the shell casing in the bag along with Mr. Bones.

"And you're just tellin' me now?"

"Yeah, well, because you were all stressed about burying Mr. Bones to begin with, I didn't say. But I think I'm going to give them to the police."

"You *kept* the evidence?"

"I was going to throw it away, but something told me not to."

"Another one of your brilliant hunches, I suppose?"

Avery didn't answer.

"So let me get this straight. First, somebody finds Mr. Bones, then the police come to your door, but as much as they suspect you're involved, without any evidence they can't prove crap. Right, so far?"

"Uh-huh."

"So instead of dumpin' the goods and leavin' the cops with nothin' to connect you to any of it, you're gonna play right into their hands and risk bein' taken to hell-knows-where by the Marshals, all because you have a hard-on for the dead guy's sister? Does that about sum it up?"

"Buck, I told you—"

"Okay, okay, so you don't, which is bullshit, and you just *like* the woman. Then out of the cosmos, a lightning bolt strikes you square between the eyes, and suddenly you've grown a conscience and decide to do the right thing? Yeah, right. Not only are you hooked, you're out of your friggin' mind."

"Probably, but with Billie involved, and because Mr. Bones is her brother, I think there's a chance it might work."

"What might work, you and her? Talk about livin' in la-la land."

"No. About finding out who killed Mr. Bones."

"And when the Marshals find out what you're up to, then what?"

"Maybe they won't have to."

Buck laughed. "I don't know what you're smokin', Ave, but whatever it is, save me some."

THIRTY

• • •

Wearing a collared shirt under a pullover sweater, and new slacks to go with his new pair of shoes, Avery sipped his coffee and watched Billie Rae's white Beamer turn into Murray Park and make its way to a parking spot.

As she exited the car, her professional attire impressed Avery, as did her shoulder-length auburn hair. He watched her long legs and the sway of her hips as she walked toward him. He could no longer deny how attracted to her he had become, and this was only their third meeting.

She placed her coffee cup on the picnic table and sat down. "I'm glad to see you kept your word by not leaving town."

"Why wouldn't I?"

"Relax, Avery, it was meant as a compliment."

Instead of "Sorry," he said, "Okay," then smiled. "Where's Detective Pearl? I thought he was going to cover your back."

"He's nearby, but don't worry, he'll keep his distance."

"What did you tell him about me?"

"Not everything. He raised an eyebrow, but gave me the benefit of the doubt."

"And what about keeping me off the radar screen? Any solutions?"

"I spoke with the D.A., and he's open to the possibility. He thinks the Police Chief would go along as well. Of course, he'd need to know more of the details before making a commitment. That's the best I could do." She drank from her cup. "I did suggest Frank be the go-between. Besides having been Parker's best friend, he's one of the department's top detectives. The D.A. agreed."

"So you told him?"

"Frank? No. You asked me not to. Just be glad I convinced him to give me several days to charm the truth out of you."

Avery laughed. "You actually said *charm?*"

"Would you prefer I beat it out of you?"

They both smiled.

"Look," she said, "if you are in Witness Protection, I want to honor that. Frank would, too. I'm sure of it."

For a few moments they didn't speak. Each time they made eye-to-eye contact, they quickly looked away. Billie Rae broke the silence. "Would you tell me where he was when you found him? Parker, I mean."

Avery fiddled with his empty cup. "Would it be enough to know he was in the house?"

"I guessed that much. But I'd like to know exactly where he was, so I can put my mind to rest. Is that too much to ask?"

Avery squirmed on the picnic table bench, which suddenly felt harder. "He, uh, he was in a bathtub."

"A bathtub, right there in the house?"

"Well, not exactly." Avery explained the renovation of his house and his grisly discovery under the master bathroom floor. To avoid the details of her brother's gruesome remains, he tried to give emphasis to the sunken, heart-shaped, black porcelain tub.

When he finished, her face showed no expression. She looked toward the Big Dam Bridge that stretched across the Arkansas River. "I've come here a lot, to stare across the river where they found Parker's car, and wonder where he was and what really happened."

Avery didn't know what to say.

Her gaze returned to him. "Tell me about the evidence you have."

He took a deep breath to regain his composure. "I found a shell casing, and a small piece of paper with writing on it that was in your brother's suit coat pocket. That's all, just those two things."

"A paper? What did it say? There had to be something or you wouldn't have kept it."

"There were several initials, I assume representing people's names, around a circle with ABC written in the middle."

"And you knew that when Frank came to your house?"

"It didn't enter my mind until after he and his partner left. That's when I remembered."

"I see," she said. "What were the other initials?"

Avery shook his head. "I didn't pay attention, except there were three sets of them." Since their meeting at Hawg's, he did climb onto the roof to more closely examine the bloodstained note, but wouldn't mention it.

Billie Rae tapped her fingers on the table. "Why didn't you put the paper and the casing in the bag along with my brother's clothes?"

Avery's foot twitched up and down beneath the picnic table. "I was going to, but in my haste to close the bag, I forgot. By the time I realized, it was too late."

"But then you kept them. That seems such an odd thing to do for a man who wants to stay hidden."

"I was going to throw them away, but I changed my mind. I thought maybe I would give them to the police if something ever happened."

"You mean if my brother was ever found in the woods?"

"Yeah, but then I froze. I was afraid I'd be recognized. That's why I'm here, trying to make it right. All I want is for the police to keep me out of it."

Her fingers resumed drumming the rhythmic pattern on the side of her paper cup.

Avery watched the breeze catch a strand of her hair. *Damn*, he thought. He *was* hooked.

Her tapping stopped. "I told you what the D.A. said. So, if you want to make this happen, you should tell Frank."

"Right, but I'm afraid he won't believe a thing I say."

"We can talk to him together."

He thought for a moment. "Okay. But when?"

"How about now, right here, before you get cold feet."

Underneath the picnic table, Avery couldn't keep his legs still. "All right, make the call."

THIRTY-ONE

● ● ●

Detective Frank Pearl said he would be there in a few minutes. Avery and Billie Rae looked everywhere but at each other. Only the sound of rustling leaves and a crow cawing in a nearby oak broke the silence.

Finally, she spoke. "This is hard to say, but I'm glad you did what you did with Parker."

Avery was taken aback. "You mean you're *happy* because I buried your brother in the woods instead of calling the cops?"

She bit her lower lip. "I would have preferred if you'd called the police, but you didn't. Yet, had you just left him under the house, I'd still be in the dark about his disappearance. But what I was talking about was the way you," she hesitated, "put him in the bag. The coroner was surprised when he examined Parker's remains. Whoever did it was very, *deliberate*, I think was his word. He said he'd never seen anything like it, 'How neatly it was done,' he said.

"But after the initial shock of Parker being found, I was relieved it was finally over. Yes, part of me was angry that someone would be so heartless as to bury him in the woods or not call the authorities. But now that I know why and how you did it, I feel better. That's why I said yes about helping you."

Embarrassed, Avery took both of their empty cups and walked

them to a trash barrel. Returning, he couldn't take his eyes off the curve of her neck and her hair as it moved with the gentle breeze.

"Since I seem to be all in, may I ask you some questions about your brother?" he said. "It might help me make sense of this whole thing."

She nodded her approval.

"Why did you suspect this Arthur Bateman guy in the first place?"

"The simple answer is, Parker was Bateman's attorney."

Avery looked puzzled. "Why would he murder his own attorney? That's crazy."

"Let me tell you what happened, then maybe it won't seem so unlikely."

Avery rested his elbows on the picnic table.

"Parker was my older brother by nine years, and ever since I can remember his dream was to become an attorney, to defend the people who needed the law on their side for a change—all that altruistic stuff. Well, he did, and from the first day he loved his job. But over time, as word spread of his legal skills, his clientele began to change. Eventually, he found himself defending mostly rich criminals, all trying to beat the system—the complete opposite of how he started. Unfortunately, Parker had developed a weakness for fancy sports cars. They cost money, and those people had it. Anyway, it all came to a head ten years ago when Arthur Bateman was indicted by the state on bribery and corruption charges. He hired Parker as his attorney.

"About the time of the trial, Parker discovered that in the past, Bateman had paid a witness to lie under oath and threatened several others if they didn't. When Parker confronted Bateman, he admitted to doing it but said it was all ancient history. He swore he was being railroaded for his past sins.

"But when Bateman was acquitted, instead of congratulating himself, Parker was sick about it. I was home from college when the verdict came down. Then one day he said he'd figured some things out and was going to make it right and quit as his attorney.

"So Parker went to Bateman's house, now your house, to give him the news. But that night he didn't come home. The next day his car was found just across the river there, in the Big Dam Bridge parking lot." She pointed. "The doors were locked and the car had been wiped clean. The only sign of my brother was his wallet in the glove box. The police searched for days, everywhere, even the river, but to no avail. And when they questioned Bateman, he admitted Parker had been to his house, re-signed as his attorney, and left. A few days later investigators found a street camera had recorded Parker's car driving in downtown Little Rock *after* Bateman said Parker left his house, except Sammy Uronski was driv-ing."

Of course, Avery thought, *S.U. on Parker's note.* "How does he fit in?"

"When Bateman was indicted, Sammy, who was Bateman's lackey, said he didn't want to be arrested for illegal things Bateman paid him to do, so he struck a deal to testify against him. He became the prosecution's big witness. But on the stand, Parker shot holes in Sammy's testimony, and Bateman got off because the jury didn't believe Sammy's story. Par-ker figured he was in cahoots with Bateman all along."

"So there wouldn't be any reason your brother would let Sammy drive his car," Avery said.

"Correct. And when the D.A. tried to get a subpoena to search Bateman's house, the judge denied it. He said there wasn't proof any harm had come to Parker."

Avery nodded his understanding. "I don't mean to be insensitive, but could your brother have been hidden in the backseat or in the trunk?"

"No. Just before the trial he bought a new, bright yellow Corvette convertible, and Vettes don't have backseats, and the trunk still had a bunch of Parker's sports gear in it. The police said there was no way he could have been in that car. And that same night, Sammy also vanished."

"And all this time you haven't had a clue what happened?"

"No," she answered. "The only thing that makes sense is, even though Parker was bound by client-attorney privilege, Bateman feared Parker would go to the authorities anyway, so he killed him and had Sammy leave Parker's car at the Big Dam Bridge as a diversion. A month later Bateman locked up his house, left the country, and never came back. But because it sat empty year after year, *and* he didn't sell it, more and more I believed that's where Parker was, buried under his house or some-where on his property. I just couldn't prove it." Billie Rae exhaled a deep breath. "Now do you think I'm crazy?"

Avery shook his head. "No, it all sounds plausible to me. And the police never found Sammy?"

"Eventually. They got a tip he was living in Memphis. They questioned him about driving Parker's car, but he said he was hanging out downtown when Parker happened into a parking space, right where he was. He said he told Parker he really liked the car, so Parker let him drive it around the block a couple of times." She threw up her hands. "But that makes no sense."

"Let me guess," Avery said. "Without any evidence, the cops had to let Sammy go."

THIRTY-TWO

• • •

Detective Frank Pearl exited his car and approached the picnic table. Avery noticed he was dressed in the same tired sports coat and tie he wore the day he came to Avery's house.

"Thanks for coming, Frank," Billie Rae said.

He smiled at her, then extended his hand across the table. "Mr. Gillis. Or may I call you Avery?"

"Sure, why not?" Avery obligingly shook hands with the detective.

Frank sat down, reached inside his coat pocket, and removed a notepad and pen. "Avery, I'm glad you've decided to cooperate with our investigation. So what do you know?"

"Not so fast," Avery said. "First, we need to talk about some guarantees."

"Guarantees? What the hell are you talking about?"

"Avery's in the Witness Protection Program," Billie Rae said. "That's why so many things didn't make sense."

Frank slapped his notepad on the table. "I knew something was funny about you from the beginning." He glared at Avery. "That's all I need, a damn Marshal telling me to butt out because you're off-limits."

"But he wants to help us, Frank, without the Marshals," she said.

"Yeah, right. And if the Marshals find out, he disappears. Not only that, anything he says isn't legally worth shit because he's really some criminal. Then where does that leave us?"

Avery's face reddened as he tried to control his breathing. He reached inside his pocket and pulled out a cell phone. He speed-dialed a number.

As he did, Billie Rae reached across the table and held his arm. "No, Avery, please. We'll work something out."

The hint of welling tears in her green eyes almost got to him.

"Hello?" a voice said. Avery pulled away from Billie Rae's grasp. "Jerry, it's me, Avery." He rose and walked a few steps from the bench, far enough for them to hear his words but not Jerry's.

"What's up?" the Marshal said.

"We need to talk, that's all."

"Is this about that new girlfriend of yours?"

"Yeah, sort of."

"Don't tell me you broke up already?"

"No, it's not that. I was wondering if you might be available later today?"

"Might be available? What is it, Avery?"

"Maybe it's nothing. I just wanted to make sure you're around."

"Of course I am. But are you safe, security-wise?"

"Yeah, yeah, that part's okay. I'll call back in an hour." Avery ended the call and returned to the picnic table.

"You've got sixty minutes to make this right, Mr. Pearl, or my *damn* friend, as you call him, will tell you to pound sand and I *will* disappear, and the evidence I have concerning Parker's murder will be gone with me." He turned his attention to Billie Rae. "I'm sorry, Billie, but I told you this would happen."

"Frank, don't you see, he's here to help," she said. "He likes it here in Little Rock and doesn't want the Marshals to relocate him. All he wants is for his name to be left out of it."

"He has a funny way of saying it," Frank said.

"Sorry if I sound melodramatic, Detective, but I could wind up dead doing this." Avery could see Frank didn't believe him. "I swear to you, someone connected with the FBI killed two of my friends and I'm next on his list, but nobody knows who he is. Any inquiry to the Feds could tip him off—especially giving them my fingerprints."

Billie Rae jumped in. "He's asking if there's a way he can give you what he has without him being in the picture—like one of your CIs."

The detective tapped on his pen on the table.

"Frank, he found a note in Parker's suit pocket with initials on it, including Arthur Bateman's company, ABC," she said.

"And an empty shell casing," Avery added.

Frank sat up and looked at Avery. "Was it a three-eighty?" he said with some enthusiasm. "That's what killed Parker."

Avery shrugged. "I don't know. I'm not a gun guy."

"Then you probably got your fingerprints all over it?" Frank said.

Avery paused. "I'm sorry, the possibility of somebody's prints being on it didn't cross my mind until later. But if it helps, I was wearing protective gloves when I picked it up. Right now it's inside a sealed baggie along with the note."

Frank grinned. "Hmm, that might could help. So what's on the note?"

"Besides the circle with ABC in the middle, three sets of initials were around it. I think one of them is S.U., which would match the Sammy guy you asked me about. The others, I'm not sure."

"That's a start," Pearl said, and wrote in his notepad. Then he looked at Avery. "Let me get this straight: you're willing to turn over this evidence if you can just walk away, no questions asked, is that it?"

"Pretty much," Avery said.

"What if I try, and through no fault of mine, somehow it doesn't work out?"

"I don't even want to go there. I just want to know, is it possible?"

Frank rubbed his chin. "It is. But before we go too far with this, how can I be certain you are who you say, that you *are* in Witness Protection, without actually talking to the U.S. Marshals?"

"I didn't say not to talk to them. It's who you talk to and what you say that counts."

"You know that won't be easy."

"I'm not saying it would," Avery answered.

"If it helps, I believe him," Billie Rae said. "Knowing all the information Avery has on me, where else could he get it but from the Marshals?"

"What information?" Frank asked.

She filled Frank in.

Detective Pearl stared at Avery. "If that's true, how did you get the Marshals to give it to you?"

Avery blushed and looked at Billie Rae. "I said I was interested in dating you, and could they check you out?"

Her cheeks turned red.

"You, date her?" Frank laughed. "That's a good one."

Her face reddened even more.

"She did give me a note to call her, you know," Avery said.

"Yes, I did," she said to Frank.

"I thought that was only to pump him for more information," Frank countered.

"Well, uh, yes. That part's true." She gave Avery a sheepish grin.

Frank cleared his throat. "Can we get back to business?" He looked at Avery. "So how do I meet this contact of yours, who I assume is Jerry?"

"He's waiting for my call."

"Okay, I meet Jerry. Then what?" Frank said.

"That part troubled me, too," Avery replied. "But I have a solution that might work if you agree to it."

"Why don't I like the sound of this?" Frank said.

"Hear me out first, then decide."

"Go for it."

"If you don't tell Jerry it was me who found Parker buried in my house, then the fact that I moved his remains to the woods would never have to come up."

Frank's mouth dropped open. "So *you* were the one. Son-of-a-bitch." Frank rolled his eyes. "Do you know how illegal that was, on several counts? And you want me to lie about it?"

"No, I'm asking you not to reveal certain facts because all you're after is the evidence I have, right?"

"And if it helps catch Parker's killer," Billie Rae added, "why not do it?"

Again Frank tapped his pen on the table. "I suppose you're right."

"What's your big worry, Frank?" she asked.

"That this blows up in my face. Then I'll look like a fool, the department as well."

All three sat without speaking. The detective continued to tap his pen.

"Frank," Billie Rae said, "what if *I* meet with Jerry to make sure his story's true?"

"Why you?"

"Because Avery contacted him on the pretense of dating me. It would only make sense for me to meet him if we were, let's say," she cleared her throat, "growing closer, and Avery said he couldn't keep lying to me about his past."

"You mean finding out he's probably a sleazebag," the detective said.

Billie Rae smacked him on the arm. "Come on, Frank, you're not helping."

Avery glared at the detective.

"Oh, I'm sorry, Mr. Gillis," Frank said. "If that hit a little too close to home, I apologize." His smile appeared insincere.

Avery pressed his fingers against the edge of the picnic table and silently began to count to 10. He only reached four when he turned to Billie Rae. "I thought you said he was different, but he's just another damn cop with an attitude, so it's clear where this is going." He took out his cell phone and dialed.

Billie Rae lunged across the table to grab his phone, but Avery pulled away.

"Jerry, we need to talk—*now*! I'll call you back in five and tell you where." Without saying another word, Avery walked to his car.

THIRTY-THREE
• • •

Behind the wheel, Avery prepared to exit the park when Billie Rae stepped into the roadway, hands on her hips, blocking his path. Avery slowed to a stop. From inside his car he heard her muted voice.

"Get out of the car."

He lowered his window and stuck his head out. "What do you want?"

"We need to talk," she said.

"It won't do any good."

"Fine, but I'm not moving."

Avery drummed his fingers on the steering wheel. "Damn," he breathed. He turned his head, searching for Frank. He was still at the park bench. Avery's eyes focused back on Billie Rae. She hadn't moved. He killed the motor, got out, and closed the car door.

She walked toward him. "Have you called Jerry yet?"

"No. I was waiting 'til I got away from here."

"Good. Then we have time to work this out."

"What about Frank?"

"Don't worry about him, he'll cool off. Then he'll be fine, I promise."

"Yeah, right. You want me to trust some cop who hates my guts?" Avery said.

"Just because he doesn't like you doesn't mean he won't do his best to protect you."

"I'm supposed to believe that?"

"If you want this to work, yes. Besides, it's true. He's one of the good guys." Billie Rae walked closer, then leaned against the car's fender. "I don't know about your past life, but at some point you're going to have to start trusting people."

"Trusting someone almost got me killed before I came to Little Rock," Avery said. "My attorney no less."

She paused. "How about your Marshal friend, Jerry? Do you trust him?"

He shrugged. "For the most part."

"But not enough to tell him about Parker," she said.

"The way things are headed, I'm about to find out."

"All right, but is it just law enforcement who frightens you, or everybody?"

Avery thought for a moment. "Mostly the law, then people who ask too many questions."

Billie Rae stepped away from the car to face him. "Do you trust me?"

He looked her in the eye. "Part of me wants to say yes."

"That's how I feel about you. My common sense says wait a minute. But like you, here I am anyway; I still want to help you."

"I know, so you can find your brother's killer."

"True, but it's more than that. I'd want you to be safe even if this wasn't about Parker." There it was again, her *almost smile*. "How about you call Jerry and we'll go see him together. It'll help Frank have a little more faith in you when I return safe and unharmed. Besides, I've never met a real Marshal before."

Avery nodded his agreement and pulled out his phone.

Billie Rae hurried back to the park bench to have a one-minute conversation with Detective Pearl.

THIRTY-FOUR
●●●

"I'm almost there," Jerry said. "I just turned off Cantrell Road."

"You know where I am?" Avery said.

"Your cell phone is on our GPS tracking system, remember? So stay put, I'll be there in three minutes," Jerry said.

"No, that won't work. Let's meet halfway, at the golf course. There's a parking lot near the clubhouse with benches by some trees."

"Right. So who is it you don't want me to meet? Is it that woman of yours?"

"Jerry, just meet me at the golf course." He ended the call.

With Billie Rae in the car, Avery turned onto Rebsamen Park Road.

"Are you sure you can pretend we're more than casual acquaintances?" she said. "Otherwise, he'll be suspicious."

Pretend? He thought. "Yeah, sure, I can do it."

Avery parked a short distance away from where the deputy waited on a green bench. "That's Jerry over there," he said.

"Good. Now come around and open the door for me."

"What?"

"My door, open it," she said. "In case you forgot, it's what gentlemen do for their girlfriends, especially when they first start dating. And smile. You look like your dog just died."

Avery complied.

As he closed the car door, Billie Rae reached out and took his hand. "What are you doing?" Avery said, as if he were practicing ventriloquism.

"Jerry's supposed to think we're in love." She too tried not to move her lips. "But loosen your grip, you're squeezing too hard."

The couple continued to walk hand in hand toward the Marshal.

Jerry stood as they approached. "I see you decided to bring her with you."

"I did," Avery said. "This is Billie Rae Robinson. Billie, this is Deputy Jerry Joyce."

She broke her grasp with Avery and extended her hand.

"How do you do?" Jerry said with a fake smile.

"Very well, thank you," she replied.

Avery and Billie Rae sat on one bench while Jerry sat opposite them.

"So how about we talk?" Billie Rae said.

"Do you have a subject in mind?" Jerry said.

"Yes, about you being a United States Marshal and Avery here being in Witness Protection."

Jerry looked around before speaking. "You don't beat around the bush, do you, Miss Robinson?"

"Not usually. It tends to waste time. Which reminds me. May I see your identification, please?"

He hesitated. "You don't believe I'm a U.S. Marshal?"

"I don't believe a lot of what men tell me. I've heard some mighty big tales, and Avery's story takes the cake. So until I see your credentials, yes, I *am* skeptical."

Jerry smirked, then reached in his jacket pocket, produced a thin black wallet, and handed it to her.

Billie Rae examined it. "Thank you, Deputy Joyce." She returned his credentials.

"Call me Jerry, everyone else does."

"All right, Jerry. So is it true about Avery?"

"I'm not sure. What did he tell you?"

"That his name's not really Avery Gillis and he's afraid for his life. Although, when we first met he did try to sell himself, but when it came to him saying he had lived in New Orleans, I can tell you, he doesn't know beans about The Big Easy, and that made me leery. So I did a little research in the D.A.'s office and found out Avery's story didn't hold water, and I called him on it. Rather than walk away, he confided in me."

"You used the District Attorney's office for your personal benefit?" Jerry said.

Billie Rae looked him in the eye. "Then report me. But I don't think you will, especially if you want to keep Avery's identity secret."

"Okay," the Marshal said, "but did he also tell you his real name or what he did?"

"No, and I didn't ask."

Jerry nodded. "That's only good up to a point. But what worries me is, Avery's complicated his life even more by bringing you into the equation, which also puts *your* life in harm's way. You could wind up an innocent victim."

"You make it sound so dramatic," she said.

"Look, Miss Robinson, it appears you mean well, but in Avery's case there are, let's say, extenuating circumstances."

"You mean an unknown agent from the FBI?"

Jerry bolted upright. "Damn it, Avery, did you have to tell her that, too?"

Avery shrugged. "I thought she should know how serious this is."

Before Jerry could respond, she said, "He's afraid we'll break up and then I'll blab whatever I know all over town."

"And you wouldn't be the first to betray someone," Jerry said.

"I'm sure it's true, but I promise, I won't do that."

"Even when you find out his real name?"

"Geez, Jerry. You make it sound like I'm a sociopath," Avery said.

"It wasn't my intention. But if you were, it would make a difference if she found out, don't you think?"

"Very funny, Jerry, because you know I'm not. So please tell her. That's one reason we're here."

"Deputy Joyce, to use your own words, it would make a difference to know," Billie Rae said. "I also agree with Avery. For the sake of our relationship, it is important."

Jerry hesitated. "All right, Miss Robinson, I will tell you this much. Avery is not in Witness Protection because of any violence on his part."

"Thank you, Jerry. That is reassuring, but I stand by my word."

"You say that now, but wait until he pisses you off someday," the deputy said.

"Don't worry, Jerry," she said. "Working for the D.A., I understand the rules of secrecy. You have my word, my lips are sealed, even if we do break up." Billie Rae reached out and squeezed Avery's hand. "But that's not going to happen, is it?" She leaned closer and kissed him gently on the cheek.

Avery blushed. "Uh, no, it's not." He returned her kiss, just above her ear. His lips lingered for a moment, pressed against the softness of her hair.

Jerry cleared his throat. "Okay, okay. Enough already."

Avery pulled away from Billie Rae.

Deputy Joyce pointed his finger. "I'm warning you both, if word leaks out and Avery's lucky enough to still be alive, for him, it's goodbye Little Rock."

THIRTY-FIVE

• • •

The couple held hands as they walked back to Avery's car. He opened Billie Rae's door without being prompted. They sat in silence and watched Jerry drive away, then breathed sighs of relief.

"I can't believe we just pulled that off," she said. "I thought the clincher was when I kissed you, but then you kissed me back. That was brilliant, Avery. Did you see the look on Jerry's face?"

He rested his forehead against the steering wheel.

She put her hand on his arm. "What is it?"

Avery looked at her. "I didn't plan anything. I kissed you because I, uh, I wanted to."

"Oh." She covered her face with her hands.

"I'm sorry, Billie, I shouldn't have said anything. I didn't mean to"

She held up her hand. "I think we should change the subject, okay?"

"Uh, yeah, good idea. So now do you believe me?"

"I thought I just said—"

"No, no. I mean about Witness Protection, and the FBI agent."

Billie Rae nodded. "I think I did from the beginning. I know this may sound strange, but I'm glad it's true. Not that I want you to be in hiding, but that you're not a, uh—"

"A sleazebag?"

She laughed. "Frank's word, not mine. But yes, something along those lines." She gave Avery's arm a gentle squeeze. "Let's go help relieve

Frank's anxiety."

The pair returned to the bench where Detective Pearl waited. They didn't hold hands.

Billie Rae confirmed to Frank the veracity of Avery's story.

The detective assured Avery he would do what he could to keep his Witness Protection status from going public. "So when I get this set up you'll turn over what you have, right?"

"Of course," Avery said. What other choice did he have? "When will I know?"

"It should be in the next day or two. Give me your number and I'll call you."

Avery recited the number of his burner phone.

"So this baggie with the note and shell casing, it's at your house?" Frank asked.

Avery hesitated, then lied, "Give me an hour and I can have it there."

"That's good. But you know you'll have to tell us how it all happened, right?"

"Everything?" Avery replied.

"Look, we're just trying to find Parker's killer," Frank said. "But I will say, if we do find the killer, you may have to testify, which means your anonymity could be compromised."

"But having me testify is the last thing you want," Avery began. "It's like you said. Me, living under an alias, lying about who I am and where I'm from, the defense would rip me apart as totally unreliable."

"But what if it does go to trial?" Billie Rae asked.

Avery paused. "I'm sorry, Billie, but your brother's death was no accident, which means the death penalty would be on the table. Rather than risk going to trial, most likely the killer would take a deal for life instead. Then I wouldn't have to testify."

"That's a good point," Frank said. "Let's hope it works out that way." He then hurried off to arrange things.

Avery walked with Billie Rae to her Beamer.

"Thank you, Avery, for trusting me."

"It's weird to hear you say that, after what I did."

"I thought we already covered that."

"Yeah, well, I still feel bad."

She smiled. "Was that before or *after* we met?"

Avery chuckled. "To be honest, both." He opened her car door. "Billie, do you think, uh, I mean, could we, uh—"

"Have dinner again? Let me think about it. Right now my focus is on Parker. First, I've got to put that part behind me." She climbed into the driver's seat. "Then if I'm ready, I might could give you a call."

THIRTY-SIX
• • •

"If she's *ready* she might call you? What the hell does that mean?" Buck said.

"How should I know?" Avery replied. "That's why I called."

"With me bein' clueless about Polly, I think I'll pass."

"Right," Avery said into his cell phone. "So how about you come over tonight? I'll barbeque a couple of steaks, you supply the beer. Then I can fill you in on what happened."

"Geez, I'd like to, but I already promised some guys I'd meet 'em for dinner. You wanna join us? It might cheer you up. That's what I'm lookin' to do."

"Thanks, but you know me, I'd feel like a fifth wheel," Avery said.

"Then how about tomorrow night? I think the Lakers are playin' and you've got the big flat screen. You cook, I'll bring the beer."

"Sounds good. What time?"

"How about six. I'll call before I get there so you know when to throw on the steaks."

It hadn't been five minutes when Avery's burner phone rang. The call number on the LED screen was blocked. He hesitated but finally answered, "Hello?"

"Avery, this is Detective Pearl. Good news, it's all arranged. Everyone agreed, your name will be kept out of it."

"Already? That wasn't four hours ago."

"I know. But the Chief and the D.A. said if this can help clear up Parker's murder, they want it done, sooner than later."

"Okay. But what about me, doing what I did? What'd they say about that?"

"Did you break the law moving Parker's remains? No doubt. But because of your cooperation and the situation you're in, they're willing to let it slide."

"Does anybody else know?" Avery said.

"Just the D.A. and his assistant. But they've done this before, so don't worry."

"What about your partner? Did you tell him?"

"Not yet. I've been too busy putting this together for us to talk. But since you asked, partners do share what's going on. It's a trust thing with cops."

"Yeah, but you promised to say something about me being in Witness Protection only on a need-to-know basis, or was that all bullshit?" Avery could hear Frank's sigh of disdain. "Sorry, Detective, I'm a little edgy. Wouldn't you be?"

"I hear you, Avery. But there's no need to get bent out of shape. My word's good. I'll work it out with Tony."

"Okay," Avery said, only half convinced.

"So do you have the stuff?" Frank asked. "I could swing by and pick it up."

"No. I didn't think this would happen so fast. I'm not even home yet."

"All right. No problem. How about I drop by first thing in the morning? That way we'll have more time to talk. You know, to go over the details."

"It's okay by me. What time?"

"How about eight-thirty?" Frank said. "You'll have the evidence by then, right?"

"Yeah, sure. I'll have it tonight."

"Good, eight-thirty it is. Oh, by the way, I promised Billie to pass on her thanks for you doing this. She really appreciates it."

"You told her already?"

"Just before I called you. I thought you'd be okay with that, seeing how she already knows it's in the works."

Damn. He hoped to tell her himself.

Avery spent the better part of an hour wandering through the supermarket, picking up an item here and there, often retracing his steps down the aisles. His mind wasn't on groceries or Frank's promise. Over and over he replayed his time spent with Billie Rae, holding hands and her kissing him on the cheek. What nagged at him most were her parting words, *"If I'm ready."* With his luck, it would be never.

He stopped for dinner at a deli and ate a tuna sandwich and chips in his car. Arriving home near dark, he put away the groceries, grabbed a beer, and walked into the living room. He didn't bother with a light, but collapsed into his favorite leather recliner.

In a few minutes he would climb to the roof and retrieve Parker's note and the shell casing from its hiding place in the chimney. He stared out the sliding glass door, beyond the pool, and watched the night swallow his long driveway and the surrounding landscape.

A flash of light disturbed the darkness as a pair of headlights turned into his driveway. First, he thought it was Buck, but remembered he was out with friends, and then he noticed the headlamps were closer to the ground—it was a car.

Still some distance from the house, the headlights went out. The hair on Avery's neck stiffened. Whoever it was meant trouble. He left his half-empty beer on the coffee table and hurried down the hall to his darkened bedroom and closed the door behind him. He felt his way along the edge of the bed and sat on the floor, his back against the mattress. His body trembled as he stared through the ceiling-to-floor glass windows into the black night.

Hopefully, they would think he wasn't home and go away. But his car was parked under the carport. If they touched the hood, it would still be warm.

The Marshals, he thought. He felt his pants pocket and cursed. His government cell phone was in his car. He checked his other pocket and found his burner phone. But did he know Jerry's number by heart? Of course not. *What about the 911?* No. Whomever he called, by the time they arrived it would be too late.

Suddenly, a series of motion detector lights attached under the eaves of the house turned on. Two men dressed in black stood outside Avery's bedroom window. The reflection of the light in the tinted, double pane glass windows acted like a mirror, preventing the pair from seeing inside the bedroom. One man was wearing a ski mask. The other held his mask in his hand and turned to put it on.

Son-of-a-bitch! Avery thought.

Detective Tony Trainer then pulled up his shirt, took out a handgun, checked the clip, and proceeded toward the front door. Avery figured he didn't have to guess the identity of the other masked-man.

For a brief moment Avery wished the U.S. Marshals had let *him* carry a gun, but being in Witness Protection it wasn't allowed. Then again, with his lack of experience with guns, he would more likely shoot his own foot before he hit anything he aimed at.

THIRTY-SEVEN
• • •

The doorbell rang. Avery didn't answer.

Thump! Thump! Thump! A fist pounded on the front door. "Mr. Gillis, we know you're in there, so open up."

Petrified, Avery didn't move.

Thump! Thump! "Come on, Gillis, don't make it harder on yourself, open the door."

First, silence. Then he heard muffled voices. They were coming from *inside* the house. Avery made himself stop thinking about how they got in and focus on how *he* was going to get out. His heart pounded like the *thump, thump, thump* on his door.

Opposite the glass wall was a sliding glass door leading to the grassy yard behind the house. Avery had used the door only twice: last summer during a tornado warning when he retreated to the underground storm cellar for safety, and again when he and Buck carried debris to the dumpster while remodeling the master suite.

He scrambled to his feet, opened the door, slipped outside, and purposely pulled the door *almost* shut behind him. Hopefully, it would be noticed.

He ran to the storm cellar that lay some 20 yards from the house, buried beneath a roundish mound in the middle of the green lawn, halfway between the house and a row of fruitless pear trees that marked the eastern boundary of the property, parallel to Arch Street. The door to the storm cellar was on the side of the mound, flush with the ground. A short way down the road a single streetlamp provided enough ambient light for Avery to maneuver.

Avery pulled open the three-foot square stainless steel door and plunged his arm into the opening. The cellar light turned on—another motion sensor device. Steep wooden steps descended into the cinderblock bunker. The shelter itself was equipped with all the basics: a flashlight, two cots, blankets, two wooden chairs, a small table, a five-gallon bottle of water, cups, a portable radio, candles, matches, a deck of cards, a bucket to pee in, a roll of toilet paper, and three Sudoku books. A #2 pencil was lodged between the pages of one of them.

Standing on the damp grass, Avery pulled off his shirt and wedged it into the opening so the door wouldn't shut completely—light leaked out around the edges. The cellar light would remain on for five minutes. *More than enough time*, he reasoned.

Avery looked back toward the house. A light was on in the kitchen and the first of the three bedrooms. Then the second bedroom light flashed on. His would be next.

He rushed to the opposite end of the house, to the aluminum ladder that lay against the foundation—the ladder he used to gain access to the roof and his secret hiding place in the chimney. He snatched it up and leaned it against the edge of the roof.

The light went on in his master bedroom. Avery hurried to scramble up the ladder. Almost at the top, his foot slipped and his face slammed into one of the metal rungs. He moaned as he clung to the ladder. His cheek was gashed and his lip cut. Blood oozed from his mouth. The pain was excruciating.

He took several deep breaths, then climbed the few remaining steps and eased himself onto the flat roof. He touched his forearm to his cheek, feeling the warm blood. He wanted to collapse but knew he couldn't.

He grabbed the ladder, moved it away from the edge of the roof, and began lifting it straight up into the air, inches at a time, higher and higher.

"Out here," a voice commanded.

As Avery raised the ladder over his head, he could see a man outside the sliding glass door of his bedroom, pointing toward the storm cellar. Had the man looked 90 degrees in Avery's direction, he would have easily spotted him. Avery rotated the ladder and lowered it onto the roof. His jaw throbbed. Blood dripped onto his bare chest.

Ignoring the pain, he peeked over the roof's edge. In the light cast from the home's windows, he watched the two men march toward the storm cellar and the light escaping from around its door. They still wore their masks.

One of the men yanked open the door.

"Come on out, Gillis," the other man shouted.

After a few moments, one of them stuck his head into the opening, then descended into the bunker, only to reappear seconds later. A short discussion ensued. Avery couldn't make out their words. They threw Avery's shirt into the hole, slammed the door shut, and returned to the house.

Avery moved to the stone chimney where he sat down and remained still. Any movement by him on the roof might be detected from inside the house. From his position he could see the skylight domes of the bathrooms, kitchen, living room, and entrance area, all lit up like giant mushrooms. He could hear the occasional sounds of crashing furniture, which meant they were taking his house apart room by room. Their purpose was clear: to find the evidence.

The bleeding from Avery's cheek and lip had lessened. He ran his tongue over his teeth. One tooth had a jagged edge. Back to the problem at hand, he pulled out his cell phone. But whom could he call, the cops? They were already here. He wondered where the Marshals would send him next.

Twenty-five minutes passed. His jaw and lip were swollen but the bleeding had stopped. Finally, he heard voices outside the front of the house. He crept to the roofline and peered over the edge. Although an overhang covered the walkway and blocked his view, he could hear them talking.

"Maybe he doesn't have it yet."

"But you said he'd get it before he came home."

"Then it should've been here. You checked his car, right?"

"Twice. There's nothin' but a phone."

"Then he's got the stuff with him."

"What if we can't find him?"

"Then you'd better hope what he has doesn't lead back to us." Their words grew faint as the pair moved down the curved walkway and into the covered carport. Their masks were gone, but he couldn't see their faces. They walked past Avery's car and disappeared into the darkness.

Avery waited.

One of the men returned. He carried something in his hand. He knelt down and reached under the chassis of Avery's car. As the man stood, any doubt Avery had was erased. It was indeed, Detective Tony Trainer. The object was missing from his hand.

A bomb was Avery's first thought, but that made little sense, considering they were after the evidence he had.

Thirty seconds later their car drove down the driveway, its lights on. From Avery's dark vantage point he watched as the car turned onto Arch Street and headed back toward town. It had almost vanished when the red brake lights flashed on. It slowed, and without signaling, turned onto a side road and stopped. The car's lights flickered off.

THIRTY-EIGHT
● ● ●

Still on the roof, Avery called Buck.

"This is Buck. Leave a message and I'll get back to you."

"Damn it," Avery whispered. Then he remembered Buck was out with friends.

Avery's mouth was bruised and swollen. His words were slow and muddled. "Buck, call me. I don't care what time it is. It's f-ing urgent."

In case he might never return to his Arch Street home, Avery removed all the items from the chimney's hiding place. After resetting the ladder against the foundation, he entered his bedroom through the sliding door.

As he anticipated, every room was a disaster. He rethought calling 911. Sure, his house had been ransacked, but by the cops? What proof did he have? Now it wouldn't matter. The Marshals would have him relocated and renamed in no time.

His mouth throbbed. He looked in the bathroom mirror. His cheek and lip were cut and swollen, his beard caked with blood. He cleansed his wounds as best he could, changed, threw some extra clothes in a sports bag, then went to his car. He placed the baggie with Parker's note and the shell casing in the car's center console.

Next, Avery checked under the car. It took a few seconds to find the small black box attached to the frame with a magnet—a GPS tracking device. He removed it. Clearly, the two intruders were hoping he would lead them to Parker's evidence. What pissed him off most was falling for Detective Pearl's line that he would be by in the morning. *Asshole,* Avery thought.

With the current turn of events, Avery needed to act quickly. What did that creep, Karl Casey tell him? Adapt, become a chameleon. *Yeah, right,* he thought. *Don't I wish?*

He placed the tracking device on the passenger seat, then drove to the end of the driveway and stopped. The engine idled while he made another call.

"Hello?" Billie Rae said.

"It's Avery. I hope I'm not interrupting anything, but I wanted to give you a message."

"No, I have a few minutes," she said. "Are you all right? Your voice sounds funny."

"I'll be fine, but I'm leaving town, and I'm taking the evidence regarding your brother's death with me. But I *will* make sure you get it, I promise."

"Leaving town? I thought Frank had this all worked out."

"So did I, until he and his pal Tony broke into my house. They were wearing masks. And I'm talking funny because my mouth got busted up."

"They broke into your house wearing masks? That's ridiculous."

"It's the truth."

She hesitated. "If they were wearing masks, how do you know it was them?"

"Because I saw Detective Tony put on his mask, not ten feet away from me."

"And Frank, too? I don't believe it. Are you sure?"

"Well, no. But I told him I would have the evidence by tonight. So who else could it be? The only reason anyone would want to steal it is because they were somehow involved in your brother's murder. Face it, Billie, they're crooked cops."

"I, I can't believe that. Especially Frank. He was Parker's best friend."

"Then give me another reason. But I bet you can't."

She paused. "Where are you?"

"I'd rather not say."

"All right. But listen, can I call you right back? It won't take two minutes."

"So you can call your pal, Frank?"

"No, cross my heart, not him. Please, Avery, two minutes. That's all."

Avery sighed. "Yeah, okay, but then I'm gone."

Ninety seconds later his phone rang. "Yes?"

"Avery, I tried to call Dianne, Frank's wife at home, but she didn't answer. That means she and Frank could be out with the kids. I left a message for her to call me. I said it was important, but I didn't mention you or Frank."

"Or she could be out with the kids, minus Frank."

"Then hang up and let me call his cell."

"And tip him off that I know he's a crook?"

"But he's not, Avery. I know him. We've worked together for years trying to find Parker's killer. What you said doesn't make sense."

Avery exhaled. "Okay, maybe it was somebody else. But until you know for sure, do you want to risk not finding out who murdered your brother?"

"No, of course not. But what are you going to do?"

"I think I have to call the Marshals and fess up. By this time tomorrow I'll have disappeared. I'll give the evidence to Jerry. You can get it from him."

"But if Frank's not involved, wouldn't that change things?"

"His partner is. I know that for sure."

"Then why not wait? Give me a chance to find out about Frank."

Avery shook his head. "I don't know. I can't wait at my place, they might come back."

Billie Rae paused. "Come to my house, you'll be safe here. Then maybe we can figure things out together."

An invitation from Billie Rae? "Yeah, okay," he said, then explained about the GPS device attached to his car. "It might take a while, but I'll be there."

THIRTY-NINE
• • •

A very arrived at Billie Rae's an hour later. She opened the door. "Come in, Avery, I was beginning to think—oh, my." She pressed her hand to her lips.

"Does it look that bad?" he said, slurring his words.

"It doesn't look pretty," she said. "Come on, we need to get you cleaned up." She led him down a hallway into the kitchen and pointed to a chair. "Sit here, the light's better."

While Billie Rae tended to Avery's abrasions, the two tried to make sense of his evening's ordeal with Detective Trainer and his accomplice.

Finished, she prepared an icepack and gently pressed it to his injured face. "Here, this should help take down the swelling."

"Thanks." Avery moved his hand to hold the icepack. Unexpectedly, their hands overlapped. Their eyes met. She smiled, then pulled her hand away.

"How does that feel?" she said.

"Better, but I think I broke a tooth."

Billie Rae's phone rang.

"It's probably Dianne," she said, and reached for her cell phone. "Hello?" Her body stiffened. "Tony?" She looked at Avery and sat down. "Frank? How should I know where he is? He's *your* partner . . . Then leave him a message." She laid the phone on the table and pushed the speaker button.

"Yeah, I, uh, I plan to," he said. "It's just that he mentioned something about picking up evidence about your brother from that jerk, Avery

Gillis, first thing in the morning. He said he was going to call with the details, but he didn't and it's getting late."

"Yes, I understand. But I can't help you, Tony."

"Yeah, sure. Say, did you just put me on speakerphone? There's an echo all of a sudden."

Billie Rae paused. "Yes, I did. Sorry, but I'm folding clothes. I need to get some chores done before tomorrow. I do have to work, you know."

"Yeah, okay. But did you hear that your office is *not* going to prosecute Gillis as long as he turns over the evidence?"

"I heard it mentioned," she said.

"Well I think that's chicken shit, especially after what he did."

"I suppose. But look, Tony, I've got to go. Sorry I can't help you."

"Okay. But let me ask you one last thing. Frank said you were the one who met with Gillis and flushed him out. Are you sure we can trust him? I mean, what if he reneges and leaves town or something?"

"Look, Tony, if Frank said he made a deal with Avery, why would he go anywhere?"

"I don't know. I guess I'm anxious to get the evidence and see if it helps find out who murdered Parker, that's all."

"All right, Tony. If I talk to Frank I'll pass along your message." Billie Rae ended the call. "Now don't you think I should call Frank?"

Avery nodded. "But wait, I'll bet Tony calls back."

"Why?"

"To see if you *are* busy doing chores. If right away it goes to voicemail he'll suspect you're calling Frank. We need him to believe he's above suspicion."

"You really think so?" she said.

"I do, because he's desperate. I know I would. He either wants the evidence or me out of the way so I don't show up with it. For him, there's no other choice."

Her phone rang again.

"Wait, let it ring a couple of times," Avery said. "You're busy, remember?"

Finally, she answered, "Hello?"

"Oh, sure, Tony, don't worry about it," she said, then hung up. "He said he misdialed."

Avery sighed. "Okay, I believe you. Call your detective friend."

FORTY

● ● ●

"Frank, you need to come over right away. Avery Gillis is here and he's been injured, and Tony's behind it . . . Yes, I'm serious . . . Frank, listen to me. It's possible Tony could be involved in Parker's murder, so if he calls, don't answer until we talk."

Fifteen minutes later, Frank Pearl followed Billie Rae into her kitchen where he exchanged a brief handshake with Avery, who had taken a break from using the icepack. She poured the two men coffee. She stayed with her favorite, unsweetened ice tea.

"All right, Billie, what's all this talk about Tony?" Frank said.

"He ransacked Avery's house. So you'd better let him explain it," she answered.

Frank took out his notepad and pen. "Okay, Avery, tell me what happened from the beginning—every detail."

Avery rattled off everything he could remember.

"How'd you lose them with the auto tracking device?" Frank said.

"To being with, I was pretty sure they wouldn't follow too close until they were ready to pounce, so I popped it off, then drove out the 30 toward Hot Springs and got off in Benton, went through the Wal-Mart parking lot and pitched the GPS under a parked car, then drove out the exit where it gets back onto the freeway. I don't think I was followed after that. I even parked two blocks away in case they came by here, looking for my car."

"And there's no doubt in your mind it was Tony?" Frank asked.

"Honest to God, Detective, he wasn't ten feet away from me," Avery replied.

"What about the other guy, did you get a look at him?" Frank said.

"No, your partner's the only one I could identify."

"Damn!" Frank pounded his fist on the table. "Why the hell did it have to be him?"

"I know how you feel," Billie Rae added.

"So where is it, Avery, the evidence?" Frank said. "I want to see what you have."

"It's over on the counter." Avery pointed.

Billie Rae retrieved the baggie, unzipped it, and slid the evidence onto the table. Avery watched as she rotated the note with her fingers, careful not to touch the part stained with her brother's blood.

"Look, Frank. It's Parker's handwriting. I'd swear to it."

Frank nodded. "And the ABC is the Arthur Bateman Company."

"And there's S.U., like Avery said—Sammy Uronski." Billie Rae's shoulders quivered. "This is creepy."

The detective agreed. "But who's A.T. and R.J.?"

Billie Rae pointed to the paper. "I hate to say it, Frank, but A.T. could be *Anthony* Trainer. Tony's short for Anthony."

"I saw that, but I didn't want to admit it," he said. "But how's he connected to Bateman?"

Avery looked at Billie Rae. "At the park you told me your brother was going to see Bateman *to make things right*. Did he say what that meant?"

She shook her head. "I thought it was about Parker quitting as his attorney. That's all."

"But it looks like Parker's note linked them all together," Avery said.

Frank nodded. "Right, but what did Parker know?"

Billie Rae shrugged. "Maybe we'll never find out. But I agree with Avery. The way Tony's acting, Parker *was* right."

"Damn!" Again Frank's fist pounded the table. "He's been my partner for eight years. I trusted him."

"I just remembered something," Billie Rae said. "Tony was the lead detective on Parker's case. He was the one who went to Bateman's house to question him about my brother's disappearance. He said Bateman was clean."

"That son-of-a-bitch," Frank said.

Billie Rae agreed. "Then who's R.J.?"

Frank shrugged. "I can't think of anyone whose surname begins with J."

Avery spoke up again. "With the quotation marks around R.J. and not the others, could it be people called the person R.J. instead of using a first name? You know, like D.H. Lawrence, or B.B. King?"

"Hmm." Frank rubbed his chin. "I hadn't thought of that." His fingers tapped on the tabletop as he began to whisper the letters RJ, RJ, RJ. Soon his tapping stopped. "Holy crap! The Honorable Robert Justin Stonehill," Frank said. "Remember? Everybody called him R.J."

Billie Rae gasped. "You're right, they did."

"Would somebody clue me in?" Avery said.

"R.J. Stonehill was the judge who denied the D.A.'s request for a subpoena to search Bateman's house after Parker went missing," Billie Rae said.

Avery looked at her. "Wait a minute. Stonehill? Is he related to Polly? Buck's—"

"He's her father," Billie Rae interrupted. "I told you Little Rock was a small town."

"You know her? Polly?" Frank said to Avery, with a raised eyebrow.

"You could say that. But not very well, which I've come to understand is a good thing."

Frank nodded. "That's for sure."

"Is there any way to nail him? The judge, I mean?" Avery said.

"Only in the hereafter," Frank replied. "He died several years ago."

"But now it all makes sense, how Bateman got off scot-free," she added.

"Billie said Bateman left the country. Can't you extradite him?" Avery said to Frank.

"Originally, we tracked him to Spain," Frank said. "But then he moved to Venezuela about two years ago, where it's next to impossible to extradite anyone."

"And that's when he sold his house to you," Billie Rae said to Avery.

Avery's cell phone vibrated in his pocket. "Can I use your bathroom?" he asked Billie Rae.

"Of course. You know where it is."

As Avery exited the kitchen he heard Frank whisper to Billie Rae. "He knows where your bathroom is? What's going on between you two?"

"Lighten up, Frank. He's only been here an hour."

Avery's mouth hurt as he tried to smile.

His phone stopped vibrating before he could enter the bathroom and close the door. He checked the LED screen. He waited a minute, then listened to Buck's voicemail.

"Jesus, Avery, answer the damn phone." Buck paused. "Come on, Ave, what the hell's goin' on? Are you okay? Call me back, damn it."

Rather than call him, Avery decided to text. If the pair in the kitchen heard him talking to someone, it could make him look suspicious, especially to Frank. But Buck hated texting. *Too bad,* Avery thought.

> I'm ok, but need to stay over tonite. IMPORTANT!

He put the phone back in his pocket and opened the bathroom door. Hearing subdued voices, he moved slowly down the carpeted hallway, but only far enough to eavesdrop, yet not be detected.

"You're right. I don't see any other way," Frank said. "But can he be trusted? He could be a big time-crook for all we know."

"Come on, Frank. I thought we went over this," she said. "He's in Witness Protection and he's afraid he'll be found out. Wouldn't you be?"

"Maybe, but being in Witness Protection, he has to be a creep of some kind."

"I think you're wrong, Frank. I kind of like him."

"Mother of God, say you don't mean that."

Avery retreated to the bathroom and closed the door. Her words ran through his head. *I kind of like him.* He flushed the toilet and ran the tap water, waited a moment, and buoyed by Billie Rae's remark, returned to the kitchen table.

FORTY-ONE
• • •

"You want me to do what?" Avery said.

"Look, Avery," Frank began, "unless Tony confesses, the only way to nail him is for you to give him the evidence, or what he thinks is the evidence, then see what he does with it."

"Isn't it obvious? He'll say I put up a struggle, kill me, then dump the evidence, and deny I ever had it. Of course, the fact that you set him up will prove he's guilty, but a lot of good that will do me. I'll be dead. No thanks, I pass."

"Frank, as much as I agree with you, he's right," Billie Rae said. "It's too much of a risk."

Frank threw up his hands. "All right, but what else can we do?"

"How about putting Tony off for a day, see if we can get a print off the casing?" she said.

Avery shook his head. "That won't work."

"Why not?" she replied.

"Let me ask you, Frank, what are the odds of getting a print off that cartridge, especially after ten years? Is it even possible?"

"Depends. Prints have been known to last for decades, but I have to admit, from what you've told me, the chances are slim."

"And being a cop, Tony would know that, right?"

"Sure."

"Which means it's about Parker's note, not the shell casing," Avery said. "Besides, the prints could belong to someone else, even if Tony did pull the trigger. So that part doesn't matter, it's all about the note."

"But with only his initials on the paper, what can we prove, legally?" Frank said.

"*We* know that, but he doesn't," Avery said. "Which says he's into Parker's murder so deep he can't take a chance on waiting to find out. Why else break into my place?"

Frank tapped his pen on the table. "I suppose, but—"

"When did you tell Tony I had the evidence?" Avery interrupted.

The detective thought for a moment. "Right after we talked."

"And what'd you tell him? That I had it, or I was going to get it?"

"I told him you'd have it tonight, and we'd pick it up first thing in the morning."

"So that was about four-thirty, five o'clock?" Avery said.

"Sounds right."

"And you told him about the shell casing *and* Parker's note?"

Frank nodded.

"Then I no sooner arrive home and he's at my house acting like a criminal. What else is that besides panic?"

"Okay, he panicked. What's your point?" Frank said.

"If you let him off the hook now, he'll have time to think. Wait twenty-four hours and he'll figure out you don't have jack, otherwise you'd have arrested him," Avery said. "Which means you have to keep him guessing; don't let him get comfy. That way he's more likely to do something stupid that would catch him out. Then you won't need the evidence."

"You sound pretty sure of yourself," Frank said.

"How do you think I wound up in Witness Protection? If I hadn't lost my cool, my two friends might still be alive." Avery cleared his throat. "And finding Parker under my bathroom floor and doing what I did—do you think that was a good decision? I freaked out and did the wrong thing again—it's the state Tony's in right now."

"So what would you do to keep him guessing?" Billie Rae asked.

"I'd call him and make up some cockamamie story that won't let him rest, and the sooner the better," Avery said. "Keep him busy all night thinking about where I am and what I've done with the evidence."

"I like it, Frank," Billie Rae said. "I also think you need to call your boss and wake somebody up to work on that casing, tonight. And while they're doing that, maybe we can figure out what to do about Tony."

"And his accomplice," Avery added.

"Okay," Frank said. "But are you willing to stick out your neck to help?"

"And get it chopped off? I already said, no."

Frank stared at Avery. "Look, pal, because Billie asked, I'm trying to get along, but you're beginning to piss me off. So I'm telling you—"

"Frank, please," Billie interrupted, "let me do this." She turned to Avery.

"Avery, if we can work out a way to keep you safe, will you help? If not for Frank or me, for Parker. You found him, remember?" She placed her hand on top of his. "Please, Avery, I'm begging you. Please."

A voice screamed in Avery's head. *Run, you fool, run! You're being played.* But because it was *her* and that inexplicable smile she gave him, he ignored the warning sirens. "Yeah, okay," he said, returning her gaze.

She squeezed his hand. "Thank you, Avery."

Frank rolled his eyes.

Billie Rae put on a fresh pot of coffee and refilled her glass of ice tea.

FORTY-TWO

● ● ●

Avery and Billie Rae sat quietly at her kitchen table as Frank called Tony's cell phone.

"Tony, it's Frank. Sorry to call you so late, but something's come up . . . It's that Avery Gillis character. He just called and said two guys wearing ski masks broke into his house and ransacked the place about five hours ago . . . No, that's just it, he called *me* instead of 911, and he waited 'til now to do it . . . He said he ran away and went back later to get his car . . . No, he wouldn't say where he was . . . What do I think? The fact he didn't call the cops when it happened says he has something to hide . . . That's what I figure. He's got to be wanted for something . . . Of course, but the weirdest thing is, he still wants to turn over the evidence. He said he owed that much to Billie. He said he'd call back in the morning with a new time and place to meet, but my gut tells me he might not show . . . The evidence? He said he's got it with him . . . I know, but if he splits we're screwed about ever finding out who killed Parker . . ..

"I hate to ask, but could you stake out Avery's place tonight, in case he stops by to pick up a few belongings to leave town . . . All right, I admit it, I do take advantage of you sometimes because you're not married anymore, but this is too important to trust to anyone else. I'd do it myself but Dianne needs me here. She's sick, so is one of the kids . . . Thanks, T, I owe you one. I'll phone Billie Rae and tell her to call me in case Gillis shows up . . . No, I'm not kidding. For some dumb-ass reason she took a shine to him."

Embarrassed by Frank's last remark, Billie Rae buried her head in her hands.

"And call me if you spot him. I don't care what time it is." Frank hung up.

Billie Rae uncovered her face. "Do you think he bought it?"

Frank nodded. "Uh-huh, I think the SOB did. Every damn word."

FORTY-THREE

● ● ●

Avery pulled into the dark and empty parking lot of Hawg's Tavern and tapped in a number on his cell phone. "Tony, this is Avery Gillis. Don't hang up."

"What the hell? How'd you get this number?" Detective Trainer said.

"That part's not important. What I'm calling about is your supposed partner, Frank."

"What do you mean by that remark?"

"Because he's setting you up. It's why I called, to warn you."

"All right, asshole, enough with the games, okay?"

"Listen, Tony, Frank's the one playing games. Right now he's got you staked out at my place in case I show up to get some of my things and make a run for it. Or do you want to tell me I'm wrong?"

Tony paused. "So?"

"Frank said he couldn't be there because his wife and one of his kids was sick. Then he told you I have the evidence with me. Right so far?"

No response.

"Tony?" Avery could hear the detective light a cigarette.

"Yeah, I'm listening. Go on."

"It's all bullshit, Tony. I gave Frank the evidence last night, after you and your pal tore my place apart trying to find it."

"Talk about bullshit, I don't know what you're talking about."

"I'm talking about you putting on your ski mask outside my bedroom window, and then when you didn't find what you were after, you planted a tracking device under my car."

Tony's breathing was heavy. "If that was true, which I'm not saying it is, why tell me?"

"Because Frank's on to you, and unless you want to spend the rest of your life in jail, we need to talk, now. By morning it'll be too late."

"Damn, that's a pretty wild story. Why should I believe you?"

"Because not one thing I've said is a lie. You're afraid the evidence I found will do you in, otherwise you wouldn't have broken into my house. So I'm telling you, your life as a cop is over, but if you'll listen, I can help you get away. I can be there in two minutes."

The detective was silent.

"Tony?"

"Yeah, I'm here."

"I'm telling you, Frank's pissed because you were in on killing Parker, his best friend. And while you've been camped out there all night, he's been busy assembling a bunch of his cop buddies to take you down." Avery changed ears with his phone. "So how about it? You want to take your chances with Frank, who knows you're a dirty cop, or with me?"

"Right, and have you show up wearing a wire? I don't think so."

"That's a laugh. With what Frank's got he doesn't need to hear you say anything. Look, Tony, I'm trying to save *both* our lives. Just give me five minutes to explain, okay? You can check me for a wire if you want, just hear me out."

"Why are you doing this? What's in it for you?" Tony said.

"Call it revenge *and* self-preservation. After I gave him the evidence, he had the balls to give my fingerprints to the FBI, which he swore he wouldn't do."

"And who fed you that info?" Tony asked.

Avery paused. "Because the evidence involves her brother, Frank called Billie to fill her in. That's when she called to tip me off. When I get there, check my cell phone. You'll see. It wasn't thirty minutes ago."

Tony laughed. "You and her? I don't get it."

"Then don't. But how do you think I found out what Frank's up to? So how about it? I'm alone and no one knows I'm here, not even Billie."

Tony took another drag on his cigarette. "Yeah, okay, come ahead, but if this is some goddamn trick, you're one dead cocksucker."

FORTY-FOUR

• • •

Avery turned off Arch Street onto the seldom-used dead end road leading to his driveway. He could see the grill of Tony Trainer's car parked on the opposite side of the road, just beyond the driveway itself.

Avery pulled onto the apron of the driveway, then turned so his headlights illuminated Tony's car. He saw two men in the front seat. One was Tony, the other had to be Sammy. Avery killed the lights and engine, and exited the car. He breathed deeply, trying to calm his nerves. Although he wore a light jacket, he could feel his body shaking. It wasn't from the chill in the air.

Tony flashed on his car headlamps.

"Hold out your hands so I can see them," Tony shouted, getting out of his car.

Avery complied.

"Okay, walk this way, real slow," Tony said.

Avery moved toward Tony's Chevy.

"That's far enough," Tony said. "Keep your hands up, and don't move."

Avery stopped 20 feet from the car, fully in the headlights.

Tony stepped into the beams, becoming a silhouette. As he did, Sammy appeared from the opposite side of the car. He held a gun in his outstretched hand, pointed at Avery.

"Whoa, there's no need for a gun." Avery took a step back.

"Keep him covered Sammy. I'll check him out." Tony flicked his cigarette onto the pavement and proceeded to pat down Avery.

"What are these?" Tony said, feeling Avery's front pants pocket.

"My car key and cell phone, okay?"

"Take them out, and let's see under your shirt," Tony said.

Again, Avery complied.

Tony finished his body search. "Relax, Sammy, he's clean. Now kill the lights, there's enough moonlight to keep an eye on him."

Sammy obeyed, then leaned against the hood of the car, his gun still at the ready.

"Okay, wise guy, let's hear it. Why should I believe you?" Tony said.

"I already said. Billie called and told me everything. Here, check it out." Avery opened his cell phone and pressed Recents. "See, she called at 2:58. We talked for five minutes."

"Uh-huh," Tony said. "So, if you two are getting it on, why aren't you at her place?"

"It's only been a week since we hooked up, and she still wants some space," he said. "And because I was afraid to come here, I was about to check into a motel. That's when she called."

Tony nodded. "Okay." He looked at Avery's phone. "I don't see any call on here to Frank. How'd you manage that?"

"My phone died. I was charging it at Billie's, so she called him. He came over to her place, and about an hour later he called you, around eleven-thirty. I was there when he did it. And by the way, I was there when you called Billie before that."

"Uh-huh." Tony nodded. "So what's this earlier call to her?"

"I busted up my face trying to get away from you two. I called her to help clean me up." Avery had deleted the calls and messages to and from Buck.

Tony laughed. "You sure someone else didn't do that to make your story look good?"

"You mean Frank? With the evidence I gave him, the only person he wants to kick the crap out of is you."

Tony lit another cigarette, tipped his head skyward and exhaled. For a moment, the particles of smoke hung in the moonlight, then dissipated into the cool night air. Tony returned his attention to Avery. "If Frank had any proof, he'd call and say me being out here was a false alarm, then wait 'til morning to grab me when I got to work. So maybe what you're telling me is pure horseshit."

"That might be true if he only wanted you, but he wants Sammy, too. This way he can nab you both at the same time."

"How could he know we're together?" Sammy asked.

"Stop me if I'm wrong, but a sheriff's deputy cruised by several hours ago, wondering what you two were doing parked out here in the middle of the night. He was just doing his job, right? You flashed your badge and said you were on a stakeout. The guy left, no big deal. But don't you get it? Frank sent him. The deputy reported that you weren't alone, and described Sammy to a tee. He's only waiting for enough daylight to make sure you both can't slip away in the dark."

"Okay, wise guy," Tony said, "if you know so much, what's all this evidence he has on me? And I mean facts, not bullshit conjecture. What can he actually prove?"

Avery cleared his throat. "I found a folded paper inside Parker's suit jacket. It connects you and Sammy with Bateman. That alone means your career is over. Too bad you overlooked Parker's note when Bateman killed him. Or was it you?"

"Nice try, asshole, but I wasn't there," Tony said.

"The hell you weren't," Sammy said.

"Not when you killed him I wasn't."

"Yeah, but you helped me stick him in the tub, so don't play all innocent."

"So you're the one who's going to get the chair," Avery said to Sammy.

"Don't listen to him, Sammy," Tony said.

Avery turned to Tony. "Is that the excuse you're going to give Frank? You weren't there when Sammy pulled the trigger? You just helped hide the body?"

Sammy stepped forward and pressed the cold muzzle of his gun to

Avery's head. "Let me do it, Tony. Let me kill 'im."

"Wait, Sammy, wait," Tony said.

"But what he just heard, he could testify against us. I'll get the chair."

"I said wait, Sammy. Give me a minute; let me think." He began to pace.

Avery didn't believe he had a minute. "Tony, I can get you out of this mess and out of the country. Sammy, too, because that's what *I* have to do, disappear. When the FBI finds out where I am, you might as well have Sammy pull the trigger. But I know how we can get away. So tell him to put the gun down."

Tony took a deep drag from his cigarette. This time he exhaled into Avery's face. "You're wanted by the FBI and *you* are going to help *me*? That's fucking nuts."

Avery coughed. "Maybe, but not if you hear me out."

Tony paused. "Okay, Sammy, back off. Let's hear what he has to say. If I don't like it, then you can shoot him. Four times if you want, just like Parker."

FORTY-FIVE

● ● ●

Avery sucked in a breath. "First off, unless you already took the fifty thousand dollars I stashed in the house, I need to get it. That's why I'm here."

"You have fifty grand in there? Where?" Tony said.

Avery hesitated. "Let's work out a deal, then I'll tell you."

Again Sammy brought the barrel of his pistol to Avery's forehead. "How about this deal? I blow your fuckin' brains out if you don't."

"I think Sammy's right," Tony said. "You tell us where the money is, *then* we'll talk about a deal."

"Okay, okay. Just put the gun away."

Sammy didn't move.

"Back off, Sammy. Let him talk."

Sammy relented.

"But if I think it's horseshit, you're done. Understand?" Tony said.

Avery nodded. "When you walk in the front door and you look up, there's a round vaulted ceiling with a stained glass skylight. Below the skylight there's a narrow ledge for recessed lighting. The money's stacked all around the ledge. I need a ladder to reach it."

"Son-of-a-bitch. Is that where you hid the evidence?" Tony said.

"No. Only the money."

Tony took a drag from his cigarette. "If what you say is true, why didn't you get the money when you left earlier tonight?"

"Because I thought I had a deal with your partner, and I wouldn't have to leave town."

Tony ground his cigarette into the pavement. "Okay, so you get the money, then what? How are you going to help *me* get away?"

"That goes double for me," Sammy said, and rubbed the gun barrel against the stubble on his chin.

"Like I told you, I need the cash. It's that simple. Sure, I could have tried to sneak in, but getting the ladder and having to turn on the lights to see, I figured you'd spot me. Then I'd never leave town. And for that, I'm willing to cut you in."

"All right," Tony said. "But you still haven't said how that helps me? Or are you planning a fast one?"

"I'm not that brave," Avery said. "But fifty Gs, even for one man, isn't going to last long in this country. I'm going to South America, and you can go with me, both of you. That's how I can help."

"South America? You *are* crazy," Tony said.

"So you're going to stay here, and maybe get the chair? Talk about crazy," Avery said.

"He's right, Tony. I *will* get the chair," Sammy said.

"What about you, Tony? I heard you're divorced with no kids," Avery said. "You got any reasons to stay?"

Tony sighed. "My mother. She counts on me."

"That's going to be tricky from prison, don't you think?" Avery said.

"You told me she's got Alzheimer's and doesn't even recognize you," Sammy said.

"Then what's the hesitation?" Avery asked.

Tony grabbed Avery's coat with his fist. "Because you just wrecked my life by giving that shit to Frank. What I want to do is let Sammy pull the trigger and waste your sorry ass."

"I'm with you, Tony." Sammy pointed his gun at Avery. "Pow!" he shouted.

Avery's body jerked. He gasped for air.

The pair snickered.

Avery tried to control his breathing. "Okay, I get your point, but are you in or out? You want to go to South America or die here? There's no time to waste."

"I hate to admit it, but maybe I'm in," Tony said. "Just where in South America are you talking about?"

"Guyana," Avery said.

"Guy what? I never heard of it," Sammy said.

"Guyana—used to be called British Guyana," Avery said. "It's next to Venezuela, and the only country in South America whose official language is English. We can blend right in."

"Maybe you've got it figured out, but how do I survive once I get there?"

"The same goes for me," Sammy said, waving his gun at Avery.

Avery wiped his brow on his jacket sleeve. "Look, I've got plenty put away, and I mean plenty. I'll give you some. But if you don't like my deal, you could look up Arthur Bateman. I understand he lives in the jungle, somewhere in Venezuela."

"That son-of-a-bitch?" Sammy said. "He wanted me dead."

Tony laughed. "And Bateman wanted *me* to do it."

"That's not funny, Tony," Sammy said.

"Maybe not, but you did kill Parker in his house," Tony said. "He was pissed."

"Yeah, but I had to. I was there when Parker showed up. He told Bateman he was done bein' his lawyer. And all the time he kept lookin' at me, funny like. I knew he'd leave and go straight to the cops—so I whacked him."

"You shot him because he looked at you *funny?* That's nuts," Avery said, not thinking.

"Yeah, that's right," Sammy said in his cocky voice, and for the third time pressed the barrel of his gun against Avery's head. "How about it, Tony, let me whack him, too, okay?"

Avery spoke with his eyes squeezed shut. "Tony, make him stop. I can't help you if I'm dead."

"Hold off, Sammy, let him finish," Tony said. "So tell me, asshole, what kind of money are you talking about, and where's it coming from?"

"I have it in a Swiss bank account. Once I get to Guyana, I'll tap into it. I can give you a hundred thousand each. You can live on that forever if you're smart."

Tony pushed Sammy aside and again grabbed Avery's jacket, this time with both hands. "Is this some kind of joke—two hundred grand?"

"I know it's hard to believe, but if the FBI catches up with me, what good is all that money? And believe me, two hundred grand is no big deal. I can get you more if you want."

"Is that why the Feds are after you, the money?" Tony said.

"What difference does it make? Do you want to get away or not?"

Tony released his grip. "Okay, Mr. Moneybags. This Guyana place, how do we get there?"

Avery straightened his jacket. As he did, his fingers detected a missing button. "We drive to the Gulf Coast. There's a guy with a boat, and for ten grand apiece he'll take us to Georgetown, the capital—but it's twenty-five hundred miles and takes over a week to get there. On the way we make one stop in the Caribbean, where for five thousand each we buy ourselves new names and passports, so when we arrive in Guyana our papers will all be in order; no one will be the wiser. And with the remaining five Gs, we stay someplace nice until I get my hands on the rest of the dough. Any other questions?"

"Yeah," Tony said. "Billie called not an hour ago to warn you, right?"

"What about it?"

"Then how is it, on the tip of your tongue, you have this run-away-to-South-America plan all worked out in less than an hour? Explain that one."

"It's a plan I've had ever since I moved here, the fifty Gs *and* South America. If too many people started asking questions, zip, I'd be gone."

Tony nodded. "Okay. But if you're so worried about being found out, why didn't you leave Parker where he was, in the tub under the floor?"

"Because I don't know jack about plumbing, and the guy was coming in two days to hook up everything. So when I found Parker, I panicked. If I called the cops, they'd find me out. So I buried him in the woods."

"Uh-huh." Tony nodded. "So *you* put in the new shower over the tub. That's what I figured when I took a pee in your bathroom."

"Yeah, but what I don't get is why you put Parker in the tub to begin with," Avery said.

Tony lit another cigarette. "Bateman called me to help clean up Sammy's mess, but the tub was his idea—Bateman's. His wife loved that tub, but after she died he wanted it gone, but it was too big to fit through the door; it was easier to have it covered over. It just happened to be almost finished when Parker showed up. So we dumped him in."

"So let me guess," Avery said. "It was you who took the search warrant to Judge Stonehill. And because he was in Bateman's pocket, you knew he wouldn't sign it and the house would never be searched."

"How do you know about R.J.?"

"It's on Parker's note I gave to your pal Frank—it ties you all together."

"Son-of-a-bitch!" Tony said.

"That's what I've been telling you," Avery said. "Now are you convinced?"

"Right, but what about Billie? Where does she fit in?" Tony said.

"Unfortunately, she doesn't."

"Does she know about South America?" Sammy asked.

"No, and she never will. Besides, when she finds out I'm helping you, it won't matter."

"So you're leaving her high and dry?" Tony said.

"Do you think I have another choice? Do any of us?"

"I suppose not." Tony took another drag and exhaled away from Avery's face. "So where do we go on the Gulf, and how do we get there without getting caught?"

Thinking, Avery hesitated, then began. "First, we take both cars, then ditch yours somewhere near Hot Springs, and when the cops find it they'll start looking for you in the wrong direction. By then we should be in Mississippi in my car."

"But they'll be looking for you, too, *and* your car," Sammy said.

"Not until later. Frank said he'd be busy with you boys all morning. He said I should lay low and meet him at the police station *after* lunch. He said he wants to thank me personally. Can you imagine that? He thinks I'm dumb enough to believe his bullshit when all he's doing is buying time to hear back from the FBI about my fingerprints. By then we'll be close to Mobile, too late for him or the Feds to find me *or* you."

"But he could track your cell phone location," Sammy said.

"Not if I dump it in the lake. You'll have to do the same," Avery said.

"Right. So Mobile, Alabama, that's where we're going?" Tony asked.

"It's close by. But if we don't take the cash and get moving, it's going to be too late to do anything." Avery took several steps toward his car.

"And have you take off without us?" Sammy said. "I don't think so."

Avery threw up his hands. "Without the money and you holding the guns?"

"I think Sammy's saying we don't quite trust you," Tony said.

"I get it, but we have to go," Avery said. "If you want, we can ride to the house together—you decide. At least let me move my car, it's blocking the drive." He opened his car door and pulled the key from his pocket.

"Keep an eye on him, Sammy," Tony said.

Avery tried to remain calm. He got in, started the engine, and began to back up in an arc, as if preparing to enter his driveway. As he did, he checked his jacket. Sure enough, his special button *was* missing. "Damn," he breathed. At the same time, Tony's car came to life and the headlights turned on. Avery saw Sammy staring him down, gun in hand.

Suddenly, on Arch Street, flashing lights appeared through the trees—the kind associated with law enforcement vehicles. Sirens split the early morning air. Frightened, Avery shifted into drive, slammed his foot down on the accelerator, and jerked the wheel hard right.

Sammy jumped out of the way, pointed his gun, and opened fire.

The first bullet shattered the driver's door window, missed Avery's skull by an inch, and destroyed the rearview mirror. A second round struck the doorframe behind his shoulder. A third bullet buried itself deep into the back of the driver's seat.

The car fishtailed toward Arch Street as Avery pressed hard against the gas pedal. His hands struggled for control. The left side of his head oozed droplets of blood from the shards of glass hitting his face. He was too frightened to even notice.

Before he reached Arch Street, another slug obliterated the rear window, two more blew holes through the front windshield, and one disappeared into the trunk.

As Avery neared the corner, he eased off the gas and tapped the brake—too little, too late. The car slid into the turn. An oncoming police car swerved to avoid hitting him head-on. Avery tried to correct his steering, but the car skidded across the road, onto the shoulder, and down a rocky embankment. The car flipped twice over, coming to rest on its top in a field.

In his haste to escape, Avery had failed to fasten his seatbelt. Inside the car he tumbled like a rag doll. His limp, unconscious body lay crumpled on the inverted roof of his sedan. The motor sputtered as the wheels turned in vain, seeking traction in the cloud of dust that mingled with the damp morning air, while 86-octane fuel trickled from the newly ruptured gas tank.

Part II

FORTY-SIX

● ● ●

A very opened his eyes. The white ceiling tiles with random pock-marked designs didn't register. He tried to lift his head. The room began to spin. He groaned, closed his eyes, and let his body go limp.

"Good morning, Mr. Gillis," a woman's voice said.

He turned his head toward the voice and saw a nurse.

"How are you feeling this morning?" she asked.

His world was still spinning. "Not so good."

"That's understandable."

"What happened?" he said. "Where am I?"

"You're in the hospital. You had a nasty accident. They said you were driving your car when it crashed and burned. Do you remember that, Mr. Gillis?"

Avery stared at the ceiling. *Mr. Gillis?* His mind was muddled. *Accident? Driving?* "Not really," he said. "How long have I been here?"

"Oh, about six hours, I'd say."

"Six hours?" He grimaced. "Did I break anything?"

"Bones you mean? No, but you do have some nasty cuts and bruises. The doctor said you probably suffered a concussion."

A concussion? No wonder he was in a fog. He attempted to touch his head but felt a tug on his wrist. Both wrists. "What's this? I'm tied up."

"My friend Sarah, who works in the ER, said you were thrashing about and talking gibberish. So they sedated you and restricted your arms so you wouldn't pull out your IV."

Avery grew anxious. "Talking?"

"She said you kept repeating, 'Malcolm, Malcolm,' and talking nonsense. Does the name Malcolm ring a bell?"

He closed his eyes. *Malcolm?* Slowly, fragmented memories seeped in. *Malcolm. Murdered. Miami.* Then he remembered another name: *John. Who's John? Oh, my God.* He was John, but not anymore. He was somebody new. Mr. Gillis, the nurse said. *Of course,* now his name was Gillis, Avery Gillis. Then he remembered, *Witness Protection,* and what might be at stake if the truth came out. "Uh, no, I don't remember anyone named Malcolm." He exhaled. "Sorry."

"No need to apologize, Mr. Gillis. Just repeating what I was told, that's all."

"Yeah, okay." He cleared his throat. "Do you know how long before I'm out of here?"

"That's up to your doctor. But I wouldn't worry, you won't be alone. You've had several visitors already. They'll be glad to hear you're awake."

"Visitors?"

"Yes. Let's see, besides the police detective, there were two other men with impressive credentials—and a woman. I think her name was Billie something. She's been in and out several times."

Billie? More of the puzzle began to fall into place. *Billie Rae. Hawg's. Mr. Bones. The bathtub. But a detective?*

"You must be somebody important," the nurse said, "because there's a policeman on the door. I suppose it's about the shooting."

"Shooting?" Avery's eyes opened wide.

The nurse stepped closer to the bed and whispered, "The police said two people were killed last night—shot, they said. Don't worry though, Sarah said you didn't do it."

People killed? Damn! He couldn't remember. Again he attempted to move his hands, but couldn't. "Can you undo these things?" he asked.

"Now that you're awake, of course. But only if you promise you won't try to pull out your IV."

"Anything. Just do it." It took him a moment to add, "Please."

"Sure, it'll only take a minute." Methodically, she unbuckled the leather strap binding each wrist. "There you go. And no pulling on your bandages either."

"Bandages?"

"Here, let me help." She held the fingers of his left hand and touched them to the white gauze bandage on the side of his face. "Sarah said they removed shards of glass, from your car wreck I imagine. And there's a bandage on the top of your head, too, covering a nasty gash with lots of stitches. Here, feel it? It's probably what caused your concussion."

Carefully, Avery traced the edges of each bandage in hopes of recalling what had happened. As his fingers felt their way he sensed something wasn't right.

"Mr. Gillis, I'm going to raise the bed so you're a little more upright. Then I'll try to find your doctor and the detective to tell them you're awake." Finished, she turned and left the room.

Avery tried to bring yesterday into focus. Bit-by-bit he began to remember more. *A park by the river where he met Billie.* Then another name popped into his head. *Parker. Billie Rae's dead brother. Oh, yeah, Mr. Bones is Parker.* Slowly, the pieces were beginning to fit. *But a car accident? People shot?*

"Avery?"

Hearing a familiar voice, Avery opened his eyes.

"The nurse said you were awake."

"Buck." Avery tried to smile, glad to remember his brother. "What are you doing here?"

Buck sat his coffee cup on Avery's tray table. "That's a dumb ass question. *Holy shit!*"

"What?"

"What do you mean, *what?* They shaved your face and cut off your hair."

Avery touched his cheek, then his head. "Crap, I knew something wasn't right."

"You think so?" Buck said with a quirky smile.

"Very funny, *Luther*." Again Avery tried to smile. He remembered the name *Luther* without thinking about it. Maybe his memory wasn't so bad after all.

"Sorry, *Norbee*, but what the hell's goin' on? Last night you call me, all panicked, then send a text—which you know I hate—sayin' you need to crash at my place, but you didn't show *or* call. Then an hour ago your girlfriend calls and says you were in a really bad car wreck and I should come to the hospital, which scared me shitless because I'm thinkin' you're on your friggin' deathbed." Buck paused to catch a breath. "And when I get here, you look like you've been on the wrong end of a street fight. That, plus the cop parked outside your door, says you're in big trouble, *again*." He heaved a sigh, and coffee cup in hand, plopped down the chair between the bed and the window. "I can't wait to hear you explain this one."

Avery moaned. "Sorry, but I can't remember what happened. The nurse said I was driving and had an accident, my car burned up, and two people died."

"People died? Damn, Avery, what did you do?"

"I don't know. It's all a blank." Avery closed his eyes.

"Is this about that FBI agent who's out to kill you?"

"No. I think it's about Mr. Bones and who murdered him."

"You found out who killed Mr. Bones, but you can't remember?"

Before Avery could answer, the door opened. It took only a moment for him to form the word, "Billie."

She broke into a big smile. "Avery, you're awake. The doctor said you might be out for days." She squeezed his forearm. "How do you feel?"

"Awful, and I don't know how I got here."

"Do you remember last night, being with Trainer and Uronski?"

Avery paused to think. "I have no idea what you're talking about."

"Oh, my," she said.

"But he hasn't lost his knack for findin' trouble," Buck added.

Her head turned in surprise. "I'm sorry. I didn't realize you had company."

"No, it's all right," Avery said. "This is Buck, Buck James, he's my—

my friend I told you about. Buck, this is Billie Robinson."

Buck stood. "Hi." He gave another halfhearted wave. "Avery talks about you a lot." Then he sat back down.

Her face reddened.

"Thanks, Buck." Avery shot him a dirty look.

Billie Rae's eyes darted back and forth between the pair before settling on Buck. "It's nice to meet you, and I'm sorry if I startled you with my call. But with everything going on, I was a little frantic myself."

"Not to worry. Avery has this habit of surprising people way too often."

"I wonder why that sounds one hundred percent believable," she said.

"Enough already. I don't need a bigger headache," Avery said.

"Fair enough," Buck replied. "But as soon as you're out of this place, you get no mercy."

"Speaking of getting out, what did the doctor say?" she asked.

"He hasn't come in. The nurse went to round him up, along with a detective, she said."

"That would be Frank," she said.

"I don't mean to pry, but can I ask what's going on?" Buck said. "The nurse told Avery he was driving and two people died. Is he any way at fault?"

Billie Rae hesitated. "No, the two died in a gun battle with police at Avery's house. He was trying to get away and was lucky he wasn't killed himself. The police want him to fill in the details about what happened before they arrived."

"Great, but I don't remember anything," Avery said.

"They won't be happy to hear that," she replied.

"What if the cops start checkin' and find out—" Buck stopped in mid-sentence.

After a moment of silence, Billie Rae said, "Are you talking about?"

"Witness Protection," Avery interrupted.

"And *he* knows?" She pointed at Buck. "You never told me that," she said to Avery.

"You didn't ask. But if you're worried about Buck, don't. He's good. He even knows about the rogue FBI agent."

Again Billie Rae scanned the two men. "Is there something else I should know that you aren't telling me, either one of you?"

A knock on the door interrupted their banter.

FORTY-SEVEN

•••

"It's probably the reporter," Billie Rae whispered.

"A reporter?" Avery said.

"Yes," she replied. "Avery, pretend you're still unconscious. And if you have to wake up, stay with the amnesia story. Buck, don't say a word. I'll handle this." She pulled the hanging curtain to partially obscure Avery's bed from view, then moved to the door and opened it.

"Well, if it isn't Gloria Dell," Billie Rae said. "What brings you here?"

"Well hello yourself, Billie. This *is* a surprise. I'm here to interview Avery Gillis, the guy in the car wreck, or do I have the wrong room?"

"No, this is it, but Avery's still unconscious. The doctor said he might have suffered a concussion, or even brain damage. We won't know until he wakes up."

"I see," Gloria said. "Do you mind if I look in?"

Billie Rae paused. "Sure. Why not?"

The *Arkansas Tribune* reporter stepped into the room.

Billie Rae pulled the curtain aside. "There he is."

"Hmm. Who's in the chair?" Gloria asked.

"Buck James, a friend of his."

Gloria nodded. "May I ask why there's a cop on the door? He wouldn't tell me diddley."

Billie Rae let the curtain fall back in place. "Until the police have a chance to interview Avery, they want to keep him under wraps."

"Which means he had something to do with the shooting," Gloria said.

"Only because he was being shot *at*," Billie Rae replied. "The police would like to hear what happened from his end."

"You mean like, what was he doing in his car outside his own house at four o'clock in the morning? That kind of question?"

"I suppose. I can't say."

"All right, but let me ask you, why are you here? Is it because you work for the D.A. and have your own questions to ask?"

Billie Rae hesitated. "No, that's not why."

"Listen, girlfriend," Gloria began, "there's something fishy going on and I can smell it. The police said the two dead men were tied to a current investigation, but refused to elaborate. I'm guessing it's about your brother, Parker, because over there is Avery Gillis, who just happens to live in Arthur Bateman's old house where Parker was last seen alive. And when I quizzed the police about any connection between the dead guys and the skeleton found in the woods two weeks back, they wouldn't say squat. And now you're here, Parker's sister, which means there's more to this than just coincidence."

Billie Rae paused. "Gloria, I'd like to help you, but—"

"Then why don't you?"

"To be frank, Gloria, it's your reputation of dragging people through the mud and making their lives miserable, no matter who it hurts."

Gloria laughed. "Get real, Billie, it's what sells newspapers."

"Then I have no comment. You'll have to wait for an official police statement like everyone else."

Gloria glared. "Okay, if that's the way you feel, fine. But you know I don't cotton to being put off when I'm this close to a story. It has a way of affecting my storyline."

"And I don't appreciate being threatened," Billie Rae countered.

"I did no such thing."

"Perhaps, but your implication was less than subtle."

"I suppose, but this story's hot, Billie, I can feel it in my bones. And with that cop outside the door and you in here, it means Gillis is part of it. So how about it, are you going to connect the dots or should I jump to my own conclusions?"

"Oh, all right. The skeleton found in the woods *was* my brother, and he *was* murdered in Avery's house." Billie Rae paused. "It's just that, uh, Avery and I are dating."

The reporter's mouth dropped open. "You two are a couple? Holy Jesus!" Gloria's exclamation was far from a whisper. "That's downright creepy."

"See, your reaction proves the exact point I'm making. Avery and me in a relationship? The press will have a field day. I'll never live it down."

Avery's eyes popped open. *Relationship? Dating?* Fortunately, the half-closed curtain hid his startled look.

"I know you always thought so, but you're sure it's where Parker died?" Gloria asked.

"One hundred percent. And because of it, you and every other reporter will hound us both for all the juicy details. 'How did you two meet?' 'Does he invite you over?' 'What kind of sick boyfriend would do that?' I can hear the questions now. I've even asked them of myself. And, of course, Avery will be painted as some kind of pervert. Gloria, I promise you, he's not like that. But as you said, him being a good guy doesn't sell newspapers."

"Hmm, you're really stuck on him, aren't you?"

Billie Rae placed her hand on Gloria's. "Enough to want our relationship kept out of the public eye, that's all."

Gloria nodded. "I hear you. But it's definitely intriguing."

"Yes, you're right, and so are your instincts. The story you're after *is* hot, and that being the case, do you want to hear it from me, Parker's sister, or try your luck with some beat cop who overheard something third hand? Do you want to be the one who breaks this story wide open, or would you rather make excuses to your editor about why you didn't deliver it first when you had the chance?"

Gloria tapped her foot on the floor. "Okay, you've got me. But why would it come out that you two are together? What am I missing?"

Billie Rae sighed. "It's about where Avery spent the night. You said you wanted to ask him why he was outside his house at four a.m., which *is* a good question, because it's relevant to how things happened. All you have to say is he was coming home from a friend's. If you can do that, there's no way to put us together. That's all I'm asking."

Buck stood and cleared his throat. "I, uh, don't mean to interrupt, but as a matter of fact, Avery was at my place last night. He tied one on and didn't want to drive home drunk, so he crashed on my couch. I'll swear to it." He gave another halfhearted wave and sat back down.

"Uh-huh, I see," Gloria said. "So off the record, Gillis spent the night with you, right?"

Billie Rae nodded. "That's why, if news gets out, it could spoil everything."

Although his eyes remained closed, Avery's heart pounded. *Me with Billie Rae? Damn, how could I not remember?*

FORTY-EIGHT

• • •

Buck waited in the hallway while Billie Rae finished speaking with the reporter.

The two women sat opposite each other near the end of the bed. Avery struggled to feign unconsciousness. Only five minutes had passed, but he couldn't fake it much longer.

"Okay, Billie, let me go over this one last time," Gloria Dell said, checking her notepad.

"Sure."

"So after Parker's remains were found in the woods, Detectives Pearl and Trainer went to Bateman's old house to talk to Gillis in hopes of finding a lead."

"That's right. Up until then, nothing had panned out."

"And Trainer went along with going there, when he was in on your brother's murder? That's hard to believe," the reporter said.

"Because Parker's remains had already been found in the woods and identified—Tony knew that. Besides, who was Avery to him? A nobody."

Gloria nodded. "Makes sense. Then Gillis remembered a paper he found behind an old bookcase. He thought it might be evidence, so he called you, and you called Detective Pearl."

"No, *Avery* called Frank. Avery and I aren't connected, remember?"

Billie Rae said.

"Right. But how did Gillis know how to call Pearl without you in the picture?"

"When Frank and Tony went to question Avery, Frank left his card. Fortunately, Avery kept it."

"Okay, got it. So Pearl gives Trainer a heads-up about picking up the evidence this morning. Then Trainer and Sammy go to the house last night to steal it, but Gillis wasn't there."

"Exactly."

"Then early this morning Gillis leaves your place—"

Billie Rae cleared her throat.

"I mean his friend's house, drives home, sees the lights on, sneaks up, and spies the two ransacking the place. But then he called Pearl, *not* 911."

Billie Rae sighed. "You're right, that part doesn't make sense. Also, why didn't he leave, like Frank told him to? It's a question the police want to ask. Anyway, somehow the pair spotted him and started shooting. He crashed his car trying to get away, just as the police arrived." She paused. "But for me, it doesn't matter what he was thinking, because now I know who murdered my brother."

"But Bateman's still on the loose," Gloria said. "And that's okay with you?"

"Not really, but with the current U.S.–Venezuela diplomacy, I'd spend another ten years trying to get him extradited and my reward would be total frustration. Besides, being that Bateman's close to eighty, he could be dead before anything happens, which he may be already. That, and the fact it wasn't him who killed Parker, it's time to move on."

"I suppose," Gloria said. "But Trainer admitted everything to Detective Pearl, right?"

"Yes. While Sammy died in a shootout with the police, Tony was trapped inside the house. Frank called him on his cell and tried to talk him into giving himself up. Tony said Sammy killed Parker, all he did was help Bateman cover it up. Then he told Frank he wouldn't spend one day in jail as a disgraced cop and hung up."

"And that's when Trainer killed himself," Gloria said.

Billie Rae nodded.

"Wow," the reporter said. "A crooked cop involved in Parker's murder and for ten years nobody knew? Damned embarrassing. No wonder the cops are trying to keep a lid on this."

FORTY-NINE
• • •

Avery stirred. If he was going to keep up his ruse, his body needed to move a bit.

The two women paused until he was still again.

"Okay, what about the evidence Gillis found?" Gloria said.

"I'm not sure about the details," Billie Rae began, "but it had to be enough to flush out Tony and Sammy, which means they're guilty as sin."

"So it would seem," Gloria said. "I can't wait to see it for myself."

"I wouldn't count on that if I were you."

"Why not?"

Billie Rae paused. "I'm not supposed to say, which means you're the first reporter to know about this, but an hour ago the U.S. Marshals took control of the entire case—guns, papers, cell phones, the lot. And using the PATRIOT Act, they can seal anything they want."

Gloria's notepad and pen fell to the floor.

"It's true," Billie Rae said. "I'm guessing it involves Tony Trainer somehow."

"What makes you say that?"

"Well, they didn't name names, but why else would the Marshals take Tony's phone and not Sammy's? Who knows, it could be about Bateman, too," Billie Rae said. "Hopefully, there'll be more in the statement they're going to release this afternoon."

"What statement?"

"According to Frank, the Marshals will say they had to step in and take control of the case because of an ongoing investigation. But no one knows any of the details."

"That's ridiculous," Gloria said. "Who do I call? I need to get to the bottom of this."

"Good luck with that," Billie Rae said. "If you call the Marshals, they won't confirm or deny knowing any name or story you throw at them. And if you're not careful, your name could wind up on some list you don't want to be on. It could jeopardize your career."

Gloria exhaled. "Thanks for the reminder. But now who's in charge, and how am I supposed to verify anything?"

Billie Rae shrugged. "To be honest, because I found the answer I was looking for, what happens between the Marshals and the police, I'll leave it for you to sort out. And because Avery's somehow a part of this, I'm on administrative leave for a month," she said. "It'll give me time to do something that doesn't remind me of work or finding Parker. Now if you don't mind, I think we're done here."

"Of course," Gloria said. "But there's one thing I can't figure out."

"What's that?"

"Well, I don't mean to be insensitive, but my source at the Coroner's Office said the skeletal remains found in the woods, which you said was Parker, couldn't have been there for more than a year or two."

"Yes, that's what I was told," Billie Rae said. "What's your question?"

"If Parker *was* murdered in Bateman's house ten years ago, what did they do with Parker's body? Leave it in the house? That's illogical."

"I agree, and unless you're clairvoyant, I doubt you'll get an answer from two dead men," Billie Rae said. "But if his remains *were* somewhere in the house, there's only one other possibility. And that's after Avery bought the house, he discovered Parker's skeleton, and instead of calling the police, he buried him in the woods. What would possess an everyday, law-abiding citizen from Davenport, Iowa to do such a thing? That's even *more* illogical."

"Hmm. I suppose. But still—"

Hearing Billie Rae's illogical tale—which was 99% true—was too much for Avery. "Ooohhh," he moaned, "Ooohhh."

The pair moved to either side of Avery's bed.

Slowly, his eyes flickered open.

"Are you okay?" Billie Rae said.

His head turned. "Who are you?" he said weakly.

"It's Billie, your girlfriend," Gloria said.

With a faint smile, he said, "Really? You're my girlfriend?"

Billie Rae squeezed his arm, harder than necessary.

"He doesn't look good, Billie. Maybe you should get the doctor," Gloria said.

Avery moaned. "Yeah, get the doctor. I need help."

Billie Rae paused, then said, "Okay, I'll go," and exited the room, leaving him alone with the reporter.

"Who are you?" Avery asked.

"My name's Gloria. I'm Billie's friend. We've never met."

"That's a relief. At least I don't know you for a reason. But where am I?"

She smiled. "You're in the hospital. You were in a horrible car crash early this morning. Do you remember anything about that?"

Avery stared at the ceiling. "No, I don't."

"Do you remember where you were last night, or who you were with?"

He closed his eyes. "Not that either." Although he would love to have said, "Alone with Billie," he honestly couldn't recall.

"Then let me ask you about two men, Tony Trainer and Sammy Uronski. Do you know them?"

He stared into space, then focused on Gloria. "Are they my friends?"

"I'm not sure. What about Arthur Bateman or Parker MacAfee? Do you know those names?"

"Am I supposed to?" he replied.

"Not necessarily. I was just asking," she said. "Now how about I bring in a photographer and we get a picture of you all bandaged up, here in bed?"

A cold chill shot down Avery's spine. "No, no. You can't. I must look awful."

"Oh, come on, your picture will be on the front page. The readers will eat it up."

Avery was saved when Billie Rae and the doctor entered the room. The doctor conducted his exam while everyone waited outside. He determined Avery's amnesia only extended back to yesterday sometime, but because he did sustain a concussion, he recommended Avery remain hospitalized until his condition improved.

The doctor gone, Buck returned and dragged a chair close to the bed.

"Ave, stop faking it. It's me, Buck."

Avery opened his eyes.

"Billie said you were brilliant, pretendin' you couldn't remember shit," Buck said.

"She really said that?"

"For sure. The brilliant part anyway. But I'm dyin' to know, did you two spend the night together or not?"

"Jesus, Buck, I'm in a wreck, my car burned up, two people are dead, and you want to know if I slept with her?"

"Well, yeah. She just told the reporter you spent most of the night at her place. So you must have."

Avery exhaled. "Honest, Buck. I don't know."

"You mean you can't remember if you got laid? Damn, Avery, you *are* hopeless."

FIFTY
• • •

Skipping the details, Avery recounted to Buck the major points of Billie Rae's exchange with Gloria Dell, including the deaths of Sammy Uronski and Tony Trainer, and it was Sammy who murdered Mr. Bones.

"What the hell were you thinking?" Buck said. "For all this time you have a secret phone, you won't use credit cards, and we bury an already dead guy in the woods. Now, in one night, two people are dead, a cop's on your door, the press is everywhere, and you can't remember shit."

"You think you're frustrated. The last thing I do remember was being at the park with Billie. That's all." Avery sighed. "Do you think we can change the subject?"

"Yeah, sure. But what about?"

"My teeth, for one thing." Avery's tongue found the problem. "It feels like part of a tooth is missing. Do you know a dentist I can see?"

"You don't have one?"

"No. I didn't want to take a chance on being recognized. Now I may not have a choice."

"Yeah. Want me to make you an appointment?"

"Not yet. Maybe I can wait 'til I grow back some hair. Then again, I may not even be in Little Rock after this mess."

"Speaking of messes, you said that cop killed himself *inside* your house?"

"That's what I heard."

"Then let me tell you, I'm not cleanin' up that shit, no way. So don't even ask."

Just then, Billie Rae reentered the room.

FIFTY-ONE

• • •

"Sorry it took so long," Billie Rae said. "I wanted to get an update from Frank on the Marshals' takeover."

"I don't understand," Avery said. "Who are the Marshals really after?"

"No one," she answered.

"But you said they were."

"I didn't, actually. I said *I guessed* Trainer was involved, and maybe Bateman—one of Jerry's ideas. And yes, I further pointed Gloria in the wrong direction by saying the Marshals took Tony's cell phone and not Sammy's. The truth is, they couldn't find Sammy's phone. But just like you, she jumped to the same conclusion. And if Gloria believes it, the whole town will."

"Then it was no accident Gloria showed up," Avery said.

"For somebody who can't remember anything, your brain seems to be working just fine."

"You *wanted* her to be here?" Buck said.

"Yes. For Avery to stay in Little Rock, we need to convince the press Avery is a victim of circumstance, nothing more."

"Then none of what you told her is true, about me spending the night at your place?"

Billie Rae blushed. "No. It was a story to help hide your

involvement in what really happened."

"What if she doesn't buy it?" Avery asked. "She sounds like a hard nose to me."

"She is, except for one thing," Billie Rae said. "When she first started with the paper, she fell in love with a lawyer whose prominent family didn't approve of her, so they launched a hate campaign, and the boyfriend caved. It devastated her. So I was pretty sure she'd empathize."

"What if she prints it anyway?" Buck asked.

Billie Rae shrugged. "Then she will. But as long as Avery's still the innocent victim and not a man hiding in Witness Protection, he's safe. As for me, my feelings won't be hurt one bit."

"That's all fine," Avery said. "But I don't have a clue what I did. The last thing I remember was meeting you in the park."

As best she could, Billie Rae related what she knew, including the fact that the slugs recovered from Avery's car matched the ones that killed her brother, Parker.

Close to finished, Avery interrupted. "I wore *a wire?*"

"Yes. A microphone disguised as a button was sewn on your jacket. But somehow it stopped working. That's when the police decided to move in."

"I still can't believe he volunteered," Buck said.

Billie Rae turned to Avery. "You said you wanted to make up for how you 'handled Parker,' I think you said, even if it meant giving up your identity."

"But why not tell the truth and say he did wear a wire?" Buck said. "Who's to know he's in Witness Protection?"

"I might agree," Billie Rae said, "except most of what transpired was recorded. And because of the Freedom of Information Act, it wouldn't be long before Gloria got hold of it, and in no time Avery *would* be exposed. But in the hands of the Marshals, and because of the PA-TRIOT Act, it can all be sealed forever. I know this sounds strange, but the Police Chief said it's a blessing in disguise—the Marshals stepping in. The D.A. agrees."

"A blessing?" Buck said.

"By the Marshals taking over, it will save the city months of investigative work by both the police and the D.A.'s office, costing millions, all coming to the same conclusions: Sammy killed my brother, and Tony and Bateman were in on it."

"Wouldn't it be easier to admit everything and have the Marshals relocate me?" Avery said.

"That was Jerry's first reaction," she replied. "But I asked him, if you—a person with high public awareness—were supposed to have fled Witness Protection, and you really hadn't, how was it going to play in the press, another arm of the Federal Government caught lying? Plus, it would alert your mystery FBI agent. And that did it. Within hours, Jerry was on his way with a team to work things out."

"You know who Avery is?" Buck said. "Who he *really* is?"

"In case he didn't tell you, I'm a sketch artist for the police department. Remembering faces comes with the job."

"How long have you known?" Avery asked.

"I had my suspicions. But last night when I was cleaning your wounds from your ladder accident, that's when I knew for sure."

A ladder? Of course, that's how it happened—another memory returned to Avery. "You knew who I was and you still wanted to help me?"

She paused. "I promised to help keep your identity secret, and I don't like breaking my promises. Besides, you wanted to help find Parker's killer."

Avery tried to give her his best smile.

"Now what happens?" Buck said.

"If all goes smoothly, very little," Billie Rae answered. "Except we need to find a place for Avery to live for a while because he can't go back to his house—it's still a crime scene."

"He can stay at my place," Buck said.

"That was my first thought," she replied, "but until this blows over he'll be safer out of town, and out of the public eye."

A sharp knock on the door announced Detectives Frank Pearl and Travis Kane. They wanted Avery to help reconstruct the events of earlier that morning, *after* his microphone button was lost. He was of no help, however. Detective Pearl said to contact him when his memory returned.

"Do you think he'll be back?" Avery asked Billie Rae.

"Unless you remember what happened, I doubt it. Just stay away from Gloria Dell."

"I understand," Avery said. "But while we're on the subject of reporters, now that it's out about Parker being murdered in my house, and then being found in the woods, what do I say?"

"That it wasn't you who put him there," she said. "If you can say it with conviction, no one could prove otherwise."

"That should be easy, because I buried your brother in the woods," Buck said. "Go ahead, ask him."

"Oh, really?" she said. "Why are you telling me this now?"

Buck shrugged. "Because it's over, and he feels bad enough as it is."

Billie Rae looked at the two in silence, then spoke. "You two are related somehow. I saw it when I came in earlier—similar cheekbones, your eyes, your build. And the way you two banter back and forth I want to say brothers, but you have different surnames."

Avery sighed. "You're close. We're half-brothers. We have the same mother."

"And the Marshals don't know?"

"Nobody," Avery said, "except you."

"That's hard to believe," she said.

"I know," Avery replied. "When the Feds checked my employment records at MUI, my grandparents were listed as next of kin. After they died, I didn't think to change it. And when Nelson and Malcolm were killed, the FBI asked if I had any siblings. I figured by them asking, they didn't have a clue, so I said, 'No.' I didn't want to involve Buck in my mess. I told the Marshals the same thing."

"What's your story?" she said to Buck.

"I was born in Australia, but my dad died before I was born. Mom was an American, so she moved us back to California. Then she married Avery's dad. But they both died when I was six, Ave was four. He talks different because he's a nerd; I hung out with normal people."

"I see," she said. "But does anyone know about Avery?"

"A while back I told a couple of friends I had a brother who lived in Florida. But since that MUI indictment thing happened, I haven't said jack to anyone."

"Then how is it you both wound up in Little Rock?"

"That's easy," Avery said. "After a car bomb almost got me in Ohio, I wanted a say in where the Marshals moved me. They offered up a half-dozen cities to choose from and Little Rock happened to be on the list. Buck was already here."

"And you got to Arkansas, how?" she said to Buck.

"Well . . ." He blushed.

"He met a girl in Minnesota," Avery volunteered. "When she wanted to move back home to Little Rock, he followed her, but it didn't work out. The same thing happened when he moved from California to St. Paul."

"Thanks, *Norbee.*" Buck gave Avery a nasty look.

"But the Marshals think living near a close relative is too risky," Billie Rae said.

"As long as the Feds didn't know about him, we figured neither would anyone else," Avery said. "Instead of being brothers, we could hang out being friends."

"If you want to keep it that way, I suggest Buck leave the hospital now," she said. "Jerry's due any time, and seeing you two together, he might make the same connection I did."

"But those two cops didn't say boo when they were here. Or the reporter," Buck said.

"My guess is they were looking for answers, not suspects. Gloria was looking for a story," Billie Rae replied. "Besides, with Avery's bruised face and the way he's bandaged up, your resemblance to one another would be harder to perceive. But still—"

"She's right, Buck. You'd better go," Avery said.

"Use the stairs and go out through Emergency," she volunteered. "You're less likely to be noticed."

"Yeah, okay." He turned to Avery. "Do you still have a phone so we can talk?"

"I don't know."

"It probably burned up in his car," Billie Rae answered. "Frank said there was nothing on you when they pulled you from the wreckage."

"Can you get me a burner phone?" he said to Buck.

"Sure, but how do I get it to you?"

"Wait a sec," Billie Rae said. She took a pen from her purse and wrote on a piece of paper and handed it to Buck. "This is my address. Buy the phone and bring it to my place, I'll make sure he gets it. If I'm not home, leave it by the back door. But you'd better do it today."

"Thanks, Billie," Buck said. "But that reminds me, how'd you get my number to call about Avery being here?"

"I googled your name and your home repair website came up, along with a listed phone number. Is there a problem with that?"

"No. Just curious, that's all." Buck said his goodbyes and hurried out the door.

Billie Rae repositioned her chair closer to Avery's bedside. "Frank said you were brave."

"For doing what? Just hearing you describe what happened makes me nervous."

"So you don't remember calling me or coming to my house with the evidence?"

"None of it."

"Hmm. But you do remember things before yesterday. Is that correct?"

"As far as I can tell."

"Good, because I have a few questions," she said, "about the story you made up to tell Tony and Sammy."

"What'd I say? Maybe it will help me remember."

"Okay, here goes. Do you really have fifty-thousand dollars stashed at your house?"

He closed his eyes for a moment. "I have the money, but Buck has it hidden at his place."

"And your escape plan to South America? That's real too, isn't it?"

Again Avery paused. "It's something I know about. But why is it important?"

"It has to do with who you are, and what makes you tick."

"That's funny, because I don't get you either."

She looked surprised. "I think I've been pretty straightforward."

Avery tried not to laugh.

"What's funny?"

"Come on, Billie. First, you spy on me, and yes, I understand why, but here you are, fudging the truth and telling people things that could get you in trouble. Why risk it?"

She paused. "Okay. You're right. But I could say the same thing of you. With no evidence to prove you buried Parker in the woods, you not only confessed, you offered to help find his killer at the risk of exposing your cover. Yes, you talked about doing the right thing, but I think there's more to it than that."

Avery paused. "Mostly, it's because I like you."

"Because you *like* me? That's it?"

"Yeah. Stupid, isn't it? I'm also tired of being the bad guy all the time."

"I already knew that—that you like me, I mean. When you showed up at The Icehouse for dinner, dressed to the nines, you weren't there to impress the *maître d*."

"Okay, but neither were you."

She smiled. "You're right. I did it to catch you off guard."

They exchanged a brief smile.

"Look, Billie, ever since I entered Witness Protection, you're the only person I've met I really like, who I could have a conversation with. So I wanted to keep seeing you. And I uh, I still do."

For a moment she sat quietly, then spoke. "Avery, if you must know, I didn't want you to leave Little Rock either." Her cheeks turned red. "Don't ask me why, but for some reason, I like you, too." She placed her hand over his. "And after last night, more than I want to admit."

FIFTY-TWO

• • •

The following morning, Gloria Dell's story exploded on the front page with two-inch headlines: **MURDER SOLVED: DETECTIVE IMPLICATED**. The last time the paper used a bigger font was for 9/11. Bold subheadings included: **REMAINS OF PROMINENT ATTORNEY IDENTIFIED**, and **U.S. MARSHALS STEP IN**. By 10:00 a.m. it became the talk of the town. According to Gloria Dell's article, in an attempt to help police, Avery Gillis was an innocent victim of happenstance, was hospitalized with a severe concussion, and suffered from amnesia.

Billie Rae was mentioned, but only as a bereaved sister, dealing with the pain and circumstance of her brother's death and grim discovery.

The hospital was deluged with flowers from well-wishers, and requests from reporters and TV stations for an interview with Avery. The clamor was intense and growing. Security on Avery's floor was increased as people tried to gain unauthorized access to his room.

Avery's memory of what happened remained in a black hole. His immediate problem was physical: standing up. He required assistance to walk. And with the unexpected attention directed his way, if he wanted to remain in Witness Protection, he needed to leave the hospital posthaste and go into hiding. Against the doctor's advice, Deputy Jerry Joyce recommended Avery sign himself out. Buck and Billie Rae concurred.

"Where can I go?" Avery asked.

"Don't worry, everything's all arranged," Billie Rae answered.

At 11:27 a.m. the hospital abruptly announced: in 33 minutes—at noon—a statement would be released regarding Avery's condition. Because of the last minute notice, two rumors quickly spread. Avery had either regained his memory, or he had died.

While Gloria Dell and other members of the press hastily gathered outside the hospital's entrance to await the news, Avery was on his way out via the loading dock behind the hospital.

A Marshal, dressed as a nurse, pushed Avery's wheelchair toward Billie Rae's waiting Beamer. Deputy Joyce was there to open the car's back door.

"What's going on, Jerry?" Avery said. "Nobody's telling me."

"In a few minutes a statement will be issued saying your memory isn't any better, and you've chosen to leave the hospital in hopes a more quiet surrounding will speed your recovery, blah, blah, blah—frigging destination unknown—and that you asked the press to honor your privacy. Of course, being pricks, they'll all ignore your request and bust their butts to find you anyway." Jerry handed Avery a new Government cell phone. "Here, I'll stay in touch."

The nurse assisted Avery into the backseat of the car.

Billie Rae brought a pillow for Avery's head, and a light blanket for him to hide under, if need be.

"Where're we going?" Avery asked.

"Hot Springs," she said. "Now lie down, we're leaving." She exited the hospital parking lot, drove to the cross-town freeway, turned west, and from Shackleford Road made her way onto Highway 430, headed southbound.

Nine minutes had passed when the car merged onto U.S. 30. "Would you like to sit up?" she called out. "It'll be another hour before we're there."

"No, I'm good right here," Avery said softly, and with the steady hum of the tires, fell fast asleep.

FIFTY-THREE

• • •

South of the city of Hot Springs, on scenic State Highway 7, Billie Rae turned onto Lookout Circle and drove out the peninsula road. Before the neck of land narrowed, she veered into a driveway that stretched 100 yards from the crest of the ridge down to a boathouse and two wooden docks anchored in the clear waters of Lake Hamilton. A stylish party barge sat between the stationary pilings. Hidden in the boathouse was a vintage 1946 Chris-Craft Custom Runabout. Its original 130 horsepower "M" engine had been silent for the past three years.

Halfway to the water, Billie Rae turned the car into a parking area behind the upper level of a two-story house.

Avery felt a gentle nudge on his shoulder.

"Avery, wake up, we're here."

"Huh?" It took a moment for Billie Rae's face to come into focus. She smiled at him. "You okay?"

"Yeah. Where are we?"

"At my place in Hot Springs, on Lake Hamilton. Actually, it was my parents' home. I was lucky enough to inherit it."

"Is this where I'm hiding out?"

"It is. Do you want to sit up and get your bearings?"

"Yeah, sure."

"Then let me help." She reached her arm over the seat. Avery grabbed hold and pulled himself up. "How's that?" she asked.

"Okay, but I'm a little dizzy," he said. Slowly, Avery scanned the surroundings: a green hedge, pine trees, an old pickup truck, and the backside of a beige stucco house. He spotted two men in overalls and ball caps approach the car. "Who's that?"

Billie Rae turned to see. "They're U.S. Marshals, here to keep you under wraps. One's a doctor. They're pretending to be workmen, in case someone like Gloria Dell shows up. They know what to do."

"You're confusing me," Avery said.

"That's all right. We can talk after we get you inside." She motioned for the two Marshals to help Avery out of the car.

Although the main entrance to the home was on the driveway side of the lower level, everyone used the upstairs door that led into the large country-style kitchen.

Down the hall from the kitchen, the Marshals guided Avery into the upstairs master bedroom suite and then onto the adjoining screened-in porch, where they sat him down in a cushioned rattan chair.

"What do you think?" she asked.

He smiled. "Wow, this is great." Before him lay a panoramic view. An expansive lawn sloped from the house to the boathouse and docks, bordered on both sides by tall pines and native dogwoods. Beyond, open water stretched to a distant tree-lined shore.

One of the two men stepped forward. "Avery, let me introduce myself. I'm Deputy Jason Moore. Call me Jay. And this here's your doctor, Francis Cadich, but he hates his first name, so call him Doc. We'll be here 24/7, so not to worry."

"I hate to interrupt," Billie Rae said, "but before I leave, I need to clear up some things with Avery. Could you give us a few minutes?"

The two men left.

Billie Rae pulled up a chair to face Avery. "You first. What do you need to know?"

"More than you probably have time for."

"Don't worry about the time. Just go ahead, I'm listening."

"To start, and it's not that I'm ungrateful, but why am I here? Why not let Jerry set me up someplace? Then you can move on with your life."

"True, but we're supposed to be a couple, remember? We need to keep Gloria Dell and the public believing it until this all blows over. Besides, I thought you might like it here."

"Who wouldn't?" he said.

"That's why I suggested it to the Marshals. All the arrangements were made yesterday."

"Thanks. But you're not staying?"

"No. Remember when Gloria was in your hospital room? I was serious when I told her I need a vacation. My life's been fixated on Parker for so long, suddenly there's this void. That's why I need to get away, to find myself again."

"Where will you go?"

"New Orleans. A college friend offered me a place to stay." Billie Rae paused. "I also have to figure out what to do about you."

"Me?"

"Yes, you. I can't deny it any longer, so I'll just say it. For some inexplicable reason we're attracted to each other. But with all that's gone on, I'm not sure if it's a temporary thing or something more. I need time and space to figure it out."

"What's to figure?"

"For starters, why I'm attracted to a man whose only history I know has been to play touch-and-go with the law. At times you're cold and calculating. Other times you're downright caring, like your concern for Buck when Polly walked in Hawg's with that guy. Or after our dinner at The Icehouse, when you politely waited for me to open my front door before you drove away. Then two days ago, you risked your life, which said a lot more than you just like me."

He was at a loss for words.

"Avery, my point is, you intrigue me. But because of our contrived meeting and the odd ways we've spent time together, I don't know the real you. Plus the fact you come with extra baggage doesn't help."

"Extra baggage?"

"Witness Protection baggage. How are you going to manage that situation for the rest of your life? And is *you* being in a Witness Protection

Program anything *I* want to deal with, even on a short time basis?"

Avery hesitated to speak.

"But to be fair, you don't know the real me, either. Until now, we've both been playing games. You, defensive, trying to hide your past, and me, obsessed with Parker. That's why I need time away from Little Rock, and my job, to sort things out. And knowing my bad history with men, if exploring a relationship with you or any man is something I want to come back to?"

Avery sighed. "Everything's up in the air for me, too. Living in Witness Protection is like being inside a giant maze with no way out. I want to change it, but I'm not sure how."

"Then we both have something to work on while I'm away."

He nodded in agreement.

"Anything else before I go?" Billie Rae said.

"Yeah. You said something about that Dell woman showing up. What for?"

"As much as she believed my story about us being lovers, she's still a reporter, and will want to hear your side of it. At some point she might remember this place. If she does, or anyone else for that matter, all they'll find is an old pickup truck, and two middle-aged men doing repairs on the house. But Doc knows what to say."

"What's he saying?"

"That we've gone someplace else, *together,* for you to recuperate. If it's Gloria, I've left a note that should keep her at bay."

"Then change your mind and take me with you," he said.

Billie Rae smiled, the same smile that hooked him the first time they met. "Don't fool yourself, Avery. For now, being apart is the best thing for the both of us."

Before she left, she slipped Avery his new burner phone.

FIFTY-FOUR

● ● ●

A few days after Billie Rae's departure, Gloria Dell did pay a visit. Doc said she was irritated not to find them. She believed his story, however, of him seeing Billie drive away with Avery lying comfortably in the back seat, destination unknown. Billie Rae's note promised when Avery was feeling better he would call her himself. "No way in hell," he told Doc.

The first week, Avery remained confined to the upstairs master bedroom and the outside porch that ran the length of the house, where he spent most of his days sleeping in a lounge chair.

The following week, as his mobility improved, Doc helped Avery negotiate the main stairs from the kitchen down to the game room, where the centerpiece was an eight-foot pool table. An oak bookcase and gun cabinet sat on opposite walls. Various sports and nature pictures were hung in the room, along with two mounted deer heads—eight-point and twelve-point bucks. A large leather couch sat in front of two picture windows, facing the lake. In the corner, a sliding glass door led to an outside patio. Near the stairwell leading to the kitchen was the front door, which no one ever used. On the opposite side of the room, a second set of stairs led to the upstairs hallway and the master bedroom. Under the stairs was the door to another bedroom and private bath.

The deputies had one rule: Don't leave the confines of the house.

As much as Avery complained of his *imprisonment,* he found the setting both peaceful and safe. Best of all was the quiet, a salve that calmed his nerves. He became thankful for Billie Rae's insistence she go off alone.

From his first day in Witness Protection, confronting his long-term future was something he promised himself he'd do tomorrow, but tomorrow was always just that, tomorrow. Coupled with a long list of past mistakes, guilt, fear, and what-ifs had consumed him.

Billie Rae was right. To move forward, it all had to change. And with nothing on his hands but time, why not now? Time to turn away from the past and spend his waking hours to prepare for the future, narrow his options, and separate fantasized fiction from hard reality. What first came to mind was the voice of Karl Casey. *Become a chameleon and make a plan to disappear.* Right, but how?

Raymond Bryce's Alabama-to-Guyana option was the only plan Avery had—one he preferred not to consider. Although, without him knowing about his attorney's South America connection, he would never have been able to convince Tony and Sammy his story was real—an encounter that became clearer every passing day.

Being at the lake reminded Avery of his boyhood, when he and Buck fished with their grandfather. In the Grand Caymans, Malcolm Westbury, Avery's dead friend, owned an upscale Boston Whaler. Avery shared expenses and helped operate the boat. They went out often, sometimes with women aboard. Unfortunately for Avery, he was better at catching fish than meeting a woman. That aside, he enjoyed being on the water.

Those memories sparked an idea. He would buy a boat, start his own business, and dream of freedom from Witness Protection. But where? South America? And when? Those answers would have to come later. But to begin, he would follow the advice of creepy Karl Casey and groom his appearance to blend in, *like a chameleon.*

FIFTY-FIVE

• • •

Avery stirred. His eyes squinted open for a brief moment as he cat-napped in what had become his favorite chaise lounge. The lake and the forested shoreline beyond were still there. Content, he reposi-tioned his body, thinking he would snooze a while longer.

"Well aren't you living a dog's life," she said.

He didn't have to look to recognize her voice. He hastened to sit upright and tried to straighten the hair on his head, now over an inch long. "When did you get in?"

"About an hour ago," Billie Rae said. "I spent last night in Little Rock, and this morning in the D.A.'s office."

"You're going back to work?"

"Only part-time, three days a week, nothing more."

"And that's okay with you?" he said.

"Yes, because it was my idea. I've decided it's time I get my life moving in a different direction, something other than law."

"Whoa, you said that to your boss?"

"Not in so many words, but I think he sensed my heart's not in it like it used to be. Anyway, I'll work this schedule for a few months, then look at it again."

"What *do* you want to do?" he asked.

"Something involving art. And right now I'm into painting."

"Seriously?"

"Yes. Growing up I wanted to be an artist, or an art teacher. I only thought about teaching because most artists can't afford to paint for a living until their work is worth something—which is usually *after* they're dead." She laughed. "But my father was against it. 'Unless you marry rich,' he said, 'you'll be poor your whole life, and wind up a lonely old maid.' That, along with the fact I idolized Parker—the altruistic, do-good attorney—pushed me into law, although I did manage to minor in art at college. Then I fooled myself into thinking being a sketch artist would satisfy my hunger." She sighed. "So I've decided I might as well have an earnest go at it. That way at least I'll have an excuse for being old and single. Does that sound crazy?"

Avery smiled. "Not to me. But are you going to manage, financially, I mean? Or is it okay if you wind up being old, single, *and* poor."

They both laughed.

"How thoughtful, Avery, but yes, I'll be fine. It seems Parker carried a substantial life insurance policy on himself. My parents tried to collect on it several years after he disappeared, but because there was no proof he was actually dead, the insurance company wouldn't pay. A couple of years later my parents passed, and I'd forgotten about it until two weeks ago. So I called the company. With an official death certificate they'll pay the full amount, and I'm the only beneficiary. And because this place is paid for, I could rent my Little Rock house for income. I should be able to survive quite easily."

"So you're moving?" Avery said.

"Not right away. I'll spend three or four nights in Little Rock and the rest here, painting. I want to see how it goes before I make anything final. The likelihood is, I'll be a complete bust, or burn out from sheer frustration. Then I'll have to look for a real job again. But what's exciting is, I've already finished several paintings."

"Good for you." Avery smiled.

She grinned. "This is when you ask if you can see them."

"Uh, yeah, but I thought artists didn't like being asked."

"It's a ruse to make themselves sound self-assured, which most aren't, especially me."

Avery sat up. "Gee, Billie, can I see what you've done?" He said with a broad smile.

"Very funny. But since you asked, maybe not." Then she laughed. "Of course. I'll show you in a bit."

Avery moved to a nearby cushioned chair at the patio table. Billie Rae joined him.

"What's your favorite medium?" he said.

Her eyebrows lifted. "Are you really interested or are you being polite?"

"I'm a nerd, remember? I like fine art."

"In that case, I'm into acrylics. I like to paint nature, with a hint of human presence. Like an overgrown field of wildflowers with a dirt road cutting through, or a vine-covered telephone pole with a single wire hanging down from the crooked cross piece, that kind of thing, with a touch of the abstract. I call it nostalgic nature with a twist."

"Is that an official art style?"

"Yes, of course. It's right up there with Picasso and Cubism. I'm surprised you haven't heard of it. It's taking the art world by storm."

FIFTY-SIX
• • •

"Can I change the subject and ask about your trip?" Avery said. "How was it?"

"New Orleans was great. That's where I got the gumption to start painting again." Billie Rae smiled. "But enough about me. How about you? Have you come to any decisions?"

"A few," he said. "First, I decided to sell my house."

"After what just happened? Isn't that going to be a problem?"

"You mean because Tony Trainer offed himself in my kitchen? No, even the Marshals agreed. And seeing as we were supposed to be together in New Orleans, they helped get the house in order and arrange the legal details. Then a few days ago I got an offer, so I took it. I'm selling at a small loss, but that's okay. I never want to set foot in that house again."

"I can't blame you. But now it's my turn to ask. Are you going to be okay, financially?"

"Yeah. In fact, I've got my eye on a house in Hillcrest. Buck's checking it out for me."

"So you've decided to rejoin civilization."

"Something like that. And I'll be closer to Buck, he's the only person I really know."

"What about me? I live there too. Don't I count?"

Avery's face looked puzzled.

"What's that look? You don't want us to be friends?"

He exhaled. "Of course I do, but is that what *you* want?"

"You really are a nerd aren't you? And I mean that in the kindest sense," she said. "Avery, we wouldn't be having this long conversation if I didn't. And to anticipate your next thought, what about us? I think we should work on knowing each other better and see where it leads, like we're doing now."

His body relaxed. "Yeah. Okay."

"So what else is running through that fuzzy head of yours?"

"I'm like you, trying to figure out where my life is going. After I went into Witness Protection, I figured I could still be involved in computer programming of some kind. But anything that interested me required a background check. And then I had a scary conversation with a man on the golf course, and that made me rethink everything."

"Because you met a man playing golf?"

"It was no accident. He knew my real name and how to find me. It still gives me chills when I think about it."

"When was this?" she asked.

Avery thought for a moment. "About a week before Parker was found in the woods."

"What'd he say?"

He recounted Karl Casey's frightening prediction if Avery didn't change his ways.

"And he found you just to tell you that?"

"Well, no, it was about some other stuff."

"Stuff?" Billie Rae said. "Look, Avery, you have to lose your filter, otherwise there's no point in our relationship. Isn't that what you want from a friend, honesty?"

"About everything?"

"At the moment I was thinking about your encounter with the scary golfer, but yes, I want to know about your past and how you got to this point. I've read the newspaper and tabloid versions, but I'd like to hear your side. I'm sure it's not nearly as sinister."

Avery sucked in a breath. "Do you know how hard that is? There are things I don't even tell Buck."

She leaned forward. "And I've never told a soul how I messed up my marriage. You're not going to like what you hear, I guarantee."

"Then don't tell me."

"A convenient out perhaps, but unacceptable. But you first, finish with your golf story."

With trepidation, Avery continued.

"Cartels, crooked politicians, *and* the Grand Caymans? Wow," she said. "And you have millions of dollars in a Swiss bank account you don't want? That's hard to believe."

Avery nodded. "I'd trade it all to make this a bad dream."

"So it's guilt money?" she said.

"Of course, look what happened. My friends were murdered and I wound up in Witness Protection. Then I found your brother buried in my house, and now two more people are dead. I know, they deserved it, but when's this nightmare going to end? I wake up every day waiting for another shoe to drop."

"Maybe you should work on it like you're in AA, one day at a time."

"That's what the Marshals tell me, but some days I wonder if it's worth it."

"I understand. But if you don't want all that money, how are you paying for a place in Hillcrest when you don't have a job?"

"I have other money." He told her about his six-figure bank account and selling his two condos for millions. "That money's all legal."

She poked him on the arm. "Don't tell me, you put it in another secret Swiss account."

"Now *you're* trying to be funny," Avery replied. "But as a matter of fact, I did. The account I told Tony and Sammy about."

Billie Rae looked surprised. "You remember about that night?"

"I remember everything except crashing my car. The fog started to lift after I stopped being dizzy."

"You should tell Frank. It would help give him some closure, especially about Tony."

"I'm not so sure," Avery said.

"But you could fill in the missing pieces for everyone."

Avery lowered his voice. "You mean pieces like a certain judge, whose initials were on Parker's note?"

"Whoa, Tony said something about R.J.?"

"Bateman, Tony, and the judge were all connected." Avery related his story.

Billie Rae collapsed in her chair. "We wondered if Stonehill's name was mentioned after you lost your button microphone. And when Frank called Tony—just before he killed himself—R.J.'s name never came up, so we let that part of it go."

"Okay. But what if I say something now?"

"It will open a Pandora's Box."

Avery looked puzzled.

"If there's evidence a sitting judge was somehow crooked, then there's reason to question the verdict of *every* case he heard from the bench. The number of lawsuits filed on behalf of convicted criminals and losing sides would be endless. Not only that, it would cost the state and county millions."

"Even after he's dead—the judge?"

"Yes, it doesn't matter." Billie Rae paused. "I just wonder what good it would serve if you did come forward, and how much damage it would inflict on the reputation of the court. It would also expose your Witness Protection cover, while Gloria Dell and the press would have a field day. They'd rip this city and everyone involved to shreds, including me."

A long silence fell before Avery spoke. "What if I choose not to remember?"

"Then it's a burden we can carry together," she said.

"What's that?"

"Guilt. Like knowing the Marshals used a phony excuse to keep you under wraps about finding Parker," she said. "But if you can rationalize it by thinking nobody went to jail if they were innocent, and only a few guilty people were set free, then it might could work."

"Can you live with that?" he asked.

"The bigger question is, can you?"

Avery thought for a moment. "Being the better of two bad

alternatives, I think I can."

Billie Rae agreed, then she stood and stretched. "I think it's time we change the subject. Are you hungry?"

After eating Chinese takeout for dinner, their conversation continued into the evening on the screened-in porch, accompanied by two bottles of wine.

Avery couldn't remember being alone with a woman for this long, ever. Billie Rae was serious; she was funny; she was—what could he say—perfect. Or was it all the result of wishful thinking and too much wine?

FIFTY-SEVEN
• • •

"She wants you to stay?" Buck said into his phone.

"Yeah, until things calm down, or another big news story comes along," Avery said. "Besides, it'll give me another month to hang out here until escrow closes on my bungalow."

"So you get to play house with Billie?"

"That's not how it is."

"But don't tell me you haven't thought about it."

"Well, uh—"

"Guilty. I knew it." Buck laughed.

"Okay. It's crossed my mind. What's wrong with that?"

"Nothing. But now you have a girlfriend, right?"

"I'm not saying."

"Up 'til three a.m. together, drinkin' wine?" Buck laughed again. "Somethin' must have happened."

"Yeah, right. Look, I called because I need to get the name of your dentist. My tooth's really bothering me; I can't wait any longer."

Buck gave him the number.

Thanks," Avery said. "I also called to tell you the two Marshals are leaving this Friday. Billie said you should come down Saturday. We'll have a barbeque. Spend the night. How about it, you in?"

"Saturday? Well, I, uh, I've got a date."

"Then bring her along."

"I don't think that's a good idea." Buck cleared his throat. "It's Polly, and she hates Billie Rae."

"*Polly?* Are you frigging kidding me, after what she did?"

"Don't go postal on me, okay? Just listen. *She* called *me.* Honest, Ave, she apologized—several times. She said she missed me and she's through with all her messin' around," Buck said. "Can you just be happy for me?"

Avery tried not to laugh. "Sure, why not? But by taking her back, you must have never stopped loving her, right?"

"Yeah, it's true. But forget about bringin' her over. I don't want to be held responsible for what might happen."

Avery's second call of the day was to the *Arkansas Tribune.* He had delayed long enough. Billie Rae agreed to listen in for moral support.

"Gloria Dell," the voice said.

"Hello, this is Avery Gillis. Billie Robinson said I should give you a call. You had some questions, she said."

"Yes, of course. Let me grab my notepad."

After a few niceties, she began with a direct question. "When you found Trainer and Uronski ransacking your house, why did you call Detective Pearl instead of 911?"

"Ms. Dell, I still have no recollection of that night or the events leading up to it. I wish I did, but I don't. I'm sorry."

"Do you remember staying with Billie earlier that evening?"

"No. I vaguely remember meeting her at the park around noon, but that's all."

"Okay." She paused. "Then let me ask you this: what's your theory about Parker's remains being in your house for all those years before they were moved to the woods?"

"I don't have one," Avery said. "But since you brought it up, I find it presumptuous to assume his body remained in the house just because he was murdered there. And unless you've discovered otherwise, there are only three men who know that answer. Two are dead, and I hear Bateman lives somewhere in South America."

"Okay, but from where I sit, I've yet to hear one plausible answer."

"Look, Ms. Dell, I'm new to Little Rock, so I wouldn't have a clue what happened ten years ago after Parker was murdered."

"All right, but one other thing. Would it be possible to come to your house, just to look around inside?"

"Look all you want, but the house has been sold."

"You sold it? It hasn't been two months."

"I know," Avery said. "But if you recall, Detective Trainer showed little regard for proper Southern etiquette by blowing his brains out in my kitchen. And if you think I want to live there every day knowing that, it's not happening."

"I see. But let me get this straight. You sold your house while you were out of town with Billie Rae? How's that possible?" she asked.

"We were in New Orleans when Billie told me how Trainer died. That's when I called the real estate agent and sent her a power of attorney to handle everything."

"You trust your agent that much?"

"Why not? She's bonded, and the agent I used to buy the house."

"All right. But if I were to check with her, she would verify the document was notarized in New Orleans?" Gloria said.

"Of course. But I'm not sure she can do that—legally, I mean."

"Hmm. You make it sound as if you have something to hide."

"Think what you want, Ms. Dell. I'm sure you'll find some way to check it out."

"Yes, but—"

"Ms. Dell, please, I understand you're chasing a story, but I'm not it. I only called because Billie promised you I would. Now, if you don't mind, I'm feeling dizzy and need to lie down." Without waiting for a response, Avery ended the call.

"You handled that well," Billie Rae said, taking his hand. "Which reminds me, did you thank Jerry for arranging to have the power of attorney letter notarized and dated in New Orleans."

"I did. I even apologized for being on his case all the time."

"Good for you."

"I suppose. But look at me, I'm shaking. Talking to her brought it all back: people dying and me telling lies. I hate it."

She nodded her understanding. "But you have to stop beating your-self up and move on."

"Where have I heard that before?"

Billie Rae reached out and took his other hand. "Maybe we can work on it together."

FIFTY-EIGHT

• • •

From a slow start of holding hands, their relationship quickly turned more amorous, with Billie Rae making most of the moves.

Initially, she spent four nights a week in Little Rock. Soon it became two—leaving Hot Springs early Monday morning and returning late Wednesday afternoon. After only one week, Avery began to accompany her. The first time his excuse was his appointment with Buck's dentist. After that, no pretense was needed.

In Little Rock they hunkered down, avoiding the limelight. While at the lake, they held hands, took walks and dined out, and made plans for their future.

She spoke of how good it felt to pick up a brush every day. Avery's idea of owning a boat was also taking shape—a far cry from writing software programs.

In Hot Springs, while Billie Rae painted, Avery spent much of his time at Bud's, a small boat repair shop with a slip on Lake Hamilton. He told Bud he wanted to learn the business and would work part-time for no pay if Bud would take him on. Fortunately, he was a quick learner, and after a short trial period, Bud gave him a job. Avery also bought himself a new car so Billie Rae wouldn't have to take him everywhere.

With every passing day his confidence grew. And being with Billie Rae, Avery's future was his to create—or so he thought.

FIFTY-NINE
● ● ●

With Avery spending most of his time in Hot Springs, his personal contact with Buck had become less frequent. Also, Buck's rekindled relationship with Polly, and her animus toward Billie Rae, meant the likelihood of the two couples ever getting together was doubtful.

Avery's newfound obsession with boating was matched by Billie Rae's passion for painting. Her efforts paid off when a popular local restaurant agreed to hang several of her smaller paintings and sell them on commission. Within two weeks, three sold. Although the money wasn't enough to buy a month's worth of groceries, their sale was reward enough.

Come August, Billie Rae would rent out her Little Rock home and give notice to the D.A.'s office. If she needed to spend time in the city, she would stay with Avery at his new place—a few short blocks from both her home and Buck's—a home where he hadn't yet spent five nights.

Avery's diligence also had its rewards when Billie Rae suggested he tackle the restoration of her father's vintage Chris-Craft Custom Runabout. With Bud's help, Avery hoped to finish by early July.

● ● ●

In mid-June Buck called to confess Polly had done it again. This time, Joe the plumber spotted her with "some dude" at an oyster bar in

Stifft Station, near downtown Little Rock. He even forwarded pictures from his cell phone. Buck was so upset he sold his guitar and said he would never play again.

"It's not like you didn't try to warn him," Billie Rae told Avery.

"I know, but I still feel bad," Avery said. "He said he canceled all his work jobs, and except for buying groceries, hasn't left his house in two weeks."

"Why don't you ask him down to the lake for the Fourth of July weekend. I'll invite a few friends over, including a couple of single women I know. That should cheer him up."

Avery made the call.

"I don't know," Buck said. "If I come, you have to promise me her friggin' name never comes up even once."

"As much as it pains me to give you a break, you've got my word, I swear," Avery said. "So how about you come down a few days early? We'll go out on the lake, just the two of us, then come back and knock down a six-pack. Billie said you should stay the weekend. We're having a barbeque on the Fourth. She asked over some friends. So how about it? Stop being in the dumps and show up Saturday morning. I have a surprise for you."

Seeing the restored 1946 Chris Craft, Buck's eyes opened wide.

"I rebuilt the engine myself," Avery said.

"The hell you say?"

"Well, Bud did give me a few pointers."

"Is it yours?"

"Don't I wish. No, it's Billie's. She got it from her old man. But she was a mess a month ago—the boat I mean. Come on, let's take her out."

They spent the morning cruising the lake, often stopping near the shore for onlookers to get an eye-full. Then Avery would open the throttle and speed off.

The brothers reminisced about their childhood and the fun times they had. Avery was pleased to see Buck beginning to emerge from under the weight of his self-inflicted doldrums. Then Buck dropped his bombshell. "I've been thinkin' about movin'."

"From your bungalow? I thought you liked it there," Avery said.

"With the shop you built in the back, you said it was perfect."

"It is if I stay in Little Rock."

"What?"

"Look at me, Avery, I'm a wreck. The woman I love is an f-in' two-timer, and I can't get over it. And now that you're doin' okay with Billie, why hang around here and beat myself up every friggin' day?"

"Where would you go?"

"Back to California, maybe. I was even thinkin' about Australia, where I was born."

"Australia? Jesus, Buck, go off the deep end why don't you?"

"I'm just talkin', that's all. But honest, I can't take feelin' this way much longer."

The two returned to the house where Billie Rae made an announcement. "Seeing how the cookout's Monday, I want to spend tomorrow afternoon on the lake. I haven't been out in weeks. Let's take the party barge, just the three of us. Then after we get back, we'll go out for dinner."

● ● ●

Around noon the next day, Buck drove his truck from the house down to the dock with a cooler filled with ice and drinks for their afternoon on the lake. Avery rode on the lowered tailgate. Billie Rae followed in Avery's car with outerwear to throw on over their bathing suits. She also brought along snacks and freshly made tuna sandwiches. Her BMW was at the dealer due to a factory recall.

They spent most of their time at Billie Rae's favorite swimming hole where the trio enjoyed lunch, swam, and laid out. Buck appeared to be the only sensible one by covering up early. He teased the pair for getting sunburned, especially Avery. "There goes your love life for the next few days," he said.

Little was discussed of Buck's fallout with Polly, except he was serious about leaving Little Rock if he didn't start feeling better.

When they returned to the dock the brothers carried the cooler and leftover goodies to the bed of the truck.

"Do you want to drive your car up the hill?" Billie Rae handed the key to Avery.

"With my sunburned back? How about you drive?"

"No thanks, I'm just as bad. That's why I asked you."

"I hate to interrupt you love birds, but is anybody else hungry?" Buck said. "It's almost dark and I'm already starved."

"Sure, I could eat," Avery answered.

"Fine," Billie Rae said. "Except we either eat out or order in a pizza because I'm not cooking. You guys choose."

"I think we should let Buck decide," Avery said. "He's always the hungry one."

"So I get to be the bad guy, is that it?"

"That's right. Just don't pick donuts." Avery laughed.

"Enough, you two," she said. "Let's go."

"Right. So walk, ride, or drive—you decide," Buck said, "because I'm leavin'. My stomach is beginnin' to growl."

"Okay," Billie Rae said, and turned to Avery. "Let's ride up with Buck and get on some lotion. We'll get your car later if Buck wants to eat out."

The pair hopped on the lowered tailgate of Buck's pickup for the short ride to the house.

SIXTY
• • •

Once inside the kitchen, Avery dropped his key on the counter, along with everyone's belongings.

Billie Rae checked her cell phone. "How about you, Avery?"

"Why bother?" he said. "The only people who call me are you and Buck."

"What about it, Buck?" Billie Rae held up his phone.

"Not me, I'm gonna shower, then it's chow time," he said, and headed to his guest room.

"Buck's in a better mood, don't you think?" she said.

"Yeah, but you heard what he said about moving," Avery replied.

"Maybe he's just testing the waters."

"I don't know, Billie, I've never seen him this serious before."

They took turns applying lotion to each other's sunburned back and legs.

"Aren't you done yet?" Buck said, as he entered the room. "I've gone from starved to famished, so I think we should eat out."

"Give us a minute," Billie Rae replied.

"Okay, but while you're gettin' your act together, I'll get the car." Buck scooped up Avery's car key from the counter and went to the door. "Make sure you're ready," he said, "because I'm not waitin'."

"Oh, Buck," Billie Rae called out, "there's a switch by the door. It's marked. It lights up the yard and dock area so you can see where you're going."

"Thanks." Buck flipped the switch and disappeared out the door.

Billie Rae moved to the kitchen counter. "Put on your shirt and come get your stuff so we don't keep him waiting."

Avery pulled on his T-shirt and joined her. She handed him his two cell phones, his burner phone and his phone from the U.S. Marshals. *How odd*, he thought, his government phone had two messages, both from Deputy Jerry Joyce. They hadn't spoken in weeks. One message might be normal, but two, close together? Goosebumps covered his sunburned arms.

The first call was two hours ago. As he listened his hand began to shake.

"What is it?" Billie Rae said.

"The guy who's trying to kill me, the Marshals think he's in Little Rock, but they don't know where."

"Oh, no." She squeezed his arm.

"Listen, here's the second call, forty minutes ago." He put it on speakerphone.

"Avery, we've got your phone's GPS in Hot Springs. We're on our way. Just stay put, but don't drive your car. Remember the bomb in Ohio? If it's him, he might try it again."

For a second the pair froze, then bolted for the living room and the door leading onto the screened-in deck. When they reached the porch, they could see Buck opening the door of Avery's car.

Together, they began to yell. "Stop! Wait! Don't get in the car!"

Buck turned and waved, but failed to understand their warnings. He climbed in and started the engine.

The ensuing explosion lifted the car a foot off the ground. The accompanying fireball shot 20 feet into the night air.

Luther Roebuck James died instantly.

Part III

SIXTY-ONE
• • •

Avery gasped for air and collapsed, his face contorted in horror. Billie Rae dropped to his side and cried, "No, no," over and over.

After a moment, Billie Rae whispered, "Avery, look. Someone just came out of the boathouse."

Still slumped on the floor, Avery peered through the fine mesh screen.

A man dressed in dark clothing walked up the drive. Suddenly, he stopped, pulled a gun from his waistband, and darted behind the still flaming wreckage of Avery's car.

Seconds later a car appeared, moving rapidly down the driveway. Its tires burned rubber as it came to a stop some 20 yards from the burning sedan. Two men jumped out. Avery recognized Jerry Joyce's balding head. The other man was his sidekick, Lance. Both men moved toward the front of Jerry's black Chrysler.

Avery cupped his hands and yelled, "Jerry, look out! There's a man with a gun behind the car!"

As the deputies turned to retreat, there were two quick pops. Lance fell to the ground, while Jerry dropped to his knees, a gun clutched in his hand. Two more shots sent Jerry sprawling. The man rushed forward and shot each Marshal once more at close range. Without hesitation the assassin turned and pointed the gun toward the sun porch and the two silhouettes.

Avery pulled Billie Rae to the floor as a bullet just missed their heads and pierced the glass door behind them. Two more shots quickly followed.

"Crawl, Billie, crawl!"

Together they scrambled into the living room.

"He's coming after us, isn't he?" she said.

"Yeah, but what can we do? Calling 911 is hopeless. We'll be dead before anyone gets here."

"The gun cabinet, downstairs," she said. "We can shoot back."

Hunched down, they hurried toward the kitchen, to the descending staircase.

"Wait," Avery said. "The back door's unlocked."

Billie Rae stopped at the head of the stairs. "Hurry," she pleaded.

Avery rushed to the door and threw the deadbolt lock.

Without warning, a bullet pierced the window above the sink, striking Billie Rae. She cried out and tumbled down the stairs, leaving a streak of red on the wall.

Panicked, Avery raced toward the master bedroom, away from the killer's line of sight. Somehow he managed to flip the light switch, plunging the house into darkness. He made his way down the back set of stairs and into the game room.

"Billie, Billie," he called in a frantic voice.

She didn't respond.

The outdoor lighting provided enough illumination for him to cross the room where he found Billie Rae lying at the foot of the stairs, motionless. He was certain she had been shot, but in this light, and with her wearing a red Razorback T-shirt, he couldn't tell where. He tried to gently shake her. She didn't move. Avery was too terrified to check for a pulse or feel for her wound.

His attention turned to the sound of the man breaking down the upstairs door. After a moment of silence, the kitchen light came on. Then a floor lamp turned on near the sofa, beyond the pool table. Avery rushed across the room and tipped over the lamp, breaking the bulb. *Escape* became his only thought. He made his way to the sliding glass door, leading to the outside. He unlocked it and pulled on the handle. It wouldn't open.

"Damn," he muttered.

"Do you want to make this hard or easy?" a voice barked from top of the kitchen stairwell. "I promise to make it painless."

"Go to hell, asshole!" Avery yelled.

"Your choice, but one way or another, you're going to die," the killer called back.

"Don't come down here, I have a gun!" Avery shouted.

The man laughed. "If you had one, you'd have used it already. You're as dumb as your shit-for-brains brother, John."

Oh, my God, he thinks it was me in the car. "I don't have a brother," Avery called out.

"Of course you do. Or should I say, *you did.* You grew up together in California. And once I found you, finding him was easy."

The killer's shadow moved slowly down the stairs. Avery could see his shoes descend step by step. Avery rushed to the pool table in the middle of the room. He pulled the rack of balls to the edge of the felt railing, grabbed a ball and threw it at the man's exposed legs. The orange five-ball missed. He hurled another and another, one finding its mark. The legs retreated back up the stairs.

Avery seized two more balls and took cover behind the couch.

The kitchen light went out.

He thought he heard faint noises in the room. In desperation he threw the balls toward the darkened stairwell. Then it grew quiet.

Suddenly he remembered: a wooden dowel at the base of the glass door prevented it from opening. On all fours, Avery felt for the round dowel and removed it, then reached up and pulled the door open. As he did, three rapid gunshots pierced the glass, just missing his outstretched arm. Avery pressed his body to the floor.

Wham!

Avery swore a canon had gone off in the room.

Wham! It happened again a split second later.

He was paralyzed with fear, but nothing happened. All Avery could hear was a ringing in his ears. The smell of burnt gunpowder permeated the air. Then, above the ringing, he heard a faint voice.

"Avery? Are you there? It's safe now."

He struggled to his feet. "Billie? Where are you?"

"By the pool table." Her voice was strained. "There's a light switch by the glass door."

He quickly found it. Canned ceiling lights flooded the room. He hurried to her side.

She sat slumped on the carpet, her back against a corner leg of the pool table. Above her head, a Remington 12 gauge double-barrel shotgun lay across the felt table.

Before Avery knelt down, he saw the gory remains of the killer on the floor. Avery guessed the Remington's first shot threw him against the now bloodied wall, while the second caught him fully in the face, leaving him unrecognizable.

Avery sat on the floor next to Billie Rae, and cringed at the sight of her wounded left shoulder. The bullet had gone straight through, front to back.

"I thought you were—" He couldn't say it.

"Me, too." Billie Rae's bloodied hand shook as she tried to wipe away her tears.

SIXTY-TWO

•••

"I came to when he was yelling," Billie Rae said. "And when the lights went out I knew I had to get Daddy's shotgun from the rack. I knew right where it was. The shells were in the drawer. Then I waited here by the pool table." She began to weep. "What else could I do?"

"Nothing." Avery helped wipe away her tears. "Nothing. But we've got to get you to a hospital."

"No, wait. I've got something to say."

"Okay, but first let me call 911," he said.

"No. If I was going to bleed to death, I'd be dead already, or at least unconscious. But it would help to get something for my shoulder. There's some towels in a drawer near the bottom of the gun cabinet."

Avery retrieved a towel and positioned it under her shirt to press against the wound.

"That's better," she said. "Now listen to me."

"All right, but make it quick. You need help."

"Avery, I know this will upset you, but hear me out. You know that man at the golf course who said you had to transform or die? Well this is it. You heard the killer, he thought you were Buck, and that Avery died in the car, *your* car. So make it real." She squeezed his hand. "Don't you see? You can become your brother."

Avery's mouth dropped open.

"I'll swear it was you in the car. I'll say Buck was here, but he left way before dark; *you* left way before dark. Because of your sunburn you weren't feeling well."

He drew back. "God, no. I, I can't."

She touched his arm. "I know it sounds awful, but now you could make Avery Gillis disappear forever."

"And pretend to be Buck? That's insane."

"What's insane is calling the police, when you could be free. Unless you think it's over, and you won't continue to be a target."

What did Raymond Bryce say? *If they ever find you, you're a dead man.*

"No," he said, shaking his head, "it'll never be over."

"Then the next time they won't miss, and Buck will have died in vain. Avery, you have to try. You just have to. And I'll help, because there's no way you can pull this off by yourself. But first I need to ask you some questions." She stopped to catch a breath. "Do the Marshals or anyone else have *your* blood sample or DNA?"

Avery shrugged. "Not that I know of, but the FBI has my fingerprints, which means the Marshals do too. And what about the hospital, when I had my concussion? They must have some kind of records."

"True, but you didn't break anything or need a transfusion. And— I don't mean to be insensitive—but the way Buck died, there *are* no fingerprints for them to check. And it would be hard for them to match your hospital x-rays with his remains. Unless one of you ever broke any bones—like an arm or a leg?"

Avery thought for a moment. "Not that I know of."

"What about being in the army or some other service? Either of you?"

Avery shook his head.

"Good, because if the only way to identify you being dead is DNA and fingerprints, it might could work."

"That's all? You make it sound so easy."

"Of course it will take work," she replied. "But right off, the police will assume it's you who's been killed because that's what I'll tell them. And because you were in Witness Protection, and how things just happened, their efforts will be to verify it was Avery in the car, not to prove anything else."

"Okay," he said. "But how?"

"To start, go to Buck's room and take his razor and comb or anything personal the police might use to collect DNA, wipe them clean of his fingerprints, and put yours all over them. Take them to my bathroom—our bathroom, and replace all your toiletries with his. Then go to Little Rock and do it again; exchange his stuff for yours. Trim your beard and make your hair all short and messed up looking—like his. The way you always pay attention to detail, I know you can do it. But it has to be tonight in case the police knock on your door tomorrow—Buck's door."

Billie Rae grimaced as she repositioned herself.

"What about his friends? They'll know I'm not Buck."

Billie Rae paused. "Yes, but in Montana or some other state, who would know? So when you leave, go to Buck's house—your house. Hunker down and don't answer the phone or open the front door to anyone."

"But what if they find out anyway?"

"Then you'll wind up in Witness Protection again, because by not protecting you from this happening, they wouldn't dare cut you loose."

He shrugged. "Maybe so. But if this doesn't work, you could be in real trouble."

"Then you'd better insist on taking me with you." She tried to smile.

Avery forced a smile in return. "Where'd this idea about me being Buck come from?"

"The killer thought Avery died in the car. And if he believed it, I thought, why can't the rest of the world? With Buck's keys and wallet and phone on the counter upstairs, it might could work out, the DNA, everything."

"If I'm supposed to be dead, what about us?"

"That part's easy. For a while we'll be platonic, grieving friends."

"Okay," Avery said. "But how are you going to explain all this, like the pool balls I threw at the guy? What if the cops check them for fingerprints? They can't be mine, because at this point I'm already dead. And what about the towel I helped put under your shirt? How'd you do that by yourself?"

"Let me think for a minute." She paused. "Do you have any blood on you or your clothes?"

Avery checked. "Not that I can see, except on my hand." He showed her.

"Turn around, let me see your clothes. And check the bottom of your shoes?"

No blood was found.

"That's good," she said. "Now go and exchange everything. By then, maybe we'll have figured out some other things. But first, wash your hands and put the pool balls back on the table. If your prints are on them, it's because you played pool sometime before this. But don't touch the shotgun; you might leave your prints. And watch for blood where you step, or this won't work."

"What about the cops? They could be here any minute," Avery said.

"If they come, they come, and we play it the way it happened. But I think they'd have been here by now if somebody called. The neighbors next to the dock hate mosquitoes and spend the summer in Maine, so they're gone. On the other side, it's a quarter of a mile to the next house, and they're not home half the time. Or maybe somebody across the lake thought it was an early Fourth of July celebration thing. It doesn't matter why, so far, no one's here but us. But hurry, I'm not feeling so good." She touched his arm. "I almost forgot, when you're upstairs, grab my cell phone."

Avery cleaned his hands and returned the five pool balls to the table and racked them, being careful to check for blood spatter on the felt. He then hurried off to stuff what few clothes Buck had into Buck's sports bag. He took his brother's toothbrush, toothpaste, hairbrush, and razor to Billie's bathroom, careful to leave *his* fingerprints on the items, not Buck's. He put his own personal items in Buck's bag, and wiped down the sink and counter space, not wanting to leave any of his loose hairs. That gave him another idea.

Eleven minutes passed before Avery returned to the downstairs room with his brother's bag in one hand and a full green trash bag in the other. Billie Rae was sitting with her back against the gun cabinet, where she had crawled. She had pulled several towels from the drawer and tried to put them over her wound—no doubt an effort to deceive authorities she had help.

"What's in the trash bag?" she asked.

"Sheets, ours and Buck's, in case they start looking for hair samples or other stuff. I'll take them with me. I laid a fresh set on each bed, so if they ask, you could say you washed them this morning and hadn't put them back on yet. I'm also taking both my phones. I already took out the SIM cards—I'll dump them later."

"Good idea," she said. "Do you have my phone?"

"Yeah, here." He handed it to her.

"And everything else Buck brought, you've got it?"

"In here." Avery lifted the sports bag. "His phone's in my pocket."

"And all your personal things they might check for DNA?"

"Also in the bag," he said. "And I made sure all the lights were out upstairs."

"Then you have to go before I pass out," she said. "Use the glass door, but leave it open, just enough to go out, and turn off the canned lights. It needs to be the way it was when I shot him."

Avery kneeled beside her. "What are you going to tell the cops?"

"I think I figured it out, but I don't have the energy to tell you. So unless you hear otherwise, it's working. And if it does, it may be days, but somehow I'll be in touch. Just remember, we have to think smart or this will never work. Now leave. You have one minute before I call 911. Otherwise, I'm going to faint."

With no parting kiss or embrace, Avery killed the lights, slipped out the sliding glass door, and hurried up the drive.

SIXTY-THREE

● ● ●

Avery climbed into Buck's F-150. Tears flooded his eyes. Why didn't he listen to the Marshals' warnings, or Karl Casey's admonition to be more vigilant? Because all this time he thought he was smarter than them. And now Buck was dead. "Son-of-bitch!" he yelled, and pounded the steering wheel with his fists.

Still unnerved, he exited the driveway and took the long way around the loop road to the highway, to make it less likely he would encounter the police. A wise decision as it turned out. Before he reached the main road he heard a siren, then another, and another. He stopped the truck, thrust open the door, and puked his guts out in the middle of the darkened roadway.

Between feelings of rage and abject despair, Avery tried to focus his thoughts on how to become his half-brother. To start, he wouldn't fool Buck's friends, who might show up anytime unannounced. As for the police or the Marshals? He pushed those fears to the back of his mind.

As easy as it was for Billie Rae to say, the odds against Avery Gillis becoming Luther James seemed astronomical. But when he mixed in the dire warnings of Karl Casey and Raymond Bryce, with the bloodbath he had just witnessed, he was convinced Billie Rae was right. He had to try. It gave him a weird, if not twisted, perspective. He should help bury Avery Gillis to bring his beloved brother back to life. Sadly, Buck didn't have a say.

Seventy-five minutes later, Avery parked in Buck's driveway, near the rear of the house. With Buck's bag in hand, Avery made his way to the back door. His fingers fumbled with Buck's key ring. It took several nervous tries to fit the key into the bolt lock. He closed the door and felt his way to the living room where he collapsed on the couch and began to whisper over and over, "I'm sorry, Buck, I'm sorry."

Close to 3:00 a.m., Avery awoke with a start from a horrific nightmare. He shook his head and rubbed his eyes. He was in Buck's living room. *Oh, my God,* he thought. His nightmare was real. He held his head in his hands and took several deep breaths to calm his nerves. What did Billie tell him? "Think smart."

To replace Buck's fingerprints with his, Avery wiped down all of the personal items in Buck's bathroom. He placed them into Buck's bag, all except for a straightedge razor that had belonged to their grandfather. He had plans for it later. Methodically, he filled five trash bags with clothing from Buck's closet and chest of drawers, including the dirty clothes from Buck's hamper.

By 4:20 the bags were in the bed of the truck. Even at this hour and with little moonlight, he worried about being recognized. He hoped wearing a hooded sweatshirt would suffice as a disguise. He drove slowly to his own house, two blocks away. He parked at the curb where he was less likely to wake the next-door neighbors. Fortunately, Buck kept Avery's door key on his key ring.

The clothing swap took 55 minutes. Just as he did in Hot Springs, he placed Buck's personal items in the appropriate places. He also vacuumed the bathroom and bedroom floors, and stripped the bed linen. If the cops came looking for Avery's DNA, it was Buck's they needed to find, yet all the fingerprints needed to be Avery's. That part was easy.

The eastern sky was beginning to glow when he carried the last two bags of his own clothing to the truck bed. Unexpectedly, three doors down, a car started, then backed out of its driveway, headlamps ablaze. Avery's heart pounded as he crouched low on the curb, beside the truck, as the car hurried by. Relieved, he climbed into the cab and drove away.

He parked the pickup in the yard behind Buck's house, out of sight if someone were to look down the driveway from the street. He moved the bags of clothing from the truck to Buck's bedroom, threw them onto the bed, and closed the door. He would deal with them later.

Once inside, Avery realized one of the knots in his stomach was due to hunger. He went to the kitchen where he downed three cold hotdogs and drank a canned soda from Buck's fridge.

At last, he turned his attention to his appearance. His propensity to notice how people looked was useful. With his trim razor he shaved off much of his beard, leaving enough to fashion a goatee. He used his grandfather's straightedge razor to make his cheeks and neck smooth. As best he could, he styled his hair, trying to capture Buck's short, unkempt look. Finished, he gathered up the clippings, along with the empty soda can, and put them in the trash.

The hand on Buck's wall clock said two minutes passed 7:00.

He stared at the image in the bathroom mirror and saw a tear leak from his eye. "Don't go there," he whispered. He turned on the shower and let hot water beat against his sunburned body. He hoped the stinging needles of water might somehow wash away his guilt—but they didn't.

What he needed was rest, but Avery knew he could never spend one second in Buck's bed. With only a towel secured around his waist, he returned to the couch, clutched his favorite bed pillow he brought from his home, and exhausted, fell fast asleep.

An hour later, Buck's phone began to ring, but Avery couldn't hear it. It sat in the cup holder of Buck's truck, while two trash bags holding bed sheets rested on the back seat.

SIXTY-FOUR

● ● ●

Buck's doorbell rang.

Avery opened his eyes. Buck's clock read 10:25 a.m.

The doorbell rang again. "Mr. James, it's the police," a voice called out.

Avery swore he would never open the door to anyone. But the police? If they thought Buck was home and he didn't respond, it could undo everything. Reluctantly he called out, "Coming." Blurry eyed, he opened the door.

Two men in suits and knotted ties flashed their badges.

"Mr. James?" the one with the gray mustache said.

Avery swallowed. "Yeah, that's me."

They hesitated, not looking at him directly.

Avery looked down. He was completely naked. "Oh, crap!" he said. His face turned the color of his sunburned body. "Give me a minute." He retreated and returned wearing an unbuttoned cotton shirt and a pair of shorts. "Sorry," he muttered. "I was sleeping."

The two men smiled politely.

"Mr. James, I'm Detective Everett Hill from Hot Springs, This here's Detective Travis Kane from the Little Rock Police Department. Sorry to disturb you. I know it's a holiday, but this is important. We tried to call earlier, but you didn't answer. May we come in?"

"Uh, yeah, sure." Avery led the men into Buck's living room where they all sat down.

"Sorry," Avery said, "but I got so sunburned at the lake yesterday and was up late—not able to sleep. I guess I'm still out of it a bit."

"Uh, we noticed," Everett Hill said with a smile.

Detective Kane leaned forward. "I'm sorry to ask, but haven't we met before? You look familiar."

Stay calm, Avery told himself. "Oh, yeah, a few months back. Weren't you one of the detectives in the hospital who talked to my friend, Avery Gillis, with the bandages on his head?"

"That's right, you were the guy in the chair, by his bedside."

Avery nodded. "Yeah, that was me. But weren't you there with another detective?" He hoped his question appeared innocent.

"Yes, Frank Pearl. The lucky stiff's on a Disney Cruise with his wife and kids to the Caribbean."

Avery sighed in relief. Pearl would have recognized him from the outset.

Detective Hill stroked his mustache. "Mr. James, you said you were at the lake yesterday. Was that Lake Hamilton in Hot Springs?"

Avery tried to control his breathing. "Yeah, I was at Billie Robinson's place, to see my friend, Avery Gillis, her boyfriend. Why, what's this all about?"

"When did you leave there to come home?" Hill asked.

"To be honest, I'm not sure, but it wasn't quite dark when I got here. That much I do remember. Why? What's going on?"

"We're trying to clear up a few things, that's all. A timeline of events," Hill replied.

Avery's eyes shifted back and forth between the two. "Events? What do you mean?"

Travis Kane sighed. "Mr. James, I don't know how to tell you this, but your friend, Avery, was killed yesterday evening."

Even though Avery knew what was coming, hearing the detective's words, he bolted for the bathroom.

His head still hung in the toilet bowl when he felt a tap on his shoulder. Detective Kane handed him a towel. "I'm sorry I had to tell you."

Back together in the living room, the two detectives explained that Avery Gillis was in the Witness Protection Program—to which Avery feigned surprise—and someone planted a bomb under his car, gunned down two U.S. Marshals, but was killed by Billie Rae in self-defense. She was also shot.

"That's, that's unbelievable," Avery said. His body quivered, and he wasn't faking it. "Is she okay?"

"She was wounded in the shoulder, but it's not life threatening," Hill reported.

Avery smiled. "That's good."

"Because you were Avery's friend, she wanted you to know before any names are made public later today. Right now, the only news being released is that yesterday evening there was an explosion and four people were killed, but none of the details. It's one of the reasons we're here this morning."

Avery's pulse quickened. "There's another reason?"

The two detectives exchanged glances. Detective Hill spoke first. "To be frank, Mr. James, because your friend died, it could be said the Marshals didn't do their job to protect him. And because an FBI agent *was* involved in the killings, they're both fighting for control of the narrative, wanting to minimize the negative impact on their respective agencies."

"Who knows? They could close ranks and whitewash this whole thing," Detective Kane added.

"You believe that?" Avery said, knowing full well how easy it had been for the Marshals to do precisely that for him months earlier.

"I wouldn't say it if I didn't mean it," Kane said.

"Mr. James, what we need is to make sure it *was* Avery Gillis who died in that explosion," Everett said.

Avery blinked twice. "Are you saying maybe he didn't?"

"I'm saying, while the Feds argue about who's to blame, we need to make sure this investigation is clean and above board," Detective Kane said. "We already collected DNA evidence from Billie's home in Hot Springs, and for verification we'd like to collect more from Avery's house here in Little Rock."

"Miss Robinson said you did some work on his place, and that you might have a key," Hill said. "And in case you're wondering, we do have a search warrant."

Avery shrugged. "Yeah, sure. I have one. When do you want to get in?"

"Now would be preferable. And because you're familiar with his place, you could go with us," Everett Hill said.

"Okay. Let me get it." Avery left the room.

When he returned, Detective Kane said, "One other thing, Mr. James. Did you see anyone or anything strange yesterday? You know, out of the ordinary, while you were at the lake house or just as you were leaving?"

Avery paused, as if thinking. "No, nothing comes to mind," he lied. "Sorry."

Detective Hill called out from Buck's kitchen. "Mr. James, are these dirty glasses only you drank from?"

Avery's heart skipped a beat. "Yeah. Nobody lives here but me. Why?"

"Because you were at Miss Robinson's yesterday, the Feds will want to separate out the various fingerprints we found at the house—Avery's, hers, and yours—to see if any other prints turn up, just in case."

"Just in case?" Avery said.

"Well, besides the killer, who else might have been there? But like I said, we're covering the bases to keep everything on the up and up." The detective pointed to a glass. "So, how about it? Then I might not have to come back with a fingerprint kit."

Don't panic, Avery thought. "Sure, take it, take them all," he said. "Do you need to see my driver's license?"

Everett Hill laughed. "No, I believed who you were from the moment you opened your front door." He put on a pair of nitrile gloves and placed two glasses in separate evidence bags.

"Do you think the Marshals want to talk to me?" Avery asked. "Or the FBI?"

Detective Hill shrugged. "I doubt it. We all know who the killer was and why he did it. We're just double-checking to verify it was Gillis who died. What else is there to know?"

"I don't mean to pry, Mr. James," Kane said, "and this has nothing to do with why we're here, but I'm curious. How is it you're sunburned all over, yet part of your face is almost pale?"

"Oh, that. My *ex*-girlfriend dumped me a few weeks back, which bummed me out. I didn't work; I didn't shave." Avery shrugged and faked a sheepish grin. "So yesterday, when we were out on the lake, I guess my beard helped protect my face from the sun. Anyway, Billie said I looked like a bum, and to snap out of it. So after I got home last night, I shaved it off except for my goatee, and tried to make it like it used to be—my hair, too."

Following a few final questions regarding Buck's time and activities at Billie Rae's, they were on their way.

The detective's DNA hunt at Avery's house was quick and simple. They took a razor, toothbrush, hairbrush, and a small bottle of men's cologne—all belonging to Buck, but with Avery's fingerprints on them.

Finished, the three climbed back into Detective Kane's car.

"Do you know if your friend had a dentist?" Hill asked. "Dental x-rays could provide positive verification. You can't fake those."

"Then the Feds can't deny shit," Kane added.

Avery's body slumped. Pretending to be Buck was doomed. Checking for dental records had never entered his mind. Then again, maybe it was for the best. Ever since Miami he tried to twist things his way, and time after time they backfired. Backfired hell, it got Buck killed, along with how many others?

"What about the hospital where he was after that car wreck?" Avery said. "You were there, Detective. They had to take x-rays. Then you wouldn't need the dentist."

Everett Hill turned in his seat to look at Avery. "I don't mean to upset you, but as badly as your friend's body was damaged by the explosion and then burned by the fire, the hospital x-rays are marginal at best—we already checked. Other than DNA, the coroner said getting his dental images was our best bet."

Avery stared straight ahead. He could say he didn't know, but eventually they'd find out, so why delay. "It's Dr. Jeffrey. I remember because his last name's like mine, usually a first name. I think his office is out on Chenal Parkway."

"Thanks," the detective said, taking out his cell phone.

Resigned, Avery's head fell back against the car seat.

"The answering machine says their office opens at eight tomorrow morning," Hill said.

"That figures, today's a holiday," Kane replied. "We can be there with a court order when they open up."

Avery suddenly paid attention. "What's that about?"

"I googled the dentist and called his office," Detective Hill said. "You heard what happened."

They pulled up in front of Buck's home.

"Thanks for your help, Mr. James. And I'm sorry about your friend," Detective Kane said, as he reached over the back seat and handed Avery his business card. "Call me if you think of anything that might help."

Avery lied and promised he would, then thanked them for the ride home. As he stood at the curb and watched the detectives drive away, his thoughts drifted to *his* dental visit with Dr. Jeffrey to repair his damaged tooth, and the x-ray lesson he got from the chatty dental tech. What he remembered most, however, was his restroom visit.

Before Avery closed the front door, his mind was changed. Buck James might not be so dead after all.

SIXTY-FIVE
• • •

Avery remembered his dental visit well.

The row of five professional offices sat perpendicular to the north side of Chenal Parkway. The 30-year-old building had been upgraded to meet the contemporary needs of its tenants. Dr. Michael Jeffrey's office was at the end of the building, farthest from the road.

"Open wide, please," the assistant said, as she maneuvered the x-ray film device into Avery's mouth. "Now bite down . . . That's it, don't move. It'll only take a sec." Moments later, with a click, the x-ray was taken. She repeated the process several times.

"Too bad your tooth couldn't wait another week," she said.

"Why's that?" Avery replied.

"No more x-ray film, that's why. It's called digital imagery. It means no more messing with chemicals to develop the film and then having to wait. One click and it's on the computer. You see it instantly."

"Does that mean you'll have to transfer these x-rays onto the computer?" Avery asked.

"No, your x-ray film will be placed into a holder, like this," she showed him, "and then go into your folder file like everyone else's. But starting next week, all new x-ray images will be kept on our office hard drive."

Other than the dentist grinding on Avery's tooth, followed by an impression, nothing else seemed memorable—except for his use of the office restroom. The following week his tooth was fitted with a gold crown. What he needed to know, however, he had already observed, and until this moment, six weeks later, he had no idea how useful it would become.

SIXTY-SIX

• • •

The idea was easier imagined than done. Exchange his dental x-rays with Buck's. His brother said Dr. Jeffrey had been his dentist for the past three years—surely he had x-rays taken. To do this, however, he must go out in public. Not an easy task, considering he must also risk being caught breaking and entering.

Wearing one of Buck's baseball caps and a pair of dark glasses, Avery drove down Chenal Parkway and turned into the long driveway of the dentist's office. He parked the truck in front of the third of the five offices, got out, and pretended to read the words on some psychologist's office door. He hadn't done anything yet and he was already nervous.

Avery walked to Dr. Jeffrey's office, the furthest from the street. As expected, the door had a deadbolt lock with a security plate. He continued into the small parking area at the end of the building—reserved for *Office Staff,* the posted sign said—situated between two other parking lots; those of a large church complex and a bank. At the back of the lot was a row of dogwoods and various shrubs.

Avery focused his attention on the end of the building itself, on the wall below the peak of the roof. There it was, just as he had hoped, a louvered attic air vent.

As happenstance would have it, when Avery visited the dentist's restroom, he noticed an attic entrance in the ceiling—something he had never seen in any restroom. It didn't appear significant until this very morning, when the detectives questioned him about Avery's dental records. It made him think: if he could gain entry to the attic, he also had access to Dr. Jeffrey's office and the files behind the receptionist's desk. Although the office door and windows were likely alarmed, Avery doubted the restroom attic opening was.

Not finding everything he needed in Buck's workshop, he would have to go out again. After some thought, he jumped on the freeway and drove southwest to Benton, a place he figured Buck never spent time. From a major hardware store he purchased an LED headlamp with adjustable focus, an extension ladder, and a 12-step rope ladder. With sweaty palms, he paid in cash. The clerk didn't give him a second look. Then he bought lunch at a drive-through burger joint, again without incident.

Safely back at Buck's house, Avery spent a short time in Buck's workshop cutting several four-foot lengths of two-by-fours.

Shortly before 9 p.m., Avery returned to the dentist's office and parked in the *Office Staff* area at the far end of the building, a perfect place not to be seen from the road, although he could easily be spotted by anyone in the church or bank parking lot. He reasoned that neither the church nor the bank would have visitors on this specific evening and time, because miles away, thousands were gathered on the banks of the Arkansas River to watch the city's annual Fourth of July fireworks show. Also, the police would more likely be assigned to help with crowd control rather than patrol the upscale neighborhoods and businesses adjoining Chenal Parkway.

Wearing blue jeans and a dark T-shirt, he pulled the ladder from the truck bed, extended it 10 feet, and positioned it under the attic vent. He took a portable drill, attached a magnetic bit, and climbed the ladder. With his headlamp in place, he turned it on and removed the eight screws holding the 24" x 28" air vent in place. Avery figured the audible whir of the drill's motor would never be heard in a passing car 80 yards away. He stuffed the screws into his pocket and placed the drill and the vent inside the attic.

One by one he placed three two-by-fours onto the floor of the attic, careful to position them to straddle the crossbeams. He would use them to walk on. One misstep and his foot would punch a large hole through the drywall ceiling of the office below. Next, he dropped in the rope ladder, then squeezed himself through the opening,

Again using his headlamp, Avery scanned the sea of yellow insulation material that covered the attic floor. At last, he spied the vacant spot that was the attic opening. Moving the two-by-fours as he went, he used the rafters above him for balance and made his way. Reaching his goal, he lifted the corner of the dusty 2½' x 3' board and shined his light into the hole.

Eureka. The dentist's restroom. He pulled the wooden cover aside, attached the rope ladder to one of the two-by-fours, and positioned it over the opening. He dropped the ladder into the hole and descended to the restroom floor.

From his hip pocket he extracted a pair of Buck's nitrile gloves and put them on. He pulled open the door, and to keep the light focused on the floor, away from the windows, he crawled into the hallway and made his way to the office area, to the cabinets housing patient folders.

As expected, they were arranged alphabetically, top of the cabinet to the bottom. It took less than a minute to find both his and Buck's folders. He marked their place, then laid them on the carpet between the desk and the wall where the light would not be seen from the outside. He opened both folders. Buck's contained three of the card stock x-ray holders, each with his name and the date of the x-rays. Because each x-ray film was so small, no identifying marks appeared on them, only on the holder. Avery had a single x-ray holder. He exchanged his x-rays with Buck's most recent ones, careful not to break off any of the tiny tabs that held each film in place.

Avery stuffed the remainder of Buck's x-rays and their cardboard holders into his hip pocket, along with a handwritten doctor's note regarding Avery's new crown.

Retracing his movements, Avery climbed into the attic, pulled the rope ladder up behind him, and replaced the restroom attic cover. He rolled up the ladder and dropped it out the vent opening onto the pavement below. He left the two-by-fours behind. The hardest part was crawling out the vent opening backward. He reattached the vent, returned everything to the bed of the truck, eased himself into the Ford's cab, and checked the time. It took him less than an hour. After several deep breaths, he started the engine, hit the lights, and exited the parking lot.

Being paranoid, before returning to Buck's, Avery discarded the x-rays, holders, note, and gloves into three different fast-food dumpsters. He also disposed of the SIM cards from both his phones, as well as the two bags of sheets from Billie Rae's Hot Springs home plus those from his Little Rock bedroom.

He parked behind Buck's house and again fumbled with the keys to open the back door. Once inside, he collapsed onto Buck's couch. He was spent, and this was only his first day of deception.

SIXTY-SEVEN

● ● ●

The doorbell rang in the early morning, scaring Avery half to death. After a moment, someone pounded on the arched wooden door. "Buck, are you in there? It's Joe, come on, open up." Eventually he left, leaving Avery wide-awake and uneasy.

An hour later the doorbell rang again, accompanied by a light tapping on the door.

"Open up, it's me, Billie," the faint voice said.

Avery's heart jumped. He rushed to open the door, then quickly closed it after she hurried in. Her left arm was in a sling. As the two embraced, she began to cry.

"I'm sorry," he said. "I'm so sorry."

"Me too."

They held each other for some time before moving to the living room couch.

"Are you okay?" he said.

Billie Rae sighed. "I'm bruised and battered, and an emotional wreck, but I'll survive." She looked at him and her eyes teared up.

"What is it?" he said.

"You look so much like Buck—your hair, your beard."

After another embrace, Avery asked about her wounded shoulder, then about her *plan* and how well it worked.

"Haven't you been watching the news?" she asked.

"I tried last night but had to turn it off. It made me a nervous wreck," he said.

"Then let me tell you." She faced him on the couch. "Two minutes after you left, the police were everywhere. I told them everything as best I could. How you went to get the car to go to dinner, and then I heard the explosion. How I ran to the porch and saw the Marshals being shot, and then the killer shot at me. I told them I ran to the back door and threw the deadbolt lock, then headed for the gun cabinet. But halfway down the stairs I remembered the kitchen lights—that I'd have a better chance in the dark—so I ran back up to turn them off. That's when I was shot and fell down the stairs. I was almost hysterical telling them, and I wasn't faking it.

"Then I said, while he was breaking down the door, I managed to get my father's shotgun, and waited on the floor at the far end of the pool table. And when the tall lamp came on, I knocked it over and broke the bulb." Billie Rae paused. "Let me catch my breath."

Avery waited patiently until she continued.

"Before long, I heard a noise coming from the back stairwell, and I knew it was him." She took Avery's hand. "I remembered your story about escaping from your bedroom through the sliding glass door, and how you left it open to lure Tony Trainer outside. So I used it for *my* story. I said I opened the door just enough to be noticed. And when I thought he was at the bottom of the stairs, I threw the dowel stick, the one that holds the door shut, and it hit the glass. That's when he fired off several shots. And like I hoped, he must have thought I'd made it out into the yard."

"Did they ask why you didn't leave when you had the chance?" Avery said.

"Yes, and I said I was too weak to go anywhere far, and I wasn't lying." She paused again. "I tell you, Avery, when it actually happened, I could barely make him out as he reached the pool table. And when I stood up, I think it surprised him, because for a split second he hesitated. That's how I got off the first shot." Tears came to her eyes. "I know I had to do it, but it was awful, Avery, God awful." She began to sob.

Avery went to find some tissues.

Drying her eyes, she continued. "But when I said you were in Witness Protection, and the two dead men were U.S. Marshals, *and* a rogue FBI agent was involved, they thought I was delusional. I had to repeat it three times and swear on my mother's grave."

"I'm so sorry you had to go through that," he said. "But did they believe you?"

"Yes, finally," she replied. "And when they realized Jerry and his partner *were* U.S. Marshals, they believed everything I told them. Then they couldn't work fast enough—they knew the Feds were coming." Billie Rae shifted her weight, trying to get comfortable. "Could you get me some ice water? My mouth feels dry."

Avery hurried to the kitchen and back.

"Thank you." She held the glass against her temple, then took a long drink. "Where was I? Oh, yes, at the hospital, after they fixed up my shoulder, a Detective Hill from Hot Springs showed up looking for clues, anything suspicious, forewarnings, things like that. Then he apologized for having to ask, and said he was looking for DNA evidence to verify it really was Avery in the car. That's the first time Buck's name came up. So I volunteered how he'd been there for a couple of days, but because of his sunburn, he went home sometime in the afternoon, way before dark. I said if it helped, Avery had a house in Little Rock and Buck had a key to get in."

"He was here with a detective from Little Rock, just like you predicted," Avery said. "I'll tell you about it, but first I want to hear about the Marshals. They were there, right?"

Billie Rae nodded. "Yesterday morning. But first it was the FBI. At least they appeared somewhat contrite, until I confronted them about their rogue agent, then they clammed up.

"As for the Marshals, they were horrible. I can understand them being upset about Jerry and his partner dying, but it felt like they took out their frustration on me." Billie Rae shuddered. "The most anxious part was, somehow they knew Jerry left two phone messages warning you, but they couldn't find your phone, his phone—and did I know where it was? 'No,' I said, and broke into tears, real tears. 'What's to know?' I said. 'Avery's dead, the Marshals are dead, and I killed the assassin.' I was hysterical; I couldn't stop crying." Billie Rae paused to take several deep breaths.

"Then one of them had the nerve to ask why I didn't yell sooner to warn Jerry and his partner, as if I could have saved them. Thank God the doctor came in and said *that* was enough, and threw them out." She finished drinking her cold glass of water.

"Later, Detective Hill said the questioning was over, and the doctor said I could leave the next day—today. I called my friend Gracie to come and get me this morning and drop me off here," Billie Rae said.

"She knows?"

"No. I said Buck was Avery's best friend and we needed to commiserate, and that he'd give me a ride back to her place."

Avery breathed a sigh of relief.

"So what happened when the police came to see you?" she asked.

He described the detective's visit, even about him opening the door, naked. Billie Rae laughed. "And then they asked about my dentist, *Avery's* dentist." He described his risky Fourth of July office visit.

"And you pulled it off? That's amazing."

"Let's just hope it works," he said. "But starting this morning it's been awful. Several phone messages to check on how Buck's feeling about his friend dying. One guy even pounded on the front door. Now I'm afraid to turn on a light, or flush the toilet, in case somebody hears and knows I'm home. I can't see any of those people, *ever.* They'll know I'm not Buck."

"Then we have to get *you* out of town. But I'm also worried about Gloria Dell."

"The reporter?"

"Yes. Now that she knows you were in Witness Protection, it'll be clear to her the Marshals weren't after Trainer *or* Bateman at all. And I'm the one who convinced her. I even bragged about it, remember? She'll crucify me for it."

"What proof does she have?"

"Come on, Avery, it's too far-fetched to be a coincidence."

"I suppose. But is it just her, or could you also be in trouble with the law?"

"What I said about the Marshals and Tony Trainer wasn't illegal, but working for the D.A., it won't sit well with the public. And now, pretending you're Buck? Yes, I could be in big trouble."

For the next hour they discussed the difficulty of keeping Luther James alive. Dealing with Gloria Dell seemed like small potatoes.

SIXTY-EIGHT
• • •

If Avery was going to survive as Buck, he had to leave Little Rock for good.

But where could he go? Where could they both go, together?

For Avery, the Caribbean, Florida, and Southern California were non-starters. Billie Rae nixed Texas because her ex-husband lived there. Avery didn't object. Beyond that, they explored their options: a place where Avery could continue his desire to be on the water, and Billie Rae, to pursue her art. Nice things to think about, but until Avery's transformation was complete, it was all talk.

Leaving Little Rock was one thing, but to assume Buck's identity, Avery needed to remain temporarily hidden in Arkansas. Fleeing the state would have to come later.

Billie Rae suggested several off-the-beaten-path places to live, one in particular. "There's a tiny town up near the Missouri border called Horseshoe Bend, about three hours from here. My parents owned a timeshare there and would invite me up every year. There's a picturesque lake, and the town is slow as molasses."

"If the dental records and DNA say I'm officially dead, it might be a good place to put things together," he said.

"I agree, but what about money?" she asked.

"Don't worry. The fifty thousand's in a sports bag under Buck's bed. I'll start using that."

Billie Rae rolled her eyes. "How could I forget about your fifty grand?"

Avery smiled. "Your forgetting reminds me. I made a will and left Buck everything. It's at my house in a desk drawer." He scratched his goateed chin. "But how do I prove I'm my own beneficiary?"

"Sounds like you need a good attorney."

"Right. But what lawyer would flat out lie and swear I'm Buck?" She smiled in a funny way. "How about me?"

"You?"

Billie Rae nodded. "I have a law license, remember? And with a power of attorney document, I can sign everything for you. Buck James never has to appear. But there will be other things you *will* have to sign, and your signature needs to be enough like his to not be questioned."

"Okay, but it looks like modern art. How am I supposed to pull that off?"

"It's called practice, so you'd better start right away."

SIXTY-NINE
●●●

Just before noon Avery ventured into the kitchen to search for something to eat. When he returned to report his findings he discovered Billie Rae had fallen asleep. He let her rest and quickly packed some of his clothes and loaded them into the cab of Buck's truck along with the sports bag containing his $50,000.

Back inside, he heated chicken noodle soup from a can, made two grilled cheese sandwiches, and then woke Billie Rae. They ate at the coffee table in the living room.

They had just finished their meal when they heard a car in the driveway. Avery hurried to the window and peeked out from behind the curtain. He saw a red Camaro convertible. "Crap! It's Polly Stonehill."

The pair waited in silence as the doorbell rang.

It rang again, followed by a thump on the door. "Come on, Buck, I know you're in there, I saw you peek through the curtain."

"Now what?" Avery whispered.

"Let me answer it," Billie Rae said.

"Are you serious? She'll see me."

"Not if I don't let her in. Quick, go to the bathroom and turn on the shower, and leave the door open."

With the shower water running, Avery hid behind the couch to listen in.

Billie Rae opened the door. "Hello, Polly. What brings you here?"

"Buck wouldn't answer his phone, so I came by to offer my condolences about his friend being killed."

"As you might hear, Buck's in the shower. I'll give him your message."

"Do you mind if I wait?" Polly said.

"Actually, I do, because he said he never wants to see you again."

Polly huffed. "He'll get over it, trust me."

"After you two-timed him *again*. I don't think so."

"I can explain that. He'll understand."

"Come on, Polly, you can't keep doing what you do and expect Buck or any man to understand, let alone forgive you."

"Look who's talking. Your boyfriend dies and two days later you're here with Buck."

"Why on earth would you think that?"

"Isn't it obvious? Buck peeks out, it takes you forever to come to the door, and now he's in the shower? I don't think you two were playing checkers."

"Holy Jesus, Polly. Not every woman is like you, getting into some man's pants at the drop of a hat."

"Why you—"

"Polly, I just killed a man for Heaven's sake. I've been shot, and my boyfriend's dead. I'm here because Buck's best friend died. We're trying to console each other."

"Make whatever excuse you want. Just wait 'til people hear about you two together, taking *consoling* showers in the middle of the afternoon."

"If you're thinking of spreading such lies, I'd think twice if I were you."

"Are you threatening me?" Polly said.

"Let's just say, Avery found a paper in his house—Arthur Bateman's old house—that ties your father, The Honorable R.J. Stonehill, to Bateman and Tony Trainer in covering up the murder of my brother. And if I hear one word of your crap, I'll give the story to the newspaper."

"Ha, that's a damn lie. If it was true, you'd have done it already."

"I did nothing because your father is dead. But I'm sure Gloria Dell and her readers won't care one damn bit. So if you want Stonehill to remain a respectable name in this town, I'd think twice if I were you. And if you don't believe me, run it past your mother.

"Now if you'll excuse me, I'm not feeling well and need to lie down. And if you really want Buck to be happy, don't ever come back here again."

If Polly was going to respond, Billie Rae didn't give her the chance. She slammed the door shut, flipped the lock, and walked to the couch where she collapsed.

Polly's muscle car laid a strip of rubber as she drove away.

SEVENTY

● ● ●

"That was scary," Avery said. "But what if she starts spreading stories anyway?"

"As much as Polly's mother flaunts the Stonehill name, I doubt it," Billie Rae said. "But if she does run her mouth, what can she say? She saw Buck looking out from behind the curtain, and then heard *him* in the shower. She could say whatever she wants, but she thinks Avery Gillis is dead, which means Buck James is very much alive. So let her talk."

Rather than risk an encounter with another visitor, he decided he should leave posthaste.

Billie Rae agreed. "Take me to Gracie's. She said I could stay with her until I can manage by myself. With her husband deployed overseas, she said she'd enjoy the company."

First, they drove to North Little Rock, another place Buck seldom shopped. Avery bought two untraceable phones, three spiral notebooks with lined paper, six pens, and a laptop computer. They returned to Little Rock where he dropped Billie Rae at Gracie's, along with the keys to Buck's house. She already had one to Avery's—a fact she hadn't shared with Detective Hill.

The pair thought it best to wait until Avery was officially declared dead before contacting each other, which could be weeks, and Billie Rae should be the one to make the first call. An ill-timed text message or call from Avery could spell disaster.

Avery headed northeast on State Highway 67 to Bald Knob, where he stopped at a fast-food restaurant for a cheeseburger, fries, and a chocolate shake. He sat in a booth and spent the next hour texting the 32 people on Buck's cell phone list, one at a time. Texting multiple people simultaneously would result in everyone knowing who else received the message, and if someone replied, everyone who got the original text would also receive the reply. Fortunately, Buck was like most people when it came to their cell phone password: 1234 worked fine.

> As you know, 2 days ago my good friend was killed. With everything that's going on, I need a break from Little Rock. Will visit old friends. May be a while before I return. Thanks for understanding.
> Your friend, Buck

He even texted Polly, but left out 'Your friend.'

Finished, he turned the phone off. He wasn't sure he would ever use it again, but kept it just in case.

Back behind the wheel, he stopped for gas, then headed north.

Later that evening, Avery checked into a motel on the outskirts of Hardy, Arkansas, a small, quaint town on a single main street with a unique dulcimer shop and eclectic antique stores, all able to interest visiting tourists long enough that they stayed to eat at one of the local cafés, often ordering barbeque and fried green tomatoes.

"Do you have a large non-smoking room? I need a place that's quiet to do some writing."

"You working on a novel?" the clerk asked.

"No. It's, uh, technical work," Avery replied, trying to keep a straight face.

An upstairs suite suited him. He booked the room for two weeks and paid in cash, as he did for everything else that day. Until his own death was verified, he wanted Buck's whereabouts to be unknown. The motel did require a credit card imprint, however, but the slip would be held and then torn up if there were no added charges. Avery would make certain there were none. The motel also required him to show his driver's license. *Don't panic,* he thought. Buck's three-year-old driver's license showed him clean-shaven with a crew cut. The clerk took the license and entered Buck's name and ID number into the motel's computer. To Avery's relief, the clerk paid no attention to the photo or checked Avery's bogus signature.

Using Buck's signature on his Arkansas Driver's License, Avery began the tedious task of reproducing it. During breaks, he scouted the area for a suitable rental house. As Billie Rae described, Crown Lake at Horseshoe Bend turned out to be ideal. She was also right about the lifestyle. The only people in a hurry were tourists. Year-round, as if infected by something in the Ozark Mountain air, the pace of locals was slower, their manners more polite. Avery took notice, and like a good chameleon, followed suit.

Newspapers and the Internet provided Avery with little information of value. Twelve days passed before his new burner phone rang.

"Is this a good time?" Billie Rae said.

"Yeah. You woke me up. I fell asleep at the table practicing Buck's signature with my eyes closed."

"How's that going?"

"The fact that it looks like chicken scratches actually helped. If it was all neat and legible, I couldn't have done it. But after several thousand tries, I think it'll pass."

"That's good, because I just spoke with Detective Hill from Hot Springs. He said the DNA and the dental records were a perfect match. By tonight it will be all over the news. Avery Gillis is officially dead."

Avery paused. "You're sure?"

"I am. And now I can tell you: the day after you left, your Marshal friend, Roger Haslock flew in to run the show. He tracked me down at Gracie's and made me go over my story again. It was horrible." Her voice was shaky. "But he did believe me. And as he was leaving, he said the killer *was* a rogue agent."

"Did he say why?" Avery asked.

"Something about him becoming a compulsive gambler and owing a huge sum of money to a shady offshore casino—plus there were threats against his family. Apparently, he was trying to pay off the debt."

"Wow. The Bureau can't be happy about that."

"I think they're both furious and embarrassed, and I can't blame them. But back to Detective Hill. He said when Roger found out the dental records were a match, he packed up and left town this very morning. So you know it has to be true."

Later in the evening, his hands trembled as he deleted Buck's business website from the Internet. Tears flooded his eyes.

SEVENTY-ONE

•••

Avery extended his stay at the motel another seven days. That same week, Billie Rae felt good enough to return home, which meant she and Avery could talk and text freely. Most of their exchanges involved missing each other, the progress of her recovery, and mutual reassurance. A few calls were more pressing: how to manage the total reincarnation of Luther Roebuck James.

"I forgot about needing Buck's Social Security card, or at least the number," Avery said.

"Please don't tell me it's in a safe deposit box somewhere," she replied.

"No, he wasn't into those. He kept everything at home in a file cabinet next to his desk, in the second bedroom. If it's locked, the key is taped to the underside of the center drawer."

"Okay. I'll check it out."

"While you're at it, get the pink slip to his pickup. It should be there, too."

"What if he owes money on it? The lender would have it."

"He shouldn't. I bought it for him. So if you can, overnight those to me. They'll help me get some things done." Avery gave her the motel's address.

"All right," she said. "Do you have Buck's checkbook? I couldn't find it."

"It was in his truck," Avery said. "Which reminds me. Did you find my will?"

"Yes, I already went over it. And I have to say, you lucked out by living in Arkansas."

"Really?"

"Yes. It was drawn up as a TOD document—transfer-on-death. It means, whatever's in the estate doesn't have to go through probate, which could take forever. Under the TOD, the beneficiary, Luther Roebuck James, can claim everything Avery Gillis owned with no waiting. Very few states recognize a TOD, but Arkansas does. All you have to do is show up with the paperwork and an ID."

"Right, but how am I going to manage that?"

"Easy. I'll send you a power of attorney document. I'll fill everything out. Just make sure your signature is notarized before you send it back to me. That way, the only person anyone will see is me, Luther James's attorney, legally acting on his behalf, because you can't ever show your face again in Little Rock."

"But doesn't the notary have to take my fingerprints?"

"They do, a right thumbprint, along with a valid driver's license. So first, if you can, get your license reissued—with *your* picture and signature."

"But won't the notary check my fingerprint?"

"Only if the notary suspected your actions were fraudulent."

Avery laughed. "Did you hear what you just said?"

"I'm embarrassed to admit it."

"I hate to ask," he said, "but did any part of breaking the law ever enter your head when you came up with this idea?"

"Other than suggesting you become your brother, clearly not. But now I'm in it up to my eyeballs."

Avery hesitated. "Does that mean if you had to do it again, you wouldn't?"

"To be honest, when I woke up in the hospital I wondered if I'd made a big mistake—if we both had. But after having to recount every detail of what happened, not just to the police, but to the FBI, the Marshals, and again to Roger Haslock," her voice quivered, "to describe seeing your brother die, the Marshals, and then me killing a man, that's when I knew I couldn't go through something like that ever again."

Avery could hear her blow her nose. "Are you okay?"

Billie Rae paused. "I'll be fine. But should I have done it? If you'd asked me a month ago, I would have said you were delusional to even think it. But now? The law-abiding side of me says I'm irrational, and by helping you pretend to be Buck, I'm looking at possible jail time, disbarment for sure. But my gut says you won't be alive very long if I don't."

"The way I see it, Avery Gillis *is* dead. So let everybody think the bad guys won. I know it's only been a few weeks, but the odds of success get better every day. Which reminds me. What do I call you?"

"Anything but Buck."

"Then it has to be Luther."

He sighed. "Because I can't think of another choice, I'll go with it."

"All right, Luther. Get that driver's license, sign the power of attorney, and follow through with our plan. I'll handle all the financial matters from here in Little Rock."

The documents arrived via FedEx the following day with a note: *At some point it might be good to have a copy of Buck's birth certificate. I couldn't find one.*

At this moment, Avery thought acquiring Buck's Australian birth certificate was the least of his worries.

The next morning he entered The First National Bank in Hardy to report Buck's credit card lost. He also said he couldn't remember the pin number. Avery presented Buck's Social Security card and driver's license as identification, and gave them his change of address. He was asked only one question. "Just for verification, Mr. James, what's your mother's maiden name?"

"Roebuck," Avery replied with ease.

The bank issued him a new credit card, with a new pin number of Avery's choosing. From here on he would use the card often, with the intent of being recognized as Luther James. Avery reasoned, by using Buck's name, the likelihood of running into one of his friends from distant Little Rock was slim at best, and was therefore worth the risk.

With his new bank card in hand, he ventured into a real estate agency in Horseshoe Bend that handled home rentals. He intended to simply enquire about availability. As it turned out, his willingness to not bicker about price, pay in cash for the security deposit and first month's rent, plus sign a six-month lease, a deal was struck for a three-bedroom home on Crown Lake with a small boat dock. Although more house than he needed, it did come furnished, move-in ready, with Wi-Fi access— well worth the extra expense, he figured.

Again, Avery had to show Buck's driver's license. But he also produced Buck's Social Security card and newly embossed credit card. The agent glanced at all three and said nothing. Avery signed the agreement with Buck's signature, and phoned Billie with the good news.

Before going to the DMV office in Ash Flat, Avery folded Buck's license in half, almost breaking the card in two—the crease conveniently distorted his photo. Even though no one else took note of the photo discrepancy, he wasn't going to chance it at the DMV. He pushed the damaged license and Buck's Social Security card across the counter to the clerk. "As you can see, I need a replacement, but I was hoping you'd make an exception and issue it showing a new picture with my goatee," he said with a sheepish grin. "I like it better than being clean shaven. I also moved and need my address changed."

"I'm sorry," the clerk said, "we're not allowed to do that."

Avery's shoulders sagged.

"You look disappointed."

"Yeah, well, I was just hoping."

"If it's that important to you, there is another way," she said. "You could apply for a Real ID Driver's License."

"I don't understand."

"Let me explain," the lady said. "In 2005, Congress passed the Real ID Act. Originally, it was intended to make military bases and nuclear facilities more secure. But its use has been expanded.

"Sometime in the next year or so, to fly within the United States, everyone must have either a passport, or a verified form of identification, and a Real ID license qualifies—a regular license will not. And by getting a Real ID, a new picture *is* required, *and* you must use your current address. For most folks it may be a bit early, but if you're serious about wanting it changed, for a small fee, here's your chance." She smiled. "For the Real ID license to be issued, all you need is your current license— your bent one would do—your social security card, *and* proof of your new residence, preferably a utility bill, or a business letter." Unlike most states, a right thumbprint was not required.

Three days later, with a letter sent to his new address from the D.A.'s office in Little Rock, and for good measure, another from his bank in Hardy, he returned to the DMV. Luther James's Real ID Driver's License would arrive by mail within seven working days, displaying *Avery's* picture and new Horseshoe Bend address along with his version of Buck's signature. It would be his first state-issued document leading to complete identity theft.

Arranging to receive Buck's Little Rock mail was even easier, a daily task Billie Rae had managed thus far. Under a program called Premium Forwarding Service, for a weekly fee, the Post Office branch in Little Rock would save Buck's mail, and every Wednesday send it to his address in Horseshoe Bend. This service could continue for an entire year, anywhere he lived in the country.

A week later, armed with Buck's laminated Real ID license and the pink slip to Buck's pickup, Avery drove the 49 miles to Batesville, where he calmly traded in the three-year-old F-150 for a reliable late model, nondescript sedan—a chameleon's perfect car.

To help disperse the remainder of his $50,000 in cash, Avery opened bank accounts in two additional banks, all in a different town. Using each bank's nighttime dropbox, once a week he began to deposit random amounts of cash, but never more than $2,000. In eight weeks, all his unspent cash would be siphoned into Buck's three accounts.

SEVENTY-TWO

● ● ●

The second week in August, Avery signed power of attorney papers in front of a Notary. While providing his thumbprint, it took all he could muster to keep his hand from shaking.

Billie Rae told him to hang onto the paperwork. "It'll give me a good excuse to come to Horseshoe Bend and pick them up myself. Besides, I can't wait to see you."

"Me too. But are you sure it's safe," he said.

"It should be fine. It's been six weeks now, and as your attorney, I'm coming to collect legal documents. As long as we don't hold hands or kiss in public, no one should raise an eyebrow. But there's something else I needed to tell you." She paused. "I had Buck's remains cremated, and I'd like to bring them with me."

Avery collapsed into a chair.

"Avery?" she said.

"Yeah, I'm here." His hands trembled. "Give me a minute."

Soon their conversation continued, but only about making plans for her to travel to Horseshoe Bend.

She intended to arrive at Avery's before noon and share a lawyer-client, friends-only lunch. But when Avery began to show her the house, they didn't get past *his* bedroom. Lunch had to wait another two hours.

Rather than eat out, they made sandwiches and enjoyed them on the lake in a rowboat, where their thoughts turned to their future.

"I've decided I want to live somewhere near water," she said. "And Hawai'i is looking better every day. And it would be perfect for your boating opportunities."

"You're right. But with all the tourists who go there, I'm afraid someone might recognize the real me, John. My picture's been all over TV and in the press in every state, including Hawai'i."

"All right, but how many people have said something to you? The motel clerk? The bank teller? The notary person? The DMV lady? *Anybody?*"

"All right, you got me. I'm being paranoid," he said.

"But if not Hawai'i, where?"

"I never thought I'd say this, but I was thinking about Guyana, in South America, where my Miami lawyer went."

"Why there of all places?" Billie Rae said.

"Let me ask you, when was the last time you saw an ad that said, *Georgetown, Guyana, vacation paradise?* The answer is never. So who from the States would ever go there? Not many."

"Hmm. You do have a point."

"All I'm saying is, the further I am from Arkansas, the less worried I'll be."

"I can agree with leaving Arkansas, that's for sure. Gloria Dell's latest *exposé* about the bombing crucified me. She blames me for going along with the Marshals about Parker, which she says, led to everyone dying in Hot Springs, as if it was all my fault. She even put my picture with the article—in color no less. And with my red hair, now people recognize me wherever I go, but no one will look me in the eye. Instead, they talk behind my back."

"Would it help if you changed your hair color?"

"Gracie suggested the same thing."

"Then we can both be chameleons," Avery added.

Rather than dine out, they settled for two frozen dinners and a bottle of wine, and pondered the best place for two chameleons to begin life over.

● ● ●

The urn with Buck's ashes rested on the fireplace mantel. The subject of what to do with him never came up.

SEVENTY-THREE

• • •

Two days later, Billie Rae had her hair cut short, but decided against dying it. Instead, she and Avery drove to Branson, Missouri. The three-hour trip took them through the heart of the Ozarks and the historic Arkansas towns of Mountain Home and Harrison.

In Branson, she found an attractive brunette wig in a boutique shop. With her new hair in place, they returned to Horseshoe Bend and dined out for their evening meal. Both were relieved when no one gave her a second look, except men checking out her shapely figure.

• • •

During the weeks that followed, to maintain their *casual* relationship, Billie Rae only spent weekends with Avery. During her time in Little Rock, when not working in the D.A.'s office, she used Buck's power of attorney to complete all the legal work to transfer Avery's estate to his sole beneficiary, Luther James. That done, she sold Avery's golf clubs and had his Hillcrest home listed for sale, just in time for the Labor Day weekend.

Only one of Avery's two secret Swiss bank accounts was mentioned in his will. He said his other Swiss account, with money from the Grand Caymans, was something he wanted to forget. True or not, the account's access code was never written down, but remained seared in his memory.

• • •

After another month, the pair believed enough time had passed for Billie Rae to take off an entire week and spend it with Avery. One morning they sat at the kitchen table having coffee when the doorbell rang. Avery went to the front door and reappeared with a package. "It's Buck's weekly mail from Little Rock." He placed the familiar USPS box on the table. "Except for the utility bills, I wish I could cancel this. It's usually just ads."

"Then let me see," she said. "I collect coupons."

"Be my guest." He pushed the box toward her and left to go shower.

It wasn't a minute before Billie Rae called out. "I think you'd better come see this."

Dressed only in briefs, Avery returned to the kitchen.

She handed him a large envelope, addressed to *Mr. Luther R. James.* The return address was embossed with the words *Embassy of Australia, Washington, D.C. 20036.*

"What the hell?"

"Don't just stand there, open it," she said.

Inside, Avery found a cover letter. It read in part, *Mr. Luther James: We are pleased to inform you . . . Please find the enclosed document along with the return of your birth certificate and your father's birth certificate . . . To apply for your Australian passport, please contact our nearest Embassy.*

"I thought he was an American citizen," Billie Rae said.

"He is." Avery paused. "He was, I mean, at least that's what he said. I know he was born in Australia, but now does it really matter?"

Together, they read the accompanying boldfaced document. **CERTIFICATE OF AUSTRALIAN CITIZENSHIP** with the name **LUTHER ROEBUCK JAMES** inscribed.

"Did you know about this?" Billie Rae asked.

"He said he was thinking about moving there, but I thought he was blowing smoke, frustrated about Polly."

They fell silent.

Billie Rae spoke first. "Are you thinking what I'm thinking?"

"Moving to Australia?" Avery smiled. "I think I am. But I wouldn't go without you."

Billie Rae sighed. "If I'm willing to move thousands of miles to Hawai'i or South America, what's a few thousand more Down Under?"

"What about your friends?" Avery asked.

"Friends? Thanks to Gloria Dell, I'm down to three. My best friend, Gracie, is moving to Virginia where her husband's been reassigned. That leaves Frank and his wife, Dianne. And because he could identify you, the only relationship I can ever have with them is without you. But wherever we go, with them it shouldn't be a problem."

Avery looked puzzled.

"Dianne hates flying, won't go near an airplane, and Frank wouldn't travel anywhere without her. They drove to Florida for their Disney vacation."

"Speaking of Frank, have you talked to him? You know, about me?"

"I did. He and his wife came by to offer their condolences. So stop worrying, Frank's convinced Avery's dead. He didn't say, but I think he was glad."

SEVENTY-FOUR

• • •

A very contacted the Australian Embassy in Chicago. In addition to filling out a Passport Application Form, he was required to bring it in person to the embassy and sit for an interview. He pulled up the app on the Internet.

"Billie," he called out.

"What is it?" she said, coming into the room.

"It says here, *a Guarantor* has to fill out one part of the application. Quote, *someone who has known the applicant for a minimum of twelve months*, unquote. And that person, *the Guarantor*, has to handwrite on the back of a photo, *This is a real picture of said person,* and sign their name in black ink."

Billie Rae sat down beside him. "Here, let me see."

Together they scanned the document's instructions. A five-minute discussion ensued.

"I think it's worth the risk," he said.

She smiled and kissed him on the cheek. "I agree."

He returned the kiss. "Then let's do it."

"All right," she said. "But are you're sure Buck didn't have some kind of social network page where the embassy could find his picture?"

He nodded. "Only on his business website, but I shut it down in July."

"Would he show up on anyone's media page, like Polly's?" she asked.

"I looked at hers when I first holed up in Hardy. It was about her kid and guitar stuff—nothing about Buck, but I'll check the Internet again."

When Avery's search turned up empty, he called the Australia Embassy to schedule an appointment for his personal interview. Eleven weeks had passed since the bombing was nationwide news, and Billie Rae Robinson became a forgotten side story, except in Arkansas and its surrounding borders, where Gloria Dell's series of exposés kept Billie Rae's unwelcome notoriety fresh in people's minds.

For that reason, Avery chose Los Angeles for his embassy visit, where the news and public interest more likely would be on the latest Hollywood gossip. His interview was in eight days. He would fly from St. Louis, not Little Rock.

● ● ●

Avery's appointment with the embassy was early in the morning.

"Mr. James, you say in your application you are a contractor," the official said.

Avery nodded.

"And what is it you contract?" he asked.

"I do remodeling, mostly kitchens and bathrooms."

"I see. So you're a woodworker of sorts," the man said.

Avery hesitated.

"You know, using dados and rabbets to help build things?"

"Uh, yes sir, that's me." Avery might have elaborated more on the subject had he known what a dado or a rabbet was. "Or should I say, I have been. When I move to Australia I plan to start a boating business to take people on sightseeing and fishing excursions. Up 'til now, boating's been a hobby. But it's something I've always dreamed of doing for a living," he lied.

"Have you chosen a home base?"

"I've decided on Sydney," Avery replied. "I know it's a big city and may take a while longer to find my footing, but I'm prepared for that."

"And you have the resources to do this?"

Avery shuffled his feet. "Well, it's, uh, kind of embarrassing. And it's not that my business hasn't done well, but I unexpectedly inherited *a very* large sum of money—*millions* in fact. So when I found out, I thought, why not go for it?" He shrugged. "I broke up with my girlfriend; all my close relatives are gone; so what better time? Besides, I've always been curious about where I was born, and with my newfound fortune I can start life over. It's like a dream come true."

"Lucky you," the official said. "And when you do settle into a home, please give our passport office a call. We'll need to have your address on file. Also, when it comes to financial issues, make sure you check with our Board of Taxation so you stay within the law." Avery understood these were not optional.

The official turned to the last page of Buck's passport application. "I assume you brought a letter from your Guarantor, as instructed?"

Avery gave the man the sealed envelope addressed *To Whom It May Concern.* It bore the return address of the District Attorney's office in Little Rock, Arkansas 72201.

The official opened the envelope. Attached to the upper left-hand corner of the accompanying letter was Billie Rae Robinson's business card along with an enlarged passport picture of Avery. The letter assured the photograph was that of Luther Roebuck James and he was indeed of good character. On the back of Avery's photograph, Billie Rae had again ascribed to the same lie.

"May I ask, Mr. James, how did you two meet?"

Avery made a face.

"It's not that I'm trying to cast aspersions, but as Miss Robinson works for the District Attorney's office and you're a contractor, what brought you together?"

Avery cleared his throat. "Through my *ex*-girlfriend, the one I mentioned. Her mother, who's a member of the Little Rock City Council, was having some uppity party, and because I was dating her daughter, I was invited. Miss Robinson was also there and somehow heard I did home repairs, so she introduced herself. Long story short, I remodeled her two bathrooms, and after that, her kitchen. Later on, I asked her if she could help me with some legal work." He forced another smile.

"I see she mentions that here," the official said. "May I ask what it entailed?"

"It concerned the inheritance I told you about, dealing with the legal details, especially with all that money." He offered a sheepish smile. "She helped me with it privately."

"I see. But I am curious, Mr. James. Why didn't you choose a business associate to be your Guarantor, someone who you've known for a longer period of time? Miss Robinson says you've only been acquainted thirteen months."

"Well, sir, most of the professional people I deal with are homeowners, on a one-time basis. So would you rather have a hand-written letter from the clerk at the hardware store where I buy supplies, or a note from my ex-girlfriend's mother, the city councilwoman—God knows what she might say—or verification from a respected member of the city's District Attorney's office, who I've known for a much shorter period of time?" Avery shrugged. "I chose her."

The official smiled. "Then I'd say you made a wise decision."

Avery sighed with relief. Surely the interview was over.

"Before we finish, I do have one last question," the official said. "Why did you choose to come to our embassy in Los Angeles rather than go to Chicago or Houston which are much closer?"

Avery nodded his understanding. "I grew up in Redlands, about eighty miles east of here. And because I'm moving to Australia, by coming here I can visit my old stomping grounds one last time, to say my goodbyes."

The truth was, Avery wasn't going anywhere near Redlands. All he needed was to run into someone who recognized him not as Buck, but Buck's half-brother, John. They would either faint or freak out, because according to all accounts, John died in a horrific car bombing months earlier.

The official closed the passport file. "It appears everything is in order, Mr. James. If all checks out, you should receive your passport by U.S. mail in two or three weeks."

"You mean something could go wrong?" Avery tried to say with a calm voice.

"Normally, no. It's just that everyone goes through the same routine screening. We call the Guarantor, in your case, Miss Robinson, to affirm her recommendation. Then we check with justice departments in cities where you've lived for the past ten years to verify you haven't committed some serious crime. In your case there's only St. Paul and Little Rock," he said. "It's our way of keeping people honest. And that's what we want, isn't it Mr. James—trustworthy, above-board Australian citizens? So I'm sure you have nothing to worry about."

SEVENTY-FIVE
● ● ●

Two days later, Avery was back in Horseshoe Bend when Billie Rae called. "I just spoke with the Australian embassy, and they believed my story."

Avery felt a giant weight lift from his shoulders. "Wow! That was quick."

"I agree, but it's a good thing they called when they did. Because of all the negative publicity I've been getting, the D.A. informed me I'm no longer an asset to his office. I have to wrap up my work by next Friday."

"You're serious?"

"I am. But it's a good thing," she said. "Because now, who can blame me for leaving Little Rock? I've been fired, my boyfriend's been killed, and thanks to Gloria Dell, everyone hates me. And now that the embassy called, I'm going to the Post Office to apply for my passport. So be happy."

Following Billie Rae's dismissal, she spent the next week with Avery in Horseshoe Bend. In public, they continued to play the roles of lawyer, client, and friends, while in private, they moved forward with their plan. Billie Rae listed Buck's house for sale and sold his woodworking tools. Avery canceled Buck's mail delivery.

Their resolve intensified with a delivery from the Australian Embassy.

"Now that I've got this passport, I'm more nervous than ever," Avery said. "Part of me's excited, but part of me is waiting for someone to figure out I'm not Buck, payback for him dying instead of me. Maybe it's karma, but I get cold chills thinking about it."

"I understand," she said. "But Avery Gillis is ancient history. It's time for the new Luther James to make his own karma Down Under. And as much as I'll miss you, the faster you leave, the sooner you can start and the safer you'll be."

Avery sold his car, gave his landlord notice, and paid the additional months due on his lease. With help from the Australian Embassy, the money in Buck's three bank accounts was electronically exchanged for Australian dollars with a branch of the Commonwealth Bank in Sydney.

He packed one suitcase with clothes, and put all the legal documents he might need into a carry-on bag. Everything else he would buy new in Sydney. Anything pertaining to his previous life as John, or his beloved brother, he could take only as memories.

As much as Avery tried to delay, time had come to say his final goodbye to Buck. One morning, at the break of day, he rowed to an open spot on Crown Lake, and with Billie Rae, scattered Buck's ashes. They both wept, but at last, Avery felt free to go.

After a lingering kiss with Billie Rae, Avery drove a rental car to St. Louis, then flew to LAX. Before boarding the QANTAS flight to Sydney, he used Buck's phone one last time to text the same people he had before—including Polly.

> I've decided to leave Arkansas and move on with my life.
> No hard feelings, Buck

With the abruptness of his text, and his non-response to occasional messages of concern over the past months, Avery hoped they wouldn't consider Buck such a good friend after all. Or better yet, say, "Good riddance."

SEVENTY-SIX

• • •

Arriving Down Under, Avery moved into a quaint hotel near the Sydney Quay with views of the famous Opera House and the captivating blue waters of Sydney Harbour. From there he would gather his bearings and search for a home to make his new beginning.

In mid-November, Billie Rae received her passport. After going online to print out an Australian visitor visa—good for a three-month stay—she booked a last-minute flight to Sydney to celebrate Thanksgiving with Avery. To the Aussies, the fourth Thursday in November was just another workday.

Avery had a surprise for her.

The waterfront home was located on the east bank of Mosman Bay, along the northern shores of Sydney Harbour. The modern four-bedroom, three-bath home was split-level. A bonus was the infinity pool off the downstairs covered deck. A lawn sloped from the house to the water's edge, to a long, deep-water pier, just to Avery's liking. Although the setting bore an uncanny resemblance to Billie Rae's home in Hot Springs, to Avery it all seemed different. Here, the trees were eucalyptus green, the sky a cleaner blue. The smell of saltwater air piqued his senses; they enlivened his hope for the future.

The home's open-plan design and bamboo floors appealed to Billie Rae. The final selling point was a south-facing bedroom, ideal for her art studio—perfect for the southern hemisphere with the sun in the north.

"It just came on the market," the agent said.

Billie Rae's only hesitation was the price. "It's a little steep, don't you think?"

"If we use the cash from the sale of Buck's and my house in Little Rock, plus the favorable exchange rate of U.S. to Australian dollars, it's almost paid for. And I still haven't touched the money from my condo sales in Miami and the Caymans."

"That's right," she said. "And with Parker's inheritance and the sale of my two homes, we can still breathe easy."

"I'm glad you think so," he said, "because I need to start looking for a boat."

Billie Rae's planned one-week stay extended to mid-December. "It's going to be painful, you know, Christmas without you," she said.

"Then stay."

She sighed. "As much as I want to, we're already pushing it. Frank and his wife were on my case from the beginning about me accepting your invitation to visit. So I asked them, with my Little Rock reputation already in the dumpster, what was I supposed to do, sit around and re-hash the horrors of Hot Springs and be in a funk the rest of my life? After all I've been through, I said I needed a break from Arkansas. Now it's time to go back and tell them I came Down Under and fell in love."

"Do you think they'll buy it?"

Billie Rae kissed him on the lips. "As long as they believe Avery Gillis is dead, it doesn't matter what they think."

SEVENTY-SEVEN

•••

With Billie Rae back in Little Rock, Avery continued to learn what he could about boating in Australia. Since landing in Sydney, he had booked numerous outings with several charter companies, eventually finding one that impressed him. He shared with the captain his eagerness to learn the business. His persistence paid off when the captain agreed to take him on, similar to the arrangement he made with Bud on Lake Hamilton. Avery would work for free, and in so doing, learn the currents, tides, and local marine rules. Of equal importance was to become enmeshed in the customs and mannerisms of the everyday *fair dinkum* Aussie.

Billie Rae returned near the end of January, several days before the date of Buck's birthday. Avery's spirit had sagged.

Billie Rae suggested, "How about every year we celebrate Buck's memory, and at the same time celebrate your good fortune to be given a whole new life?"

Avery embraced the idea, and within the week he was back on the water. Billie Rae divided her time between learning her way around the city, decorating their new home, and turning a spare bedroom into her art studio.

One small problem did arise. According to Australian law, even with her newly issued visa, Billie Rae, not being an Aussie citizen, was limited to a six-month stay. Then she would have to leave the country until the following year. Immigration *was* possible, but a tight quota kept the number of people moving to Australia small, and because of the large number of applications each year, and her being an unemployed artist, her chances of being accepted were unlikely. *Except,* the married spouse of a citizen and resident of Australia could apply without restriction.

Following research on the Internet, in mid-April the pair flew to Hawai'i to tie the knot. Unlike Australia and most American states, Hawai'i required no waiting period, blood tests, fingerprints, birth certificates, or a document to prove Billie Rae's eight-year-old divorce was final. Following a simple ceremony, they spent a romantic week on the island of Kaua'i.

Avery returned Down Under, while Billie Rae made one last trip to Little Rock to announce the good news to Frank and Dianne Pearl. The tricky part was showing pictures of the wedding to Frank's wife without him seeing them. She had never met Buck or Avery.

Also, Billie Rae would sign papers for the sale of her two homes, file her and Buck's tax returns, sell her father's Chris-Craft Custom Runabout, discard her wig, and say her goodbyes. Then she would fly to Sydney in time to celebrate her birthday in early May, and together with Avery, begin life anew.

SEVENTY-EIGHT
• • •

Avery had just finished breakfast when the doorbell rang. He opened the door to find a deliveryman. Avery looked puzzled.

"G'day, Mr. James. It says here," the man pointed to his clipboard, "a fortnight ago the lady of the house bought a rug and wanted it delivered."

"That's right, she did," Avery said. Prior to their trip to Hawai'i, Billie ordered a large area rug for their living room. After the deliveryman left, Avery moved the coffee table and several chairs to the edge of the room, then dragged the rug into place, ready to unroll.

The doorbell rang a second time. Avery opened the door, expecting to see the deliveryman again. Instead, another man removed his designer sunglasses and Panamá hat. "Hello, I'm looking for Luther James." Although he now sported a short crew cut, there was no doubt it was the muscular man from the golf course in Little Rock, Arkansas, Karl Casey.

Avery's knees buckled.

For a moment, they both stood speechless.

Karl spoke first. "Son-of-a-bitch! You're supposed to be dead."

Avery staggered backward. *It's over,* he thought.

"Damn. If I wasn't standing here I wouldn't believe it," Karl said.

Avery forced a grin. "Really? You're the one who suggested it, remember?"

Karl nodded. "Right. But I never thought you'd pull it off." He pushed past Avery and entered the house. "Now I should call you Buck, I suppose?"

Avery struggled to regain his composure. "No. I, I don't use that name."

"Then it's Luther, isn't it? *Lucky* Luther as it turns out, the chameleon."

Even though the morning air was cool, Avery was beginning to sweat. "Who sent you, Nylander?"

Karl laughed. "Didn't you hear me? Until a minute ago I thought you were dead."

Avery threw up his hands. "Then why are you here?"

"Are you alone?" Karl asked. "I'd like to keep our conversation private."

"Yeah, it's just me."

"What about your girlfriend, Billie Robinson?"

Cold chills ran down Avery's spine. "You know about her?"

"Of course. I'm not stupid, you know."

Perhaps, but you are ignorant of the fact that we're now married, Avery thought. "She's in Arkansas."

"Good. So how about you make us some coffee. Then we can talk things over."

"Do I have a choice?" Avery said.

"Will you give it a rest? I'm trying to make nice, okay?"

Avery sighed and led the way to the kitchen.

"While you're making the joe, I want to look your place over," Karl said.

Avery stiffened. "I'd prefer you didn't."

"What are you hiding?"

"Nothing, it's just that—"

"It's that strangers shouldn't be snooping around somebody's house unless they're invited. Right?"

"Something like that."

"What are you going to do about it, call the cops?" Karl laughed. "That's a good one." He left the room.

Ten minutes later Avery poured two cups of black coffee and sat down at the kitchen table opposite Karl Casey.

"Damn nice digs," Karl said. "I should take notes."

"Am I supposed to say thank you?"

"Jesus, Luther, *lighten up*. I told you already, your secret's safe with me. Washington thinks I'm here on vacation. Nobody knows about you *or* Luther James, and I'm not telling a soul, that's for damn sure. It's not in my vested interest."

Avery shrugged. "I still don't get it."

Karl sipped his coffee. "I'll explain. But first, how in the hell did you become your brother? The dental records, the DNA, they all said you burned up in your car."

Starting with witnessing Buck's death, Avery told a short version, enough to satisfy Karl's curiosity.

"Damn, that's some story."

"Uh-huh." Avery nodded. "Now it's your turn. How in the hell did you find me?"

"Well, it wasn't so much that you died, but somehow that asshole FBI agent was able to find you, and it got under my skin. By the end of the year, when it was still a mystery, I was even more pissed. I guess it was an ego thing—a scumbag like him outthinking me. That's when I decided to figure it out.

"So like everyone else, I tracked his whereabouts before the bombing. I narrowed it down to a weeklong trip he made to L.A. in June. The FBI said he went to a conference, but it only lasted three days, not a week. So what'd he do the other four days? Disneyland? Sightseeing? That's what the Bureau said." Karl smiled. "But then I remembered, you were born and raised in Southern California. So on a hunch I made my own trip and started knocking on doors in the town where you grew up. Sure enough, some old woman three doors down from where you lived made an unusual comment. She remembered you *and* your brother, said you two were a handful. I couldn't believe it. You had a half-brother, Buck James. That's how that FBI prick found you, by finding him."

"Please don't remind me," Avery said. "But what does that have to do with you being here? And what's this *vested interest* crap?"

"Don't you see? It's the money from the Grand Caymans, the money you said you didn't want. What happened to it? With half a brain you would've left it—and your other millions—to somebody, but because you had no living relatives, I figured it was gone. But then, when Buck entered the picture, I knew it had to be him. But by the time I checked, he was gone. On one hand, I understood. His brother died a horrible death and he wanted a new start. But he didn't just move, he fucking disappeared. No traceable credit cards, no phone records, nothing. And in trying to find him, I stumbled onto your girlfriend, who not only had the power of attorney to sell Buck's house, but *yours* as well."

Karl slapped the table. "Bingo! That's when I knew for sure she had to be in on it, too. But damn, I couldn't find her either." Karl asked Avery for a refill.

"Not to belabor you with more details," Karl continued, "but when I discovered Buck was born in Australia, I pulled a few strings, and sure enough, he used an Aussie passport to leave the States, all legally done. And the way he did it meant he had the money and he didn't want anyone else to know.

"Then, when she applied for a second visa, it listed this address as her contact point—Luther James's address. I had to wait a while to take more vacation time, but here I am. The funny thing is, until you opened that door, I thought *she* was playing Buck for the money. But damn—you and her together, you pulled it off and I didn't see it. Nobody did." Karl shook his head. "Son-of-a-bitch. That was brilliant."

"Okay, you found me. Now what?" Avery said.

Karl smiled. "It's like I said, I'm here for the money from the Cayman Islands."

"What the hell?" Avery stood up and pointed. "I think you should leave."

"And maybe you should sit back down before you screw everything up and piss me off."

Fearful of Karl's anger, Avery complied.

"Look," Karl said. "I'm almost fifty, and I'm tired of all the cloak-and-dagger shit they have me do. In many ways I'm like you, always pretending to be somebody I'm not. I want it to be over. But idiot me, I invested in Enron. Add to that the economic collapse, and I was financially screwed. Then what did I find? A pot of gold, and you have it. Or did you spend it already?" He pointed his finger in Avery's face. "And don't even think about lying to me."

Avery shook his head. "No, it's, it's all there. But because of the taxes and penalties there's only about ten million."

Karl smiled. "That's what I figured. So here's the deal. First, you give me two million, which leaves about eight. And at three percent interest, the yield should be around twenty thousand a month, every month, while the principal remains the same, *forever*. And that's what you're going to pay me, twenty big ones every month, like clockwork, into *my* Swiss account. You can set it up electronically so we never have to communicate. Just keep the money coming and you can forget about ever seeing me again. That's a promise. Then I get to retire in luxury, play golf, and surround myself with beautiful women, while you keep living your life as Lucky Luther James, and no one will be the wiser." He laughed. "What a fucking deal."

"So just like that you switch sides and now you're a bad guy? I don't get it."

"If you think I've been Mr. Nice-Guy-secret-agent for the last twenty years, think again. You wouldn't believe the shit I've done for governments under the guise of justice. So save your morality speech for somebody else."

Avery hesitated. "And if I say no?"

Karl's eyebrows lifted. "Then I blow your cover. But I won't tell Nylander or the Marshals. I'll tell the cartels, and they won't stop with just killing you. I'll make sure they start with your sweetie, Billie Bob, and make you watch while they—"

Avery raised his hands. "All right, all right, you win. Stop already."

Karl laughed. "I knew you'd cave. But don't you see, by doing it my way we both win, so why fight it?"

Avery slumped in his chair. "Yeah, whatever, but I need time to set it up."

"All right. How about we meet again on Monday?"

Avery sighed, then agreed, and wrote down Karl's Swiss account information.

"So, do you work, or just hang around that boat all day?" Karl asked.

"You know about my boat?"

"Of course. I've been watching you for two days. You leave your house around nine, go to the marina, climb on the boat, take a long lunch, go back to the boat, then return here about five. I'm just wondering, is it a job or do you just fart around?"

"Why should you care?"

"I care because I don't want you blowing your fortune and my retirement. Like I said, I want us both to be happy."

"If you must know, I have a harbor tour business. Some fishing, but mostly I tour rich people around in luxury. Three good tours a week and I'm well into the black."

"So that's *your* fancy boat?"

"Actually, *she's* a yacht, and she does everything but walk on water."

"Nice. Then you can take me out, show me the sights. We can discuss the finer points of our deal."

Our deal? Avery thought.

"Buy the way," Karl said, "do you, or should I say, does Luther have any loose connections to worry about?"

"Meaning?"

"I'm guessing Buck's Aussie father's not in the picture, but what about other relatives? Did you think about that?"

"I did. Buck's father died before he was born. And from what I could find, his father had one older sister who married a Kiwi and lives in New Zealand. So even if she found me, without a DNA test, how would she know I'm not Buck?"

Karl nodded. "But what about your business? The name I mean. Luther or Buck James is rather unique. Why wave it around for everyone to see—especially if you're not him."

"I'm already one step ahead of you. The business name is MacAfee Harbour Tours. Already the locals call me Mac, not Luther." Avery picked MacAfee to honor Billie's brother, Parker. Also, it was Billie Rae's maiden name. She loved it, and thought Mac was a perfect name to call him. Henceforth, *Luther Roebuck James* would be reserved for legal issues only.

"Good thinking," Karl said. "But what if someone says, 'You're a dead ringer for John.' Then what?"

Avery smiled. "I'd say they were right, except John was my brother, who was born in California. And because we were so close, and looked so much alike, I moved Down Under—to *my* birthplace—hoping to not be reminded every day of his tragic death in faraway America."

After setting a time to meet in three days, Avery escorted Karl to the front door.

"What would you have done if Buck answered the door?" Avery asked.

"Here, at this house? It's a dead giveaway he had the money."

"But what could you do?"

"Bottom line? I'd ask him a simple question, which was my original plan. Do you want to wind up the same way your brother did in Hot Springs? Or your wife or kid? It might have been a harder sell, and my cut would have been smaller, but he would have caved, just like you. But that's not your worry, is it? He's dead and you're not. Like I said, *Mac,* you're one lucky asshole."

"And you're a real prick, you know that?" Avery countered.

Before Avery could blink, Karl's large hand grabbed him by the neck and thrust him against the wall. "You're goddamn right I am. And if you *ever* think of reneging, I'll come down on you like your worst fucking nightmare come true."

"Okay, okay, I get it," Avery said in a choking voice.

As Karl loosened his grip, Avery pushed hard against Karl's chest. "Just get the hell out!" he yelled.

Caught by surprise, Karl stepped back to steady himself, but his foot caught the edge of Billie Rae's new rolled up rug, causing him to lose his balance and fall backward. As his body twisted in the air, he tried to extend his arms to break his fall. Instead, his head struck hard against the corner of the quarter-inch-thick glass coffee table—the same table Avery had moved against the wall to make room for Billie's new rug.

Karl landed with a thud on the bamboo floor.

Avery froze.

After a moment, Karl's body jerked, then remained perfectly still.

Avery bent down by Karl's limp body, and saw the bruise on his left temple. He shook the man's shoulder. "Karl, wake up, damn it, wake up!"

Avery felt for a pulse but couldn't find one. He ran to the bathroom, returned with a small mirror, and held it under Karl's nose. No moisture appeared on the glass.

Avery sat on the floor, his back against the cushioned couch. "Holy shit," he whispered.

Karl Casey was stone dead.

SEVENTY-NINE
• • •

What the hell do I do? Avery thought. For the second time in his life, here he was with a dead man on his hands. First, Mr. Bones, a skeleton, and now Karl Casey, his body still warm to the touch. Buck was right about Mr. Bones: Avery should have called the cops.

But now, call the police? And tell them what? Karl just blackmailed me for millions of dollars, but when he left, he tripped over the rug, hit his head on the coffee table and died, saving me a shit load of money—what fortuitous luck!

'Blackmail?' they would ask. Yeah, because I wasn't born in Australia and I'm pretending to be my dead brother. What could go wrong?

Or I could say Karl stopped by to book a boat tour. That's plausible. Then again, when the CIA, or whatever secret agency Karl worked for, finds out he's dead, they'd be sure to ask questions. Let's see, Karl died in the home of Luther James, a sudden made millionaire, recently arrived from Little Rock, Arkansas, and newly married to Billie Rae Robinson, known for her connection in the Hot Springs bombing and the death of four individuals, including her Witness Protection lover, Avery Gillis, Luther's best friend. No, that wouldn't raise anyone's suspicions.

His cell phone rang in the kitchen. Panicked, he ran to answer it, thinking if he didn't, whoever was on the other end would somehow know what had just happened. The LED said the call was from Billie Rae. He hesitated, then let her call go to voicemail.

Avery had to act quickly, but how? One thing was clear, however. Whomever he told, his account of Karl's death would not ring true, regardless of his story.

Karl Casey said it himself, *"Son-of-a-bitch."*

EIGHTY

• • •

Thirteen days had passed since Karl Casey's accidental death. South of Sydney, on the northern banks of Botany Bay, Avery drove his metallic-blue Holden Sports Wagon into the parking structure at the city's International Airport to await the arrival of Billie Rae's QANTAS flight from Los Angeles. Counting the time for her to disembark, collect her luggage, and clear customs, it would be another forty-five minutes. Trying to remain calm, he decided to wait in the car.

Next to him, on the passenger seat, was the first section of a three-day-old *Morning Telegraph* newspaper, opened to an article on page three. Avery glanced around to make sure no one was watching. He picked up the folded paper, checked his surroundings one last time, and began to read the column—he couldn't count the number of times he had read it before.

Mystery Surrounds Missing Tourist Authorities, SIS Release Findings

SYDNEY - The search for an American tourist, Karl Casey, has been abandoned. He was first reported missing Tuesday of last week. Authorities indicate Casey, age 49, likely drowned in the ocean in the vicinity of Bondi Beach. The desk agent at the Harbour Arms Hotel, where Casey was registered, indicated he was here on holiday. "To enjoy the beach, swim, relax, and see the sights," he quoted Casey as saying.

The initial sign of Mr. Casey's disappearance came from Luxor Car Hire of Sydney, when he failed to return his car at the appointed time. Luxor then waited the customary 24-hour period before notifying the authorities. The following day, authorities discovered the car parked on Ramsgate Ave. near Bondi Beach. It was locked, but nothing appeared suspicious. A hotel key from the Harbour Arms was found in the center console. In the boot, police found shoes and socks, a flower print shirt, plus other clothing, sunglasses, and a Panamá hat. Inside one of the shoes was a wallet containing

$280AUD and $130US, and a Rolex watch. The second shoe held a United States passport and a tube of sunblock.

An employee of the Harbour Arms said Casey last slept in his room the previous Thursday night. With the help of the hotel management, police gained access to Casey's room as well as the room's locked security safe. One look inside the safe and the police contacted SIS, Secret Intelligent Service

A spokesman for SIS stated the safe contained four other passports from four different countries, all with different names, yet all bearing Mr. Casey's photo. Officials contacted the corresponding embassies, but each denied knowledge or record of the individual named. The passports were identified as one from an African nation, two from Europe, and one from a nation in the Caribbean. These were in addition to his U.S. passport. SIS said it had no plans to release the various names given on each passport, and declined to say whether any of the undisclosed countries were Commonwealth nations.

Other papers found in Mr. Casey's safe indicated he was scheduled to fly from Sydney to Mumbai last Saturday, final destination, Zurich, Switzerland. A spokesperson for the airline stated Mr. Casey was absent from the flight.

U.S. officials in Washington, D.C. did confirm Mr. Casey was an employee of their Department of State, but did not elaborate. They acknowledged awareness of Casey's planned holiday to Sydney but expressed shock over the findings in his hotel safe. SIS received a request for two members of the American CIA to assist with the investigation.

Mr. Casey's picture was distributed to media outlets with an appeal to the public seeking information leading to his whereabouts. Hospitals were also contacted, all to no avail. The only valuable clue came from a surfer who found an orange swimsuit in the surf at Bondi Beach. In the suit's waterproof pocket was found an automobile key. An official with the investigation revealed the key did fit the ignition of the car hired by Mr. Casey.

A sea search was launched, but from the outset, authorities said because of the delayed timing, the possibility of finding Casey alive was nil.

Finding his remains was also unlikely. After five additional days of inquiry, and lacking any evidence of foul play, Sydney Police, SIS, and American official concluded Mr. Casey likely drowned accidentally in the ocean waters off Bondi Beach, or had an unfortunate encounter with a shark, although there were no shark sightings reported during that time, which is not unusual for April. No further follow-up was anticipated. An unnamed SIS source was heard to state, "Unless he was abducted by aliens, no other conclusion appears plausible."

Who was this mysterious Karl Casey, or was Casey his real name? American officials won't say. Was he truly a low-level employee of the U.S. Government, or an international spy?

Wearing a Rolex watch and in possession of five various passports, all with different names, there appears to be more questions about Karl Casey than answers, accidental death or not.

EIGHTY-ONE

• • •

Setting aside the paper, Avery began to remember the events of that fateful day. He wasn't worried if he had made the right decision, but if he had made any mistakes.

With Karl dead on the floor, Avery let Billie Rae's call go to voice mail. He walked to the outside deck and stared across the water. His heart pounded. *What to do?* Then he remembered Karl's own words: "If ever the opportunity strikes, be ready to do the most unlikely of things," although Avery wouldn't characterize Karl lying dead on his living room floor as an opportunity. Then again, it's exactly he did when Buck died—the most unlikely thing. *So why not again?* Besides, what other choice did he have? Calling the police would unravel everything. What he needed now was a plan—not perfect, but one that worked.

By 10:00 his heart rate slowed and his breathing became deep and deliberate. He walked back into the house and returned Billie Rae's call. He said all the appropriate words with all the right inflections. Hanging up, he walked past Karl and out the front door. He was relieved to see Karl's car in the circular drive, not parked on the street. Inside the car, he opened the glove box. As expected, it was a car for hire. The return date was in two days.

He reentered the house and methodically stripped the clothes from

Karl's body, a task he found more gruesome than cutting the clothes from the bare skeleton of Mr. Bones.

Returning to Karl's car, he opened the boot—the trunk—and carefully placed Karl's shorts, shoes, hat, and other personal items inside. From Billie Rae's art room, he put on a thin pair of nitrile gloves, dampened a dishtowel, and returned to the car to wipe clean all the places he may have left fingerprints. He reopened the boot and cleaned Karl's sunglasses, wallet, money clip, and Rolex watch, plus the tube of sunblock taken from Avery's own bathroom, and placed them neatly in and around Karl's shoes.

In the living room, next to Karl's body, Avery unrolled Billie Rae's new rug. He spread out a king-size bed sheet on top of the rug and first wrapped Karl's body in the sheet, then rolled him up in the rug. He dragged the rug across the wooden floor and down the stairs, to a door leading to the pool deck.

Avery dressed in a nondescript T-shirt, shorts and sandals, and placed the damp dishtowel into a small sports bag. Wearing sunglasses, he exited the house with his bag, climbed into Karl's car, and drove out of the circular drive.

He made his way south, across the Sydney Harbour Bridge and onto the Cahill Expressway, which skirted the Circular Quay and the Sydney Opera House. He wound his way to Bondi Beach where he purposely found a parking place two blocks away. "This will do," he mumbled, having no desire to be photographed by a beach web-cam.

Avery checked in the mirrors and scanned the surroundings. When it appeared safe, he wiped the steering wheel clean with the damp towel, exited the car and locked it, slipped the towel and the car key into his bag, and casually strolled away.

He walked a dozen blocks before he stopped in a large sporting goods store where he bought a pair of bright orange swim trunks. Also a tube of sunblock, to replace the one he left in Karl's car. He paid cash and put them into his bag. Three blocks later he boarded a bus to the Circular Quay, near the Opera House, where he went to Wharf Number Four to catch the ferry for the 20-minute ride to the Mosman Wharf, and reached his yacht well past lunch. Even so, he wasn't hungry.

"You goin' out today, Mac?" Thomas, a worker at the marina asked.

"I am," Avery replied.

"You picked the right day for it. Tomorrow's gonna be a bugger."

"Yeah, that's what I hear."

"Is Harry tagging along?"

"No. He said it's time I take her out alone, at night, to help build my confidence."

"So am I right in guessing, going out on Friday evening, either you're in the doghouse with your new Mrs., or she ain't back from the States yet?" Thomas said.

"For the moment, I'm good. She's still in Arkansas."

Thomas laughed. "If she's a keeper, then you'd better be good, 'cause if you're not, she just might stay there. I know my Mrs. would." He laughed again.

You don't know how prophetic that is, Avery thought, then grinned and lied, "Trust me, I've got nothing to worry about."

The boat, a 75-foot all-water craft with a 1,200-mile reach—deemed a yacht by its builders—was luxury at its finest. Harry Winslow, the former owner had suffered a stroke. His doctor ordered Harry not to drive or operate any machine-powered equipment, the yacht included. Avery bought it in early February. Part of the deal which cost him most all of his 5.8 million dollar Swiss bank account included not only the yacht, but Harry's business and previously scheduled bookings. Avery would continue to employ Harry's crew when needed. Part of the agreement was for Harry to teach Avery everything he could about the yacht, and to share his 35 years experience of navigating Australian waters. Thanks to him, Avery was quickly becoming more than an able boat captain.

An hour passed before he pulled the yacht alongside his home's private dock. To single-handedly secure the yacht was no easy task, but with the help of calm waters, Avery managed. As he entered the house, his frantic imagination half expected to find Karl at the kitchen table demanding another cup of coffee. To his relief, Karl's body hadn't budged an inch.

Although the yard was secluded, Avery used a truck dolly to move a few boxes from the house to the yacht, pretending to take supplies aboard; paranoid someone might be watching. Finally, he dragged the rug with Karl rolled inside onto the pool deck and maneuvered the dolly into place. With no boats passing by, he wheeled the wrapped body onto the dock alongside the yacht's railing. One tip of the dolly and the rug tumbled onto the deck.

Avery unrolled Karl from the rug, but left him wrapped in the bed sheet. He dragged Karl into the main cabin, re-rolled Billie Rae's rug, and wheeled it and all the decoy boxes back to the house. Nearing half past three, he decided he needed a breather and something to eat. What he wanted was a good stiff drink.

• • •

Thirty-five miles east of Sydney Harbour, in the Tasman Sea, Avery slowed the yacht and adjusted the controls to automatic pilot. The yacht's instruments showed no other craft within a three-mile radius. Fifteen minutes of natural light remained.

He pulled Karl onto the deck, near the aft railing, and unrolled him from the sheet. Seeing the large bruise that had formed where Karl struck his head on the coffee table, Avery's stomach churned. Regaining his focus, he went to one of the yacht's storage bays and removed two large diving belts and accompanying weights.

Avery struggled to attach the diving belts around Karl's waist. In each of the belt's five pockets he placed the various small weights. With an added 50 pounds, and not wearing a wetsuit, Karl would slowly sink to a depth of 50 or 60 feet, then drop like a brick, straight to the bottom, 17,000 feet—3.2 miles—below the water's surface, where he would become fish food, leaving his bones to gradually dissolve over the next 75 years.

It took every ounce of Avery's strength to drape Karl over the railing, half in, half out of the yacht. As Avery stopped to catch his breath, he pulled a small knife from his pocket. He intended to make cuts on Karl's legs and torso to entice sea predators to hasten Karl's complete and total demise. Avery shuddered. "Damn," he said, and hurled the open blade into the blackened sea. Even without the help of Avery's knife, the chances of ever finding Karl Casey's remains, unlike those of Mr. Bones, would be infinitesimal in the frigid, two million square mile, pitch-black world known as the Tasman Basin.

After several deep breaths he checked in all directions, as if afraid he might be seen, then grabbed Karl by the ankles and heaved him overboard. Avery's body trembled as he stared into the black water. Had their roles been reversed, he knew Karl would have done the same to him and thought nothing of it. For Avery, quite the opposite.

Hours later, before he reentered the harbor, Avery steered the craft a quarter-mile off Bondi Beach. He sealed the key to Karl's rental car in the waterproof pocket of the newly purchased swim trunks, then threw the suit overboard. Hopefully, being bright orange, someone would spot it in the water, or find it washed ashore, adding to the speculation that Karl had drowned or ran afoul of a great white.

He moored the yacht to his dock shortly after midnight. Rather than go into the house, he tumbled onto the bed in the yacht's master suite. His sleep was disturbed by a worrisome dream that Karl had somehow survived his watery grave.

When he awoke, the sky was gray. He returned the yacht to the marina, and by afternoon the storm arrived in full force from the Tasman Sea. Avery hoped the heavy downpour might somehow cleanse his transgression—as if that was even possible.

● ● ●

Five days passed before the news broke of a missing American tourist. Karl's photo appeared in the newspapers and on TV. **HAVE YOU SEEN THIS MAN?** the caption read. To Avery's relief, there was no report of a man wearing sunglasses buying bright orange swim trunks at a local sporting goods store.

Avery continued to cover his tracks as he prepared for Billie Rae's return, leaving no reason for her to ask about unwelcome visitors. He did deliberately spill red wine on her new rug, however. He allowed the stain to dry, then gave it to a charity organization. He wasn't going to spend every day for the rest for his life having to see *that* rug—knowing the secret it held. He would apologize to Billie Rae and buy her a new one.

Avery washed the sheet and gave the entire set to a Goodwill store. Paying in cash, he bought an identical new set and washed it several times to take away its newness. He put the new tube of sunblock in the bathroom medicine cabinet. He even replaced the two diving belts and the weights that were now residing with Karl at the bottom of the Tasman Sea.

To keep things routine and help secure his identity as "Mac," the repatriated Aussie, he made sure he was at the helm on the five, already scheduled half-day harbor cruises. The last one, two days before Billie Rae's return, was in the company of Harry Winslow, who came along to check on Avery's progress at becoming a *fair dinkum* captain.

"Say, Mac," Harry said. "Did you read about that American bloke who drowned? The one with those five passports, all from different countries, usin' different names?"

Avery tried to remain calm. "I did."

"Struth! You never know about those bloody Yanks, do you?" Harry said. "Any one of 'em could be a fuckin' nut-job and you wouldn't know it."

You don't know the half of it, Avery mused.

EIGHTY-TWO

•••

It was time.

Leaving his car, Avery took the newspaper and stuffed it in the nearest trash bin. As the light mist turned to rain, he tugged on the brim of his cap and quickened his pace to reach the terminal overhang. The automatic doors opened, inviting him in.

Do I tell her? he thought. *Of course not . . . What if she finds out? . . . How? The paper said the case is closed. Why would it ever come up?*

For the same reason Harry Winslow said something. Karl Casey was an American, Billie Rae's an American, and Luther James lived in America. Sometimes people ask questions. Then what?

Deny even knowing about it . . . But Billie Rae reads you like a book. What if she doesn't believe you?

Confess. Karl's death was an accident. What I did wasn't about right or wrong, it was about survival. How many times had he said it? *What other choice did I have?* Except, this time he really believed it, in his mind, and in his heart.

There, in the thinning crowd, he spied a wisp of her auburn hair. He took several deep breaths. *Relax. Be ready. Be the chameleon . . . be the chameleon.*

Any moment now she would wave and flash her compelling smile. One last breath. *Be the chameleon.*

He exhaled, slowly.

Now Mac James waited alone.

Avery Gillis had vanished.

Acknowledgments

Foremost, I thank my wife, Chief Editor, and heroine, Billie Rogers, for her never-ending support in completing this story. That said, her first comment was, "You're writing *another* novel?" She's the best!

I would like to thank my editing crew for their invaluable input: Milan Hamilton, Joseph Karcher, Sylvia Karcher, Carol Pool, Christine Rodgers, and Rayanne Scofield. I'm blessed they put up with me. Thanks to my writing teachers Pat Teeters and Cora Lee Brown for their instruction and continued moral support, and Cora Lee's class for their insightful comments.

For law enforcement and firearms information, I am indebted to Officers John Boyd and Robert Dotts, both Assistant Sheriffs for the State of California, stationed in Riverside, CA.

The Honorable Gordon Burkhart, Judge of The Superior Court, State of California, provided legal advice.

I would like to acknowledge certain members and offices of the U.S. Marshals Service and the FBI for their assistance, but because I was not given their permission, I won't. You can therefore assume everything I wrote about these agencies is what I learned from watching fictional movies, television, and reading other books of fiction.

Thanks to Joseph Karcher, MD for medical advice, and Jeffery Deledonne, DDS for his bathroom that has an attic opening in his office restroom—it changed the storyline. (FYI, his attic opening is to the *roof* and *is* alarmed.) Additional thanks to Anne Hoquist, Dental Assistant, for dental x-ray information, and explaining the world of digital technology in dentistry.

Thank you, Ms. Chris Maynes, with Whole Hog Enterprises, Little Rock, Arkansas, for permission to set Chapter 15 inside the Whole Hog Café on Cantrell Road, Little Rock. (I can never decide which I like best, their pulled pork sandwich or rack of ribs.)

Help regarding the finer details of Little Rock and the state of Arkansas came from Cathy DuPont—thanks, Cathy—and my wife, Billie, who was born and raised in Little Rock. And, no, her middle name is not Rae.

Thanks to Michael McCabe in Tennessee for technical support.

Thanks, Hawai'i, for your marriage laws.

A special thanks goes to Ann Aubitz and Kirk House Publishers. Without Ann's help and guidance, *On the Run* would still be in a folder on my computer. Thanks, Ann, you're the best!

And to the great state of Arkansas, thank you for being so diverse—which helped make the storyline so plausible—for your simple inheritance laws, 86-octane gas, and not requiring a person's fingerprint for every dang thing under the sun. Go Razorbacks. *Sooooo pig!*

Although I spent part of my life living Down Under, immigration information came from Australian Embassies in Chicago, Illinois, and Washington, D.C., as well as from their Internet website.

Finally, here's a special salute to the house on Arch Street, named the Buffalo house after the architect who designed it. My wife and I once owned this story's stone and glass home in south Little Rock, with its towering oak, and overlooking the small lake. The black, step-down, heart-shaped bathtub remains hidden under the floor of the master bathroom, too big to be removed. Wow, what a great prompt for a story.

Notes and Storyline Inspirations

Choosing Arkansas: The primary motivation was the home on Arch Street. And because of my frequent visits to the state of Arkansas, from Hot Springs to Horseshoe Bend, it was a perfect fit.

The Australia connection: To fill a teacher shortage, the state of Victoria, Australia flew 495 American teachers from San Francisco, CA to Melbourne via QANTAS Airlines in August of 1972. I was one of them. I taught music in the country town of Wangaratta.

In case you didn't know, QANTAS is an acronym: Queensland and Northern Territory Air Service. In reference to Buck's father's death: in January 1977, there *was* a horrific tram disaster in the western Sydney suburb of Granville.

The Tasman Basin: Its vast area would cover over half the size of the United States.

Hot Springs, Arkansas: One of my favorite cities. My editors decided to leave this tidbit on the cutting room floor. The reason: it didn't advance the story. Fair enough. Yet, it is of historical interest. The 143°-Fahrenheit springs produce nearly one million gallons of water per day, and was first recorded in Spanish explorer Hernando de Soto's journal in 1541. In 1832, four years before Arkansas statehood, President Andrew Jackson designated Hot Springs as America's first National Reserve. It became a National Park in 1921. Definitely worth a visit.

A curious discovery: A person in Arkansas is issued a Driver's License, while a person in California is issued a Driver License. In other states? Check 'em out.

About the Author

This is Dennis Smith's second novel. His first, *Lighthouse on the Hill*, was published in 2018. It is available on Amazon in paperback and e-book formats.

His creative activities began in the music world: teaching, writing children's music and lyrics, and arranging and composing adult choral literature. While living in Australia, he wrote a series of beginning etudes for classical guitar. One of his more successful choral pieces is *May Your Sun Forever Shine*, which, the last we checked, can be googled or found on Facebook® and YouTube®. Many of the lyrics to his children's songs were published and made into Reader's Theater scripts.

Prior to writing *Lighthouse on the Hill*, he published short stories and poems in local anthologies. *Challenger*, a sonnet written as a tribute to the crew of the Challenger spacecraft, was combined with three NASA photos as posters.

When not traveling the world or doing volunteer work at Ghost Ranch Conference and Retreat Center in Abiquiú, New Mexico, he lives with his wife and best friend, Billie, in the foothills of the San Bernardino Mountains in Southern California. He continues to compose and arrange music, participate in writing groups, does fine woodworking, and *tries* to keep up with four grown children and their families.